In the Inner Quarters

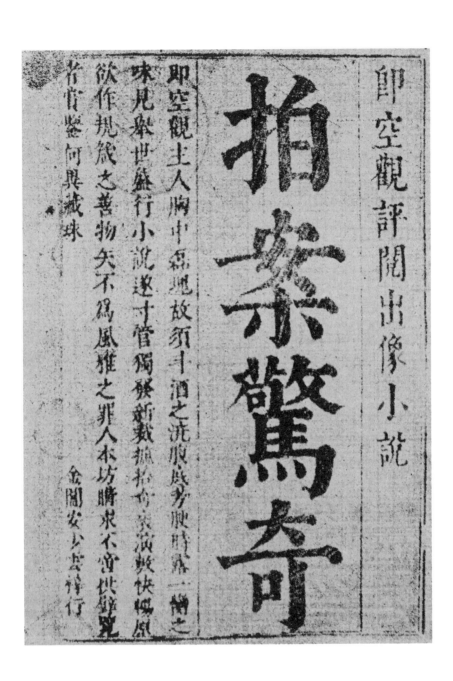

即空觀評閱出像小說

拍案驚奇

即空觀主人胸中磊塊故須斗酒之澆庶幾乎便時舍一閱之
味見拳世蓋行小說遂寸管獨發新裁抚拾爵臺演數快惕風
欲作規範之善物矢不爲風雅之罪人本坊購求不實供鋟覽
若肯鑒何興滅珠

金閭安少雲梓行

cover of *Slapping the Table in Amazement, 1st Collection*

In the Inner
QUARTERS

Erotic Stories from

Ling Mengchu's

TWO SLAPS

translated by
LENNY HU

in collaboration with
R.W.L. GUISSO

ARSENAL PULP PRESS
Vancouver

IN THE INNER QUARTERS
English translation copyright © 2003 by Lenny Hu

ARSENAL PULP PRESS
103, 1014 Homer Street
Vancouver, B.C.
Canada V6B 2W9
arsenalpulp.com

The publisher gratefully acknowledges the support of the Canada Council for the Arts and the British Columbia Arts Council for its publishing program, and the Government of Canada through the Book Publishing Industry Development Program for its publishing activities.

Cover and text design by Solo
Printed and bound in Canada

CANADIAN CATALOGUING IN PUBLICATION DATA:

Ling, Mengchu, 1580-1644
    In the inner quarters : erotic stories from Ling Mengchu's Two slaps /
Lenny Hu, translator.

ISBN 1-55152-134-2

    I. Hu, Lenny. II. Ling, Mengchu, 1580 - 1644. Two slaps. III. Title.
PL2698.L55A3 2003   895.1'346   C2003-910030-8

Contents

PREFACE 7

INTRODUCTION

Ling Mengchu: An Overview 13

Ling Mengchu's Erotic Stories 34

Notes 62

EROTIC STORIES FROM TWO SLAPS

Fatal Seduction 87

One Woman and Two Monks 115

The Wife Swappers 137

The Elopement of a Nun 157

In the Inner Quarters 191

Notes 218

BIBLIOGRAPHY 233

GLOSSARY 247

ACKNOWLEDGMENTS 254

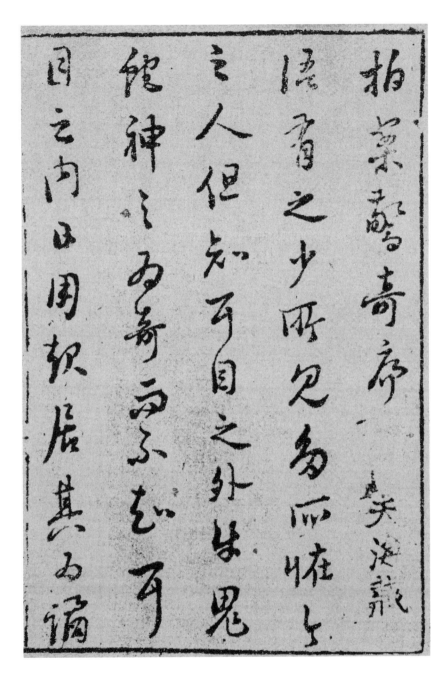

拍案驚奇序 即空觀主人

語有之少所見多所怪
之人但知可目之外皆異
物神之而奇而不知可
目之内日用积居其不禍

first page of Ling Mengchu's preface to
Slapping the Table in Amazement, 1st Collection

Preface

Ling Mengchu (1580-1644), whose erotic stories we present here, lived in the later period of the Ming dynasty. His life spanned an age which may have been as insignificant as the year 1587 described by Ray Huang in his book *1587: A Year of No Significance*, but it was nevertheless a time of peace and economic prosperity before the peasant leaders Wang Jiaying and Li Zicheng rose in rebellion, which resulted eventually in the collapse of the Ming House in 1644.

The Jiangnan region of the lower Yangzi, where Ling was born and brought up, had been regarded by Northern scholars since the Tang dynasty (618-907) as "indolent" and "given to luxury", and the flood of recent academic scrutiny has borne out this view. During Ling's lifetime, the Chinese polity experienced a variety of traumas ranging from palace scandals, the power struggles of top officials, the spread of corruption, and the stirrings of class and racial conflict. Yet far removed from Beijing, Jiangnan retained a high degree of optimism and prosperity, and as the fiction of Ling and his contemporaries makes clear, the social dynamics of the region had a life of their own.

Throughout the Ming, Jiangnan had been China's leader in both economic and social development, and it had paid the highest tax quotas of the fifteen provinces. The economy of this so-called "rice-bowl-of-China," bolstered by the rise of legume and especially cotton production, was then in a state of flux, and gave rise to the flight of peasants from the land in pursuit of the greater excitements of urban life. As the famous literatus He Liangjun (1506-1573) observed:

> [Taxes and labour service] have exhausted the endurance of the people. They now change occupations; and while in the past, few became retainers of community leaders, [now] ten times more people have left farming to become retainers. In the past, the number of persons employed by the authorities was limited. [Now] five times more persons have abandoned farming to live off the authorities. . . . Three times more people have left their farms to become artisans and merchants. In the past, there were no idle hands, but now, of every ten persons, two or three live in idleness (see *Siyou zhai congshuo*, pp. 111-112).

Ling's stories, set against such a social backdrop, largely reflect the life of people in a peaceful time: their enjoyment of pleasure and leisure, their excitement in pursuing something new and adventurous, and their indulgence in excessive or deviant carnality, despite that they also reveal the fears of a world where both values and practices of tradition were constantly called into question.

There is, in the stories chosen for translation in this volume, a distinct conflict that arose between the sober and constraining sexual morality of Neo-Confucianism and the cult of *qing*. According to Dorothy Ko (see *Teachers of the Inner Chambers*, pp. 68-96), the cult of *qing* was the pervasive "hallmark" of Jiangnan urban culture in the seventeenth century. Referring mainly to loving affection, *qing*, without which "no human beings could be created" as Feng Menglong (1574-1645) claims in his *Qingshi* (History of Love), had an explicitly carnal side in a very full sense. Women of the late sixteenth and early seventeenth centuries, especially those in Jiangnan, increasingly crossed the gender boundary as they followed the "teaching" of *qing*, disregarding the old notions of women being relegated to "inner" spheres of activities. Reflecting the erotic ethos of the time, almost all the female characters in Ling's stories translated here openly acknowledge their lusts, and satisfy, regardless of the dangers, their sexual desires in the illicit joys of the bedroom.

Ling, however, was a Confucian author, and there is usually, if not always, retribution for those who have deviated from traditional ethical principles. The retributive denoument, as well as the authorial didacticism, constitute a conflicting and repressive aspect of his stories, though it seems sometimes little more than the conventional nod to a *de rigueur* Confucian morality.

Dr Lenny Hu first drew my attention to the *Two Slaps* anthologies when he was casting about for a suitable dissertation topic. I was charmed by the tales but was often puzzled by the difficulty of their language. Dr Hu was able to solve that problem. My own long-standing interest in gender issues in pre-Modern China, and Lenny's interest in the tradition of Chinese eroticism let us focus upon five tales which are among the most salacious. We spent many hours in enjoyable debate on the nature of eroticism versus that of pornography in the context of Ming China. We discussed the validity and possible application of analytical tools of the post-modernists and deconstructionists, and decided finally that it would be better to just let the history and its documents speak for themselves, instead of using them as illustrations of the theories of Derrida, Foucault, Kristeva, or Lacan.

Chinese is not an alphabetical language. By virtue of its age and its creative use over time, it produces words and expressions redolent with association and allusion, which are difficult to render into English. Style of translation is another problem. Although the stories were written largely in the vernacular, the vernacular is, after all, not same as that used in Modern China. Our greatest wish, ever since the first days of our collaboration in this joint project, has been to produce a translation both faithful to the original and familiar to the contemporary ear. Anything inappropriate is due to our failure to achieve this goal, and our Chinese author must be exempted from responsibility.

R.W.L. Guisso
Toronto
May, 2002

Introduction

The function of literature is to convey
the tao (the Confucian philosophical and moral principles).
  – Zhou Dunyi (1017–1073)

To literature we must look if we hope to discover
the inward thought of a generation.
  – A.N. Whitehead

Ling Mengchu

LING MENGCHU: AN OVERVIEW

Ling Mengchu was a prolific writer. Fiction was but a small fraction of his voluminous writings. The thirty-odd works he wrote, edited, and compiled include short fiction, drama, poetry, popular songs, prose, literary criticism, political treatise, and exegetic studies of the classics, if we don not take into consideration some possible unattributed pieces that are not registered in local gazetteers.

The works mentioned in *Huzhou fuzhi* (The Local History of Huzhou Prefecture) and *Wucheng xianzhi* (The Local History of Wucheng County),[1] recategorized in the following list, are generally held to constitute his major oeuvre.

COLLECTIONS OF POETRY & PROSE
Guomeng ji (The Gate of the Capital, 1st Collection)
Guomeng ji yiji (The Gate of the Capital, 2nd Collection)
Jijiangzhai shiwen (Poetry & Prose from Jijiang Studio)
Yan Zhu ou (Songs to Yan Zhu)

STUDIES OF THE CLASSICS
Shengmeng chuanshi dizhong (*The Book of Poetry* Handed Down from the Direct Disciples of Confucius)[2]
Yan shiyi (Guide to the Understanding of *The Book of Poetry*)
Shini (Some Inquiries into *The Book of Poetry*)
Shijing renwu kao (Study of Historical Figures in *The Book of Poetry*)
Zuozhuan hezheng (A Joint Study on *The Commentary of Zuo*)
Houhan shu zuanping (History of the Latter Han with Annotations and Commentaries)
Ni Si Shi-Han yitong buping (Ni Si's Supplementary Commentaries on the Difference between *Records of the Grand Historian* and *History of the Latter Han*)
Shanding Songshi buyi (Supplementary Material to Song Poetry, A Revision)

POLITICAL TREATISES
Jiaokou shice (Ten Suggestions for Eradicating the Rebels)

MISCELLANIES

    Jibian dudan (A Collection of My Old Manuscripts)

    Dangzhi houlu (A Late Record of my Debauchery)

    Yingteng sanzha (The Three Precious Letters)

ANTHOLOGIES

    Xuan fu (Selected Prose-Poems)

    Heping xuanshi (Selected Poems with Collective Commentaries)

    Tao Jingjie ji (Works of Tao Jingjie, with introduction)

    Dongpo Shangu chanxi ji (Su Dongpo and Huang Shangu's
Inner Bliss from the Chan Meditations)

    Nanyin sanlai (Three Kinds of Southern Sound)[3]

Also attributed to him are another two works, *Huoni gong* (Confessions of My Indulgence) and *Guoce gai* (A General Introduction to *Intrigues of the Warring States*).[4] We have no doubts that he had a hand in editing *Wusao hebian* (The Combined Edition of the Songs of Wu) and *Dongpo shuzhuan* (Collection of Letters of Su Tongpo).[5] Fu Xihua claims that Ling is a likely candidate for a work on drama entitled *Qulü* (Rules for Libretto). Patrick Hanan, however, doubts his authorship due to the lack of reliable evidence.[6]

Twelve plays, so far as we know, have been regarded as Ling's, of which nine are northern plays and three are southern plays.

NORTHERN PLAYS

    Mang ze pei (Choosing a Spouse in a Hurry)

    Qiuran wen (Curly-beard Man)

    Song Gongming nao yuanxiao (Song Gongming Throws the
New Year Festival into an Uproar)

    Diandao yinyuan (Reversed Destiny in Marriage)

    Mohu yinyuan (A Temporary Union)

    Juedi baochou (Digging a Hole in the Ground for Revenge)

    Ni Zhengping (Ni Zhengping)

    Liu Bolun (Liu Bolun)

    Taohua zhuang (The Peach-Flower Village)

SOUTHERN PLAYS

    Xuehe ji (Snow Lily)

    Hejian ji (The Match of the Swords)

    Qiaohe shanjin ji (The Lapel)

In addition to his script writing, Ling penned a number of *sanqu* verses (lyric-songs). Two sets of *sanqu* are found in *Taixia xinzou* (Celestial Air), a *sanqu* anthology compiled by Feng Menglong, and another three sets are included in *Wusao hebian* (The Combined Edition of the Songs of Wu), an anthology Ling edited in collaboration with Zhang Xuchu. Ling was also a *fu* (prose-poem) writer. Some titles of the *fu* he composed, such as "Zhushan fu" (Rhapsody on Mount Dai) and "Beishu fu" (Songs on the Successful Transportation to the North), were recorded by Zheng Longcai in his tomb inscription.

However, a large part of Ling's oeuvre is not extant and the majority of his non-fiction is not easily accessible since little of it was reprinted after its original publication. Ling's main extant works, which were not included in any local histories but have been read with pleasure from the time he was alive to the present day[7] and have endeared him to modern readers, are his two *huaben* story collections, *Pai'an Jingqi* (Slapping the Table in Amazement) and *Erke Pai'an Jingqi* (Slapping the Table in Amazement, 2nd Collection), usually collectively referred to in abbreviation as *Erpai* (Two Slaps).

Composed in the style and format set up by Feng Menglong's *Sanyan* story collections, each collection of *Two Slaps* contains forty stories. In all, *Two Slaps* is supposed to have eighty stories. Yet the best editions of the two collections that we now have, the Shangyoutang editions printed in the late Ming,[8] which have been preserved in Japanese libraries and upon which this translation is based,[9] have left us with only seventy-eight stories, because the twenty-third story in the second collection, without having been "slightly abridged,"[10] was merely repeated from the first collection, and the last chapter "Song Gongming nao yuanxiao" (Song Gongming Throws the New Year Festival into an Uproar) is a play, ostensibly added to round out the number.[11]

Biographical Sketch[12]

A biographical sketch is necessary for a better understanding of Ling's erotic stories. Ling Mengchu, known also by his styles Ling Xuanfang and Ling Chucheng,[13] was a native of Huzhou prefecture in Zhejiang province. He was born in 1580 in the district of Shengshe in the eastern section of Wucheng county, a scenic spot under the administrative jurisdiction of Huzhou, close to Lake Tai and remarkable for its abundance of agricultural products. His family had lived there ever since his great-great-grandfather Ling Fu married into the Mins, a clan very distinguished in the local area.

Ling's grandfather, Ling Yueyan, was a *juren* (second-degree holder in the Civil Service Examinations), and the family seemed to reach the peak of its prosperity when he served as Vice Director of the Board of Justice in Nanjing. Ling's father, Ling Dizhi, passed the State Examinations, receiving the highest academic *jinshi* degree. But he was not very successful in his official career, and despite his promising start as the Supervising Secretary of the Bureau of Construction in the Board of Works, soon lost his much-treasured position due to his handling of construction materials during the period when he was superintending the building of ten prayer-altars.[14] He was demoted to an assistant prefectship in Dingzhou, and later years saw him transfer in succession from one post to another at the same level[15] before his retirement at an early age.

Ling's uncle, Ling Zhilong,[16] was a committed scholar and renowned publisher. His published works include not only editions and versions of the early histories with collected commentaries, but a number of general reference books as well. Ling's father, often in collaboration with his brother, enjoyed very much the life of collating, editing, annotating, and compiling classics[17] after he had officially retired. Among Ling's generation, his two elder brothers, who were born to his father's first wife and died young, were both recognized as fine essayists, skilled especially at classical prose composition. And Ling also had a cousin from the Mins who was rather well-known for initiating fine editions.

Ling seemed to be a very gifted child. He was admitted into a local official school when he was only eleven, much earlier than ordinary students, and became a salaried licentiate (*lingshan sheng*)[18] at the age of seventeen. This means, in modern phraseology, that he passed the entrance examinations and entered college in his early teens, and began to live on government scholarship before even reaching adulthood. As a precocious adolescent, he was not only unusually brilliant, but appeared to be immensely ambitious, driven by an urge to succeed. Prior to his participation in the Provincial Examination, he had already made a name for himself among scholars and officials with a well-written letter he addressed to Master Liu, Chancellor of the National Academy, who praised him highly in front of his colleagues for his astonishingly excellent writing.[19]

Ling lived a fairly hectic life in his twenties. Being a young man of talent, he seems to have been an "ethical hedonist" as well, romantically inclined and experienced in sexual adventures. After having observed a three-year mourning period for his father's death, he married a woman surnamed Shen, who bore him a son just after he turned twenty-five. Later he took a concubine surnamed Zhuo, who bore him another four sons.[20]

It was during this period that he began to travel around in the Lower Yangtze River area, where he made many friends, including such literary celebrities as Feng Mengzhen (1546–1605), Wang Zhideng (1535–1613),[21] Chen Jiru (1558–1639), Tang Xianzu (1550–1616), and Yuan Zhongdao (1570–1623).[22] It is also likely that he was associated with Feng Menglong.[23] Suzhou, where Feng lived, was the destination of the first journey Ling made after his mourning period was over, and thereafter he went to Nanjing via Suzhou several times.[24] As his senior by six years, Feng was an established writer of popular literature whom Ling greatly admired. Hanan has pointed out strong resemblances between these two men in their background, quest for official careers, and their literary achievements.[25] We might add one more similarity: Ling also resembled Feng in what some might call libertinism.

While Feng was notorious for frequenting brothels, there is no definite evidence regarding a similar proclivity in Ling's life.[26] However, one of his stories, "The Elopement of a Nun," might be read as autobiographical. Master Wenren, the hero of the story, is also a resident in Huzhou. A seventeen-year-old, "he looked like Pan An and was as gifted as Zijian." He is not only handsome, refined and romantic, but also knowledgeable and experienced; none of his friends fail to respect him. With the only picture left to us showing an old, magisterial Ling wearing his official cap, we are not certain if Ling in his youth could be likened to the handsome protagonist in his story. Yet he did bear a resemblance to Wenren in talent and scholarship, as well as in friendship with a large circle of literati, who admired him so much as to "come visiting him from a thousand miles away."

Moreover, both Ling and Wenren shared a very similar family background. Wenren moves with his grandfather from Shaoxing to Huzhou because his grandfather receives a place as a tutor in a family there, while Ling's family migrated to and settled in Huzhou because, as mentioned before, Ling's great-great-grandfather married into a local distinguished family. Wenren seems to have lost his father at a tender age, and so did Ling, who was bereaved of his father when he was only twenty and was thereafter left alone with his mother. Wenren's mother possesses the title of *anren* (serene lady) for the wife of a rank 6b or 6a official, which is approximately equal to the honorific title *yiren* (delightful lady) granted Ling's own mother, who, as a daughter of the director of one of the Six Boards, was the wife of a rank 5 official. Wenren's uncle (or adoptive father) is a Supervising Secretary in the central administration, while Ling's father once served as Supervising Secretary of the Bureau of Construction in the Board of Works. And lastly, Wenren's wife, the former nun Jingguan, is about the same age as Wenren, whereas Ling's own wife Shen was only a few months older than Ling.

Given these striking analogies, we have reasons to infer that Wenren's familiarity with a sexually hedonistic life style, his formation of intimate relations with a host of nuns during his sojourn in a nunnery, and his ability as a satisfactory lover without becoming a Don Juan, are probably drawn from his own personal experience.

Some scholars suggest that a major characteristic of Chinese autobiographical fiction is its indirectness, that is, the self is presented through a third-person fictional persona.[27] This is an acute observation. Although Ling had no intention of writing an autobiography of himself and was obviously forced to look elsewhere for subject matter after "all the source materials had been collected" by Feng, there is, undeniably, an autobiographical element in the above-mentioned story, an element that shines a light onto its author and the enigmatic facet of his libertinism.

However, Ling's failure in the Provincial Examination, by which he was plagued almost all his middle life, changed him tremendously. We have no information as to when he took the Provincial Examinations; we only know that he took them four times and failed four times. His biographical epitaph, written by his contemporary Zheng Longcai, gives us a more detailed account: "Lord Ling participated twice in the Zhejiang Provincial Examination and was successful only in getting his name listed on the supplementary announcement notice as a candidate of good academic standing.[28] Later Lord Ling took the examination at the National Academy in Nanjing and then at the National Academy in Beijing, and both times he received the same result."

Because of his failure to earn the second degree, Ling was denied access to an official career. He was no longer a romantic enthusiast, nor did he entertain his previous political ambition. He wanted to be quit of the examination, of the "vanity fair," to lead a reclusive life. He had always been very interested in Buddhist teachings. In one of the sutras he had commented on, he had described himself as a "disciple of Buddha." Yet never before had he wanted to follow the Buddhist sages as he did now. After due consideration, he wrote a farewell letter to his fellow students, ready to settle back in Huzhou, where in the valley between Mount Zhu and Mount Dai he planned to build a retreat of cultivation for his later years. To record his determination, he wrote a prose-lyric, an essay, and a poem under the titles "Zhushan fu" (Rhapsody on Mount Zhu), "Daishan ji" (A Sketch of Mount Dai), and "Daishan shi" (Ode to Mount Dai).

Whether or not he became a Buddhist *jushi*[29] in the mountains remains to be investigated. However, judging from the pseudonym Jikongguan Zhuren (Master of the Temple of Emptiness) he used for *Two Slaps* a few years later, he seems to have turned towards and then away from Buddhism and finally to have arrived at a kind of intellectual transcendence that was characteristic of a syncretist rather than a devout disciple of Buddha.

The credit for discovering Ling's identity should go to Wang Guowei (1879 – 1927), who was the first scholar to link this pseudonym with Ling Mengchu.[30] Later more evidence was found by Ma Lian,[31] which, together with Ye Dejun's study on *Lingshi zongpu* (The Clan Genealogy of the Lings), finally established Ling's authorship.[32] However, the discovery had a deplorable effect on his pseudonym: it has been forgotten, or relegated into a simple verbal sign which no longer shows the manner in which its polysemous ambiguity was implied.

Few, if any, scholars have ever troubled to raise questions as to why Ling used the pseudonym Jikongguan Zhuren, and none have explored its meaning. "Jikong," the first two characters, represents, in fact, an elliptical expression of "jiyou jikong" (literally, "possession and loss"), a Buddhist term which, according to the *Prajnaparamita Sutra*, can be interpreted as follows:

> Since materials in the world and bodies of human beings are insubstantial entities, compounded by the essential four elements, earth, water, fire, and air, we may regard void (emptiness) as being (material existence of things). But when the four essential elements are disintegrated, everything again comes to nothing. So we may also regard being as void.[33]

As an essential concept in the Doctrine of Void, this term basically conveys the idea that no particular thing is real, and what our senses (*se*) provide us is only the experience of transient phenomena. One might tend to think that Ling, by using the latter half of this term, was probably stressing the negativism or nihilism of its metaphysical assumptions. This, however, is only partially true.

If he espoused only a transmundane world outlook, why did he deliberately choose "guan" as the third character for his pseudonym? "Guan," literally meaning "Daoist temple," was ostensibly meant to imply an aspect of his non-Buddhist thought, that is, the thought of his Daoist eremitism. To the Daoist escapists, especially those of the Wei-Jin type who regarded void as a correct stage in experiencing "being" rather than absolute extinction of desire, the Buddhist quest for void was simply an ideal too high to be practicable. If they concealed themselves in mountain retreats, it was not principally for the purpose of their religious pursuit, but for seeking peace of mind after they had failed the examinations. They might appear transcendental, but they could also be pragmatic and secular; they might live as a recluse, eschewing social and political involvement, but they could also seek the consolations of good wine and beautiful women: all depended on what they naturally needed.[34] "Jikong-guan," a seeming oxymoron that juxtaposes the Buddhist term with a word of Daoist flavour, reveals Ling's ideological ambivalence about being a faithful follower of one single dogma.

Yet there was an even deeper contradiction in him. On the one hand, he seems to have been disillusioned with the corporeal world and desirous of spending the rest of his life in seclusion, but on the other, he still wished to "be helpful in the difficult times" which the late Ming regime was facing. After all, Ling was a Confucian scholar infused with a tradition of social responsibility. Many years of orthodox Confucian cultivation finally sent him on the journey to Beijing to seek a vacancy, in any possible office, through recommendation, the only way left for the failures of the Provincial Examination to enter the civil service. Ling travelled on the same boat with Zhu Guozhen, the newly-appointed Director of the Board of Rites, who, having heard of Ling's fame, was very glad to have the opportunity to talk to him and consult with him about the "art of government."

However, Ling was not successful in securing a position. In 1627, he returned to Nanjing and began writing *Slapping the Table in Amazement*. "In the autumn of Dingmao (1627)," he wrote in the preface, "I tarried in Nanjing after 'grazing the skin' and 'missing the mark' in my affair."[35] These obscure allusions refer to his abortive attempts to gain an appointment. He was, of course, rather piqued at failing to receive a nomination for public service, and he made his discontentment quite explicit in his preface. In one of his stories, he even went so far as to vent his spleen by bluntly criticizing the Civil Service Examination system.[36]

But on the whole, *Two Slaps* shows Ling as a Confucian writer who, if not without occasional mockery and superstition, was sympathetic, positive, humanistic, and open-minded, rather than as an aging man full of disgruntlement and cynical pessimism.

It took him a year (1627–28) to finish the first collection; the book was, by all accounts, well received. Thus, at the urging of his publisher, Ling wrote its sequel *Slapping the Table in Amazement, 2nd Collection*. The great commercial success, however, could not cover his mixed feelings in composing the stories. He might have, in his private moments, enjoyed pursuing aesthetic pleasure and financial profit, but he never took his fiction writing as a *pure* literary or economic activity. Reading his *Two Slaps*, we can see that he was still under the sway of the prevailing bias against men of letters[37] and was eager to endow his stories with a sense of engagedness. One may say that "popular fiction" at its earlier stage had already become mingled with didacticism. Yet in his stories Ling began to approach a new notion, the notion that fiction should become a special commitment to Confucian political and moral missions. His *Two Slaps*, by and large, are a record of his attempt to wrestle with the problems of accomplishing such a mission.

Ling's Confucian esprit was clearly displayed during his tenure of official positions in his later years. Some Chinese scholars tend to criticize his career, especially his suppression of peasant uprisings, and avoid characterizing him as a man of integrity who stayed loyal to the Ming and died at his post. In fact, it was simply for his martyrdom, rather than his "meritorious" feats in putting down the peasant rebellions or his literary accomplishments in writing *huaban* stories, that he received accolades in local histories.

In the seventh year of the Chongzhen reign (1634) when Ling was fifty-four, the imperial government, in selecting capable *fugong*[38] for lower ranking positions, appointed him as an assistant magistrate for Shanghai county (then only an insignificant small town). His dream of becoming an official had at last come true. This was a turning point for him, which marked the end of his life as a writer and publisher[39] and the inauguration of a new career. At the beginning, he was in charge of coastal defenses,[40] but soon became the surrogate of the magistrate who was on leave for eight months. As an acting magistrate, Ling was diligent and conscientious, collecting land taxes and other levies and straightening out the difficulties of ordinary people. Owing to his remarkable services in Shanghai, he was promoted to an assistant prefectship in Xuzhou, a position much more responsible and important. The day he was leaving Shanghai for Xuzhou to take up his new post, so many local people with tears in their eyes came to see him off that they almost blocked the road.

Ling's two years in Xuzhou were perhaps the most challenging period of his entire life. By that time much of the country was in turmoil and rapaciousness was everywhere, threatening the tottering Ming house. The crisis was not confined to the North and the West, but was also felt in Xuzhou where Ling worked. In 1643, Ho Tengjiao, the newly-appointed Military Defense Circuit (*bingbeidao*), was sent to Xuzhou with a commission to exterminate the rebels headed by Chen Xiaoyi, who had captured fort Fengcheng and proclaimed himself King Xiao. When

21

the first battle was lost, Ho convened an emergency meeting and new strategies and tactics were put forward and discussed. Unlike most of his colleagues present at the meeting, Ling kept silent from beginning to end. That night he was invited to council with Ho at his residence. "Aren't you Ling the Nineteenth from the west Zhejiang?" Ho asked. "I have heard of your literary reputation and have long been your admirer. Why didn't you say something to help me straighten out my muddled mind?" "As an official of lower rank," Ling replied, "I was not in a position to offer different opinions. But I had a feeling that you might wish to talk to me on this subject, so I have prepared a draft, which I hope can catch your attention." He then presented to Ho his treatise *Jiaokou shiche* (Ten Strategies for Eradicating the Rebels), and Ho, after reading it, exclaimed, "If we do as you suggest, we may even wipe out the ringleaders in Gansu and Sicuan,[41] not to mention the insignificant clown in our Xuzhou!"

Ling was grateful for Ho's appreciation and pledged that he would do whatever was necessary to aid him, even at the expense of his own life. Ho then deployed his troops in the light of Ling's suggestions and this time the rebels were indeed defeated. Seeing many of them fleeing, Ling said to his superior: "Now that the rebels are panic-stricken with the defeat, please allow me to go to the Chen encampment and persuade him to make an early capitulation." Ho was greatly surprised to hear this, and dissuaded him from taking such a hazardous mission. Still, Ling insisted. "If I fail," he said with firm resolution, "I shall die for you!" The next morning he mounted a horse and ventured alone into the city where the rebels were stationed. Chen, sitting on a raised chair with bodyguards protecting him on both sides, shouted loudly at Ling: "Are you courting death?" "If I were afraid of death," Ling replied, showing no sign of fear at all, "I wouldn't have come here!" With his convincing argument, he finally compelled Chen to submit.

The next year was *jiashen* (the Chinese cyclical year corresponding to 1644). Li Zicheng, having conquered a large part of the country, proclaimed himself Emperor of the Shun. At his order, one of his detachments approached Xuzhou, and the district along the river that was within Ling's jurisdiction[42] became the first target to be attacked. There is a very moving passage in Zheng's epitaph, describing how Ling dedicated himself at his last moments to the Confucian principles of duty, loyalty, integrity, honour, justice, and courage when he and his townspeople were besieged by Li's insurgents:

> On the morning of the ninth day of the twelfth month, the insur-
> gents called out, "We wish to see Lord Ling!" Lord Ling, standing

behind the battlements of the city wall, shouted back angrily, "You want me to surrender? What do you think I am? A cowardly rat whose purpose is just to keep on living?" He shot several men dead with his fowling piece. The insurgents flew into a storm of rage and attacked the city even more fiercely. Lord Ling said to the townsfolk, "I shouldn't let you fall victim because of me. Please allow me to jump off the building to kill myself so that you can be saved." People cried and swore that they would defend the town to the death. Lord Ling said, "I have been working here for three years. Although I haven't helped you much, I am most unwilling to do you a great injury by throwing you into a dangerous situation. If I die, you can survive." He then refused to eat and drink. His servants tried to dissuade him, but Lord Ling replied, "Fighting is now breaking out all over the country. In view of the possibility that there will be no space to bury my corpse in the future, it is wise for me to choose to die at this place!" The servants delicately called his attention to the fact that the position he held was rather insignificant. Lord Ling said, "No matter what position I hold, low or high, I wish only to maintain my integrity!" After saying this, he spat out a large quantity of blood.[43] He then spoke to his people, "Since the rebels called me 'Lord Ling,' they might not have lost all their sympathy. Please help me up to speak to them." He called out to the insurgents, "I am on the verge of collapse and shall die tomorrow. I entreat you to spare ordinary people!" In the early morning of the twelfth day, Lord Ling spat blood incessantly. Still he addressed his people in a loud voice, "Since I can't protect you when I am alive, I shall kill these rebels for you after I have become a ghost!" Blood gushed out with his speech. His last words were: "Spare my people!" which he shouted three times before he died.

23

In the above portrayal, we have tried to show that Ling was a many-sided man and that Confucianism was an essential factor in his thought. It seems clear now that throughout his entire life, despite his probable dissipation in early manhood, his failures in the Provincial Examination, and his attempts to become a Buddhist recluse, there had been one thing that remained constant: that is, his conviction to Confucian ideals and principles. If we view him basically as a Confucianist, we may interpret his pseudonym Jikongguan Zhuren as a passive endorsement of the Confucian doctrine that in times of peace and good government it is a scholar's honour and obligation to seek official appointment, while in times of decay and disorder it is no dishonour but a sign of personal integrity to reject government service.[44] And we may see, therefore, a logical link between his pseudonym and the moral stance that he assumed in *Two Slaps*. This moral stance is not only a conspicuous feature of his erotic stories, but owing to his influence, spawned a similar didacticism in the erotic fiction of this type written by authors of later generations.

Social Milieu of the Late Ming

24

Ling's Confucian leanings and sentiments, manifested especially in his life as an official and in the moral concerns that permeate his erotic stories, may, as previously indicated, be attributed to his family background and the education he had received. But this explanation will be incomplete if we do not point out its origin in the larger social background constructed by the state orthodoxy.

The state orthodoxy in the Ming was Neo-Confucianism. A philosophic school formed in the Northern Song dynasty (960–1127) and systematized in the hand of the great synthesizer Zhu Xi (1230–1300), Neo-Confucianism was far more sophisticated than the heritage from which it developed. Despite its metaphysical orientation which blends Buddhist and Daoist philosophy, Neo-Confucianism essentially concentrated on the rationalization of ethics and personal cultivation of morality. Its elaboration on the *a priori* "principle of heaven" provided for the traditional ethical hierarchy an unprecedentedly solid theory, a cosmology that reinterprets the Three Bonds and Five Relationships (*sangang wuchang*) as manifestations of the one single principle in the universe[45] and emphasizes the absolute necessity of their maintenance. One of the major founders of the school, Cheng Yi (1033–1107), even brought up such an extreme proposition: "Starving to death is incidental, whereas the loss of chastity is a matter of great consequence."[46] Later, in a similar vein, Zhu Xi also commented: "The sages might have said thousands of words, but they are only meant to teach people to revere the 'principle of heaven' and restrain their desires."[47]

Nevertheless, these orthodox attempts at re-examining and revitalizing the classics were for a long time regarded as "false learning" and suffered proscription in the State Examinations.[48] Although toward the end of the Southern Song, Neo-Confucianism "gained wide acceptance and great prestige" and enjoyed steady development even under the Mongol occupation, it was not until after the founding of the Ming dynasty that it finally became the predominant ideology sanctified by the imperial government.[49]

It is true that the rulers of the Ming regime were interested in Buddhism or Daoism or in both. The founder of the Ming, Zhu Yuanzhang, had himself been a Buddhist monk before rising to power,[50] and his successor Emperor Chengzu (r. 1403 – 1425) was a great believer in both religions. Emperor Shizong (r. 1522 – 1567) was so committed to the attainment of Daoist immortality that he devoted much attention to unusual elixirs, almost oblivious to his duties as a monarch. But the personal ideological favour of a sovereign does not necessarily represent state orthodoxy.[51] State orthodoxy is part of a superstructure,[52] linked with the power of the ruling class and enforced through means such as legislation, decrees, and education. Of the Three Teachings (*sanjiao*)[53] prevailing in the late imperial China, only Neo-Confucianism, due to the efforts the Ming emperors made in building their empire on Confucian thought patterns, gained political or institutionally authoritarian status.

25

The founding emperor, Zhu Yuanzhang, after defeating the Mongols and restoring Chinese sovereignty, enjoined that *The Four Books* and *The Five Classics* with Zhu Xi's commentaries be studied in the National Academy as basic texts, and that topics for the Civil Service Examinations be drawn from these canons. He also instructed that the curriculum in prefectural and sub-prefectural schools, official and private alike, should rest on the Confucian classics,[54] and even elementary education should be no exception.[55] When his successor Chengzu[56] ascended the throne, he had *The Three Great Collections* compiled,[57] stipulating that examination papers be judged according to their standard interpretations. Meanwhile, Confucian ethics were codified in *Da Ming lü* (The Legal Codes of the Ming),[58] and edicts were issued to the effect that, among other things, all widows who lost their husbands before the age of thirty but did not remarry until after fifty should be praised in their neighbourhood and the corvée of their households should be exempted.[59] All these educational, political, and legal measures consolidated the status of Neo-Confucianism as the state orthodoxy, making it not only accepted by the scholar/official class, but spreading it to the common people as well.

During the sixteenth century, however, various aspects of this dominant ideology were challenged by the Wang Yangming school. As a "monistic idealist" giving a new direction to Neo-Confucianism, Wang Yangming (1472 – 1529) emphasized perception rather than cultivation, and stressed reliance on the innate knowledge of the individual mind rather than reverence for the universal principle. He may still be considered as a moralist working "within the universe of Neo-Confucian discourse,"[60] yet his insistence on the autonomy of individual consciousness was eventually developed into a revolutionary "mass" philosophy represented by such populist thinkers as Wang Gen (1498 – 1582), Luo Rufang (1515 – 1588),

He Xinyin (1517–1579),[61] and Li Zhi (1527–1602). Li Zhi, "the greatest heretic and iconoclast,"[62] was the most outstanding among them. He carried Wang's epistemology so far as to criticize Confucius, renounce the classics as the criteria of right and wrong,[63] and openly profess that selfishness, sexual satisfaction, and the pursuit of profit are integral to human nature.[64] This iconoclasm was so influential at the time that it formed an intellectual trend and obtained a widespread following. Little wonder that some scholars call the latter half of the sixteenth century the "Li Zhi period."[65] During this period, oxthodox Neo-Confucianism was bogged down in stagnancy, and individualism and humanitarianism grew ever more prevalent along with the disintegration of traditional morality.

We agree, however, with the Ming-Qing scholar Bao Zunxin that ideas and trends in the seventeenth century were different from those in the sixteenth century.[66] Li Zhi's suicide in prison in 1602 and the founding of the Donglin Academy in 1604 actually marked the end of a nonconformist epoch and the inception of a Neo-Confucian moral crusade.[67] Gu Xiancheng (1550–1612), the major leader of the Donglin movement, made it clear at the Donglin inaugural meeting that they were to follow the lineage of Cheng-Zhu Neo-Confucianism, defend conventional moral principles, and redress Wang Yangming's errors.[68] The Donglin denunciation of Li Zhi's attitudes and their opposition to heterodox eclecticism were not just partisan passions; they actually represented a general tendency in the last few decades of the Ming. As Bao points out, the seventeenth century was a period in which strong efforts were made by politicians and scholars to return to the old tradition, and Neo-Confucianism was again elevated to the orthodox status politically and ideologically. We should not regard the publication of Nüsishu (Four Books for Women)[69] or the propagation of 27,141 exemplary women (lienü)[70] in The History of Ming, the writing of which began in the seventeenth century,[71] as isolated phenomena. They, in fact, reflected a growing ideological emphasis of the time.

This brief delineation of the state orthodoxy may account for Ling's Confucian leanings and for the moral stance he took in writing his fiction, but it certainly cannot explain why at the same time he made so many of his stories erotic. To look into the reasons for his eroticism, we must shift our attention to the economic and social changes that had occurred and continued during the period in which he lived.

According to Ray Huang, there were at least three economic "booms" in Chinese history, one in the Han dynasty, one in the period from Tang to Song, and the last one in the late Ming.[72] The flourishing economy of the Ming, starting from the early sixteenth century as what

26

W. G. Skinner has called the "ascending phase of the second great macrocycle,"[73] should be ascribed to a large extent to the founding emperor of the dynasty. Zhu Yuanzhang, who seems to have deemed it advisable to adopt a laissez-faire attitude in socio-economic spheres of government policy, said, "When stability has just been achieved in the country, people are physically exhausted and financially deficient. They are like birds starting to learn to fly, or trees newly planted, so we must not pull out their feathers or shake their roots. We should instead let them lead a pacific and restful life."[74] He encouraged people to migrate from overburdened arable land to open up virgin soil,[75] financed construction projects for water conservancy,[76] and alleviated levies to entice escapees in the dynastic war to return to their homeland. He also liberated slaves and simplified commercial taxes[77] to facilitate handicraft manufacture and internal trade. Thus agriculture, rural industry, and commerce began to recover during his reign, and continued to maintain a slow but steady growth in much of the next century (i.e., the 15th century). From the time Emperor Xiaozong (r. 1488 – 1506) was on the throne, the pace of the economy picked up, and it is a general consensus of historians that when Emperor Wuzong (r. 1506 – 1522) was in office there appeared a marked economic transformation, a sharp upsurge which in historiography in China is referred to as the "spouts of capitalism."

It was for some time argued that China's self-sufficient agrarian economy was predominant at the time, and most inland regions were still too backward to "interest merchants in visiting and buying their food crops and commodities."[78] However, in economically advanced areas, especially along the Southeast Coast, the Lower Yangtze River, and the Grand Canal,[79] great changes did occur. We see an ostensible shift from the traditional agricultural basis of social and economic structure to something akin to a market economy.

The development of subsidiary industry is regarded as important evidence of such a transformation. As productivity increased by the sixteenth century, a large part of the handicraft sector began to separate from agriculture and become an independent productive entity. Its rapid growth was most clearly reflected in textiles, and concrete examples of this are well-documented by, among other things, the meteoric rise of some cotton textile titans.[80] One Ming story, found in Feng Menglong's *Xingshi hengyan* (Constant Words to Awaken the World), is a vivid portrayal of how a weaver named Shi Fu starts from scratch and in the course of a few years grows into the rich owner of a fairly large weaving workshop.[81] This is fiction, of course, but we can find a more reliable source in Zhang Han's *Songchuang mengyu* (Reminiscences Written in My Study). Zhang Han

27

(1502 – 1589), a State Graduate who once served as Director of the Board of Personnel, describes his ancestor thus:

> "My ancestor Yizu, suffering from the family's financial decline in the middle of his life, was forced to live on a wine-selling business. But he gave up that business in the last year of the Chenghua reign (1487) because of a great flood. He bought a hand loom and began to weave linen in different colours. The quality of his cloth was so good that every time he had a bolt made it was sold immediately. The profit he gained from selling a bolt was equal to one-fifth of the value of his weaving instrument. After having worked about twenty days, he saved enough money to buy another loom. Later he owned as many as twenty-odd looms. Still he could not meet the demand of merchants who were crowded around his workshop waiting to purchase his cloth. His financial situation greatly improved. My later four ancestors who inherited his business all became rich."[82]

At the same time as this significant textile expansion, other handicraft industries such as metal smelting and casting, salt processing, and porcelain manufacturing also showed notable development. In the same period and later, some previously underdeveloped trades and professions like sugar extraction, cotton ginning, papermaking, printing, and publishing also began to burgeon, and printing and publishing were especially thriving. "When I was a youth studying for the Provincial Examination, there were no guide books whatsoever," wrote Li Xu (1505 – 1593) in his *Jie'an manbi* (Random Jottings of Li Xu). "Now such books published by commercial publishing houses can be found everywhere."[83] Although government agencies for publication are still active, they can no longer compare with commercial firms in terms of the volume of books published.[84] The rise of the commercial publishing business,[85] as the Ming scholar Hu Yinglin (1551 – 1604) observed, was fastest in three regions: Wu, Yue, and Min,[86] and the advanced printing techniques they applied included not only various movable type-faces,[87] but multi-coloured printings as well.

Commercialization that reached a full-fledged stage of develop-ment was probably the most conspicuous sign of the economic changes. The agrarian idyll that "women wove, men worked outside, and servants did household odd jobs" seemed to be diminishing rapidly in certain areas and was replaced by the commercial com-petition of a market economy. It goes without saying that the man-ufacture of handicrafts, on a scale much larger than before, was for public consumption rather than for private use. Even agriculture, the basis of the traditional imperial order, began entering commerce. Cash crops appeared in response to increasing market demand,[88] and a part of the rice that was a staple everywhere was now commercialized.

Interregional and, to some extent, international trade showed that commercialization, if not new in kind, was at least new in magnitude. "People in the north who are good at cultivation but clumsy at spinning will ship their cotton to the south for sale, whereas people in the south superior at weaving but uninterested in cultivation will transport and sell their cloth to the north."[89] Mercantile exchange at the time was so broad[90] that one could even find a variety of fish in the food stores in Beijing that previously had had no fish markets at all.[91]

As more and more people engaged in commercial activities and left their land unattended, trade was not only carried on in the "three macroregional cores,"[92] but was also expanded overseas. One of the stories by Ling Mengchu, often cited as a description of maritime business adventures, can at least verify that private junks did go as far as to Southeast Asia for trading during the middle and late Ming.[93] The wide use of silver bullion[94] and the adoption of the single-whip method of taxation (*yitiaobian fa*) by the end of the sixteenth century, which commuted labour levies to monetary payments,[95] were actually a reflection of the demand resulting from this large-scale interregional and international commerce.

Also worth note is urbanization, a phenomenon that was concomitant with the flowering of industry and commerce. Urban-ization appeared at its inception to be related to the migration of peasants from countryside to city, a migration that began as early as the fifteenth century, apparently the result of malpractice on the part of collateral and junior members of the ruling clan and rich and powerful landlords who joined in abusing land policies.[96] It was not until the sixteenth century, when the commercial economy was flourishing, that forced migration gradually turned into conscious settlement. As a large number of landless farmers and farmers with small landholdings, now having seen the alluring prospect of making money in industrial and commercial sectors, were willing to move out of the countryside to pursue a better life, cities underwent an unprecedented increase of population and expansion.

The two metropolises, Beijing and Nanjing, were no longer political and cultural centers only; they also became the biggest commercial distributing cities, functioning as national economic hubs respectively in the north and the south. Regional centers had a similar evolution.

Suzhou,[97] for instance, had always been the administrative capital of the prefecture, and since the Hongzhi reign (1488–1506) an army of labourers appeared. The workers employed for weaving and dyeing alone numbered nearly ten thousand. Another city, Linqing, located along the Grand Canal, was so economically developed that by the end of the sixteenth century, shops and stores spread everywhere, and grocery, draper, and satin stores alone numbered one hundred and seventy.

30   While large and medium-sized cities were undergoing a marked development, the rising prosperity of market towns was even more conspicuous. Market towns were usually smaller than cities in population. Some might have had only a few hundred households, whereas large ones could have more than ten thousand. Quite a few towns had previously been the seats of district yamen or garrison posts, while the majority of them developed from former villages, desolate fishing ports, or settlements dependent on rural periodic markets. One good example is Shenze Zhen:

> [It] was, at the beginning of the Ming, a village where there were only fifty to sixty households. During the Jiajing reign (1522–1567), its population doubled and people began to live on the man-ufacturing of damask silk. Then it was given the status of 'town.'[98]

Newly developed market towns like Shenze Zhen, which were mostly concentrated in the regions of the Lower Yangtze Delta where the commercialization of agriculture was more popular and the cotton textile industry was more advanced than in other parts of the country, are too numerous to be listed. Some of the towns grew so big and prosperous that it was hard to tell them from cities. In a typical large town, weaving workshops, dye-houses, restaurants, teahouses, pawnshops, grain stores, herbal medicine stores, hotels, and vegetable markets lined the streets, and "buyers and sellers from all over the country were crowded together on roads like bees and ants, leaving virtually no room for one more person to squeeze by."[99]

    Whether or not one agrees that the late Ming economic changes were "sprouts of capitalism,"[100] it is undeniable that there was at the time a convergence of industrialization, commercialization, and urbanization. This trend toward the dominance of a fledgling market economy fostered the beginnings of a generalized materialism in society.

    What we call materialism refers mainly to the pursuit of luxury, love of pleasure, and the striving for money and profit. As the traditional emphasis on spiritual life began to disintegrate with material abundance, people became more and more fond of extravagance.[101]

Lavish dining was one of the hallmarks of this new ethos. Rich househoulds, no longer considering thrift a virtue, would treat their guests with exotic delicacies from land and sea. Following in their wake, lower-middle class households would also give expensive dinner parties in order to flaunt their wealth.[102] He Liangjun (1506–73) accurately observed that in his youth the banquets for four to six people in the Songjiang area usually had only five main dishes and five side dishes, and sumptuous repasts were held once or twice a year in gentry households. In the last years of the Jiajing reign (1560s), however, even ordinary people would host a small festive board, capable of serving ten or more main dishes, while wealthy families would offer a distinguished visitor a grandiose feast that could have as many as a hundred dishes with all kinds of delicacies.

31

The new impulse to luxury was also manifested in fashion. In the early and middle Ming, women were accustomed to wearing dresses in drab colours; but now they favoured elegant attire with lighter shades and shorter sleeves. Their shoes became more elaborate with high heels, and their hairdos and jewelry were constantly changed. A similar phenomenon occurred in men's clothing. The corrugated bristle hat, as was officially stipulated in *Taizu shilu* (The Factual Records of Emperor Taizu), was designed for those who were above the status of licentiate. Gradually, however, men of wealth without scholarly attainment began to wear it as an emblem of nobility, and later its use extended to all classes of people.[103] Silk clothing, a previously frivolous luxury, became prevalent even among servants and workers, and the fine, glossed, silk-lined garments for lowest-rank civil servants like government runners were now disdained in favour of Yang-ming dress, the Eight Scholars' dress, and the Twenty-four Seasons dress.[104] Even scholars would find cotton gowns, their standard dress, too cheap to wear. Fan Lian (1540–?), for instance, was an "extremely poor" literatus who had the highest regard for economy and simplicity. Yet he finally had to force himself to wear "decorated" garb.

Material enjoyment in the late Ming was not confined to lavish dining and expensive clothing. Living in magnificent mansions,[105] using silver tableware, and furnishing rooms with elegant furniture were not unusual. It was a natural progression that sex also became integrated into this material world. No longer seen simply as a procreative function in marriage, it now began to be perceived as a pleasure as satisfying as the finest silk or the most savoury of dishes. The growing openness of women toward sensual enjoyment, and even a sort of sexual licence, which had previously been limited to males of the elite orders, was a symbol of this new development.

One of the most striking examples was a woman known as the Wife of Wang Ke who was mentioned by the scholar Gui Youguang (1507–1571) in his *Gui Zhenchuan wenji* (Literary Works of Gui Youguang). A promiscuous woman, the Wife of Wang Ke was fond of liaisons with young men. She often invited her paramours to come to her house and drink and sleep with her when her husband, an elderly drunkard who hardly paid attention to her, was away from home. Once she was taking a bath with a youth of the streets and bade her daughter-in-law to bring water to them. The young man, upon seeing her daughter-in-law, immediately showed an interest in her. In order to satisfy him, the Wife of Wang Ke insisted that her daughter-in-law drink with him and another four men and then forced her into intercourse with all of them.[106]

Not only did women of wealthy families spend more time and energy purchasing fashionable dress and seeking intimate male company, but "girls in the fields and crones in the brush," to use Fan Lian's words, "craved to be seductresses." The strangest phenomenon, according to this eyewitness, was that there even appeared "female knights-errant" who were willing to help men in sexual matters:

> Although Songjiang [prefecture] has been called licentious and extravagant, we had never before had the term "surrogate mother." From the time that Saleswoman Wu came on the scene and saw that the physician Gao Heqin had no offspring and rented herself out to beget a child with him, she became famous as a female knight-errant. Families of wealth and official connections competed to engage her. Wherever she went, households treated her as especially valuable.
>
> On the pretext of being a business woman, Wu made her daily living as a hanger-on in rich houses. She was skilled in making sexual devices and aphrodisiacs and leading people to indulge themselves in wine and wallow in pleasures. From this she accumulated an estate of several thousand taels. She came and went in a palanquin and was called "Triple Wife."[107]

This propensity for sexual openness has usually been ascribed to the "lecherous" lifestyle of emperors and their advocacy of the art of the bedchamber.[108] Nevertheless, we must reiterate that in spite of the influence of the emperors and their high-ranking officials on general sexual practices, the change of morality could not have been so dramatic and so widely accepted without the longer trend of materialism generated by the economic prosperity.

Materialism was virtually ubiquitous; even in literary spheres one could feel its impact. Writing, especially fiction writing, was now not merely a creative activity; it was also a production aimed at making money. It is true that, unlike poetry,[109] vernacular fiction was invested from the very beginning with an entertaining mission. Literary historians, by quoting scholars like Duan Chengshi (fl. 843 – 863), Meng Yuanlao (fl. 1126 – 1147), Wu Zimu (fl. 1270), and Guanyuan Naideweng (fl. 1235), have already indicated its origin, that is, the commercial story-telling undertaken at market-places in Tang-Song times. But never before had fiction been so heavily subjected to literary middlemen – the publishers – and to the control of economic laws as in the late Ming when the printing and publishing industry was experiencing an unprecedented prosperity. As literati, particularly hacks, were writing for profit in a slipshod way at the urging of their publishers, they, together with their "Master Manufacturers," gradually turned fiction into a commodity.

33

"Writing," Daniel Defoe writes in 1725 about the situation of literature in England, "is become a very considerable Branch of the English Commerce. The Booksellers are the Master Manufacturers or Employers. The several Writers, Authors, Copyers, Sub-writers, and all other Operators with Pen and Ink are the workmen employed by the said Master Manufacturers."[110] To an uncanny extent, what Defoe describes was also true of the changes taking place in the Chinese literary environment at the turn of the seventeenth century.

As a market commodity, vernacular fiction was produced for a broad range of consumers. Writers no longer aspired to satisfy the elite in order to achieve literary fame.[111] They first and foremost pandered to the public. Most of them, contrary to what some Ming-Qing fiction scholars tend to believe, wrote not only for the gentry class, but also for people with less education;[112] not only for readers of different levels, but also for an audience who might be semi-literate or even illiterate.[113] It was likely that they did not strive for high literary standards when they were set to writing by their "employers" with the stimulus of a lucrative profit, but there was one thing they would never or would never be allowed to sacrifice, that is, their commitment to amusement. From the titillating or diverting titles of *huaben* story collections (including the titles of Ling Mengchu's story collections), we can easily see that there was a commercial orientation in the majority of the late Ming fictional works.

The foregoing analysis outlines the underlying social forces that drove Ling to be a Confucian apologist and at the same time an erotic writer. This seeming contradiction reflected, in fact, the contradiction between the traditional state ideology based on the "timeless" agrarian mode of production and the newly-booming economy characteristic of more modern "bourgeois" mercantilism. It seems that superstructure is not always determined by economic base. Although there is no doubt a certain relationship between superstructural ideology and material productive forces, their relationship, as Max Weber tried to point out, is characterized more by *interaction* than by *determination*,[114] and this holds especially true in a period of social and economic change. In the latter half of the Ming dynasty when such changes were underway, it was understandable that there was an ineluctable conflict between the spiritual intercourse of men and their material behaviour. The tension between eroticism and morality in Ling's sexual stories was therefore not just a personal quandary of the author; it was determined by the contradictory tension of his contemporary society.

LING MENGCHU'S EROTIC STORIES

In his preface to *Slapping the Table in Amazement*, Ling writes:

> After a long period of peace and tranquility, people are loose-living
> and licentious. Some young neophyte writers of frivolity have no
> sooner learned how to hold a brush than they begin to defame
> the world, writing sheer fabrications that are either too absurd to
> believe or too obscene to read.... Officials of insight concerned
> with social mores have suggested that such publications be rigor-
> ously banned, and I think they are right.

Judging from this disapproving comment, Ling seems to have had no intention of writing erotica. In fact, however, we find him still unable to get rid of eroticism. Erotic fiction, treated in a broad fashion,[115] describes activities that are sexual or sexually affiliated. With their focus on the presentation of such activities, Ling's five erotic stories included in this book all possess the characteristics of this genre. These five stories, due to the conventions of the *huaben* style, actually contain ten tales, for each story is made up of two independent tales: the prologue and the main tale.[116] Though varying in complexity and differing in length, there is one feature that the author has made common to all of them: that is, their preoccupation with sexuality.

Aspects of Sexuality

One of the characteristics of erotic fiction, according to the Kron-hausens, is its exaggerated depiction of "supersexed males" who are extraordinary in virile stamina and have an enormous male organ.[117] Whether or not the heroes in Ling's stories are so sexually endowed we cannot tell, for such information is not provided except in the case of a young monk who has a penis seven or eight inches long and is able to have sex with ten women in a single night. Most of Ling's male characters, however, can at least be called libertines, renowned not for their physical attributes but for their seductive skills. They usually appear as scholars preparing for the Civil Service Examinations, but in courting a woman they like, in order to seduce her into surrendering her chastity, they are bold, aggressive, and cunningly capable of seductive savoir-faire.

35

Tangqing, the protagonist in the prologue of "The Wife Swappers," is such a scholar unfettered by traditional sexual restraints. Sex appears to him simply as a natural impulse, and once aroused, it seeks fulfillment regardless of obstacles. Another Casanova is a handsome young man called Teng in the prologue of "Fatal Seduction." In comparison with Tangqing, Teng seems a more experienced seducer, capable of using his wits and patience to steal another man's wife. Though there is no reference in the story as to his phallus – size, shape, or the degree of tumescence – we do see that he has his own unique strength, that is, his expertise in the art of the bedchamber.[118] With his lovemaking skills, he is able to set his partner "atingle," making her feel extremely satiated after having had sex with him.

According to Ding Yaokang (1599–1671), there were three types of libertine. The first was the "scholar-libertine" (*caizi yin*), who tended to be handsome and talented and was interested only in the most beautiful of women; the second type was the "profligate libertine" (*dangzi yin*), who spent a fortune on pretty women in the pleasure quarters; and the third was the "indiscriminate libertine" (*xionghuang yin*), who was so shamelessly obsessed with sex that he would copulate with any woman regardless of age, beauty, or social class.[119] If Tangqing and Teng belong respectively to the first two categories, we may regard Bu Liang, a character notorious for his ceaseless dissipation in "Fatal Seduction," as an example of the third type. One of his unfortunate victims is Madam Wu, the chaste wife of Licentiate Jia, and Bu Liang is so crazed for her that he even rapes her in sleep during her sojourn at a nunnery as she prays for a child.

> The door was closed. Bu Liang pulled aside the bed curtain and
> was assailed by a strong smell of alcohol. Madam Wu, her cheeks
> charmingly red like a tipsy crabapple, looked to him even more
> beautiful than before. In an agony of desire, Bu Liang planted
> a kiss on her lips, and she showed no reaction. He then gently

removed her lower garments, laying bare before him her pale-white thighs. Having swiftly parted her legs, he mounted her, inserted himself, and started to thrust.

Swollen with pride, Bu Liang said to himself, "Pity, my little creature! You are now in my hands!" Although too inebriated to move, Madam Wu neverless experienced a dreamlike sensation that someone was making love to her. But she mistook her ravisher for her husband and let him use her at his will. Soon she was aroused by his fierce ramming. In spite of being in a hallucinatory state, she began to moan as her passion reached full flow. A wild surge then ripped through him, and Bu Liang was unable to restrain himself any longer. Clutching her in his arms, he cried, "My dearest, I am dying!" And then he ejaculated, his sperm shooting like a water-spout.

In Ling's erotic stories, chaste women like Madam Wu are as few as morning stars, and the majority of his females are women of easy virtue, highly passionate, sensual, or sexually insatiable. The episode from the prologue of "In the Inner Quarters," in which the author describes sexual combats between a group of concubines and a scholar, provides us with a glimpse:

He squatted uncomfortably in the cave, with no doubt that it was a safe place. Nevertheless, as the saying goes, "Events are unpredict-able and enemies are bound to meet on a narrow road." To his great surprise, he found that the red gauze lantern was, too, advancing toward the pavilion. Watching from the darkness of the grotto, which made the lantern and its surroundings even brighter, he caught sight of about ten young women outside, all in beautiful attire, and all coquettish, frivolous, and seductively charming. He peered in fascination, having no expectation that this flock of women would swarm to the cave, and reaching out their hands, lifted the felt blanket. All of them, to be sure, were taken aback as they found a stranger inside.

"How come this gentleman is not the one we are expecting?" they said, looking at each other in great confusion. A mature woman among them seized the lantern and cast its light upon the scholar.

"This one is not bad!" she said, after having taken a close look at him.

With her delicate hand she grabbed him by the hand and pulled him out of the cave. Submissively the scholar let her lead him and did not even dare to ask her where they were going. Yet he was certain that nothing untoward would possibly occur.

He was ushered into their boudoir where a feast of wine and delicacies had been laid out. Each of the beauties vied to entertain him, as if they wished to win in a *liubo* game. They began by exchanging cups with him, and then proceeded to encircle his neck with their arms, stroking his face, and kissing him on the mouth. A few cups of wine were sufficient to render them bubbling with lewd excitement, and finally, without observing proprieties, they forced him onto the bed.

Some of them, having crawled inside the bed curtain, busied themselves with the removal of their clothes, while others were active around his waist. With no idea how to take turns, they had to start with whoever was in the closest proximity to him. The moment he ejaculated, they used their tongues to clean him and fondled his organ until he was brought once again to erection. Fortunately, he was a young man capable of releasing twice more his "string-of-beads" arrows. Without, however, even so much as a minute's recuperation between such strenuous bouts, even a man of iron could hardly endure. He felt sick and tired. Yet the women did not disperse till about the fifth watch. By that time the scholar was utterly depleted, his whole body listless and numb, and his limbs too weak to support him.

As a recurrent motif, female obsession with lust and amorous adventurousness features in almost all of Ling's erotic stories. The nun Jingguan in "The Elopement of a Nun," though only about seventeen years old, is nevertheless sexually mature. When she is camouflaged as a "priest" and is invited to share the bed with a young man she fancies, she immediately begins her caresses between his legs. Like Fanny Hill, she grasps the function of "that instrument" and keeps on nudging it until her bedmate wakes up.

Lady Di, a cultured and conventional wife, seems to have been a victim of Teng's stratagem at the beginning. But after the loss of her chastity, she no longer remains passive. The sexual pleasure given her by her rapist, something that she has never before experienced as a respectable married woman, is so ecstatic and so satisfying that she cannot resist the temptation to continue. Being conquered sexually as well as emotionally, she finally draws herself away from the moral values she has previously cherished.

The most lecherous female seems to be Madam Jade, the

nymphomaniac in the story "In the Inner Quarters," whose goal is to reach all the satisfactions of carnality. As an adulteress, she is very different from Lady Di. She conceives the idea of seducing Ren Junyong, a retainer of her husband; she makes a rope ladder – an indispensable device for her liaison; and she has her maid set a tryst and badgers her reluctant fornicator as he is frightened halfway through and wishes to renege.

Lady Di, after her intimate relationship with Teng has been cut off by her husband, falls ill and expires. Yet affection and sentimentality are almost unknown to Madam Jade. She is not only much more daring and strong-willed, but also more rational and practical. To her, men are just tools. She wants them more for fulfilling her sexual desires than for so-called love. She hardly cares whether her maid Rosy Cloud wants to share Ren Junyong. As long as she can keep the man and indulge herself in fleshly enjoyment, anything else is of incidental consideration. She even helps Madam Beautiful Moon have intercourse with her lover and invites other concubines into her lascivious orgies. However, she does care about one thing: the phallus. After her husband returns home and has his retainer castrated, she loses interest in him immediately, for she knows that without his "snake" to play with, he is uterly useless to her.

Ling, in his erotic stories, hardly devotes himself to concupiscent routines between husband and wife. What he describes is mostly sensual pleasure unbounded by matrimony. Adultery was one kind of extramarital sex, but for men of the gentry class, the more common form was visiting prostitutes.

While covertness and deceitfulness were marked features of adultery on the part of wives, a man's dalliance with prostitutes was permissible (if not legal) and therefore was often carried on in an open manner except for officials. This should be attributed to the privilege male adults enjoyed in the traditional patriarchal society that gave them the right to freedom and granted them the benefit of infidelity.

Ren Junyong, Commander Yang Jian's "outer-house guest" in "In the Inner Quarters," often drags his friend out to haunt the licenced quarters. In order to seduce him at her mistress's bidding, Rosy Cloud teases him as he returns to his studio early in the morning: "Sir, you are coming back in the early morning, so you must have spent the night outside, I suppose?" Ren Junyong feels unashamed about his whoring and frankly admits: "Yes, I did. It's agonizing to sleep alone."

Another client of brothels is Yi, the main character in "The Wife Swappers." As a scion of a rich family, he is lavish in his spending, and any beautiful courtesan, no matter how far away she lives, will receive his patronage. With his substantial family property, he can afford to stay in the pleasure quarters for days on end. He never needs to conceal this from his wife. In fact, his wife often encourages him to stay in a brothel for a longer period. No doubt Yi is very appreciative of her generosity. It is just that this generosity is not entirely selfless.

The story of Yi and his wife Di is far more complicated. It tells how an intended wife-swapping transmutes into double liaisons and ends in a tragicomedy. Swapping, or the practice of swinging,[120] was very popular in the late Ming. *Yiqing Zhen* (A Joyful Array), a short novel by an unknown author which is remarkable for its ribaldry and its explicitly erotic details, offers us a most vivid picture in this regard.[121] What, by comparison, makes the wife-swapping in Ling's story different is its half-transparency, its deceptiveness, and its Machiavellianism, although in view of the lack of a simultaneous exchange by both parties, it is not typical of group sex.

In the various forms of group sex, the carnal orgy is prominent in erotic fiction. The orgy is similar to swapping in that it often involves two couples copulating together. But it is wilder and has more people: maids and menservants in addition to the participating husbands and wives, as is depicted in *Yiqing zhen*. Ling offers no graphic elaboration of the orgy in his stories. Only in "The Wife Swappers" does there appear a brief scene of an orgiastic party, which is held in Yi's house, and the participants include high-class courtesans, Yi's friends notorious for their debauchery, the two husbands Yi and Hu, as well as their wives Di and Men. Di and Men take no real part in sexual intercourse. They are simply voyeurs hiding themselves behind the screen to watch their husbands and other people flirting with the courtesans and engaging in all kinds of lewd activities. In this sense, their orgy is different from those that function as a dramatic climax in the majority of erotica: it is only a preparation, designed to release the two wives from their inhibitions about sex with each other's husband.

Ling's most frequent reference to group sex is the *menage à trois*. Because of the system of concubinage in imperial China,[122] it was not unusual for a man to sleep with two or more women at the same time,[123] and therefore it is quite natural that Yi, after his sexual conquest of Men, wishes to take her as his concubine and engage her in a threesome to satisfy his erotic desires. "My wife is not jealous," he tells her. "The other day she proposed that I take you to my home and she would help me seduce you. After we get married, we may live together and the three of us may enjoy mutual pleasures. Isn't it wonderful!"

In fact, the *menage à trois* was not confined to polygamous marriage; it often occurred outside the concubinage system. A maid could become her mistress' bedmate in the lovemaking trio, and concubines could enter into an alliance for the sake of joint seduction, as we see in "In the Inner

Quarters." What strikes us most about the maid/mistress relationship in this story is the active role the maid Rosy Cloud plays and the generosity her mistress shows toward her. It is interesting to note that Madam Jade's seduction of Ren Junyong is first suggested by her maid, and moreover, even before her mistress puts her seductive plan into action, Rosy Cloud has made it clear to her that later she would also like to share the man. "Ma'am," says she, rather daringly, "you really should devise a plan so that he can enter and we can both of us enjoy some recreation together."

Rosy Cloud is not the only one who joins Madam Jade in her bed. There is another woman, Madam Beautiful Moon, who also envies Madam Jade and wishes to share her lover. When they are alone together, she asks Madam Jade to give her a chance, and to her surprise, gets her consent:

"Is he coming this evening, Sister?" she asked.

"Why should he not?" said Madam Jade. "To be frank with you, he visits every night, and it is unlikely that he'll fail to come tonight."

"When he comes, you will still keep him all to yourself?" asked Madam Beautiful Moon.

"Sister," said Madam Jade, "you said yourself that you wouldn't take part in such activities."

"Well, I was not being honest when I said that," Madam Beautiful Moon explained. "In fact, I would also like to join the fun, should you permit me."

"Certainly I am very willing to accommodate you if that's what you want," Madam Jade replied. "Tonight I shall send him to your room when he arrives."

"But I don't even know him," said Madam Beautiful Moon. "I would feel most embarrassed if he comes directly to my place. I only wish to be your helper."

Madam Jade smirked. "I hardly need a helper, you know," she said.

"I tend to be timid at the beginning," murmured Madam Beautiful Moon. "So perhaps I shall take your place in your bedroom? You just keep it secret until he and I become familiar with each other."

"Such being the case, you simply need to hide yourself somewhere first," Madam Jade told her. "After he gets into bed and removes his clothes, I will extinguish the light and let you replace me."

"Sister, are you sure you will really do me this favour?" asked Madam Beautiful Moon.

"Of course!" said Madam Jade.

Also interesting in this story is a similar complicity between the concubines Sister Smile and Aunt Flower who develop a companionship for the purpose of collaborative seduction and copulation. With no other suitable male in the household, they, too, have to settle upon their husband's retainer. In order to seduce him and taste the delights of a *menage à trois*, they intercept him one night. Ren Junyong, fearing that they may report him to the steward, has to follow their instructions to sneak to Sister Smile's boudoir, where Aunt Flower joins them and the three share the bed together. This form of enjoyment is indeed a novel experience for the women, who, happy and sastisfied in making love in a threesome, "toss and turn like clouds and rain raging in a fury, like mandarin ducks in heat in their conjugal felicity."

The relationship of camaraderie or "sisterhood," found between Sister Smile and Aunt Flower, also features Ling's other female characters. Unlike the viragos or shrews in some famous late Ming novels, women in Ling's stories are usually not jealous and sometimes even regard it as a virtue to share their male partners with each other. The wealthy woman in "The Elopement of a Nun" is another such example, so generous as to offer to share her lover with a nun. Being a licentious abbess, the nun shows very strong interest, although not without suspicion that the offer might not be genuine. The rich lady then assures her: "It is I who want your help, so you needn't worry that I'll be jealous of you. After you come to my house, I may even ask you to sleep with us in the same bed." Later she does invite the abbess to join them in her bedroom. The abbess teaches the lady various lovemaking skills and they find an immense sensual delight in their *manage à trois*, in which – if it is not an exaggerated description – nothing "was superfluous and no body part could not be brought into play except for one of their heads."

There is, in Ling's erotic stories, also a "reverse" *menage à trois*. Most commonly, *menage à trois* consists of one man and two women, while the reverse *menage à trois* is made up of two men and one woman, opposite to the norm of gender combination as is presented in "One Woman and Two Monks":

> After supper the three of them slept together. Du put her arms around Zhiyuan's neck as soon as they got into bed, paying no attention to his master. The Old Monk had ejaculated during

the day and was unable to achieve erection. Thinking that their intercourse might help stimulate his own sexual desire, he decided to let them begin. Their ecstatic moans, accompanied by the lubricious sounds of sex, indeed excited him. In a fever, he started to savour her charms here and there, and then threw one arm around her and with the other pressed her to his bosom. His caress of her vagina, now filled up by Zhiyuan's member, made him feel so aroused that his own penis, urged on by his hand, became semi-hard. He tried to push his disciple aside to replace him, yet Zhiyuan, having just reached the summit of his ecstasies, was unwilling to give way to him, and meanwhile, with both her hands Du also clutched the Young Monk tightly, protecting him from being pushed away.

What is worth noticing in this passage is the voyeurism on the part of the Old Monk. In a morally open period like the late Ming, in which both men and women seemed to love observing others in action, voyeurism became an indispensable component of group sex. Madam Jade, for instance, is so aroused by seeing Madam Beautiful Moon in intercourse with Ren Junyong that she strips her clothes and jumps onto their bed. Lady Di in "The Wife Swappers," incapable of controlling herself after watching Hu's flirtation with the courtesans, resolves to commit herself to adultery. If there is anything that can explain why Ling's characters are so fond of *menage à trois*, it is probably the voyeurism it involves, or rather, the sexual stimulation provided by voyeurism.

The monks' illicit sex brings our attention to a conspicuous feature of Ling's stories: the description of the carnal activities of the clergy. In theory, clerics were supposed to lead an ascetic life of religious cultivation; in reality, however, sex of various sorts was common to them. Ling, in spite of his Buddhist leanings, seems not to have had a favourable impression of monks and nuns, and in his fiction, nearly all of them appear as "hungry devils of lust."

The monk Guangming, in the prologue of "One Woman and Two Monks," seems outwardly a hospitable man inclined to make friends with both officials and scholars, yet secretly he is an abductor of women. Similarly, the abbess of the Green Duckweed Nunnery in "The Elopement of a Nun" is notoriously lecherous, though on public occasions she appears quite respectable. She forces her novices to behave like prostitutes, and she herself, taking advantage of her senior position, is usually the first one to sleep with any man they lured into the temple. While Gaungming is clandestine, the abbess is quite overt about her sexual activities. "You think we are celibates?" she confides to her friend, the rich woman from the south. "To be honest with you, we have patrons to keep us company from time to time." Her analogous but more clever counterpart is the supervising "nun" of the Nunnery of Merits and Virtues in the prologue of the same story. As a man in female disguise, "she" has a huge penis and is superbly skilled in the art of the bedchamber, capable of seducing both village housewives and ladies from good families and copulating with as many as ten in a single night. While the Green Duckweed Nunnery functions as an unlicenced brothel for men, "her" convent is a *de facto* bawdyhouse for women, where female "pilgrims" can stay for one night or for several days on end, to immerse themselves in the pleasures of sex.

43

Similar to clerical sex, albeit in a completely different category, is homosexuality, for legally speaking, neither could bring about an institutional union.[124] While the frequency of illicit sex occurring among Buddhist priests and acolytes was often ascribed to the notion that most of them came from the lowest rungs of society and had not yet reached the stage of absolute extinction of desire, the origins of the popularity of male same-sex relationships in the late Ming seems also to have related to a specific class of people at the bottom of the social scale who are historically referred to as *jianmin* (pariahs).[125] Because Fujian province was the home of *jianmin* and was best known for its homosexual practice, people in Ming times euphemistically called male homosexuality the "southern custom" (*nanfeng*).[126] This "southern custom," according to Xie Zhaozhe's (1567–1624) *Wu zazu* (The Five Miscellanies), had become such a fashion by the end of the sixteenth century that it could be found in northern cities as well.[127] From Xie's account as well as from some other sources, we can infer that in the late Ming male same-sex relationships were generally tolerated by society. Van Gulik believed that lesbianism in the Ming was "quite common,"[128] whereas male homosexuality was relatively rare. His assumption, however, has not been borne out and all the evidence that we have from late Ming erotica points to the contrary.[129] In Ling's stories, at least seven men, including Judge Lin, Guard Yu, Commander Yang Jian, Ren Junyong, Zhiyuan, the Old monk, and Wenren, engage in sex with each other, whereas we find only two "lesbians:" Madam Jade and her maid Rosy Cloud.

As the sole example of lesbianism, the relationship between Madam Jade and Rosy Cloud is quite enlightening. It suggests that female same-sex encounters are simply a poor substitute for sex with a man. Madam Jade, as we have seen before, is a woman with strong sexual desires. As she finds her "widowed" nights too lonely to bear, she invites her maid Rosy Cloud to sleep with her. To give vent to her suppressed libido, she talks to the maid about sex, and when aroused, has the maid take out a dildo, put it on, and make love to her as if she were a male. Rosy Cloud does as she is told, making her mistress moan and groan with pleasure.

What is of particular interest here is the way they perform coitus. We notice that they use a dildo, whereas there is no mention of cunnilingus. Other late Ming erotic works also confirm that the dildo was a sexual instrument commonly used by women engaging in same-sex activities and that cunnilingus, often a feature of Western erotica, is hardly ever applied. This dildo phenomenon, we believe, can be explained by the fact that most of the late Ming lesbians were bisexual, lacking a deep affection toward their partners. They took homosexuality as an imitation of heterosexuality and resorted to it only when they were alone at home and needed to allay their erotic hunger, although as a "stand-in" it could not really satisfy their "sexual appetite," as is shown by the dialogue between Madam Jade and Rosy Cloud in the midst of their sex play:

> "Is this dildo as good as a real man?" Rosy Cloud asked.
> "It is only for fun and can't really satisfy our sexual appetite," replied her mistress. "The feel of a real man is of course much better."

Comparing lesbianism with male homosexuality that was prevalent in the late Ming, we might remark on one similarity: while the former was a vicarious means of sensual pleasure for lonely women confined in the inner quarters, the latter seems to have been practiced by men mainly to add variety to their sexual lives. Of all the men involved in the "southern custom" in Ling's stories, none are "gay" in today's sense of the word and none show any commitment toward their partners. For example, Wenren is a romantic youth with some bisexual proclivities, and the Old Monk enjoys having sex with women more than with men, preferring to eat "chick" (female) than "homely food" (man). Commander Yang Jian, a married man with a bevy of wives and concubines, is cruel enough to castrate his ex-catamite Ren Junyong, and Judge Lin, in spite of his ostensible affection toward his young partner Guard Yu, hardly feels guilty when he sends him away for some minor transgressions. To them, homosexual relations are simply situational and hedonistic – for fun rather than for a stable loving partnership. This hedonistic attitude is, in effect, not only accountable for their lack of love, but also helps explain why trans-generational sex[130] is invariably more common among them and why those senior in age or position always play the role of penetrator, whereas young men or boys can only serve in the passive role.

Of Ling's five erotic stories, we can make one flat generalization: all are marked by a focus on sex rather than on love. Men esteem women according to their sexiness; women select men in the light of their virility and the size of their penis. Men seduce women in order to possess their sexual organs; women make liaisons with men for the sake of enjoying the pleasure of orgasm. To satisfy their erotic appetites, men go whoring and indulge themselves in group sex or same-sex relations; to quench their lust, women are as daring as Pan Jinlian (Golden Lotus) in committing adultery and feel free to use lesbianism as a convenience when a male partner is not available.

Sex and love are not always clear-cut concepts.[131] "Love," in common euphemism, "is used to cover all the manifestations of sexual impulse" in the West,[132] while in China "sex" was once also connected with sentimental passion (*qing*).[133] It included love or generated love rather than being an antithesis to it.[134] In Ling's erotic stories, however, sex is quite detached. It is treated as an urge of the body and erogenous zones and all feelings other than lust are almost excluded or de-emphasized. As Hu Shiying perspicaciously notes, Ling in his erotic stories does not describe loving affection between men and women. What he describes is their "sexuality in its naked form."[135]

Pleasure and Repressive Mechanisms

We might be giving the impression that Ling wrote soley within the framework of erotic fiction. In fact, he simultaneously followed another tradition, the tradition that used literature as a vehicle for instructive purposes. If he cared about a wide audience of readers and tried to get them interested in his *Two Slaps* by using sex as a topic, he was equally or even more concerned with their moral education. Eroticism constitutes only one plane in his writings. All his erotic stories consist of two planes: one is devoted to the depiction of fleshly enjoyment, and the other is reserved for his commitment to the containment of that pleasure for ethical purposes. To those critics who focus only on the eroticism without giving due attention to its repressive mechanisms, Ling's erotic stories seem to have been written only to present the enjoyment of sex. Yet we do not have to go to the other extreme and apologize for them by overemphasizing their moralistic implications. What distinguishes his erotic stories is simply the tension between sexuality and morality. This tension, from a formalist point of view, may be described as an interaction between the story *per se* and the way of representation. However, given the fact that sexuality was socially embedded and moral constraint is basically a deliberate textual deployment by the author, it is more appropriate to see it as a result of chiasmic formulations between "historicity of texts and textuality of history."[136]

There is not always a clear division between "textuality" and "historicity." In its actual presentation we see that it is often the situation that these two planes are intermingled with each other. Before we turn to the didactic sections of his stories which are relatively detached and independent, it is necessary for us to first attend to the authorial controlling mechanisms, the "textuality" in "historicity," which Ling himself called "decent ways of writing" (*bimo yadao*).[137]

46

In the "Introductory Remarks" (*fanli*) to his stories, Ling says that he was determined to follow the "decent ways of writing" in order not to be condemned as a "guilty writer." In following this standard, especially in the sections in which sexual description might "corrupt customs and damage [readers'] health," he often applies linguistic containment. His frequent change to *wenyan* (the literary language) from *baihua* (the lingua franca) clearly manifests his stratagem of using linguistic means for sexual repression. *Wenyan* and *baihua*, though sometimes not quite distinguishable,[138] are commonly used by modern Chinese scholars as functional concepts to designate the two sign systems, the bookish language system and the colloquial language system. Since Ling wrote in the vernacular, one may be inclined to agree with some scholars that colloquialism is a marked feature of his stories. In fact, however, to point out that there is a salient colloquial or dialectal element[139] in the linguicity of his stories seems to be insufficient. In many places his stories are also strongly characterized by their use of the literary language. If we compare *Two Slaps* with the source materials, we will find that Ling appropriated numerous *wenyan* sentences or even passages from the original texts.[140]

A considerable amount of *wenyan* in Ling's erotic stories is related to sex. In referring to sexual parts, he usually resorts to old medical terms derived from ancient books on the art of the bedchamber, such as "*yangwu*" (male endowment), "*yangju*" (male organ), "*yangdao*" (virility), "*rouju*" (fleshly organ), and "*nanxing*" (male form), which, with their scientific tinge, are surprisingly reminiscent of such similar words as "machine," "engine," and "instrument" used by Cleland in referring to male genitals in his *Fanny Hill*. Such stylized medical vocabulary is also applied when Ling describes certain skills of intercourse, and "*caizhan zhi shu*" (the art of obtaining female essence through intercourse)[141] and "*suoyang zhi shu*" (the art of contracting the male organ) are two prominent instances. In addition to the *wenyan*-styled scientific phrases, Ling is equally fond of employing euphemisms and metaphors. For example, "*hanhua weiguan feng he yu*" (a flower that is not yet accustomed to wind and rain) alludes to "the vagina whose hymen still remains intact," "*qiqiang*" (flag and gun) to "penis," and "*jiaofeng*" (cross swords) to "engaging in a sexual bout." The more common euphemistic expressions in Ming times were "*yunyu*" (clouds and rain, referring to lovemaking), "*yunshou yusan*" (clouds have dispersed and rain has stopped, referring to coitus that comes to a pause), "*houting*" (rear courtyard) or "*houting hua*" (rear courtyard flower) to "anus," "*nanfeng*" (male custom, referring to homosexuality), "*nanfeng yidu*" (practicing male custom, referring to homosexual intercourse), and *dianluan daofeng* (referring to the sixty-nine position). All these phrases also appear in the sections of *Two Slaps* in which lovemaking is implied. Ling never broke his rule of avoiding slangish salacious words. "*Bi*" (cunt), "*luan*" (cock), and "*ri*" (fuck), which can be found everywhere in some late Ming novels, are absolutely excluded from his stories. Perhaps the only exception is "*luandai tou*" (the head of a cock), a ribald phrase of the Wu dialect used by the page Ah Si in "The Elopement of a Nun." But we must note that in the original context this abusive expression is a pun referring to the monk's bald head rather than the head of his penis.

47

The poems (*shi*) in Ling's stories, of which there are a large number, are all written in *wenyan*. Using a high literary language, these poems in the presentation of sex adventures usually give readers a degree of aesthetic pleasure instead of inciting their lust, and it is in this poetic form that Ling on many occasions describes amatory behaviour. In "In the Inner Quarters," after "Madam Jade was so stirred up by her companion's [Madam Beautiful Moon] sexual pleasure that she also stripped her clothes and jumped onto their bed," Ling refrains from getting directly into a detailed narration of how Ren Junyong copulates with these two women simultaneously. Instead, he uses the following quatrain to portray, in a symbolic way, their *ménage à trois*:

> Kissing green and hugging red are most exciting
> On Mount Wu enveloped by clouds and rain.
> The romantic aroma that butterfly is stealing,
> Shuttling from east to west simply for a change.

If we understand that the symbolic words "green" and "red" stand for the two women, Madam Jade and Madam Beautiful Moon, and "butterfly" for their partner Ren Junyong, and if we understand that the allusion "Mount Wu" refers to a place famed for sexual encounters and the metaphor "shuttling from east to west" to Ren Junyong's dealing with his two paramours, we can easily construct an amorous picture from this poem – a picture of their making love in trio!

The employment of poems seems to be a felicitous way for the author to avoid explicitly erotic scenes. In "One Woman and Two Monks," an overt description of the anal sex between the two young males, Guard Yu and Zhiyuan, would have been inevitable as they slept together, had there not been a four-line verse that "bears witness" to it, though in comparison with the poem just quoted it is relatively plain and less allegorical:

> Both young men are an equal match,
> Taking turns a good time they catch;
> To have sex, Zhiyuan is the first one,
> Yet he offers his partner the same fun.

Ling was a versatile writer, equally capable of composing fiction, drama, and poetry. And his versatility can also be seen in the writing of verse, in which he had a perfect command of not only *shi* (poem), but also *ci* (lyric), *qu* (song), and *duiyu* (set-piece, to use Hanan's translation).[142] In his stories the more common poetic form he assigned for sexual description is not "poem" or "lyric," but "set-piece." The set-piece, according to Chen Shidao (1053 – 1101), is an imitation of the language of Tang classic tales.[143] It may not have a fixed number of words in each line nor adhere to literary language throughout, but it does generally observe the standard prosody by using rhythms, similes, metaphors, and parallel or antithetical constructions. Because of their analogy to *pianwen* (parallel prose), which to some extent resembles Shakespeare's blank verse, we have rendered the set-pieces into lines with some metrical patterns:

> One at the height of his passion dashes madly to fight,
> The other is lethargic, reluctant her partner to satisfy.
> One feels lucky to taste the fruit without much ado,
> The other by wrongly offering her flower makes herself a fool.
> One is so fervent as to gasp like a fire-fanning bellows,
> The other is listless as a sack that blood and bone holds.
> For all the tasteless rashness they have undergone,
> This momentary enjoyment is a love affair on every account.

Another example:

> He meets the beauty like a starving tiger devouring a lamb,
> As a thirsty dragon seeks water, so is she crazed for the young man.
> Lustful, the village wench cavorts wild and promiscuous,
> Experienced, the Buddha man conquers the lecherous.

> One thrusts hard and the other strives to receive him,
> Both of them vie to be triumphant, with equal enthusiasm.
> Although her gate is thrust wide open by the old master,
> From the "Boddhisattva," the young novice obtains more water.

Both of these set-pieces are taken from "One Woman and Two Monks," respectively describing the village woman Du's sexual intercourse with two monks – one with the master Dajue and the other with his disciple Zhiyuan. Ling, like his predecessor, the author of *Jin Ping Mei* who seems to have been the first in depicting coitus in set-pieces,[144] was apparently a virtuoso in this special literary genre. In the passages cited above (quite magnificent pieces of work, we should say), he uses a variety of rhetorical techniques, recounting the erotic scenes in such a coded way that one can hardly feel their lubricity. Unless one is familiar with the Chinese poetic tradition, one probably will not easily associate the metaphors "food" and "flower" with the woman Du and her vagina, nor will one fully appreciate the graphic similes "like a fire-fanning bellows" and "as a sack that blood and bone holds" that illustrate the two parties in action: one (the Old Monk) is sexually incompetent and out of breath, and the other (Du) is reluctant and languid, almost corpse-like. In the latter piece, the author shows an even more marvelous craftsmanship in his implication of erotic connotations. A pair of puns, "*di*" and "*tiao*" (literally, "buy rice" and "sell rice"), is exploited to refer implicitly to the copulation between Du and Zhiyuan, or to be more specific, to the act of their "thrusting into" and "being thrust into" (this pair of puns, unfortunately, has to be sacrificed in the translation). And in the final couplet, one may have already noted, the ordinary word "door" and the religious allusion "Boddhisattva's water" are dexterously transmuted into the emblems for "vagina" and "a large quantity of female fluid flowing in orgasm."

As sexuality is narrated indirectly in literary language, its linguistic opaqueness sometimes achieves such an intensity that it is comparable to that of Joyce's *Ulysses*. In *Ulysses*, Joyce often writes in an obscure style in order to present his characters' stream-of-consciousness. Yet while Joyce's manipulation of language has something to do with his artistry, Ling's shift from *baihua* to *wenyan* was simply for the sake of morality – for making the actual sex play appear less transparent. We certainly cannot deny that Joyce sometimes stretched linguistic amorphism to such an extent that it becomes too difficult to understand. But generally his shapeless language allows him to present intermittent and irregular psychological activities in a more genuine way. On the contrary, the high literary vocabulary that Ling chose has only a distancing effect, and it never completely rises to the level of fusing with the real sexual behaviour of his characters.

The incongruity between language and reality occurs in the poems and set-pieces as much as it does in the narratives. The dialogue between Tangqing and the boatman's daughter, which is written in *wenyan* style, may catch our special attention due to its refined diction:

> "You are both beautiful and clever," said Tangqing. "You should
> find yourself a good husband who is worthy of you. What a pity
> it is that a colourful phoenix should be confined to a hen-house by
> mistake!"
>
> "I am afraid you are not quite right," said the girl. "A beautiful
> woman usually has an unfortunate life, and this has been so ever
> since time immemorial. I am not the only one who suffers this fate.
> We are all predestined; how can I complain about it?"

To carry on a conversation in *wenyan* is not always impossible. Tangqing, as a well-educated scholar, may indeed be able, if he wishes, to speak in a genteel way by using literary language throughout. Nevertheless, even though we consider it likely for him to address the girl he fancies in the polite form of second-person pronoun "*qingjia*" (you) and describe her as "guose" (a national beauty) and "wenyuan caifeng" (a colourful phoenix), we can hardly imagine that the illiterate daughter of the boatman, who has received no formal education, should also be capable of speaking in such an elegant manner and using literary phraseology (such as "*junyan*" and "*jieyuan*," meaning "your words" and "complaints") and bookish expletives (such as "*zhi*" and "*yi*," meaning "of" and "indeed"). These are surely not compatible with her social status and education.

This is not meant to be a critique of Ling's artistry. By pointing out his non-realistic usage of language, we simply wish to call attention to the fact that the author of *Two Slaps* did not aim at what we usually call "realism."[145] What he aimed for was the goal of "decent ways of writing."

His insistence upon "decent ways of writing" is, of course, not confined to linguistic containment. Behavioural containment is also a common strategy he applies in sexual description. His erotic stories, read in their entirety, may appear as a panoramic picture of illicit sex in the late Ming times, peopled by men and women engaging in physical enjoyment as has been previously analyzed. In fact, however, this picture is not all-inclusive. What is conspicuously absent in it is sexual behaviours that may be called aberrant. By "aberrant," we do not connote anything like "sinful" or "degenerate." The term rests on biological, psychological, and sociological premises rather than on moral ones. In terms of different abnormalities, sexually deviate acts can be divided into three categories: heterosexual/homosexual mouth-genital contacts, sadism/masochism/sadomasochism, and incest/pseudo-incest.[146] All of these aberrations, however, are carefully avoided by Ling in his stories.

Unlike most *erotikers* who show a strong interest in the "French way" of having sex, Ling never tried to go directly into the depiction of fellatio and cunnilingus, no matter whether they are female-male, or male-male, or male-female or female-female activities. Cunnilingus is conspicuous by its absence in the scene in which it is most likely to occur, as Madam Jade and Rosy Cloud are performing lesbian copulation. Similarly, in the prologue of "In the Inner Quarters," we are almost on the verge of seeing a vivid portrayal of "*pinxiao*" (taste a "flute," i.e., fellatio) as a group of women are licking up the semen of their playmate, when the author comes to a stop, holding himself back from proceeding any further than that.

As a Confucian writer, Ling seems to be more careful about *who* performs coitus than about the *way* coitus is performed, hence he never allows himself any freedom to approach incestuous or pseudo-incestuous taboos. This can be seen more clearly in the intertextuality of late Ming erotica. One might agree with Andrew Plaks on the "relative paucity of direct treatment of incest in Chinese literature." But after skimming over the major erotic novels or novellas, one would certainly be struck by the high incidence of pseudo-incest, which, according to Plaks, is based on ties by marriage and adoption, figural submissions, and retroactive changes of status.[147] Ample pseudo-incestuous cases, such as sex between daughter-in-law and father-in-law as in *Chipozi zhuan* (Story of a Woman of Incontinence), between brother and adoptive sister as in *Langshi* (History of Amorous Adventures), and between son and stepfather as in *Xiuta yeshi* (The Embroidered Couch), set off sharply Ling's discreet abstention from depicting this type of moral impropriety. Ling's avoidance of anything that is related to pseudo-incest or incest makes him seem almost puritanical.

Also worth noting is his effort to avoid flagellation or any infliction of pain. Sadism or masochism, or sadomasochism, being psychologically abnormal, may further break down into two sub-groups: one is performed out of anger or jealousy, and the other is playfully administered with affection. Appropriate examples are provided not just by de Sade, but by a range of his Chinese predecessors. Ximen Qing's stripping off Lotus' clothes to lash her naked body for her infidelity in *Jin Ping Mei*, and the female emperor Wu Zetian's burning a ring on the penis of her partner Xue Aocao in *Ruyijun Zzhuan* (Story of the Lord of Perfect Satisfaction) can be regarded as two cases belonging respectively to these two sub-groups. But we witness no example of either type in Ling's fiction, be it playful sadism or brutal torture. Some readers might disagree. They might argue that Yi's instigation of his wife to have sex with his friend is a covert kind of psychological sadism, and the disguised "nun" Wang's sexual congress with ten women in a single night to absorb their female essence constitutes a form of sexual vampirism. But in these stories we see no description of Yi's attempt to degrade his wife by treating her like a whore, nor are we provided with any detailed information as to how "nun" Wang strengthens his health at the expense of the female partners with whom he has intercourse.

This classification of sexual aberration may seem imcomplete, for it does not include homosexuality (in which anal sex and pederasty are often involved) and group sex (or sex in the presence of others). It would be true if we used as a reference John Gagnon and William Simon's typology that defines both of these sexual acts as "socially structured deviance," that is, behaviour which is strongly disapproved of by society and is often in overt conflict with other components of the social structure.[148] But in view of the unique background of Ming China, in which homosexuality was not uncommon and was generally tolerated by the whole society, and polygamy with legal guarantees was so popular as to make group sex increasingly acceptable, it is not completely arbitrary to exclude these two socially-established sexual behaviours from the category of aberration.

This explanation is subject to one more qualification. One might think that homosexuality and group sex, not as aberrant as is imagined, would have received explicit portrayals in Ling's fiction. This is not the case, though. Ling may have given them fairly extensive attention, but he never allowed himself to use more than "a limited number of words" for the presentation of these erotic activities.

The employment of "a limited number of words" for an implicit sexual description is a *simplification* principle Ling employed. "In some stories," he explained in his introductory remarks, "there may be some amorous flirtations, but I have given them only a factual delineation, with a limited number of words implicitly referring to the sexual act itself."[149] This principle, as a common method of achieving behavioural containment, is as worthy of notice as his avoidance of describing what we have called sexual deviation. In traditional Chinese fiction criticism, the antithetical concepts "*xu*" and "*shi*" are often used to refer to "fictional fabrication" and "factual recording." Quite frequently this pair of terms also stands for two different modes of representation – "diegesis" and "mimesis." To restrict himself to "a limited number of words" is actually to apply the *xu* technique (or the technique of diegesis). Ling rarely 'showed' lovemaking in mimesis. Instead he tried to keep it to the minimum and make it happen offstage if he could. Homosexuality and group sex are briefly treated, and so are the more usual scenes of sexual intercourse.

For instance, in "In the Inner Quarters," ample space (thousands of words) is given to Madam Jade's seduction of Ren Junyong. Once Ren Junyong has been lured into her bedroom, the narration is drastically reduced to a short passage:

> It was now completely dark and silence reigned over the rest of the household. When delicacies and wine had been quietly laid out by Rosy Cloud, the lady and her guest, sitting face to face, began to drink, while at the same time conversing in sweet and tender voices and interchanging glances. After three cups of wine, their passions were aflame and they embraced each other. The pleasure they enjoyed in bed afterwards is beyond description.

This is not the only example. A similar technique can also be found in "The Wife Swappers." When one day Yi is drunk and gives his wife Di and Hu a chance for flirtation, the reader might expect to see a sustained erotic scene. The story, however, does not turn out that way. Once their "foreplay" is over, the mimetic presentation ceases, too. Their intercourse, in fact, is only implied in transient and euphemistic language:

> She removed her pants and reclined on a lounge chair placed in the middle of the room. Then she raised her legs, making herself ready for doing the work of clouds and rain.

Immediately after this summary narration, with a poem following in its wake in a routine manner, their "clouds and rain" are formally brought to an end:

> No stranger to pleasure, Hu was an expert in the art of love. By bringing into play all his skills, he offered Di the most overwhelming sexual delights she had ever experienced. She felt total satisfaction.

To the morally-oriented writer Ling Mengchu, even the reliance on "decent ways of writing" – that is, on linguistic and behavioural containments – was not enough to achieve his educational goal. We often see him assume the role of an omniscient moral pedagogue, stepping out of his stories to preach! In reading *Two Slaps*, it is our common experience that no matter how we may be entertained by a sensual story, we will sooner or later be taken onto another track – to listen to the author's admonition and instruction. For this, Ling has been accused by the modern scholar Lu Xun of being too didactic.[150] Yet Ling himself believed that didacticism was a major function of fiction, a function which was even more important than that of entertainment. In the twelfth story of *Slapping the Table in Amazement, 2nd Collection,* he clearly states that the best story should teach audiences (or readers) something: "It has been our tradition that stories told by professional storytellers are either concentrated on seduction and dissipation or on occurrences extraordinary enough to attract an audience. But the most valuable story is the one that shows the ways of the world and illustrates karmic principle, capable of making the audience change their indecent thoughts after they have heard it." Late Ming *huaben* story writing after Ling tended to be didactic. Whether or not this is an artistic defect is beyond discussion here. But there should not be too much controversy if we say that Ling was an initiator in making the composition of fiction move further forward toward this tuitionary goal.[151]

Huaben stories were written not only for readers, but were performed for audiences as well. To maintain silence or to give the audience a break in the narrative, or to provoke their interest, professional storytellers often made use of formulaic practices such as beginning with an introductory comment, singing in verse, and making some digression. If these formulaic practices had previously been only formal elements, that is, the elements that were conducive to the unfolding of the story proper *only* in a technical sense, we may say that it was Ling who greatly changed their nature. In his *Two Slaps* they are no longer formal elements only; they are also thematically integral parts of a story, serving as the author's tools for his didacticism. The most useful and effective tool for his didactic imposition is the introduction. In a typical Ling story, as Hanan has observed, the introduction presents the theme, and the prologue and main tale illustrate it.[152] The introduction, with which almost all his stories begin, is usually a disquisition or miniature essay, elaborating on the author's moral philosophy. For instance, in his introduction to "The Wife Swappers," a story that warns readers against the seduction of good women and its disastrous consequences,[153] Ling remarks:

> A romantic youth, passionate and highly predisposed for sexual
> enjoyment, will find it hard to keep his mind focused. Yet sex
> is something indirectly related to the moral merits of the nether
> world. Men keeping away from the wives and daughters of others
> and respecting their chastity have mysteriously been recompensed
> for their goodness with divine benefaction. Some won the highest

places in the examinations, some gained important positions
with handsome emoluments, and some fathered eminent sons.
There is no need to recount these stories, for most of them can be
found in the biographies of dynastic histories. As for those who
indulged themselves in sex and conceived ruses for seduction and
violation of good women, they either died an untimely death, or
lost their official posts, or brought disaster to their own wives
and daughters. There are none who have not received their just
desserts.

One point that needs to be explained here is the nature of his moral teaching. On the surface, the foregoing introductory comment seems to be rather
Buddhistic with its emphasis on the retributive principle. But retribution
was actually common to several systems of belief due to the unification of
the Three Teachings in the Ming. As Ding Kangyao remarks in his *Xu Jin
Ping Mei* (Sequel to *Jin Ping Mei*), no matter whether it was Buddhism or
Daoism or Confucianism one wanted to preach, one must first of all start
with the preaching of karma.[154] With this in mind, we can see that in the
preceding introduction, Ling, with his emphasis on the cultivation of self
and the regulation of family, is more concerned with worldly affairs than
with the afterlife, with Confucian secular ethics than with the Buddhist
transcendental world outlook. This is not to say that the Buddhist ingredi-
ent in the story is merely a camouflage for the author's Confucian concerns.
We simply intend to emphasize that in spite of its karmic veneer, Ling's
introduction to "The Wife Swappers" gives people very practical advice
on sexual management (albeit as somewhat of a platitude): seduce no good
women and you will be amply rewarded – not in the other world after you
have died, but in this world while you are still living!

The opening section is not the only domain in which the author
openly promotes moral regeneration. His didacticism also appears in the
main body of his stories. Quite frequently in the middle of narration, he
will suddenly step out of his story and make comments to his readers/
audience directly:

> Gentle reader take note. Men and women who wish to become a
> monk or a nun must reach the stage in which the four elements are
> not present. That is to say, they must purge their desires and be
> down-to-earth in their determination to join the Buddhist clergy.
> Only when they are cleansed and with no desires, and are resolute
> to cultivate themselves day and night in earnest according to the
> religious doctrines, will they succeed in attaining enlightenment.

Nowadays it is too often the practice that parents rashly send
their young children into the gateway of the void, little realizing
that it is easy to begin but difficult to persist, especially when their
children have grown up and experienced the awakening of love.
After they have tasted sexual passions, even though they may still
be able to contain themselves, they will feel that it is religious
obligation that forces them to do so. That is the reason why those
who loath to resign themselves to the rules and regulations would
often go so far as to desecrate the meditation rooms and Buddha-
halls. Indeed, this is precisely the meaning of the proverb: "You
begin with a search for happiness, yet finish enmeshed in crime."
So, pray take my advice: Do not send your sons and daughters on
that path!

Hanan refers to this kind of narrative commentary, prefaced often with
the storyteller tag "*kanguan tingshuo*" (gentle reader or audience take
note), as "digressions," and he is quite right to call our attention to Ling's
innovative use of them. The digressions, as Hanan has noted, used to be
employed only as a means of "providing general information" or "solidi-
fying the social context of the story," and it is Ling who applies them to
"drive home his own ideas." Although the digressions are admonitory or
hortatory, they nevertheless do not merely duplicate the moral inculcation
offered in the introduction. While the introduction expounds the retribution doctrine, digressions, generally in a more random manner, pass on
the author's practical wisdom which often only complements the theme.

True, digressions only marginally serve an expository purpose for the
moral significance outlined in the introduction, but we shall see that Ling
never misses a chance to return to his major topic and beef it up. Reading
his stories, we will notice that he tends toward repetition thematically.
After having expounded upon the theme of retribution at the outset, he
will reinforce it when the prologue or the main tale is finished. In "The
Wife Swappers," for instance, the theme of warning against adultery and
sexual licence reappears in a poem when the prologue draws to an end:

If I defile not another's wife,
He will not defile mine;
But if I defile another's wife,
In turn, he will do so to mine.

The poem at the end of "Fatal Seduction" summarizes the story and reit-
erates the author's expostulation for women:

A good flower withers and loses its scent,
For it has exposed itself to an alluring light.
Remember this important piece of advice:
Women should stay home and not go outside.

As these above-cited poems are "extratextual" in nature,[155] we might call them *epilogues*. The first poem, inserted between the prologue and the main tale, may be called an *intermediary epilogue*, whereas the latter one, appearing at the termination of the whole story, is obviously an *end epilogue*. When the epilogues are moralized, we seem to have no reason to doubt that the offering of moral advice "for three times in each story," as is claimed by the author in his "Introductory Remarks," is not true. In fact, there is little hyperbole in this claim. Given the fact that all Ling's erotic stories, from introduction to epilogue, are "fully loaded with admonitions and exhortations," this is actually a minimalist statement.

57

In addition to these moralizing discourses which may be called *direct* didacticism, Ling also resorts to *indirect* didacticism to persuade people to suppress their improper sexual desires. What we call indirect didacticism refers to the arrangement of characters' fates, to which Ling paid particular heed. This is not to say that Ling was a realistic writer committed to the representation of his characters in a faithful manner. In his aesthetics of fiction, little emphasis is placed on the description of characters and their world for its own sake. The revelation of a particular character's fate is simply a symbolic expression of the author's own moral intent. In order to enforce the value structure of society, Ling would sometimes rather sacrifice verisimilitude to arrange a punitive denouement for the ethical violators. In his stories, poetic justice always prevails. Those who indulge in illicit sex will eventually receive their "heavenly retribution" in one way or another, and the punishment befalling them will always take place when they are still alive rather than after they have died.

The most severe punishment is death, of course. Guangming is killed for abduction, the Old Monk is executed for rape-murder, and Bu Liang is flogged to death for seducing good women. The female characters involved in illicit sex, like Du and Nun Zhao, also end up tragically. Ren Junyong, the protagonist in "In the Inner Quarters," seems to succumb to depression, yet his depression apparently results from the castration he receives for his adulterous liaisons. The same is true of Hu, who, despite a minor illness at the beginning for stealing his friend's wife, dies in the end.

Retribution does not always take the form of death. There are other alternatives. *Tuoyang* (the collapse resulting from overindulgence in sex and seminal depletion)[156] is one of them, from which a number of libertines, such as Yi, Wenren, and the scholar in the prologue of "In the Inner Quarters," suffer as a punishment owing to their intemperate debauchery. In addition to *tuoyang*, lighter disciplines include failure in the Civil Service Examinations, setbacks in official careers, and cuckoldry. On the surface, it seems that the different punishments are meted out arbitrarily without sufficient justification by the author's moral principle. Why, for example, is Commander Yang Jian only cuckolded for taking dozens of concubines, whereas Ren Junyong is penalized by castration and death? And why does Hu lose his life for stealing another man's wife, whereas his counterpart Yi is pardoned after a short period of suffering from his *tuoyang* infliction? Given that concubinage, detrimental as it might be to the husband's health, was sometimes necessary for the reproduction of posterity and hence accorded with filiality,[157] and given that Hu is a duplicitous man who violates the basic moral principle, honesty, as is pointed out in the marginalia,[158] we can see that the seemingly arbitrary arrangements of the scenario for these characters are not at all arbitrary: they reflect the author's moral stance as a Confucianist![159]

With all these repressive mechanisms imposed upon the narratives, Ling's erotic stories are caught between teaching and pleasing, between nostalgia for and withdrawal from the world of sexuality. So in spite of the familiar features they share with erotic stories in general, they are nonetheless not *pure* erotic stories, but erotic stories that are *moralized*.

An Enclosed Typology

Rereading Ling's erotic fiction with a historical perspective, we believe that it ought to be considered in view of its historical, social, and entertaining values as well as its literary merits. The foregoing discussion concentrated on its nature, or to be more specific, on a paradoxical phenomenon – the tension between sexuality and morality and this tension, in our opinion, is the most distinguishing feature of his erotic works, though a great part of late Ming erotica is, to some extent, also tinged with a moral colour. We have approached this tension both textually and contextually. That is, we have not only analyzed the textual aspects of sexuality and of morally repressive mechanisms, but have also explored, with the intention of shedding light on the cause of this tension, contextual factors: the author and the social milieu in which he lived.

The historical significance of the tension in Ling's erotic fiction lies largely in the way that it reveals his quandary in the handling of illicit sex both as an orthodox intellectual brought up in the Confucian tradition and as a commercial writer living in a socially transforming era in which the economy was booming and materialism, including the enjoyment of sexual pleasure, prevailed to an unusual degree. This personal predicament made him vacillate between sexuality and morality, and that is why he only *contained*, rather than totally *abandoned*, sex in *Two Slaps* in order to fulfill his moral mission. Such a containment endows his erotic stories with a distinctive quality, making them quite different from the similar works previously produced.

However, these erotic stories of Ling's have long been an "unwelcome muse," and scholars have hardly paid attention to their nature, especially to the repressive mechanisms that make them different from other types of sexual fiction. Robert van Gulik, as a pioneering sexologist, had, admittedly, a traditional literary connoisseurship of Chinese erotica. Yet in his book *Sexual Life in Ancient China* he mentioned only two types of erotica in the late Ming. One he called "pornographic" and the other he defined as "erotic," refer respectively to such erotic novels as Li Yu's *Carnal Prayer Mat* and Xiaoxiao Sheng's *Jin Ping Mei*. The former, in his view, is "a literary genre,"[160] whereas the latter is not necessarily a genre of its own, but a part of the total literary pattern, and therefore the fiction falling into this category, like *Jin Ping Mei*, can be works of "great literary merit," "important sociological documents," and gold mines of "information on Chinese private and public life, manners, morals, and sexual habits of that time."[161]

Van Gulik's classification, due to the nature of his work and the limited space allotted for the discussion of late Ming erotic literature, is preliminary. He obviously did not take into consideration Ling's erotic stories that were very typical in the last few decades of the Ming dynasty. According to his division, we certainly have no reason to put Ling's stories in what he called the "pornographic" category. Yet if we classify them as "erotic," how can we distinguish them from *Jin Ping Mei*, a work that is sharply different?

A more complicated cataloguing schema, as put forward by Lin Chen (1928 –), a scholar well-known in the Ming-Qing fiction field, began to pay heed to the uniqueness of the didactic type of erotic fiction. In his short note on *Langshi* (History of Amorous Adventures), Lin divided Chinese erotic fiction into the following six types: (1) sexual relations are mentioned but there is no graphic description of intercourse, such as in *Yanyi bian* (Collections of Amorous and Unusual Stories); (2) the theme of the story is non-erotic, yet erotic descriptions appear in some paragraphs, such as in *Guilian meng*; (3) sexual behaviour is philosophically presented in an allegoric form, such as in *Hou xiyou ji* (A Sequel to the Journey to the West); (4) sexual indulgence is described with an admonition intended to put a stop to it, such as in *Wutong ying* (The Shadow of

Wutong Tree);[162] (5) sexual activities are portrayed simply for the purpose of exposing social maladies, such as in *Jin Ping Mei*; and (6) purely erotic, that is, the presentation of sex is intended only to arouse the lustful desire of the reader, such as in *History of Amorous Adventures*.[163]

Although Lin Chen did not mention Ling's erotic stories, we can place them into his fourth category, a category which is equivalent to what we might call the didactic type. However, it should be pointed out that Lin's categorization is largely based on so-called authorial intention rather than on the text, such as the features of style and motif that constitute the tension noted above. The problem, however, is how to know the intention of the author. Who can say that the intention of *History of Amorous Adventures* was to arouse sexual desire, whereas that of *Jin Ping Mei* was not? Even if we do know the intention of an author, it is not, by any means, a reliable criterion for judging the difference between one work and another. In terms of intention, both *Two Slaps* and *Jin Ping Mei* should belong to the same group, that is, to the fourth category in Lin's classification.[164] His grouping cannot really help us understand the textual features of Ling's erotic works.

Actually, it is the textual features, or rather, the repressive mechanisms, rather than the admonitory *intention* of putting a stop to illicit sex, that made Ling's stories idiosyncratic, distinguished not only from *Carnal Prayer Mat*, but from *Jin Ping Mei* as well. To divide late Ming erotic fiction into three categories – (1) lust, (2) lust-love, and (3) lust-sex[165] – may demonstrate more clearly the nature of Ling's fiction. In this tripartite typology, lust is a common property shared by all three divisions. What makes them different is the ways of presentation. The first category is basically focused on lust itself, whereas the second category expands lust to include other feelings and acts such as loving affection and love-making, and the third category illustrates lust with physical sexual intercourse. In other words, we can also say that the first category is a basic form, whereas the second and third categories are respectively its enlarged and concretized versions. Using literary terminology, we may refer to the first category as the *didactic mode*, for it has the least sexual description and the most didacticism. The second and third categories, which are characterized less by didacticism and more by naturalistic or hyperbolic presentation, may be called the *realistic mode* and the *melodramatic mode*. Both are explicit in sexual depiction, though the former is closer to serious erotic fiction like *Saline Solution* by Marco Vassi, and the latter is more similar to entertaining hard-core literature.

Jin Ping Mei and *Carnal Prayer Mat* represent, so to speak, the realistic and the melodramatic types of erotic fiction, while Ling's stories fall into the didactic type. To be sure, this typology is by no means an estimation or a ranking of the literary value of different kinds of erotica. Erotic fiction of the realistic type is not necessarily better than that which is melodramatic or didactic, and the same holds true the other way around. In each type we can find both masterpieces and inferior works. By establishing this new taxonomy, we intend only to define the nature of different major erotic works more accurately, to give Ling's erotic stories a more distinct identity.

Opinions may differ on how the artistry of Ling's erotic stories should be evaluated, but it seems less controversial that his *Two Slaps* ought to take the blame for the decline of late Ming erotic literature. Erotic fiction in the West began with Boccaccio's *Decameron*, developed in its middle stage through Cleland, de Sade, and Walter,[166] and finally reached its culmination in the twentieth century. If this indicates a three-phase evolution – from a humanistic emancipation through a moral repression to an unconstrained prosperity[167] – then in Chinese erotica, such a three-phase development appeared as an opposite movement. *Story of the Lord of Perfect Satisfaction, Story of a Woman of Incontinence, Jin Ping Mei,* and *The Embroidered Couch* undoubtedly represent an auspicious start. But immediately following such a jump-off, an ostensible reaction took place, seeking Confucian moral regeneration rather than further sexual liberation. Morality eventually triumphed over sexuality, making erotica vanish from the literary arena completely and for good.[168] This is the process that Chinese erotic literature underwent – a process of rise, decline, and extinction.[169] Ling's stories, with the characteristic paradox as has been indicated, had, at the moment of their birth, planted seeds for a more puritanical future.

Lenny L. Hu
Surrey, B.C.
December, 2001

Notes

Introduction

[1] See *Huzhou fuzhi*, juan 59; *Wucheng xianzhi*, juan 31.

[2] "Shengong shishuo" (The Poetics of Master Shen Pei) is attached to this book.

[3] His work on drama "Tanqu za zha" (Notes on the Southern Drama) is attached to this book.

[4] See Wang Gulu, "Benshu de jieshao" (Introduction to *Erke Pai'an Jingqi*), *Erke Pai'an Jingqi*, Zhang Peiheng, ed.

[5] See Ye Dejun, "Ling Mengchu Shiji Xinian" (A Chronological Account of Ling Mengchu), in *Xiaoshuo Xiqu Congkao* (Assorted Studies on Fiction and Drama), vol. 2, p. 586; Shi Changyu, "Ling Mengchu," in *Zhongguo Gudian Xiaoshuo Baike Quanshu* (An Encyclopedia of Classical Chinese Fiction), p. 304. According to Ling's tomb inscription written by Zheng Longcai, the title *Dongpo shuzhuan* should be *Su Huang Chidu* (Letters of Su Dongpo and Huang Tingjian). Ling also edited *Shiliu Guo Chunqiu Shanzheng* (A Revised Edition of the Annals of Spring and Autumn of the Sixteen States). See Zhou Shaoliang, "Qumu congshi" (Some Additions to the Titles of Drama), in *Xuelin Manlu* (Random Records of Scholars and Academic Works), no. 5, 1982, p. 100.

[6] See Patrick Hanan, *The Chinese Vernacular Story*, p. 234.

[7] Ling's *Pai'an Jingqi* achieved great commercial success after its publication. Encouraged by his publisher, he wrote a sequel, *Erke Pai'an Jingqi*. Whether the second collection was as successful as the first one, we do not know. But judging from the popularity enjoyed by the anthology *Jingu Qiguan* (Unusual Stories Old and New) which contains eleven stories from *Erpai*, and also judging from the publication of some imitation works such as *Sanke Pai'an Jingqi* (Slapping the Table in Amazement, the Third Collection) written by Lu Yunlong (fl. 1628) and published also in the Chongzhen period (1628 – 1644), we have reason to assume that *Erke Pai'an Jingqi* must have been well-received, too.

[8] The best edition of *Pai'an Jingqi* was discovered by Toyoda Minoru of Tokyo University in 1941. Toyoda Minoru came upon a copy of a forty-chapter edition in the library of a temple in Japan and then reported it in an article entitled "Minkan yanjikkanban hakuan kyoko oyobi suiko shiden hyorin kan no shutsugen" (The Discovery of Both the Ming Forty Chapter Edition of *Pan'an Jingqi* and the Complete Text of *Shuihu Jichuan Pinglin*). Before the discovery of the original Shangyoutang edition, what had been available to Chinese readers were mainly Qing reprinted editions, which contain only thirty-six stories.

[9] In the 1950s two versions of *Erpai* based on the Shangyoutang edition were

published. One is the version collated, punctuated, and annotated by Wang Gulu and published by Renmin wenxue chubanshe in mainland China, and the other is collated and punctuated by Li Tianyi (without annotation) and published by Zhengzhong shuju in Taiwan. Both were abridged editions, in which all sexual words or sentences are removed (the exact number of the words expunged are indicated). The best version now available is the unabridged edition collated and punctuated by Li Tianyi and published by Youlian Chuban Youxian Gongsi in Hong Kong.

[10] See Hanan, *The Chinese Vernacular Story*, p. 143. Zhang Peiheng, after checking with the original Ming editions in Japan, found that the two stories are exactly the same. Since the modern reprinted edition was based on the version manually transcribed by Wang Gulu from the Cabinet Library's copy, there are quite a few copying errors, which include the missing passage. In fact, the story in the second collection is exactly the same as the one in the first collection. See Zhang Peiheng, "Jiaodian shuoming" (Explanatory Notes on Collation and Punctuation), in *Erke Pai'an Jingqi*, p. 2.

[11] Judging from the central margins, story 23 was taken from the first collection, and the play also came from another source. In addition, story 5 and story 9 have different imprints on the central margin, and therefore are probably not the original stories. See *ibid.*

[12] For this part, I relied heavily on Zheng Longcai's tomb inscription and Ye Dejun's article.

[13] Ling's other less-used courtesy names include Ling Bo and Ling Bo'an. Since he was the nineteenth child among his generation in the Ling clan, he was sometimes called by his contemporaries Ling Shijiu (Ling the Nineteenth). In order to avoid Emperor Kangxi's taboo name in the Qing dynasty, Ling's courtesy name Xuanfang was changed to Yuanfang in *Huzhou fuzhi*, *Wucheng xianzhi*, and some other books.

[14] According to *Huzhou fuzhi*, the building of ten prayer altars required three million earthenwares. A certain high-ranking official concealed some ready-made earthenwares and asked for new ones. Ling Dizhi checked the inventory of the goods in stock and discovered the concealed earthenwares. Because of this, he offended that official, who later slandered him and had him demoted to a lower position.

[15] Ling's father Ling Dizhi also served as Assistant Prefect of Daming, Acting Prefect of Kaizhou, and Assistant Prefect of Changzhou. See *Huzhou fuzhi*, *juan 75*. Patrick Hanan, who checked with some local gazetteers, said that the string of "higher positions" (actually they were positions of the same level) given by the genealogy is not borne out by the local histories, because these positions are not mentioned by the 1854 *Daming fuzhi* (The Gazetteer of Daming Prefecture). But in the case of Ling Dizhi, a native of Huzhou prefecture, *Huzhou fuzhi* is perhaps more reliable than *Daming fuzhi*. According to *Huzhou fuzhi*, Ling Dizhi did assume all the official positions listed in the genealogy.

[16] Ling Zhilong was originally called Ling Yuzhi. The old *Huzhou fuzhi* (i.e., the

one published in the Wanli reign of the Ming dynasty) says that Ling Zhilong was Ling's father, but Ye Dejun made a point of bringing our attention to this mistake. This, perhaps, is not simply a mistake. Judging from the collaboration of Ling's father with his uncle in the studies of the classics, Ling might have been adopted by his uncle after his father had died. Whether or not this is true remains to be investigated.

[17] The works Ling Dizhi wrote, edited, or collated include *Daxue Yanyi Bu Yingcui* (A Supplement to the Elaborations on *The Great Learning*), *Wanxing Tongpu* (Biographies of Ten Thousand Historical Figures), *Lidai diwang xingxi tongpu* (Biographies of the Emperors in Previous Dynasties), *Wenlin Qixiu* (Selections from the Literary Classics), and *Mingshi Lieyuan* (Biographies and Anecdotes of High-ranking Officials). See *Huzhou fuzhi*, *juan* 58.

[18] This is the highest grade of licentiate (*shengyuan*). In the Ming, students of official schools sponsored by prefecture or sub-prefecture government are divided into three categories: *lingshan sheng* (salaried licentiate), *zengguang sheng* (licentiate without salary), and *fuxue sheng* (licentiate on probation). In the early Ming, all the students of official schools received financial aid from the government. Every month the government provided students with 6 *dou* (decalitres) of rice as well as meat and fish. But later more and more students wanted to get into official schools and the enrollment was therefore enlarged. The students who were admitted on the basis of the enlarged quota were called *zengguang sheng*, and were not eligible for government financial support. Later, still more students wanted to get into official schools. Those who were admitted outside the quota for *lingshan sheng* and *zengguang shen* were called *fuxuesheng* and could only be placed on a probationary basis. Usually newly admitted students were put on probation first. It was only after taking the annual examination that they could fill vacancies for *zengguang sheng* and *lingshan sheng* if they showed that they had a good academic standing. If a *lingshan sheng* spent ten years at official school without making marked progress, the government could punish him by demoting him to the rank of secretary for *yamen* or demanding that he return the financial aid he had received from the government. But if a *lingshan sheng* was excellent in his studies, he could enter the National Academy at the recommendation of his local official school.

[19] Chancellor Liu was surprised by Ling's well-written letter, which he showed to his colleague Geng Dingli. Geng told Liu that his elder brother Geng Dingxiang, Vice Censor-in-Chief in the Wanli reign, had once highly valued Ling as a would-be nationally famous scholar. Ling thereafter became well-known among high-ranking officials. See Zheng Longcai's tomb inscription.

[20] The genealogy does not mention when Ling took his concubine Zhuo. Based on the birthdate of the first son born by this concubine, their union must have taken place before Ling was thirty-five. Whether Ling had other concubines we do not know, for usually the genealogy only lists the names of the concubines who gave birth to sons.

[21] Wang Zhideng, a native of Changzhou county, enjoyed great popularity as a famous writer. He wrote a preface for Ling's first publication, *Hou Hanshu Zhuanping* (The History of the Latter Han with Annotations and Commentaries).

[22] Yuan Zhongdao was the youngest of the three Yuan brothers. In 1609, he visited Ling at Zhenzhu Bridge in Nanjing. He only recorded the picture by Liu Songnian which Ling hung on his wall. See Yuan Zhongdao, *Youju shilu* (A True Record of My Travel and Sojourn), *juan* 3, in *Kexue zhai ji* (Works of Yuan Zhongdao), vol. 3, p. 1151.

[23] Hanan thought it was likely that Ling met Feng in Nanjing in 1627. The evidence is that Feng's preface to his third collection of *huaben* stories was dated mid-autumn of 1627 in Nanjing, where in the same year Ling began writing *Pai'an Jingqi*. See *The Chinese Vernacular Story*, p. 145. Feng Baoshan in his article, "Ling Mengchu jiaoyou xintan" (A New Investigation of Ling Mengchu's Friends), also indicates that Ling might have known Feng. He gave his reasons as follows: (1) both Ling and Feng were about the same age; (2) Feng lived in Changzhou county of Suzhou prefecture, while Ling lived in Huzhou, and these two place are very close, separated only by Lake Tai; (3) when Ling visited Suzhou in 1604, Feng was also in Suzhou; (4) they thought highly of each other; Feng selected two sets of Ling's *sanqü* verses in *Taixia xinzou* (Celestial Air), and also wrote the following comments: "Chucheng (i.e., Ling Mengchu) is brilliant, capable of writing fine songs at will" (*ibid*, *juan* 6, p. 230); Ling in his preface to *Pai'an Jingqi*, praises Feng as a writer whose *Sanyan* story collections "maintain a rather high moral tone and consistently offer moral precepts which demolish the vicious practices of the day." See *Ming-Qing xiaoshuo yanjiu* (Studies of Ming-Qing Fiction), no.1, pp. 75–76, 1995.

[24] Ling lived in Nanjing several times, which was mentioned by himself and others. His mother Lady Jiang died in Nanjing, and Ling carried her coffin back to Huzhou. Perhaps the reason he lived in Nanjing was to fulfill the residence requirement as a student at the National Academy. In one of his *sanqu* verses, "Xibie" (With Reluctance to Part), Ling describes himself as "a traveller in Nanjing" and mentions that he "attended the National Academy there and liked to hum verses in the courtyard when having spare time."

[25] See *The Chinese Vernacular Story*, p. 140.

[26] Although Ling wrote "Huoni gong" (Confessions of my Indulgence), a work possibly about his sexual dissipation, this piece of writing is not available (most likely it is not extant). In his *sanqü* verses "Xibie," however, he mentions that his wife and family lived in Huzhou and he, alone in Nanjing, fell in love with a woman. Judging from his descriptions of the way the woman greeted him and of her consummate skill at playing a lute at midnight, she was perhaps a high-class courtesan.

[27] See Martin Huang, *Literati and Self-Re/Presentation*, p. 8.

[28] If the candidate's name was listed on *fubang* (supplementary announce-ment notice), he was recognized as having good academic standing in spite of his

65

failure in the examination. This is a euphemistic way of saying that Ling failed the Provincial Examination.

[29] *Jushi* means a Confucian scholar living in the Buddhistic way without becoming a monk. Lin Yutang (1895–1976) thought this a most peculiar Chinese invention, for it allowed a follower of Buddhism to live a married life and become a vegetarian for periods at leisure. See Lin Yutang, *My Country and my People*, p. 125.

[30] See Li Tianyi, "The original edition of *Pai'an Jingqi*," note 5.

[31] Ma Lian also found Ling Mengchu's seals under the signature of Jikongguan in Min Chiji's edition and hence confirmed Wang Guowei's discovery, although Ma Lian thought that to establish Ling's authorship for *Erpai*, further studies were still necessary.

[32] *Lingshi Zongpu* contains Ling's tomb inscription, in which it is clearly recorded that Ling Mengchu was the author of *Erpai*.

[33] See *Foguang Da Cidian* (A Great Dictionary of Buddhist Illumination), vol. 4, p. 3478.

[34] For the difference between Buddhism and Daoism, Dao-an (312–385) has a very succinct explanation: "Buddhism looks upon life as illusory and a void and therefore ignores the body to benefit others. Daoism takes one's self as true reality and therefore consumes elixirs to nourish life." See *Guang hongming ji* (The Further Collection of Essays of Spreading and Elucidating the Buddhist Doctrine), *juan* 8.

[35] The translation is Hanan's. See *The Chinese Vernacular Story*, p. 144.

[36] See *Pai'an Jingqi*, story 29: "It was the practice of the pre-Han and Han dynasties that qualified personnel could be either recommended for or appointed to government posts. That is why the titles *xianliang fangzheng* and *maocai yideng* were designed for men of virtue and persons of ability, and the special honour *buqiu wenda* granted those sterling recluses who sought no fame. So at that time the worthies were not left unused, nor were the men with expertise. All human resources in the country were utilized to the best advantage. Down to the Tang and Song dynasties, however, a great emphasis began to be placed on the Civil Service Examinations, and though one could reach a higher position without passing the examinations, only those having the degree enjoyed the most envious glory. In order to achieve academic success, it was not unusual that scholars grow old and die in the capital. True, at the beginning of our reigning dynasty, three different ways of selecting officials were put on an equal footing, and quite a few renowned scholars and ministers, who performed meritorious deeds for the court and were therefore recorded in history, were not State Graduates. Who can say that only State Graduates can do things best? But recently stress is put more and more on academic credentials, and officials not chosen from degree holders are only allowed to assume minor positions. Even if some of them might have been lucky enough to hold power in some places, the location or the administration would have been bad or problematic, and there have hardly been any exceptions. Those who have lower degrees suffer all the same. They would be dispatched to undesirable regions, and quite often they

were dismissed after only a short period of service. In a word, these people have not been taken seriously. Little wonder they could hardly accomplish much, despite being men of superior capacity."

[37] The prevailing prejudice against men of letters, best represented by the Song Neo-Confucianist Zhu Xi's opinionated comment that "a person who engages in writing literary works [i.e., fiction and drama] is not worth serious attention," had a great influence upon Confucian scholars. That is why the authors of "popular" fiction, usually the literati holding the first degree in the Civil Service Examinations, tended to make their works didactic, to teach, rather than to merely entertain, readers and audiences.

[38] A student of the National Academy who failed the Provincial Examination yet was considered as having good academic standing.

[39] Ling was a well-known publisher in the late Ming. He usually published books in two colours: black and red. But some books, like *Shishuo xinyu* (A New Account of Tales of the World), were printed in multi-colours. The books he published were mainly fiction and drama, which include the famous play *Xixiang* ji(The Western Chamber) and his own short story collections *Erpai*. Ling's publications, usually with illustrations, were good in quality, representing the highest achievement in the golden era of Chinese printing history.

[40] Ling worked in Shanghai for eight years, mainly in charge of coastal defense. He took strong measures against malpractice on salterns. For his meritorious service, he received a number of commendations from the central government.

[41] The ringleaders refer to Li Zicheng and Zhang Xianzhong, who carried on most of their activities in Gansu/Shanxi and Sichuan provinces. The late Ming peasants' rebellion began in the first year of the Chongzhen reign (1628) under the leadership of Wang Jiayin. After 1632 Li Zicheng and Zhang Xianzhong began to play more and more important roles. It was Li's army that destroyed the Ming House in 1644.

[42] Ling was in charge of Fangcun located on the bank of the Huai River when he was working in Xuzhou. Fangcun was a region which often suffered from floods caused by breaches of the Huai River, and Ling's work was to bring that part of the river under control.

[43] "He spat out a large quantity of blood" is in the original text "*Ouxue shusheng*" (literally, he spat out several pints of blood). Although this kind of exaggeration is rhetorically permissible in the Chinese, it has been modified in this translation to avoid unnecessary misconceptions by Western readers. I surmise that Ling probably had tuberculosis. It seems that this was a hereditary disease in his family, for his uncle Ling Zhilong, the famous writer and editor, also "spat out several pints of blood" in his later years before he died. His two elder brothers both died young, around the age of twenty, and their death was probably related to this disease, too.

[44] In *Lunyu* (The Confucian Analects), book 5, chapter 28, Confucius remarks: "When good order prevailed in his country, Ning Wu acted the part of a wise man. When his country was in disorder, he acted the part of a stupid

man. Others may equal his wisdom, but they cannot equal his stupidity." In book 5, chapter 7, Confucius says: "My doctrines make no way. I will get upon a raft, and float about on the sea."

[45] See *Zhu Wengong wenji* (Works of Zhu Xi), *juan* 70. In another place Zhu Xi makes a more detailed elucidation on how the real and perceptual innate laws of human ethical relationships demonstrate the absolute, rational, and noumenal principle: "The mandate is like a command and nature the principle. Heaven uses yin-yang and the Five Elements to create things and *qi* to produce forms. The endowed principle is like an order or a command. When people are born and things are made, they receive their own endowed principle to serve the Five Relationships." See *Zhongyong Zhangju* (The Commentary on *The Doctrine of the Mean*).

[46] See *Henan Chengshi yishu* (Posthumous Works of Cheng Brothers), *juan* 22.

[47] See *Zhuzi yulei* (Classified Conversations of Master Zhu), *juan* 12.

[48] See James T. C. Liu, "How Did a Neo-Confucian School Become the State Orthodoxy?" *Philosophy East and West*, 1973, p. 485.

[49] The issue of when Neo-Confucianism became state orthodoxy is a matter for debate. For example, James T. C. Liu maintains that Neo-Confucianism, after having overcome the crisis (i.e., the persecution of the Qingyuan Party), was dominant in state ideology in the Southern Song. But Tang Yuyuan, whose point of view has been adopted here, argues that Neo-Confucianism did not become state orthodoxy until the Ming dynasty: "Cheng-Zhu Neo-Confucianism, upon its formation in the Southern Song, was not immediately accepted by the ruling class as state ideology or as official philosophy. After the proscription of the Qingyuan Party was lifted, Cheng-Zhu Neo-Confucianism was no longer banned, and like other schools of Confucianism, began to enjoy a respectful recognition from the ruling class, although this sort of recognition should not be regarded as equal to state orthodoxy. Later, in the Yanyou reign (1314–1321) of the Yuan dynasty, it became an officially acknowledged school, and students were tested in the Civil Service Examinations for their knowledge of Zhu Xi's exposition of Confucianism. But as an officially acknowledged school, the Cheng-Zhu Neo-Confucianism was authoritative only in terms of interpretation of Confucian classics and it had not yet reached the status of the orthodox state ideology. It was only in the early Ming, when Emperor Chengzu had *The Three Great Collections* compiled and published, that Cheng-Zhu Neo-Confucianism finally became what is called state ideology or the predominant official philosophy of the ruling class, providing not only standardized interpretations for the examinees but also 'statecraft' for emperors." See Tang Yuyuan, "Cheng-Zhu Lixue Heshi Chengwei Tongzhi Jieji De Tongzhi Sixiang," (When Did Neo-Confucianism Become the Predominant Ideology of the Ruling Class?), *in Zhongguo shi yanjiu* (Studies in Chinese History), no. 1, p. 125, 1989.

[50] For a biographical account of the founding emperor Zhu Yuanzhang as a Buddhist monk, see Wu Han, *Zhu Yuanzhang zhuan* (Biography of Zhu Yuanzhang).

[51] James T. C. Liu points out that the state orthodoxy was characterized by three elements: (1) the selection of one particular school or set of interpretations and commentaries as the officially approved ones in the Civil Service Examinations; (2) official proclamation of the same in the name of the state, for presumed application throughout the government, not just the state examination; and (3) other efforts, parallel to the state efforts, in getting the same to be accepted by the whole society, led by some elite and spreading downward among the common people.

[52] According to Marx, ideology, along with legal and political institutions, is part of superstructure: "The totality of these relations of production constitutes the economic structure of society, the real foundation, on which arises a legal and political superstructure and to which correspond definite forms of social consciousness." See *A Contribution to the Critique of Political Economy*, p. 20.

69

[53] Scholars vary in opinions as to whether Neo-Confucianism was a religion (in the Western sense of the word). I find Hu Shi's explanation of this issue quite enlightening: "The Chinese word for 'religion' is *jiao*, which means teaching or a system of teaching. To teach people to believe in a particular deity is a *jiao*; but to teach them how to behave toward other men is also a *jiao*. The ancients did say that 'the sages founded religions (*jiao*) on the ways of the gods,' but it is not always necessary to make use of such supernatural expedients. And the Chinese people make no distinction between the theistic religions and the purely moral teachings of their sages. Therefore, the term *jiao* is applied to Buddhism, Daoism, Mohammedanism, and Christianity, as well as Confucianism. They are all systems of moral teaching. Teaching a moral life is the essential thing; and 'the ways of the gods' are merely one of the possible means of sanctioning that teaching. That is in substance the Chinese conception of religion." See *The Chinese Renaissance*, p. 79.

[54] See Fu Weilin (fl. 1646), *Mingshu* (History of the Ming), *juan* 62.

[55] In Ming-Qing times, elementary education usually used *Sanzi jing* (The Three-Character Classic) as a major primer, which, originally written in the Song dynasty, consists of approximately 356 three-word lines and contains 500 different characters. It begins with a famous Mencian tenet, and the entire text blends moral teaching with historical information, with a special emphasis on the Confucian reciprocal obligations of parents and sons, teachers and students, and elders and juniors.

[56] The appointed successor was actually Zhu Yunwen, not Zhu Di. It was through a civil war that Zhu Di, the fourth son of Zhu Yuanzhang, usurped the throne from his nephew and became the successor to Zhu Yuanzhang. Zhu Di was originally Prince of Yan. After Zhu Yuanzhang died and Zhu Yunwen (r. 1399 – 1403) ascended the throne, he rose in rebellion, launching his three-year military campaign against the throne under the pretext of getting rid of treacherous court officials. He finally defeated Zhu Yunwen and became emperor himself.

[57] These three collections are *Sishu daquan* (The Great Collection of Commentaries on the Four Books), *Wujing daquan* (The Great Collection

of Commentaries on the Five Classics), and *Xingli daquan* (The Great
Collection of Neo-Confucianists' Works).

[58] The subject must obey his ruler, son and daughter must obey their parents,
wife must obey her husband, and students must obey their teachers. Any
violation of these Confucian relations is considered as "disobedience to a
superior" (*fanshang*), and it was one of the "ten crimes."

[59] See Li Dongyang, *et al.*, eds., *Da Ming huidian* (The Political Institutions and
Administrative Statutes of the Great Ming), *juan* 20.

[60] See Andrew Plaks, *The Four Masterworks of the Ming Novel*, p. 17.

[61] Wang, Luo, and He were representatives of the Taizhou school, while Li has
been controversial as to whether he should be considered as its member.
While most scholars consider the Taizhou school a left-wing branch of the
Wang Yangming school, some experts on Chinese intellectual history deny
their relationship. For instance, Hou Wailu says: "We do not agree that the
Taizhou school should be generally called a left-wing branch of the Wang
Yangming school, because this appellation still has an implication that they
were related. Actually the difference between them was already noticed by
[the late-Ming scholar] Huang Zongxi (1610–1695)." See Hou Wailu, *et
al, Zhongguo sixiang tongshi* (A General History of Chinese Thought),
vol. 4, p. 972. The Taizhou school might have been unrelated to the Wang
Yangming school, and my usage of the term the "Wang Yangming school" is
simply a convenient rubric to describe general ideas and trends of the era.

[62] See Wm. Theodore de Bary, "Individualism and Humanitarianism in Late
Ming Thought," in *Self and Society in Ming Thought*, p. 188.

[63] "If all people take what Confucius said as the standards of right and wrong,
then actually they have no standard of right and wrong." See Li Zhi,
"Cangshu Shiji Liezhuan Zongmu Qianlun (Foreword Placed Before the
Table of Contents of *The Book to be Burned*).

[64] See Li Zhi, *Fengshu* (Works to be Burned), *juan* 1, "Da Teng Mingfu" (Reply
to Teng Mingfu).

[65] See Dong Guoyan, *Dangzi, Rouqing, Tongxin: Mingdai Xiaoshuo Sichao*
(Libertine, Sentimentality and Child's Mind: The Trend of Fiction in the
Ming Dynasty), p. 78.

[66] See Bao Zunxin, "Ming-Qing Zhiji Shehui Scao Yu Wenyi Fuxing" (The
Social Trend and Renaissance in Late Ming and Early Qing), in *Zhongwai
Wenhua Bijiao Janjiu* (Comparative Studies of Chinese and Foreign
Culture), p. 265 and *passim*.

[67] For detailed discussions of the Donglin movement, see Charles Hucker,
"The Tonglin Movement of the Late Ming Period," in *Chinese Thought
and Institutions*; Carsun Chang, *Development of Neo-Confucian Thought*,
chap. 6; Jerry Dennerline, *The Chia-Ting Loyalists: Confucian Leadership
and Social Change in Seventeenth-Century China*, chaps. 1 and 2; Wang
Tianyou, *Wan Ming Donglin dangyi* (The Donglin Party in the Late Ming).

[68] See Gao Tingzhen, *Donglin Shuyuan zhi* (The Records of the Donglin
Academy), *juan* 2.

[69] The four books, *Nüjie* (Lessons for Women) by Ban Zhao, *Nü lunyu* (The

Analects for Women) by Song Ruohua, *Nü fanjie lu* (Biographies of Exemplary Women) by Wang Xiang's mother, and *Neixun* (The Internal Instructions for Women) by Emperor Chengzu's wife, were published in the seventeenth century in a bound volume titled *Nü sishu*.

[70] Zhu Yilu provides us with a chart from which we can see the number of chaste women in different dynasties: 6 in Zhou, 1 in Qin, 22 in Han, 29 in the Six Dynasties, 32 in Sui and Tang, 2 in the Five Dynasties, 152 in Song, 359 in Yuan, 27,141 in Ming, and 9,482 in Qing. See Zhu Yilu, *Rujia lixiang renge yu Zhongguo wenhua* (The Confucian Ideal Personality and Chinese Culture), p. 147.

[71] The compilation of the *Ming shi* (History of the Ming) began in 1678 by order of the Kangxi emperor, though it was not completed until the early eighteenth century.

[72] Ray Huang, *Fangkuan lishi de shijie* (Broadening the Horizon of Chinese History), p. 3.

[73] See William Skinner, ed., *The City in Late Imperial China*, p. 28.

[74] Quoted from Han Dacheng, *Mingdai chengshi yanjiu* (Study of Cities in the Ming), p. 14.

[75] For example, Zhu Yuanzhang once said to the officials in the central administration: "In Suzhou, Songjiang, Jiaxing, Huzhou, and Hangzhou there is not enough arable land, and people there have to engage in commerce. But in Linhao, my native place, much of the land needs to be reclaimed. So we should make an announcement to those living in the above-mentioned five prefectures with no real estate of their own that if they are willing to move to Linhao to reclaim the wasted land, they will be given rice, seeds, cattle, and boats for their financial support, and in the first three years of their settlement there they will be exempted from taxation." After this announcement had been made, more than four thousand households moved to the region where the emperor had been brought up. See *Taizu shilu* (Factual Record of Emperor Taizu), *juan* 53.

[76] Zhu Yuanzhang once told local officials that any written suggestions from the residents for water conservancy must be submitted to him immediately. He took the matter seriously and during his reign a number of construction projects, often financed by the government, were undertaken for that purpose. For example, in the first year of the Hongwu reign (1368–1398), the dam as well as its embarkment (about a hundred kilometers in length) in Tongcheng of Hezhou sub-prefecture was repaired; in the fourth year of the Hongwu reign, the main irrigation canal in Xing'an county of Guangxi province, which could water ten thousand hectares of land, was repaired; and in the nineteenth year of the Hongwu reign, a sea embarkment in Changle county of Fujian province was built and thereafter the arable land of the county no longer suffered from the damage caused by the immersion of sea-water. See Zhang Tingyu, *Mingshi* (History of the Ming), *juan* 88.

[77] Zhu Yuanzhang not only simplified the old complicated levy duty on commerce, but also reduced commercial taxation to one-thirtieth. In one of the decrees he issued, he stipulated that nobody was allowed to charge more

71

than one-thirtieth for tax and violators would be punished.

[78] See Huo Yuxia, *Huo Mianzhai ji* (The Works of Huo Yuxia), *juan* 18. For the underdevelopment of commerce in the north, see also *Yongping fuzhi* (The Local History of Yongping Prefecture), *juan* 5.

[79] Judging from Portuguese trade at Macao and the increase in the number of private academies, the Lingnan regional economy, for instance, might also have experienced growth and prosperity from the onset of the sixteenth century. See Evelyn S. Rawski, "Economic and Social Foundations of Late Imperial Culture," in *Popular Culture in Late Imperial China*, p. 5.

[80] Through the rapid rise of textile towns and a large number of workers employed in the weaving and dyeing trade we can see how fast the textile industry grew. For instance, an official named Cao Shiping reported that, according to his eyewitness, there were at least several thousand weaving and dyeing workers in the city of Suzhou. See *Shenzong shilu* (The Factual Records of Emperor Shenzong).

[81] See Feng Menglong, ed., *Xiangshi hengyan*, story 18.

[82] Zhang Han, *Songchuang mengyu*, *juan* 6.

[83] Li Xu, *Jie'an manbi*, *juan* 8.

[84] Some commercial publishing firms were very large in scale, and the Mao Jin Publishing House was one of them. It consisted of a large printing workshop, a building of stacks named Jigu Ge, and nine storage rooms mainly for keeping plates. See Qian Yong, *Luyuan conghua* (Collected Essays of Qian Yong), *juan* 22. For more infornation on Mao Jin and his publishing enterprise, see Tsien Tsuen-hsuin, *Paper and Printing*.

[85] By "commercial publishing business," I refer to both the commercial press (*shufang*) and the private studio (*sijia*). Some experts on the history of Chinese books divide the publishing houses in Ming times into three types: (1) government agency, (2) commercial press, and (3) private studio. But I myself do not see how the commercial press was different from the private studio. Tsien Tsuen-hsuin maintains that private studios "were motivated by altruism toward the spread of literature and did not act for profit or because of official obligation." From a variety of accounts written in Ming-Qing times, however, private studios were also commercially oriented rather than "altruistic." It is true that they paid great attention to the quality of printing, but as Luo Shubao points out, their emphasis on printing quality grew simply out of competition with their rivals. See *Zhongguo gudai yinshua shi* (A History of Printing in Ancient China), p. 349.

[86] See Hu Yinglin, *Shaoshi Shanfang Bicong* (Notes from Shaoshi Shanfang), *juan* 4.

[87] There were wood movable type, copper movable type, tin movable type, and in Dantu of Jiangsu province, one could even find lead movable type. yet despite the invention of movable type, woodblock printing or xylography remained the dominant printing method in the Ming times.

[88] For example, the planting of tobacco in Fujian province occupied 60 or 70 percent of the total land. And in counties like Fanyu, Yangchun, and Donghuan in Guangdong province, the size of the field for growing sugar

cane was almost equal to that of the rice field. See Li Tiaoyuan, *Nanyue biji* (Notes about Southern Yue), *juan* 14.

[89] See Yao Zhiyin, *Yuan Ming Shi Leichao* (A Categorized Account of the History of the Yuan and the Ming), *juan* 24. See also Xu Guangqi, *Nongzheng Quanshu* (Complete Treastise on Agriculture), *juan* 35.

[90] See Song Yingxing, *Tiangong Kaiwu* (The Exploration of the Works of Nature), preface: "In a most prosperous age under the reign of your Majesty, in which I was luckily born, carts and carriages from southern Yunnan [province] travel as far as to Liaoyang [i.e., Jilin province], and merchants from the border of Guangdong [province] walk on streets in the north of Hebei [province]." See also *Hejian Fuzhi* (The Local History of Hejian Prefecture), published in the Jiajing reign (1522–1567), *juan* 7: "The merchants in Hejian who sell silk, rice, salt, iron, and timber usually come from other parts of the country. The sellers of silk are from Nanjing, Suzhou, and Linqing, the sellers of rice are from Weihui and Cizhou, the sellers of iron (most of them sell farm tools which they carry on their own carts), from Linqing and Potou, the sellers of salt, from Cangzhou and Tianjin, and the sellers of timber, from Zhending."

73

[91] See *Crisis and Transformation in the Seventeenth Century China*, p. 148.

[92] Three macroregional cores refer to the North China core along the Grand Canal, the core of the Lower Yangtze, and the Southeast Coast. See William Skinner, "Regional Urbanization in Nineteenth-Century China," in *The City in Late Imperial China*, p. 217.

[93] In the first story in *Pai'an Jingqi*, the protagonist Wen Ruoxu and his friends take a business trip by boat to a country called "Jiling guo" for trading their goods: "They sailed before the wind for several days – how far exactly they could not tell. Then they sighted land and saw from the junk a populous city with towering walls, which they knew must be the capital of some country." See *Courtesan's Jewel Box*, p. 410. The maritime trade was also recorded in other sources. Zhang Xie (1574–1640) in his *Dong Xi Yang Kao* (Records of East and West Oceans) mentions that in Fujian province wealthy families sometimes took a huge junk and went abroad for trading.

[94] In the early Ming two kinds of money were used: one was copper coins and the other was paper money. The use of gold and silver as currency was strictly prohibited. But from the mid-Ming onward, silver became the main curency. Paper money was no longer used, and copper coins were only supplementary in actual circulation.

[95] For example, the Ming founder had continued the Yuan practice of registering certain households for special service as salt producers, soldiers, or artisans, but this system was replaced in the late sixteenth century by the single-whip tax collection. Goods obtained for Imperial Household use with corvée labour in the early Ming were now acquired through subcontracts to private firms using wage labour.

[96] See Zhang Tingyu, *Mingshi* (History of the Ming), *juan* 208: "During the Zhengde reign (1506–1521), it often happened that eunuchs illegally took land from its owner and made it part of the manors of imperial families."

Malpractice of this kind became worse during and after the Jiajing reign (1522 – 1566), especially in Henan province where a number of princes were enfeoffed. See Wang Jieren, *Zhongzhou Zazu* (Miscellanies of Zhongzhou), *juan* 1. According to Zhao Yi, some palace officials (*jinyiwei baihu*) even seized land from people in the Lower Yangtze Delta. See *Nian'er Shi Zhaji* (Notes Taken for the Twenty-Two Histories), *juan* 34.

[97] For example, the commercial prosperity of Suzhou is described by a poem in story 26 of *Jingshi tongtyan* (Popular Words to Warn the World) as follows:

> Three thousand courtesans, up and down, served inside the houses,
> Millions of taels, carried by boat, flowed in from east and west.
> Merchants and vendors sold their goods early in the morning,
> Peddlers coming from all over the country spoke different dialects.

[98] *Wujiang xianzhi* (The Local History of Wujiang County), *juan* 4.

[99] See *Xingshi Hengyan* (Constant Words to Awaken the World), story 18.

[100] Opinions vary regarding the sprouts of Capitalism. Some scholars maintain that they appeared in the late Ming, whereas others argue that evidence of the development of commercial capitalism can be found even in the Tang and Song periods (but Tu Wei-ming points out that *commercial* capitalism was not the same as *industrial* capitalism, i.e., the bourgeois capitalism which appeared in the late Ming). There is also another group of scholars who simply deny the sprouts of capitalism in Ming-Qing times.

[101] According to Shen Chaoyang (fl. 1599), social customs before the Zhengde reign (1506 – 1521) were simple and plain; but during and after the Jiajing reign (1522 – 1567) they tended toward luxury; people liked to show off and regarded frugality as despicable. See *Huang Ming Jia Long liangchao wenjian ji* (A Factual Account of the Jiajing and Longqing Reigns), *juan* 6.

[102] Tao Shiling offers a similar account: "In recent years, the banquet has become so lavish that it requires several days of preparation, and it is considered impolite to invite guests to dinner unless the menu is extensive, including the produce of land and sea. Soups and dishes are served one after another, too much to eat and even too many to count. A banquet as such usually costs at least several taels of silver." See Wu Han, "Wan Ming Shihuan jieji de shenghuo" (The Life of Official and Gentry Classes in the Late Ming).

[103] See Fan Lian, *Yunjian jumu chao*, *juan* 2.

[104] See John Meskill, *Gentlemanly Interests*, p. 142.

[105] It seems that the building of magnificent mansions did not become popular until the Jiajing reign (1522 – 1566). In the early Ming, ordinary people usually lived in thatched cottages, and even well-to-do families would hide their brick houses by building a thatched structure in front of it, lest officials think they were rich. No one but extremely wealthy people built storeyed houses. Tao Shiling, a scholar who was born around the mid-16th century, also said that when he was young, he did not see any mansions in Zhejiang province. But in the late sixteenth century, even a *yamen* runner could

afford to live in a house with "a scenery garden."

[106] See Gui Youguang, "Shu Zhang zhennu sishi" (A Report of the Death of the Chaste Woman Zhang) and "Zhang zhennu yushi" (The Case of the Chaste Woman Zhang), in *Gui Zhenchuan wenji, juan* 4.

[107] Quoted, with minor changes, from John Meskill, *Gentlemanly Interests*, p. 149. "Triple wife" refers to the wife of the Mongol leader Altan Khan. After he died she became the wife of his son and later of his grandson.

[108] See Lu Xun's argument, *Zhongguo xiaoshuo shilue* (A Brief History of Chinese Fiction), pp. 182–3: "During the Chenghua reign (1465–88), the alchemist Li Zi and the Monk Jixiao meteorically rose to eminence by teaching the art of the bedchamber; down to the Jiajing reign (1522–67) Tao Zhongwen, owing to his compounding of the 'Cinnabar' pill (an aphrodisiac made from the hymenal blood of young girls) won such favour from Emperor Shizhong that he was promoted to the rank of the highest official and ennobled. And it seems that these decadent trends gradually spread to scholars. Although Chief Censor Shen Duanming and High Commissioner Gu Kexue became officials via the State Examinations, they nevertheless achieved high ranks with unusual speed by presenting to the throne an aphrodisiac called 'Autumn Stone' (made from a substance extracted from children's urine). Since such sudden prosperity and fame gave rise to envy, opportunists tried in every possible way to obtain unusual prescriptions. As a result, people no longer considered it indecent to talk about sex and aphrodisiacs." Lu Xun's opinion has been most influential. Other scholars like Hu Shiying, Ren Jiyu, and Vivien Ng all echoed the view that Emperors Wuzhong, Shizhong, and Shenzhong were responsible for the "social anomies" in late Ming times.

[109] The history of Chinese literature shows that the major function of poetry was different from that of fiction. It was for self-expression rather than for entertainment. Mao Heng was the first literary critic who stressed this function of poetry. His famous dictum that "poetry expresses the self's intent" (*shi yan zhi*) was repeated by later poets and critics and had a very strong influence on the development of Chinese literature.

[110] Quoted from Ian Watt, *The Rise of the Novel*, p. 53.

[111] The most obvious evidence was the fact that the late Ming fiction writers never used their real names to publish novels and short stories, and a great number of their pseudonyms are yet to be identified. The reason for them to use pseudonyms was mainly because they regarded fiction as a debased kind of writing. Ling Mengchu, for example, candidly admits that he did not take his fiction writing seriously. His "vulgar" book *Slapping the Table in Amazement* was, in his modest opinion, "not good enough even to be used as covering pieces of paper for the soy-paste jars." It could not compare with his high-brow literary and scholastic works "on which he spent so much time and energy conceiving and writing that he spat blood and wore out his brush and ink stone."

[112] Most Japanese and Western scholars believe that the Ming vernacular fiction was part of elite literature rather than popular culture, intended mainly

for the enjoyment of the gentry and well-to-do classes. Their arguments are based on two kinds of evidence: (1) some editions of vernacular fiction were "relatively fine printings, apparently expensive and meant only for a limited circulation," and (2) "literacy was only one percent" and therefore, the reading ability of folk readers is "questionable." In my opinion, the quality of the edition does not necessarily determine its content and readership in economically flourishing times when ordinary people can afford to buy fine editions (some popular Western magazines like *Vogue*, *Cosmopolitan*, and *Playboy* are also relatively fine printing, but they are obviously not circulated only among the elite). In fact, most editions of fiction or drama published in the late Ming were inexpensive. For instance, a selected anthology of librettos from the drama entitled *Xindiao wanqu changchun* (Ten Thousand Newly Attuned Songs on Eternal Spring) cost only 1.2 mace. As for literacy, "one percent," a late Qing statistical figure, should not be diachronically applicable. I should also call attention to a very simple fact: To read vernacular fiction does not need profound knowledge; functional literacy (i.e., simple reading and writing) is good enough for rough understanding. It is a general consensus of scholars that functional literacy in late imperial China could be as high as 30–45 percent among men and 2–10 percent among women. This certainly does not deny that fiction could also be enjoyed by upper classes. Emperor Wuzhong's purchase of the novel *Jin tong can Tang* (The Romance of the Unification of the Remaining Tang by Jin) at the incredibly high price of 50 taels of silver is perhaps the most well-known example. But I wish to point out that fiction in the late Ming was not intended only for the elite; it was for all classes.

[113] Most of the Chinese Ming-Qing fiction scholars believe that *nihuaben* (simulated *huaben* stories) were written only for the reading public, not for an audience. These scholars were probably misled by the term *nihuaben* coined by Lu Xun in his *A Brief History of Chinese Fiction*. But Lu Xun did not claim that the simulated *huaben* stories were produced only for the reading public. From the formal features (digressive discourse, among others), and especially the phrases such as "storyteller" (*shuohua de*) and "insignificant person" (*xiaozi*) used by the authors to refer to themselves, we can see that the authors addressed themselves more to an audience than to readers. External evidence also tells us that simulated stories like *Sanyan* were indeed used by storytellers as "base-texts" (*diben*) in their storytelling performance in late Ming times. And their audience included not only people of the lower social strata but also members of scholar-gentry classes. Wen Zhengming (1470–1559), a literatus well-known for his calligraphy and painting, admitted that he "was fond of listening to the stories about Song Jiang [a hero in *Water Margin*] when he had spare time." This was also mentioned by other famous scholars such as Yuan Zhonglang (1568–1610) and Zhang Dai (1597–1679).

[114] Although Max Weber did not directly deny Marx' thesis that super-structure is determined by economic base, he nevertheless tried to bring our attention to the phenomenon that the formation of superstructure was also

influenced by some other factors. "Among other circumstances, capitalistic interests have in turn undoubtedly also helped, but by no means alone nor even principally, to prepare the way for the predominance in law and administration of a class of jurists specially trained in rational law. But these interests did not themselves create that law. Quite different forces were at work in this development. And why did not the capitalistic interests do the same in China or India? Why did not the scientific, the artistic, the political, or the economic development there enter upon that path of rationalization which is peculiar to the Occident?" See Weber, *The Protestant Ethic and the Spirit of Capitalism*, Talcott Parsons, trans., p. 25.

[115] In my discussion, I avoid fine distinctions between "pornographic" and "erotic," and use the term "erotic fiction" in such a broad fashion that it includes not only relatively "high-brow" erotica but also the so-called hard-core literature.

[116] Strictly speaking, a *huaben* story usually consists of four parts: introduction or introductory comments (*ruhua*), prologue (*touhui*), main tale (*zhenghua*), and epilogue (*pianwei*). The introduction is a poem (*shi*) or lyric (*ci*) followed by an explanation, which either focuses on the theme of the story or summarizes the main plot. The prologue is a short, simple story (occasionally several short, simple stories), which, though independent in terms of plot, is thematically connected to the main tale. The main tale (or the story proper) is the body of the story. Sometimes it is divided into two parts, as we see in the story "Nianyu guanyin" (Jade Carver), or several parts, as we see in some of Li Yu's stories. The epilogue is an attached part – always written in verse(s) – for the recapitulation of theme and the like. Of these four parts, the prologue and the main tale are obviously the most important.

[117] See Eberhard and Phyllis Kronhausen, *Pornography and the Law*, p. 221.

[118] The art of the bedchamber has been generally regarded as a practice for enhancing health and promoting longevity. It was also intended for increasing sexual pleasure. As Douglas Wile in his *Art of the Bedchamber: The Chinese Sexual Yoga Classics* points out, the art of the bedchamber, described in the Ma Wang tui and *Ishimpo* (The Essentials of Medical Prescriptions) texts, strongly emphasizes prolonged foreplay, female orgasm, and male *reservatus* as promoting not only superior health but also greater pleasure than ejaculatory sex.

[119] See Yenna Wu, *The Chinese Virago*, p. 126.

[120] The reason for using the term "swinging" is not because "wife swapping" implies sexual inequality, and male property rights of wives as some scholars claim, but because in late Ming erotica there are various kinds of mate swapping, and "swinging" is perhaps a broader word in connoting different kinds of activities.

[121] See *Yiqing Zhen*: "The story goes that Bai Kun and his wife Li invited Jing Quan and [his wife] Jade Sister to move into their house. Li found Jade Sister pretty and Jade Sister was also impressed by Li's beauty.... In the evening, when the dinner was ready for serving, Bai Kun and Jing Quan

took the seats of honour, and Li and Jade Sister sat at the opposite side. The maids Laurel and Rue served them tea, one with a teapot in hand and the other holding glasses. After four glasses had been poured out, Bai Kun passed one to Jade Sister with both hands, which she took with courtesy. Bai Kun noticed that her hands were very white and her fingers as thin as green onions; gazing at her under the light, he was enamoured with her charming looks. Feeling as if he had been carried away, he almost lost control of himself. Jade Sister, being so amorously gazed upon, felt rather abashed. She cast a quick glimpse back at this handsome man as she took the glass, and then lowered her head wihtout saying anything. 'Why so shy, Younger Sister?' said Li. 'Elder Brother is no stranger.' 'She is shy because this is her first time getting together with you.' Jing Quan replied for her. 'Next time she should feel fine.' Bai Kun said, 'Sister-in-Law, I am going to say something ungenteel to you, and I hope you will not mind.' 'You shouldn't worry about that,' Jing Quan said for his wife. 'We are all friends, aren't we?' Bai Kun then said, 'Sister-in-Law, I can't stand any more. My prick is hard and I want to fuck you!' Jade Sister blushed all over upon hearing this and rose to leave. Li, however, caught her by the arm. 'Don't be so ashamed,'' she said, laughing. 'Don't be so ashamed. Every woman does this.' Laurel and Rue, who were standing to the side, burst out laughing. Jing Quan said with jest, 'Elder Brother, you are really far too ungenteel and unscholastic.' Bai Kun said, 'We are doing unscholastic things, so what's the need to show off our knowledge of the classics to them? In terms of conventional principles, I shouldn't have fucked your asshole and you shouldn't have screwed my wife's cunt to begin with.' 'You are right,' said Jing Quan. 'In that case, I have no reason to restrain myself any more. My prick is rising too. Sister-in-Law, could you please let me stick it into your cunt? I am very horny.' Li said, 'You have done it with me before. But your wife is still reluctant. You should talk her around first.' Jing Quan said to Jade Sister, 'It's no use being so shy. You can't escape anyway.' Jade Sister said, 'You have deceived me.' Laurel broke in, 'This is something delightful. Why so stubborn?' Rue also poked fun at her: 'You came here yourself. Who else can you blame?' Jade Sister cursed, 'You oily mouths! Don't you know that you have between your thighs only a small pussy, and I'll never need your comments, eh?' 'My good sister,' said Li with a smile, 'please don't say it any more. You'd better be quick to strip off your clothes and let your Elder Brother give you a thrust.' Although Jade Sister was still unwilling to comply, she was in fact quite aroused now, doing nothing to resist Li as she stretched out her hands to pull at her lower garments. While Li continued her stripping work, Bai Kun gave Jade Sister a quick kiss on the mouth and carried her to the bed. Now Jade Sister was stark-naked. She covered her eyes with her hands, rather shamefaced. Bai Kun, after having removed his own clothes, lifted her legs and started to ram his shaft into the fissure between her thighs. . . . Jing Quan kept looking on as Bai Kun was fucking Jade Sister. Seeing his beautiful wife immersed in wanton frolics of copulation, Jing Quan became jealous and excited. Catching hold of Li, he pressed her down onto a bench, and then both of them cast their clothes off, naked. Jing Quan held Li's face in his hands and kissed her twice on the mouth. Li said, 'Honey, let us have a chat first to renew our sweet experience. You know your precious cock is way too large for me. You must go slow, okay?"

[122] Strictly speaking, polygamy in China was one husband and one wife, plus one or more concubines. Imperial Chinese law prohibited bigamy, but allowed men to take concubines. According to *Ming Huidian* (The Collection of Statutes of the Ming), the number of concubines was legally restricted: ten for princes and four for their posterity (they could take two concubines first when they had no son at the age of twenty-five and two more when they reached the age of thirty but still had no son), three for generals (they were allowed to take two concubines first when they had no son at the age of thirty and one more later when they reached thirty-five and still had no son), and one for common people when they had no son at the age of forty.

[123] The most extreme example can be found in the novel *Xinghua Tian* (When the Apricot Trees Were in Bloom), in which the protagonist has a special bed made, big enough to allow himself and his twelve "wives" to sleep in it and make love together.

[124] I should point out that in Fujian province gay men did have a "bond" ceremony if they wanted to win social recognition for their homosexual relationship. Still, their relationship was informal. When the younger "bond brother" reached the age for marriage, he would finally break up with his elder brother.

[125] According to Xiaoming Xiong, *jianmin* could be "barbarians" from the south by origin, or Mongols who had migrated to Fujian and Guangdong provinces. Although the Mongols enjoyed high social status in the Yuan dynasty, they were nevertheless forced to live as pirates in the Ming, and their social position was no better than slaves. When their boats were at anchor, they sold their bodies as male prostitutes. *See Zhongguo tongxing'ai shilu* (A Historical Account of Homosexuality in China), p. 149.

[126] "Male homosexuality" and "southern custom" are homophones in Chinese and can be used interchangeably.

[127] See Xie Zhaozhe, *Wu zazu*, *juan* 8, p. 209. In the Ming dynasty, especially in the late Ming, homosexuality was so popular among literati that they humorously called their homosexual behaviour "*waijiao*" (external intercourse) and their heterosexual relation with their wife and concubine(s) "*neijiao*" (internal intercourse). The majority of literati enjoyed both internal intercourse with their wife and concubine(s) and external intercourse with handsome young men from outside.

[128] See *Sexual Life in Ancient China*, p. 163.

[129] Male homosexuality is mentioned or described in almost all late Ming erotic fiction, and there are three erotic story collections exclusively centering around this theme: *Bian Er Chai* (Hairpins Beneath his Cap), *Yichun Xiangzhi* (Fragrant Bodies Suitable for Lovemaking), and *Longyang Yishi* (Anecdotal History of Male Love). On the contrary, lesbianism, to my knowledge, appears only briefly in Ling's story, in *Xu Jin Ping Mei* (A Sequel

to *The Golden Lotus*), and in *Xinghua Tian* (When Apricot Trees Were in Bloom).

[130] David Greenberg in his *The Construction of Homosexuality*, divides homosexuality into four categories: "trans-generational homosexuality," "trans-genderal homosexuality," "class-structured homosexuality," and "egalitarian homosexuality." In trans-generational homosexuality, the older partner takes the active role, with the younger one acting in the passive role.

[131] For a detailed discussion, see Liu Zaifu, "Guangyi qingyu lun" (On the Generalized Concept of Love-Sex), in *Shengming jingshen yu wenxue daolu* (The Spirit of Life and the Road of Literature), pp. 43 – 54.

[132] See Havelock Ellis, *Psychology of Sex*, p. 323.

[133] This can be seen from what Disenchantment (Madam Fairy) says about "lust" *in Honglou meng* (Story of a Stone): "There are always any number of worthless philanderers to protest that it is woman's beauty alone that inspires them, or loving feelings alone, unsullied by any taint of lust. They lie in their teeth! To be moved by woman's beauty is itself a kind of lust. To experience loving feelings is, even more assuredly, a kind of lust. Every act of love, every carnal congress of the sexes is brought about precisely because sensual delight in beauty has kindled the feeling of love." See David Hawkes, trans., *The Story of the Stone*, vol. 1, p. 145.

[134] See Patrick Hanan, *The Invention of Li Yu*, p. 123.

[135] See Hu Shiying, *Huaben Xiaoshuo Gailun* (A General Introduction to the *Huaben* Story), vol. 2, p. 463.

[136] I borrow this phrase from Louis Montrose, the meaning of which he explained as follows: "By *the historicity of texts*, I mean to suggest the cultural specificity, the social embedment, of all modes of writing – not only the texts that critics study but also the texts in which we study them. By *the textuality of history*, I mean to suggest, firstly, that we can have no access to a full and authentic past, a lived material existence, unmediated by the surviving textual traces of the society in question – traces whose survival we cannot assume to be merely contingent but must rather presume to be at least partially consequent upon complex and subtle social processes of preservation and effacement; that these textual traces are themselves subject to subsequent textual mediation when they are construed as the 'documents' upon which historians ground their own texts, called 'history.'" See *The New Historicism*, p. 20.

[137] See Ling Mengchu, "Fanli" (Introductory Remarks) to *Pai'an Jingqi*.

[138] This is a controversial point. In his article "Buddhism and the Rise of the Written Vernacular in East Asia: The Making of National Languages," Victor Mair says: "It must be pointed out that difference between *wenyan* and *baihua* is at least as great as that between Latin and Italian or between Sanskrit and Hindi. In my estimation, a thorough linguistic analysis would show that unadulterated *wenyan* and pure *baihua* are actually far more dissimilar than are Latin and Italian or Sanskrit and Hindi." *Journal of Asian Studies*, vol. 53, p. 707, 1994. But in his essay "Wenyan he baihua"

(Literary Language and Vernacular Language), Lü Shuxiang (1904 – 1998), a distinguished Chinese philologist, says that he once gave his friends some paragraphs taken from a variety of old sources, asking them to ascertain whether or not these paragraphs were written in *wenyan*, and their answeres differed. For a detailed discussion of the difference or similarity between *wenyan* and *baihua*, see the aforementioned article by Lü Shuxiang, in *Lü Shuxiang wenji* (The Works of Lü Shuxiang), vol. 4, pp. 67 – 86.

[139] Wang Gulu in his introduction to *Chuke Pai'an Jingqi* remarks that Ling Mengchu's language, in spite of being smooth and natural, is blended with dialectal words and phrases used in Zhejiang and Jiangsu provinces. These words and phrases may not be difficult to understand to the southerners, but are barriers to those living in the north or other regions.

81

[140] Ling may have been guilty of running the gamut from "plagiarism" to "subtle transformation," although he claimed that he just followed the general practice of fictional composition. For instance, the beginning lyric (*ci*) of "The Wife Swapper" was obviously taken from *Jin Ping Mei* (chapter 1). Yet, according to Patrick Hanan, the author of *Jin Ping Mei* appropriated this lyric from a story entitled "Wenjing yuanyang hui" (A Tryst for Which the Lovers Lost Their Heads) in the collection *Qingping Shantang Huaben*. Hanan also pointed out that the original author of this lyric was a Song poet named Zhuo Tian. See Hanan, "The Sources of *Jin Ping Mei*," *Asian Major*, vol. 10, 1962, pp. 32 – 34.

[141] *Jiji zhenjing* (True Sutra of Assistance) has an exposition on how to obtain female fluids through intercourse. According to it, female fluids include saliva, milk, and vaginal secretion: "The upper is called the Red Lotus Peak, its medicine is named Jade Fountain, Jade Fluid, or Fountain of Sweet Spirits. This medicine emanates from the two cavities under a women's tongue. Its colour is grey.... The middle peak is called the Double Lotus Peak and its medicine is called Peach of Immortality, White Snow, or also Coral Juice. This medicine emanates from the breasts of a woman. Its colour is white, its taste sweet and agreeable.... Of the three peaks, this one should receive attention first. A woman who has not yet borne a child and who has not yet milk in her breast will give the most benefit.... The lower is called Peak of the Purple agaric, also the Grotto of the White Tiger, or the Mysterious Gateway. Its medicine is called White Lead."

[142] See *Tower for Summer Heat*, p. xii.

[143] See Chen Shidao, *Houshan shihua* (Houshan's Remarks on Poetry).

[144] For example, in chapter 13 of *Jin Ping Mei*, Ximen Qing has a tryst with Li Ping'er, and their lovemaking is presented in a set-piece: "When she [a maid] saw that the two of them were going to engage in an illicit liaison that night, she stealthily pulled a hairpin out of her headdress, poked a hole in the paper of the lower part of the casement, and peeked inside. Truly, what were the two of them doing with each other? Behold:

By the gleam of lamplight,
Amid mermaid silk curtains;

One comes, the other goes,
One butts, the other lunges.
One of them stirs his jade arms into motion,
The other raises her golden lotuses on high.
This one gives vent to the warbling of an oriole,
That one gives voices to the twittering of a swallow.

See *The Plum in the Golden Vase*, David Roy, trans., pp. 264–266.

82

[145] Rolston's explanation, which I paraphrase as follows, may help understand why Ling in his stories tends to slight the so-called "realism" or "reflectionism": While faithful representation of the world was long held to be the highest goal in art in the West, little emphasis, in mainstream Chinese aesthetics, was placed on the description of the outside world for its own sake; Chinese aesthetics tend to favour expressionism or impressionism (*xieyi*) over realism (*xieshi*); details from the outside world were incorporated into literary works as part of the symbolic expression of the author's intent. See David Rolston, *Traditional Chinese Fiction and Fiction Commentary*, pp. 166–7.

[146] Cf. John Gagnon and William Simon's categorization of sexual deviance. The first kind includes masturbation, premarital coitus, and heterosexual mouth-genital contact, which, generally disapproved of but performed by large numbers of people, is called "normal deviance." The second kind is called "pathological deviance," and examples include incest, sexual contact with children of either sex, exhibitionism, voyeurism, and aggressive or assaultive offenses. The third kind involves behaviours that generate specific forms of social structure, such as female prostitution and both male and female homosexuality. See *Sexual Deviance*, pp. 7–11.

[147] See Andrew Plaks, "The Problem of Incest in *Jin Ping Mei* and *Honglou Meng*," in *Paradoxes of Traditional Chinese Literature*, p. 126.

[148] See Morton Hunt, *Sexual Behavior in the 1970s*, p. 298.

[149] See Ling Mengchu, "Introductory Remarks" (*fanli*) to *Pai'an jingqi*.

[150] See Lu Xun, *A Brief History of Chinese Fiction*, p. 264.

[151] In my view, late Ming fiction can be divided into four types: realistic, allegoric, moralistic, and idealistic. The first two types, represented respectively by *Water Margins* and *The Journey to the West*, are mainly entertaining, whereas the latter two are largely didactic. *Xu Jin Ping Mei* can be considered as a representative work of the moralistic type, and *Yu Jiao Li* (Strange Tales of the Two Beauties) is perhaps one of the most famous idealistic novels (the difference between the didactic type and the idealistic type is that the former imposes moral teaching on the story through the intervention of author/narrator, whereas the latter lets the story demonstrate a moral theme by setting up a good example of ideal love, usually between a scholar and a beauty). From the early 17th century onward, due to Ling Mengchu's influence as well as to other factors, didactic fiction (both the didactic and idealistic types) gradually became a mainstream, and even an

explicitly erotic novel, after depicting all kinds of sexual indulgence, would offer readers some moral clichés.

[152] *The Chinese Vernacular Story*, p. 149.

[153] I should point out that despite his warning against seduction and other illicit sexual activities, Ling was by no means an advocator of asceticism. Unlike the Song Neo-Confucianists who stressed the necessity of getting rid of "*yu*" (desire) in order to obtain "*li*" (principle), Ling seemed not to be entirely negative about sexual desire. He only opposed, as is shown by his erotic stories, indulgence in illicit sex. So we may say that his attitude was closer to the attitude of the ancient Confucianists than to that of the Neo-Confucianists. The Confucianists in the Warring-States period were hedonistic, favouring moderate enjoyment of desire over absolute abstention.

[154] *Xu Jin Ping Mei*, p. 2.

[155] According to David Rolston, there are two kinds of commentarial modes, the "narratorial commentarial mode" and the extratextual commentarial mode, and the major difference between them is that the latter is not part of the oral storyteller context.

[156] The most serious *tuoyang* instance can be found in *Jin Ping Mei*, chapter 79.

[157] Confucian filiality emphasizes the family line more than anything else. "Mencius said, 'There are three things which are unfilial, and to have no posterity is the greatest of them.'" See *The Works of Mencius*, in *The Chinese Classics*, James Legge, trans., vol. II, p. 313.

[158] The marginal and interlinear comments were all made by Ling himself.

[159] It seems that in deciding whether his character should receive light or heavy punishment Ling was strongly influenced by *Gongguo ge* (Ledgers of Merits and Demerits). These ledgers are predominantly Confucianistic, though they were also equally popular among Daoists and Buddhists.

[160] See *Sexual Life in Ancient China*, p. 299.

[161] *Ibid.*, p. 288.

[162] *Wutong ying*, the authorship of which is unknown, is a novel published in the Qing. It has twelve chapters. The first three are largely introductory, with the story proper beginning from the fourth chapter. The story is about Sanzhuo, a son born into a store-owner's family in Suzhou. In his childhood he is sent into a monastery. After having grown up, he meets with a Daoist adept, who teaches him the art of the bedchamber. Later he gets acquainted with a young man named Wang Runguan. Wang is an actor who is handsome, smart, and popular among women from official and rich families. Sanzhuo teaches Wang love-making skills, and they indulge in sexual pleasures and often make love together. In the end, both are arrested and punished for their notorious behaviour.

[163] See Lin Chen, *Mingmo Xiaoshuo Shulu* (An Annotated Bibliography of Late Ming Fiction), pp. 400–401.

[164] In his preface to *Jin Ping Mei*, Xinxin Zi, the Master of Delight (who has been considered to be the author himself by some scholars), remarked that

83

the author of the novel intended to make a contribution "to the moral reformation of the age, the reproof of vice and encouragement of virtue, the purification of the mind and cleansing of the heart." Ling Mengchu, in his "Fanli" (Introductory Remarks) to *Pai'an jingqi*, also made it clear that "this collection [of my stories] is intended for admonition, and that is why moral advice is offered three times in each story."

[165] These three types also represent the three grades of the explicitness in erotic description. The first type "lust," is the least explicit, the second type "lust-love," is fairly explicit – between the first type and the third type; and the third type "lust-sex," is the most explicit.

84

[166] *My Secret Life* was written by an unknown author. Since it is autobiographical and the hero is called Walter, I, like Western scholars, also refer to its anonymous author as Walter for the sake of convenience.

[167] The literary representation of sex in these three stages are different too. In the Renaissance period that is known for its humanistic emancipation, sex is undifferentially treated as part of love; in the repressive 17 – 19th centuries, sex begins to be separated from socially accepted behaviours and becomes an underground activity; and in the 20th century in which erotic literature has reached its unrestrained prosperity, sex is regarded as integral to human nature and is consciously intermingled with love and marriage.

[168] While erotic literature suffered repression in the West in the nineteenth century, it had a worse fate in China: after an ephemeral prosperity in the late Ming, it completely disappeared. The nineteenth-century novels such as *Pinghua Baojian* (A Precious Guide to the Appraisal of Flowers), *Haishang Hualie Zhuan* (Stories of Prostitutes in Shanghai), and *Jiuwei Gui* (The Turtle with Nine Tails) are not erotic fiction, and there has been no erotic literature of any kind produced in the twentieth century.

[169] In terms of the literary representation of sex, the process of the rise, decline, and extinction of Chinese erotic fiction can also be described as a process of portraying sex in three different forms: (1) sex as pure carnal enjoyment (often portrayed realistically in juxtaposition with loving affection and other activities), (2) sex in constant conflict with social mores (often portrayed repressively), and (3) sex occurring offstage only (largely replaced by love, or to be more specific, by spiritual love).

In the Inner
QUARTERS

Fatal Seduction[1]

The monk may be a hungry devil of sex,
But the nun is no less so.
When she finds her way into a boudoir,
Seduction and violation are sure to follow.

There are three kinds of "aunts" and six types of "crones"[2] whom one should most carefully avoid. These women have abundant idle time to fritter away and are shrewd, skillful, and scheming. Having visited thousands of households, they are rich in experience and familiar with all walks of life. Indecent women, nine out of ten, will be duped by them. Even ladies who are blameless and unspoilt will frequently fall victim to their wily intrigues. They are as artful as the master strategists Zhang Liang and Chen Ping[3] and enjoy the repartee that can be found only in such famous sophists as Sui He and Lu Jia.[4] Given their ability to make trouble out of nothing, official households who value propriety are forced to put a large sign on their gates prohibiting their visits.

Of all these aforementioned women, the nun is the most vicious. On the pretext of preaching Buddhism and having the advantage of a private sanctuary, she is able to attract both women to come and burn incense and youths to visit and take pleasure. If the visitor is a man, she will greet him and talk to him like a monk, without feeling awkward by the difference in their sexes. As a woman, she naturally feels more comfortable in intimate situations with her female clients as she chants sutras to them in the meditation room. The nun is a notorious go-between who has been involved in most of the liaisons known to us, with the nunnery serving as a place for trysts with paramours.

In the Tang dynasty there was a woman from a distinguished family whose surname was Di[5] and whose marriage to a high-ranking official in the central administration entitled her to be addressed as "Lady."[6] Lady Di was famed in the capital for her outstanding beauty, and women of imperial and aristocratic families would often say, in the midst of jealous squabblings, "You think you are elegant and can put on airs for me? You are certainly not up to Lady Di!" In spite of her reputation as a peerless beauty, Lady Di was nevertheless a woman of demure disposition, decorous, and lax neither with speech nor smile.

It was the spring season when our story unfolds. Flushed with pleasure, literati and their wives gathered at the Western Pond, and colourfully painted and gaily curtained carriages filled with princes and dukes and the like arrived in an endless stream. Lady Di, who was very conventional socially, also joined this spring excursion.

A handsome young man by the name of Teng, who was sojourning in the capital as a candidate for an official post, was at the pond, too, on that day. When he saw Lady Di, he was so transported that it was as if his soul had taken flight. He followed her wherever she went, his eyes focused on her all along the way. Lady Di, at one point, looked around and caught sight of him. Though she noticed that he was handsome and entrancing, she did not pay him much attention. Teng was completely captivated, though, and stood gazing at her in a daze, dreaming that he might find some cold water to gulp her down, clothes and all! He inquired of the passing strollers and was informed that she was a well-known beauty in the capital.

The carriages and horses had dispersed. Teng returned to his lodgings, dejected. Thinking of her kept him from sleep all night, and from that time on, he longed so much to see her that he would forget to eat in the middle of a meal, or keep going onward after he had reached his destination, as if a lost treasure were weighing each moment upon his mind. As he could no longer bear the distress, he went to the area where Lady Di lived and inquired about her throughout the neighbourhood. Yet he was told nothing more than that she was a virtuous woman, very difficult to approach.

"She must have some close friends," thought Teng. "If I can discover who they are, I should be able to make their acquaintance."

One day he saw a nun leaving Lady Di's house. He followed her and learned from those on the street that her name was Huicheng. They told him that she was the abbess of the Nunnery of Tranquil Happiness and often came to visit her patron.

"Excellent!" Teng exclaimed.

He hastened back to where he lodged, took ten taels of silver, and wrapped them up. Then he went hurrying to the nunnery.

"Is the abbess in?" he asked.

Huicheng came out and saw that the caller was a youthful gentleman. She invited him in for tea, and after they bowed to each other, asked, "Sir, may I know your honourable name and the purpose of your visit?"

Teng told her his name and explained, "I have no particular business. For a long time, I have heard of the reputation of your holy place, and today I came simply to present you a small pittance in the hope that I may worship and burn incense in your sanctuary afterwards."

He removed the silver from inside his sleeve[7] and handed it over to her. As an experienced woman, Huicheng could tell, with a single sweep of her eyes, that with such a heavy packet of money the man was bound to ask her a favour.

"Please don't bother!" she declined, but at the same time her hands had already seized the offering. "Sir, I appreciate very much your generous bounty," she said. "Perhaps you would like to talk to me?"

Teng prevaricated, pretending that he had nothing special to say, and that the money was just a little token of his sincerity. With this, he took his leave and returned to his lodgings.

"What an odd thing!" thought Huicheng. "He is such a dashing youth and I am just an elder nun. It is unlikely that he has taken a fancy to me. But why would he leave me so much money without saying a word?" She pondered, but found no reason.

Teng visited the nunnery every day, and on each visit displayed more congeniality and gallantry. Soon he and the nun became very familiar with each other.

One day Huicheng brought up her question again. "Sir," she said, "you appear restless, and I suspect that you have something on your mind. Should there be some confidence you can entrust to me, I would assuredly do my best to help you."

"I was not sure that you could be of help so I haven't said anything to you, "Teng replied. "But since this is a matter of life and death to me, I shall seek your assistance, no matter how trifling it might be. If I fail to achieve my goal, I shall surely languish and die."

The abbess could make neither head nor tail of what he was saying. "In a matter of such gravity," she said, "you must first of all make clear to me what exactly you wish me to do for you."

Teng then told her that he had encountered Lady Di at the Western Pond and had been pining for her ever since. If he could enjoy her favours, he said, he would gladly offer her ten thousand pieces of gold.

"Your wish is not easy to fulfill," said Huicheng, smiling. "She is indeed very beautiful and I have had some acquaintance with her. But given her unblemished virtue, I doubt that I can aid you in this matter."

Teng mused for awhile and asked, "Since you know her well, do you know of anything that would give her great pleasure?"

"Nothing particular as far as I can see," Huicheng replied.

"Has she ever asked you to do something for her?" Teng pressed.

"Well," said Huicheng, "not many days ago, she asked me several times to look for some fine pearls for her. That's the only thing."

"Splendid! Splendid!" Teng exclaimed. "As luck would have it, I have a relative who is a jeweller and has a stock of fine pearls. I am now lodging

89

with him, and can obtain as many fine pearls as you wish."

With this he went hurrying out, hired a horse, and sped off. Soon he returned with two bags of large pearls and handed them to the abbess for inspection. "These pearls are usually priced at twenty thousand strings of cash,"[8] he said. "Since she is so great a beauty, I would be willing to reduce the price and ask only for ten thousand."

"But there is a problem," said Huicheng. "Her husband is currently on a diplomatic mission in the north, and she, after all, is only a woman, who probably can't lay her hands on so much money in his absence."

"Then I will let her have them if she can afford only four or five thousand," said Teng. "Or she may pay me a thousand or even less. Should she agree to grant me her favours, I won't ask her for a single penny."

"Ridiculous!" the abbess smilingly chided him. "But now that you have these pearls, I will surely exercise a tongue as glib as Zhang Yi and Su Qing[9] and devise 'six ingenious stratagems'[10] for you. I will see to it that she at least comes to the nunnery. Once she is here, I will set up an occasion for you to meet her. You must be most tactful once she is in your hands, for you know a successful seduction depends wholly on you and I can do nothing about it."

"I will entrust my life to you, Abbess!" Teng exclaimed.

Greatly pleased, Huicheng hastened to Lady Di's residence, carrying the bags of pearls with her. After the customary exchange of greetings, Lady Di asked, "What do you carry inside your bags?"

"The pearls you asked me to look for the other day," the nun replied. "These are very fine pearls and today I have made this trip especially to let you take a look."

The bags were opened. Lady Di spilled the pearls into her hands to examine them. "They are indeed very fine!" she sighed, gazing at them over and over and fondling them in admiration.

"How much are they?" she asked.

"Ten thousand," Huicheng answered.

"But that is only half the usual price," said Lady Di. "It seems impossible to me that they are so inexpensive! Unfortunately, my husband is away from home and I can't obtain so huge a sum immediately. What shall I do?"

"Permit me, Ma'am, to speak to you in private," Huicheng said, tugging at Lady Di's sleeve. They then went to an inner room, where there were no maids. The nun continued, "If you like these pearls, you may have them and needn't pay a penny, for they belong to a young scholar who is seeking your help."

"Story-teller," you may protest, "how dare the abbess so plainly proposition a lady of good family, asking her to sacrifice her virtue for the sake of a love affair?"

Gentle reader, please have patience. The silver-tongued nun cer-tainly knew how to disguise her intention in appropriate words.

"What help does he expect from me?" asked Lady Di.

"The young gentleman was previously an official," Huicheng told her. "He lost his post due to a false accusation by his enemy. In order to get a chance to defend himself before the Board of Personnel[11] for re-instatement, he is willing to give these pearls to whomever might secure him a hearing. Since your husband, brothers, and uncles are all high-ranking officials, you should be able to instruct him on how to solve his problem. If you agree to his assistance, then these pearls will be yours free."

"Such being the case," said Lady Di, "return them to him temp-orarily and ask him to wait until I have thought the matter over. I am sure I can do something on his behalf."

Huicheng was persistent. "This gentleman can't delay," she said. "He will seek help elsewhere with the jewels if I return them to him, and then you will never see them again. I suggest, ma'am, that you accept them, tell him that you will somehow find a way, and ask him to await your reply tomorrow."

"You are right," Lady Di agreed. "I will do as you say."

Huicheng then took her leave, and told Teng of their conversation.

"What should be done next?" Teng asked.

"Since she loves the pearls and has accepted them," said Huicheng, "you may trust me to ensure her appearance tomorrow at the nunnery!"

Teng gave the nun another ten taels of silver, begging her to pay an early visit to Lady Di the next morning.

Lady Di, after the abbess had left, once again gazed upon the jewels. The more she looked at them, the more beautiful they seemed. "To think, I only have to request a small favour from my brothers and these pearls will be mine," she mused.

One should not have covetous desires. A greedy craving may lay one open to vulnerability and one will therefore fall prey too easily to deceitful trickery. Had Lady Di not asked the nun to look for pearls for her, this unexpected turn of events would not have occurred. When she had seen fine pearls, she could have purchased them if she had had the money. Otherwise she could have chosen to live without them. Had she been able to manage on her own, no man, however skilled, could have touched a single fine hair of hers. Lady Di, however, was wholly seduced by the gems yet could not afford to purchase them. As a result, she was to fall into the trap that the nun had set for her, and her jade body, as transluscent as ice, would become entangled in the web of an an illicit affair.

The next day Lady Di was still preoccupied with thoughts of this matter when Huicheng arrived. "Have you found how to help the young gentleman?" she asked.

"Last night," replied Lady Di, "I devoted careful thought to his problem, and am certain now that I can use some connections to pull a few strings on his behalf."

"Still, there remains one more difficulty," said Huicheng. "This transaction is large, involving a huge sum of money. As an insignificant nun with but a few pounds of flesh on her body, how can I convince him, if he doesn't know you personally, that you will keep your word?"

"That's true," said Lady Di. "Do you have a solution?"

"Yes, I have a silly idea," said the abbess. "In order to meet him, you could perhaps visit my nunnery. You could pretend that you are there to observe a fasting ceremony and have met him only by coincidence. That way you can make his acquaintance. What do you think?"

Lady Di was a decent woman. The nun's suggestion that she meet a male stranger in the convent brought a blush to her entire face.

"This is out of the question!" she said, with a dismissive wave of her hands.

Huicheng's face fell. "Why are you so upset?" she said. "A meeting would do no more than give him a chance to speak to you so you might assure him that you have found a way to help him, lest he be filled with misgivings. If you think you oughtn't see him, then, let's proceed no further. I have no intention of forcing you to do something unwillingly."

Lady Di could not make up her mind. Upon second thought, she said, "Since you are experienced, Abbess, I will take your advice. Two days from now is the anniversary of my late brother's death, and I will visit your nunnery to carry out the praying. But you should advise the young man that our talk must be brief and that he must leave as soon as the business is finished. I have to take care to avoid scandal."

"That's what I would like you to do," Huicheng assured her. "He certainly has no reason to remain once your conversation is completed. So you needn't concern yourself about that."

The date having been set, Huicheng returned to tell Teng this news. Teng had reached the nunnery ahead of her, and after hearing her detailed account, bowed deeply to her, saying, "You did so well that only Su Qing and Zhang Yi could equal your skill!"

The day came. Huicheng rose early in the morning and prepared vegetarian dishes. After concealing Teng in a quiet, infrequently used room where she had laid out a table of wine and delicacies, she closed the door behind her and strolled out into the reception hall to wait for her guest. Truly:

> The fragrant bait is assaulting the nose,
> Specially made for the lady whale to use.

As expected, Lady Di arrived in the afternoon, dressed in splendid attire. To shun gossip, she dismissed her male servants and entered the nunnery only with a young maid. No sooner had she stepped into the gate than she saw the abbess.

"Has he come?" she asked.

"Not yet," Huicheng replied.

"Good," she said. "Allow me to finish the fasting ceremony first."

When prayers had been made and sutras had been recited, Huicheng bade her young novice take Lady Di's maid to amuse themselves somewhere else. She then said to Lady Di, "Let's find a small room to sit for a while."

Following several narrow corridors, they reached a secluded alcove. Lady Di, upon pulling the curtain aside and entering, was startled to find that a young man was sitting by himself at a table fully laden with wine and food. She was about to withdraw when Huicheng interposed.

"My venerable sir," she addressed Teng, "this is the lady whom you wish to speak to. Please be quick to bow to her!"

Teng rushed forward upon hearing this and fell gallantly to his knees before Lady Di, who felt compelled to return the obeisance.

"This young gentleman," Huicheng went on to say, "has specially prepared this banquet in honour of your kind visit. It is his humble wish that you accept his sincerity. Please don't reject him!"

Lady Di then turned and looked up, and was greatly taken aback as she found that the young man before her was none other than the scholar she had encountered at the Western Pond. Observing his elegant handsomeness, she became less rigid, and in a delightful tone, still somewhat timid and affected, stammered, "Please, sir, tell me what you wish me to do for you."

Huicheng pulled at her sleeve, saying, "Why are you both stand-ing? Conversation is better conducted in seated comfort."

Teng, smilingly bowing his gratitude to Lady Di, filled a wine-cup to its brim and presented it to her with both hands. Lady Di found it difficult to resist and took the cup and drained it. Huicheng then raised the wine pot to pour herself a cup; out of courtesy, Lady Di drank a toast in return.

Her manner was now less controlled and reserved than it had been before, and she even winked at Teng.

"What post do you wish to obtain, sir?" she asked.

Teng gave Huicheng a look. "I am afraid I can't tell you with Abbess present."

"I will leave you to talk," said Huicheng immediately. She then quickly rose to her feet and slipped out, closing the small door behind her.

In less time than it takes to tell, Teng moved from his seat to the other side of the table and took Lady Di into his arms. "Since I first saw you at the pond, ma'am," he said, "I have been longing for you day and night, pining away. I am now on the brink of dying and only you can save me. Ma'am, should you permit me to fulfill my desires, then both my body and my life would be yours. As for an official position, I really care little."

He fell to his knees. His masculine beauty and abject pleadings, sprinkled generously with plenty of "madams," filled Lady Di with both joy and alarm. She wanted to scream for help, but knew that no one would come to her rescue. She then struggled to get out of his embrace, but Teng's hands clutched her tightly. Taking advantage of his kneeling position, Teng succeeded in carrying her in his arms and throwing her onto the bed, and then in total abandon, began to pull at her underwear. By now Lady Di had become inflamed and was no longer able to control her raging passions. She writhed about for only a short while before yielding to him, letting him make free with her. Young as he was, Teng was a veteran in the art of the bedchamber. With his lovemaking skills, he set her atingle and soon her female essence flowed out. In spite of the conventional joys of her married life, Lady Di had never experienced so ecstatic a sensual delight as she did this time. She felt immensely satiated.

After they had finished the work of the clouds and rain,[12] Lady Di clasped Teng's hand and asked, "What is your name, sir? If it hadn't been for today's meeting, I would have spent my whole life in vain. From now on we must be together every night!"

Teng told her his name and thanked her profusely. At this moment Huicheng opened the door and came in. Perceiving Lady Di too embarrassed to speak, she said, "I hope you will forgive me! This gentleman has been slowly killing himself on your account, and as a sympathetic nun, I wished only that you save him. To build a seven-storeyed pagoda is, no doubt, not as meritorious as the benefaction you have just now granted him."

"You have deceived me and made me the victim of a hoax!" Lady Di returned, pretending to be vexed. "Now I want you to send him to my house every night!"

94

"That's no problem," said Huicheng.

They parted company in the evening.

Since their first meeting, not a single night passed that did not see Teng slip in through a side door to meet his paramour. Lady Di, who had fallen deeply in love with him, tried her utmost to please him lest he grow tired of her. Teng, too, exerted himself to make her happy and satisfied. They were as thick as thieves for several months until Lady Di's husband returned home. Now Teng could no longer visit her regularly. But whenever her husband was away, Lady Di would send for him, and their trysts went on in this fashion for almost a year before her husband caught wind of something and took precautions, which fi-nally made it impossible for them to continue their intimate relations. Lady Di missed her lover so much that she soon fell sick and died.

It was because of the nun's meddling that Lady Di, always before that a virtuous woman, fell into illicit ways and expired. Of course, her loss of moral rectitude and her submission to lust must, too, be ascribed to her own fickle nature.

There was, by contrast, a woman of integrity, who, in spite of having been violated through a nun's vicious trickery, persisted in the pursuit of her vendetta and eventually, in co-operation with her husband, made her seducers pay for their evil. This is a most exciting story, extraordinary and amazing. It tallies exactly with what the "Pumeng pin" (Universal Gateway of the Boddhisattva)[13] predicts:

> With poisonous drugs and curses and spells
> Someone intends to injure your health.
> Owing to the power of the Perceiver of Sound,
> The mishap will return to the prayer himself.[14]

In Wuzhou[15] there lived a young licentiate[16] named Jia who was both eru-dite and intelligent. His wife, née Wu, was both beautiful and demure. Hus-band and wife, like fish in water, enjoyed a happy conjugal life and never had they had even half a bickering word with each other. The Licentiate, working as a private tutor, resided in a rich household and returned home only twice a year, while his wife, Madam Wu, in the company of her maid Spring Flower, led a domestic life, occupying herself with household work.

Madam Wu was skilled at needlework. She once embroidered a depiction of the Boddhisattva Guanyin,[17] which, vivid with colours and solemn and dignified in expression, appeared as if it were real. She was very proud of her work and had the Licentiate take it to a frame shop to mount it. People there who saw the embroidery all gasped in admiration.

It was made into a scroll, and Madam Wu, after bringing it back home, hung it in a freshly-cleaned room, and burned incense and prayed before it every morning and evening.

Since Madam Wu was a devotee of the Boddhisattva Guanyin, a certain nun by the name of Zhao of the Nunnery of the Perceiver of Sound located on the same street often dropped in on her. She would sometimes stay for a couple of days, providing Madam Wu with company when the Licentiate was not home, and sometimes she would invite Madam Wu to the nunnery. As a woman of decorum, Madam Wu rarely went out. She visited the nunnery at most once or twice a year.

On one spring day when the Licentiate was away, Nun Zhao called upon Madam Wu, and after a brief chat, rose to leave. "What a beautiful day!" she said. "Let's go outside to take a look!"

Madam Wu saw the nun to the gate. As ill-luck would have it, just as she popped her head out to look around, she saw what seemed to be a rogue swaggering down the street. He caught a glimpse of her before she could shrink back and hide behind the door. Nun Zhao, however, stood still, brazenly staring at him.

The man, in fact, knew her.

"Mother Zhao!" he called, "I have been looking everywhere for you and had no idea that you would be here! I have something to ask you."

"Let me take leave of the lady of the house," Nun Zhao replied. She went in and said some parting words to Madam Wu, who, after her guest had left, closed the door and returned to her room.

The foppish-looking man who had accosted the nun was called Bu Liang.[18] He was a tireless dissolute notorious in the town. Every pretty woman he saw would stimulate his seductive desires, and there were few who had not fallen prey to his lust. Since he sought only sex, he did not much care whether his partner was beautiful or ugly; and his promiscuity made him a quite popular figure among the nuns with whom he associated. Sometimes they acted as his panders, and sometimes they crawled into bed with him themselves.

Nun Zhao had a beautiful novice, about twenty years of age, whose ecclesiastical name was Benkong. It was, perhaps, more appropriate to regard her as a whore supported by the elder nun than as a tonsured member of the Buddhist order, since secretly she prostituted herself and took money for selling her body. Bu Liang was actually one of their clients.

After having parted with Madam Wu on that day, Nun Zhao caught up with him. "Mr. Bu," she called, "what do you wish to ask me about?"

"Was that Licentiate Jia's residence that you were just visiting?" he asked.

"Yes?" said Nun Zhao.

"I have heard that he has a pretty wife," said Bu Liang. "I suppose that she must have been the woman who just escorted you out and stood behind the door?"

"Goodness me!" said Nun Zhao. "Do you think there is another beautiful woman in his house? On this entire street you will never be able to find a woman as beautiful as she is!"

"She is indeed beauteous and deserves the reputation she enjoys," Bu Liang agreed. "I wish I could see her just one more time so that I could look at her more closely!"

"That's not difficult for me to arrange," Nun Zhao declared. "The nineteenth of the second month is the birthday of Guanyin, and since there will be parades through the streets, multitudes of people are bound to come to watch. You may perhaps rent an upper room on the opposite side of her street beforehand. She is alone at home and I will invite her out for the festival. It should be all right for her to watch the parades from her own doorway, and I wager she will watch them for some time. As she stands there, you may spy on her through a window until you have fed your eyes to the full."

"Wonderful idea! Wonderful idea!" Bu Liang exclaimed.

Taking Nun Zhao's advice, Bu Liang rented an upper room from which he could obtain a clear view of the Jia house located on the other side of the street. As promised, he saw the nun go into the house and emerge with Madam Wu. The poor woman, having not yet realized what trickery was involved, feared only that by standing at the doorway, she might be seen by men passing by. Never did she suspect that someone would stealthily gaze at her from a window on the upper floor opposite! Involuntarily she offered herself, from beginning to end, for the scrutiny of a voyeur, who watched her until she went in.

When Bu Liang descended the stairs, Nun Zhao, fresh from the Jia house, encountered him. "Now you must have had a close look at her, haven't you?" she asked, grinning.

"Yes, I did have a close look," Bu Liang replied. "But just looking and thinking of her will do nothing but drive me crazy. I wish to find a way to have her."

"You live in the gutter yet want to taste the flesh of a swan!"[19] said Nun Zhao. "She is the wife of a licentiate and dwells in the inner chambers. You are not a relative of her husband, nor do you have any other relationship with her. How can you make her acquaintance? You can but look upon her."

So saying, she turned and walked away, and was soon back in the nunnery. Bu Liang, following on her heels, knelt before her once they were inside the temple. "Mother," he implored, "you often visit her, and I beg you to think of a stratagem to bait my hook."

Nun Zhao shook her head. "Difficult, difficult, difficult!"

"I would die content if I could only have a taste," Bu Liang insisted.

"Madam Wu is no ordinary woman," said Nun Zhao. "It's not even easy to strike up a light conversation with her, let alone engage her in an illicit liaison. Even if you laboured for ten thousand years, I doubt that you would succeed. But if you want only a taste, I might be able to coax her into submission. You must be patient."

"Are you suggesting that I rape her?" asked Bu Liang.

"You needn't rape her," said Nun Zhao. "Instead, she will submit to you."

Bu Liang was curious. "What is your magic plan then, my brilliant advisor?"

"As the old saying goes," said Nun Zhao, "'Paddle the boat slowly and you will catch the drunken fish.'[20] That is to say, you must make her drunk in order to achieve your goal. What do you think?"

"The idea is not bad," said Bu Liang. "But how might it be carried out?"

"The problem is that the woman does not drink wine, not even a drop," Nun Zhao told him. "You must not force her if she is unwiling, for if you press her over and over, she may become suspicious and angry, and as a result, will certainly refuse to comply, which you can do nothing about. If she drinks only a cup or two at your persuasion, she will become sober just as quickly as she gets drunk, and you won't have an opportunity to lay your hands on her."

"Then what should we do?" Bu Liang asked.

"I know what I am about and you don't have to bother your head about it," said Nun Zhao.

Bu Liang, however, insisted that she reveal the scheme to him. Nun Zhao then whispered something in his ear, and asked, "How is it?"

Bu Liang gave a great guffaw. "A wonderful plan! A wonderful plan! From ancient times to the present I have never heard of a scheme as good as this one!"

"But there is one thing that still worries me," said Nun Zhao. "I may manage to take her in, but once she wakes up, she may be angry with me and may never again speak to me. I don't know yet what I should do to deal with that scenario."

"The only thing that concerns you is to get her for me," said Bu Liang. "Once she has fallen into our trap, I don't think she will kick up a rumpus and fall out with you. Keep plying her with words of honey and you may perhaps even enable the two of us to establish a long intimacy. If she does blame you, I shall repay you amply for your kindness to me. But should I in any case carry on intimately with her, I shall ensure that she maintain a closeness with you as she did before!"

"How glibly you speak!" said Nun Zhao.

They continued in this jocular vein for some time before breaking up. From then on, Bu Liang went to the nunnery every day to inquire about Madam Wu, and Nun Zhao racked her brains every day to devise a plan for him. A few days later she prepared two boxes of sweets to pay a visit to Madam Wu, and was invited to stay for dinner. This gave her a fine opportunity for intimate conversation.

"Madam Wu," said Nun Zhao, "you and your husband are a young couple, and you should have had a child by now, since you have been married for quite a long time."

"I wish I could," said Madam Wu.

"If you are serious, why don't you pray for it?" Nun Zhao asked.

"I did, as a matter of fact," Madam Wu replied. "Every morning and evening I burn incense before my embroidered Boddhisattva Guanyin, and I also pray silently whenever I can. It is just that my prayers haven't been answered yet."

"Madam Wu," said Nun Zhao, "you are perhaps too young to know properly how to pray for a child. If you wish to conceive, you must pray to Guanyin-in-White. There is a scripture called *The Sutra of Guanyin-in-White*, which is not usually recited nor is *The Universal Gateway of the Boddhisattva*. *The Sutra of Guanyin-in-White* I am talking about contains words of great power, which I can't show you at the moment, for this sutra is in the last few fascicles and I didn't carry them with me today. Although I cannot speak for elsewhere, I can at least assure you that in our town there is no one who has read it or copied it out without having given birth to a child. It is indeed no exaggeration to say that when there is a prayer, there is a response."

"Mother, since this sutra is so effective, may I ask you to lend it to me so that I may read it at home?" asked Madam Wu.

"You are not familiar with the text," said Nun Zhao, "and might feel it too difficult at the beginning. I should first invite you to our nunnery so that I may inform Guanyin-in-White that you are going to read it. Only after I have prayed on your behalf and recited the first few chapters for you can you begin your own study at home and perform the daily recital by yourself."

"All right, I will do as you say," Madam Wu agreed. "I will fast for two days beforehand and then I will come to your temple to make a pledge before the Guanyin-in-White that I am going to read the sutra you have chosen for me."

"A two-day fast is sufficient to show your sincerity," said Nun Zhao. "During the period when the daily ceremony is performed, it is necessary that you adhere to a vegetarian diet in the morning before you begin your sutra-reading. After your prayers, if you wish some meat or fish, it is permitted."

"If this is how things should be done, it does not seem difficult," said Madam Wu.

The date of her visit having been set, Madam Wu gave the nun five maces of silver toward the expense of preparing the food for the ceremony. Nun Zhao then left and told Bu Liang the good news.

Madam Wu ate vegetarian meals for two days. On the third day, she rose at the fifth watch, and after dressing herself, went to the nunnery in the company of her maid Spring Flower. It was early in the morning and there were few persons on the streets as they made their way to the convent.

Gentle reader take note. A nunnery[21] is a place which women from good families should avoid at all costs! Had I lived in that time and at that place and been informed of the visit, I would have barred the door to stop her. That way, Madam Wu might have preserved her chastity and Nun Zhao might have also been saved from her mishap. It was only because of this appointment that:

> The pretty woman of fine pedigree
> Will be defiled like a sullied jade tree;
> And the malicious crone of the nunnery
> Will like a maple be all over bloody.

This, however, will unflold only at the end of the tale, and now allow me to pick up where we have left off. With great glee, Nun Zhao greeted Madam Wu and invited her to take a seat in the reception room. After tea had been served, she led her patron to pay homage to the Guanyin-in-White, in front of whom Madam Wu prayed silently by herself for some time. Nun Zhao then made a formal prayer on her behalf, helping to convey her sincere wishes to the Boddhisattva. "This devotee, née Wu, of the Jia house," she prayed, "wishes to recite *The Sutra of Guanyin-in-White* in the hope of having a son as early as possible and enjoying a felicitous and satisfying family life."

When the prayer had been made, she beat the wooden fish and fell to chanting. She first chanted the "Mantra for the Purification of the Mouth," and then the "Mantra for the Protection of the God of Earth."[22] Only after she had remained prostrate before the Boddhisattva for a long while did she start her recitation of *The Sutra of Guanyin-in-White*, which she did breathlessly over twenty times.

Nun Zhao was skillful in deceit. She knew that Madam Wu had fasted for two days and had come to the nunnery early in the morning without having had breakfast. So she purposely brought her nothing to eat, nor did she even mention a word about the morning repast, pretending to be completely oblivious to it. She intended, as she deliberately whiled away time, to make her guest weak with hunger.

Madam Wu was a frail woman. What with her early rising and empty stomach, and with the many kowtows and bows she had been obliged to make to the Buddhas and Boddhisattvas, she felt extremely tired and hungry. But she could not complain, and could only whisper to her maid Spring Flower, "If you find some hot porridge in the kitchen, please ladle out a bowl for me."

Overhearing her conversation, Nun Zhao apologized: "I have been so preoccupied with the sutra-reading that I forgot to ask you if you have had breakfast."

"No, I didn't," said Madam Wu. "I came here early and haven't eaten anything yet."

"You see how muddle-brained I was!" said Nun Zhao. "I didn't even prepare breakfast for you and now it is very late. What should I do? Perhaps we should eat our midday meal a little earlier?"

"To be honest with you, I am starving," Madam Wu told her. "If you have some light snacks, or anything at all, I would like to eat some now."

Nun Zhao deliberately murmured some self-deprecatory words before going off to her own room. She remained there for some time, and then made her way out to the kitchen. After awhile a tray of food, together with a pot of tea, was ready for serving, which Nun Zhao had Benkong take out and set on the table. The various kinds of fresh fruit on the tray were designed to be unsuitable for Madam Wu whose stomach was rumbling with hunger. Only the hot cake appealed to her, and she took a piece and found it both soft and sweet. Starving, Madam Wu wolfed down several pieces in succession, and after drinking some of the tea that Benkong had poured for her, ate another few pieces. Then she poured out more tea for herself and drank again, until her face grew red and she felt as if the ceiling and the floor were rotating around her. She yawned and collapsed in her chair.

Nun Zhao pretended to be startled. "What has happened to her?" she asked. "Perhaps she is feeling dizzy because of her early rising this morning? Let's help her to bed so that she might sleep for a while."

She and her disciple then lifted the chair Madam Wu was sitting on, and carried it to the bedside. They lay her in the bed and positioned her head on the pillow to make her sleep comfortably.

Do you know why the cake had such power? It was because it had been specially baked by Nun Zhao for the poor woman whom she knew could not drink alcohol. To make the cake, Nun Zhao first ground sticky rice into fine powder, then mixed it with wine and baked it until it was completely dried. She then repeated the process of grinding and mixing and baking twice more before adding some herbal medicine she had herself concocted. Then she steamed it to ensure that the cake, when eaten with hot tea, would have a soporific effect as strong as the yeast for brewing liquor. An ordinary person might become inebriated after eating the pastry, not to mention the starving Madam Wu who could not even endure food pickled in wine. No wonder that after having had several pieces along with hot water, she was utterly under the sway of its effects. Truly:

> You may be smart and keen and witty as an imp,
> Your aunt can make you drink the water in her footbasin.

Now Madam Wu was completely in the power of Nun Zhao, unable to resist her manipulations. Spring Flower, taking advantage of her mistress's sleep, had disappeared with the young nun to eat and amuse herself somewhere else. She was neither taking care of her mistress nor could she come to her rescue.

Wasting no time, Nun Zhao dragged Bu Liang out from a shadowy corner. "The woman is now in bed ready for your enjoyment!" she said. "Don't forget that it is I whom you must thank for this!"

The door was closed. Bu Liang pulled aside the bed curtain and was assailed by a strong smell of alcohol. Madam Wu, her cheeks charmingly red like a tipsy crabapple, looked to him even more beautiful than before. In an agony of desire, Bu Liang planted a kiss on her lips, and she showed no reaction. He then gently removed her lower garments, laying bare before him her pale-white thighs. Having swiftly parted her legs, he mounted her, inserted himself, and started to thrust.

Swollen with pride, Bu Liang said to himself, "Pity, my little creature! You are now in my hands!" Although too inebriated to move, Madam Wu neverless experienced a dreamlike sensation that someone was making love to her. But she mistook her ravisher for her husband and let him use her at his will. Soon she was aroused by his fierce ramming. In spite of being in a hallucinatory state, she began to moan as her passion reached full flow. A wild surge then ripped through him and Bu Liang was unable to restrain himself any longer. Clutching her in his arms, he cried, "My dearest, I am dying!" And then he ejaculated, his sperm shooting like a water-spout.

When Bu Liang had finished, Madam Wu was still not awake. Bu Liang lay down beside her, and with his arm over her body and his face close to hers, fell into sleep. After the spell of the medicine wore off, Madam Wu woke up. Opening her eyes, she was stunned to find a stranger sleeping right beside her in the same bed.

103

"My goodness!" she cried, breaking out into a cold sweat. She sat up swiftly, now having entirely come to her senses. "Who are you?" she screamed at him in a loud voice. "How dare you defile a good woman!"

Frightened, Bu Liang hastily knelt before her, begging her for clemency: "Please forgive me for my offence."

Seeing her pants removed, Madam Wu knew that she had been debauched. She ignored his pleadings and called out for Spring Flower, and in the meantime, pulled up her pants and leapt from the bed, staggering out of the room. For fear of being seen, Bu Liang dared not follow her. He remained in the room while Madam Wu pushed the door open and rushed out.

"Spring Flower!" Madame Wu called once again.

Because of her early rising, Spring Flower was dozing in the novice's room. When she heard her mistress calling, she yawned and hurried to her immediately.

"You damned slave!" Madam Wu scolded. "Why did you not accompany me while I was sleeping in that room?"

She was about to beat her to vent her spleen when Nun Zhao came and dissuaded her. This made her even more angry. She gave the maid two resounding slaps on the face.

"Go! Go home right away!" she shouted.

"But we haven't recited the sutra yet," Spring Flower meekly reminded her.

"You lousy meddlesome slave!" Madam Wu cursed. "That's none of your business!"

Madam Wu was so furious that her face turned purple. She neither castigated nor said goodbye to the nun, leaving the temple with the maid. She hastened back home without even pausing to catch her breath, and as soon as she opened the door, dashed into her room and sat sullenly by herself. Only after a long while did she begin to cool down.

"I remember only that I was hungry and ate the cake," she said to Spring Flower. "How was it that I ended up sleeping in that bed?"

"After you had eaten the cake and had drunk some tea, you fell asleep in the chair," the maid told her. "It was Nun Zhao and her disciple who put you in bed."

"Where were you then?" asked Madam Wu.

"You were sleeping and I was hungry," said Spring Flower, "so I first ate some of the cake you had left behind and then went to the young nun's room for tea. I felt tired and was napping when you called me."

"Did you see somebody come into the room where I slept?" Madam Wu asked.

"No, I saw no one but Nun Zhao and her disciple," said Spring Flower.

Madam Wu made no comment. Some vague recollections about what had happened during her sleep appeared before her eyes as she thought back. She felt her privates and found a stickiness still there. "I was duped," she sighed. "Who would have thought that the old nun was so vicious as to let some damned knave ravish my chaste body. How can I live on?"

Tears came to her eyes. Overflowing with regret, she wanted to commit suicide. Yet she wished to see her husband and tell him the truth, and was therefore unable to make up her mind to take her life immediately. She went to her embroidered Boddhisatva Guanyin, and in tears, wept: "This disciple of yours burns with resentment and seeks your aid in finding a way to avenge her insult."

She sobbed while praying, and the thought of her husband made her cry bitterly for a long time. Despondent, she finally fell asleep. The maid was greatly bewildered, capable of making neither head nor tail of what had really happened to her mistress.

Let us put aside the story of the remorseful Madam Wu for the time being.

Our story continues that Nun Zhao, seeing that Madam Wu was wrathful and had left without even saying goodbye to her, knew that Bu Liang must have had what he desired. She entered the room and found him still lying naked in bed, staring pensively ahead with his finger in his mouth. The old bawd was so stirred that she leapt upon him at once.

"Now it is the time you thank your matchmaker!" she said, burning with lust.

Her hands stroked his crotch as she rode up and down on him. Since Bu Liang had just spent, his penis was rather limp, refusing to stand up no matter how it was manipulated. Nun Zhao, as her frustration grew, bit on him. "You have got what you wanted," she complained, "but do you know how much I have been suffering for you?"

"I am very grateful to you," said Bu Liang, "and I will keep you company tonight, making you as happy as I can. I shall also consult you about my future plans."

Nun Zhao was confused.

"Your future plans? You said all you wanted was just a taste, so what are your future plans about?"

"It is understandable that one will covet Sichuan after capturing Gansu,"[23] said Bu Liang. "Now that I have had a taste, why shouldn't I take a big bite? This time I raped her. But I intend to engage her in real lovemaking, so that she will do it of her own accord, happily and delightfully."

"You are hard to please," said Nun Zhao. "You have had intercourse with her, making her so angry with me that she didn't even bid me farewell as she left. I can't predict what she will do next, so how can I be of assistance in your future plans? You must wait until I discover if she is still on good terms with me before I can pursue your quest."

"Good," Bu Liang agreed. "Anyway, I will trust your brilliant strategies."

Full of gratitude, Bu Liang concealed himself that night in the nunnery and tried his best to make his matchmaker satisfied. It goes without saying that they spent a fine time indulging in sexual pleasures. But let us say no more of this.

Our story goes that Licentiate Jia, who lived in his employer's residence, had a dream that night. He found himself at home and saw a woman in white come in through the front door. He went up to greet her, and she disappeared into another room. Hastily, he rushed forward to catch up with her, only to crash into his wife's embroidered Guanyin scroll. Looking up, he found that there were a few lines of words on it, which, upon closer scrutiny, revealed themselves to him as follows:

> What has been gained through a mouth
> Will be lost through a mouth
> It is only via the novice
> That your revenge will be carried out.

After reading these words, Licentiate Jia turned around and found his wife down on her knees before him. He raised her to her feet and then suddenly woke up. "I cannot understand this dream," he reflected. "Perhaps my wife is indisposed, or has had an accident, so she asked Guanyin to convey this message to me?"

The next day he took leave of his employer and returned home. On his way back he tried once again to solve the puzzle of his dream, but without success. He felt rather worried. When he arrived home, Spring Flower came out to open the door for him.

"Where is my wife?" asked the Licentiate.

"Mother has not risen yet," Spring Flower replied. "She is still lying in bed."

"But it is very late," said the Licentiate. "Why is she still sleeping?"

"Mother is not happy," said Spring Flower. "She keeps calling your name and sobbing."

Upon hearing this, the Licentiate rushed into the bedroom hastily. At the sight of her husband back home, Madam Wu sat up immediately, her eyes still red and her hair dishevelled, and plunged herself from the bed to the floor before him, wailing and weeping.

The Licentiate was shocked. "What is this about?" he asked, helping her to her feet.

"I beg you to avenge me," she implored.

"Has someone bullied you?" asked the Licentiate.

Madam Wu sent the maid away to the kitchen to prepare tea and lunch.

"Since I married you, my husband," she said, "I have neither bickered with you nor have I been unfaithful. But now I have been guilty of a horrible sin and deserve the death penalty. I have been longing for your return so that I can explain to you. If you avenge me, I shall die with my eyes closed."

"Please don't say such inauspicious words," said the Licentiate. "Tell me truthfully what has happened to you."

Madam Wu then related to him how Nun Zhao had enticed her to read sutras in her nunnery and how she had provided her with the drugged pastries and had allowed some man to rape her while she was asleep. When she had finished her story, she burst into tears and fell to the floor.

Her account of the incident filled the Licentiate with such anger that his hair stood on end. "What an astonishing misfortune!" he roared. "Do you know who that man was?" he inquired.

"How could I know?" said Madam Wu.

Licentiate Jia drew a sword out from its place at the head of the bed and drove it into the table. "If I fail to destroy these people, I cease to be a man!" he bellowed. "However, since you don't know who he is, we are bound to make mistakes if we act rashly. Let me conceive a plan before taking action."

"Now that I have made a clean breast of everything," said Madam

Wu, "I feel complete and can say no more to you. I ask you to give me your sword so that I may kill myself, here in front of you!"

"Don't be so short-sighted!" said the Licentiate. "It was not that you sought to lose your chastity, but rather it was that misfortune befell you. You have made it clear to me that you were innocent; if you were to die, I would suffer greatly."

"You may suffer," said Madam Wu, "but that can't deter me."

"If you committed suicide," said the Licentiate, "your parents and other relatives would surely demand that I give them a reasonable explanation of your death. If I were to tell them the truth, both your good reputation and my future career would be destroyed. But if I were to hide the truth, it is likely that your kinsmen wouldn't let me off, nor would I feel comfortable taking revenge for you when I have lost the appropriate moral reason."

"If you wish me to live on," said Madam Wu, "you must kill that malicious old baggage and her damned ruffian for me."

The Licentiate brooded over the possibility for quite some while. "What did you say to the nun after you found that she had tricked you?" he asked.

"I was so angry at the time," said Madam Wu, "that I just returned home without speaking a single word to her."

"Such being the case," said the Licentiate, "our revenge can't be taken openly. Open revenge would bring us to court and make it impossible for us to cover the truth. People then would know what really happened to you, and your good fame would be ruined. Now I am thinking how I might contrive a scheme by which I might avenge you but without destroying your reputation nor letting any of these evil-doers escape alive."

He bowed his head and remained deep in thought for some time. "I have it! I have it!" he suddenly cried. "My idea tallies exactly with what the Boddhisatva revealed to me in my dream. A wonderful plan! A wonderful plan!"

"Could you please tell me about it?" Madam Wu asked.

"My wife," said the Licentiate, "if you wish to clear the matter and avenge yourself for your humiliation, you must obey me in each and every respect. Should you fail to do so, I will not be able to avenge you nor to trust that your fidelity to me is unsullied."

"You are making a decision for me," said Madam Wu, "and certainly there is no reason for me not to follow your instructions. Please just make sure that all will go well."

"Good," said the Licentiate. "Since you didn't heap blame on Nun Zhao, she must have thought that you rushed back home out of embarrassment, and that like other women of easy virtue, will eventually change your mind. Now, you should entice her to our home, and here is how we should deal with her."

He whispered in her ear, saying thus and thus and so and so. "I can guarantee," he finished confidently, "that she will fall into our trap."

"Your plan is a most cunning one," said Madam Wu, "but I feel embarrassed about my part in it. However, revenge is now uppermost in my mind and I must ignore any secondary considerations."

The plan had thus been designed between husband and wife. The very next day, the Licentiate hid himself in an inconspicuous corner behind the back door while Madam Wu had Spring Flower invite Nun Zhao to visit her home for a chat. Nun Zhao was glad to see the maid and even more pleased by the invitation.

"The woman must have actually enjoyed herself last time," she thought, "and can't resist the temptation to repeat the experience." She then swaggered along the way to the Jia house, with Spring Flower taking the lead, scampering as if she were flying. The moment she saw the mistress, she apologized, "Please forgive me for my offending you and entertaining you so shabbily the other day."

Madam Wu dismissed the maid, and taking Nun Zhao's hand, inquired in a low voice, "Who was that man, may I know?"

"He is Mr. Bu, a romantic young gentleman living in this neighbourhood," Nun Zhao told her, delighted to find that she was interested in him. "His full name is Bu Liang, and he is very popular with women who are associated with him. Since he was so smitten by your beauty, he had been begging me day and night to help arrange an assignation with you. I was deeply touched by his sincerity and wished not to dash his hopes. Besides, you were on your own and must have felt very lonely. I thought that you ought to have the right to take the occasional lover and enjoy life to the full while you are still young. That is why I made this arrangement for you. Is there any such thing as a cat which gives up eating fish and meat? I know the ways of the world, and you shouldn't be too serious. What harm will befall you if you have someone who loves you dearly without reserve and venerates you so much as if you were his Buddha?"

"But you should have advised me beforehand rather than set up the trap for me without my knowledge," said Madam Wu. "Now it's over and we needn't discuss it further."

"But you didn't know the man," said Nun Zhao. "You might have refused my arrangement had I put it to you bluntly. Now that you have met him, you may well wish to consider a long-term relationship."

"I made such a spectacle of myself," said Madam Wu, "and didn't even allow myself a chance to observe his countenance or his temperament. Since, as you say, he loves me dearly, you may invite him to my home so that I may look at him more closely. If indeed he is a handsome man, I may permit him to meet me in secret."

"She has again risen to the bait," thought Nun Zhao.

"Well," she said, both delighted and trustful, "if this is what you wish, I will ask him to visit your house this evening. The man is indeed comely. The more closely you see him, the more your attraction will grow."

"I will await him behind the door at the hour of lamp-lighting," said Madam Wu. "But he mustn't enter until after I cough as a signal."

Nun Zhao, rapturous, sped back to the nunnery and informed Bu Liang of this good news. He, shaking his head and wagging his tail, looked forward in anticipation for "the golden bird to fall from the sky and the jade hare to leap from the ground."[24] No sooner had night fallen than he was at the doorway of the Jia house, looking jerkily around. He was in such a frenzy of desire that he was even ready to poke his engorged penis through the gate.

It was now pitch-dark. The door suddenly slammed shut. Bu Liang was rather anxious and began to suspect that the nun had deceived him. At that very moment, however, a cough came from inside, the signal that he had long been waiting for! Bu Liang hastily returned a cough and the door opened a crack. He coughed again, and upon hearing the second cough, swiftly slipped in. He found himself inside a small walled courtyard and could, by starlight, see the silhouette of a woman. He strode forward and took her into his arms.

"Ma'am," he husked, "I am so very grateful for your benefaction!"

Despite the fullness of her resentment, Madam Wu did not push him away. Instead she responded by drawing herself closer to him. This triggered Bu Liang's ardent reaction. He kissed her with fervour and thrust his tongue into her mouth. Madam Wu hugged him even more closely, licking and sucking hungrily upon his tongue until he grew wild with sensual delight. His penis erect, Bu Liang drove his tongue deep into her throat. Madam Wu had by now mustered her courage. With all her strength, she bit at his tongue, gnawing off half an inch. The pain was so excruciating as to force Bu Liang to stagger away from her and rush for the gate.

Madam Wu, spitting the tip of his tongue into her hand, slammed the gate shut and went hurrying to the back door. "Here is the rapist's tongue," she said to her husband who was awaiting her there. Delighted, the Licentiate took the tongue and wrapped it in his handkerchief, and then, with the dim light of the stars and the moon above him, made his way to the Nunnery of the Perceiver of Sound, carrying his sword with him.

Nun Zhao, who had taken it for granted that matters would go smoothly and that Bu Liang would sleep in the Jia house, had retired to her room for the night. Suddenly, there was a knock on the door. The novice had been sound asleep already, and once her head had hit the pillow, even a loud bang could not wake her up. Nun Zhao, however, was still wide awake. She was fantasizing about the couple cavorting in bed and therefore felt quite aroused. When she heard the knocking, she thought that it must be Bu Liang returning. She called her disciple to open the gate for him but there was no response. She had to get up herself. No sooner had she pulled the gate ajar than Licentiate Jia darted in, and with sword in hand, struck her on the head. The nun fell backward onto the ground, her blood spattering like a flood. She died on the spot.

The Licentiate closed the gate, and sword in hand, rushed inside.

"I shall kill that son-of-a-bitch if he happens to be here," he thought. Seeing the permanent flame that burned before the Buddha, he grabbed it and cast it upon every corner of the room, only to discover a young nun, still in sound slumber. He gave her a stab, ending her life at once. After having adjusted the wick to make the lamp brighter, he unwrapped the handkerchief and, taking out the tongue, pried open the jaws of the novice and inserted it into her mouth. He then extinguished the lamp, closed the door, and returned home.

"Both of the nuns have been killed and your revenge is complete," he told his wife.

"What a pity that I only bit that ruffian's tongue off instead of slaying him," said Madam Wu.

"Relax. Someone will kill him for you," said the Licentiate. "From now on you should just feign ignorance and make no mention of the matter."

Now the sun was three yards high in the sky. The neighbours around the Nunnery of the Perceiver of Sound, seeing its gate closed and no sign of anyone entering or leaving, suspected that something might be amiss. Trying the gate, they found it open, for it had not been bolted, and before their eyes appeared the old nun, sprawled across the doorway, obviously dead. Alarmed, they hastened into the building, only to encounter another murdered corpse. One had been bludgeoned to death and the other had had her throat slit. Frightened out of their wits, they rushed in a flurry to fetch the co-ordinators in charge of residential security affairs, whose responsibility it was to make a formal inspection and report the case to the local authorities. Upon their arrival, the co-ordinators inspected the corpses and noticed something between the young nun's tightly clenched teeth. They removed it and discovered that it was a human tongue.

"No doubt this is a rape-murder case," they said. "Since we don't know who the murderer is, we must report it immediately to the local authorities."

It so happened that the district magistrate was presiding over court that very day. The co-ordinators submitted their report to him the moment it had been completed.

"It shouldn't be difficult to apprehend the murderer," the magistrate declared. "He must be that man whose tongue has been bitten off. Be quick to find him! Make sure you go to each and every place, whether in town or village, and check with the residential security co-ordinators one by one. I demand you arrest him quickly."

Shortly after the official order, a suspect was indeed arrested and brought to the yamen.

Bu Liang, after the injury to his tongue, realized that he had been tricked. He fled helter-skelter, paying no heed to directions. Soon he got lost in the labyrinth of small alleys, incapable of telling east from west and north from south. Fearing that he might be mistaken for a thief, he had to hide in a deserted lane, where he crouched under the eaves of a household to spend the night. When day dawned, he dragged himself out, trying once again to find his way home.

Perhaps Heaven wanted him to be arrested. He wandered back and forth in the narrow lanes looking for an exit to a main street, but without success. To make things worse, he could not open his mouth to ask directions. The residents of the area found him very suspicious, and one officious-looking man started to cross-examine him just as the news of the murder was spreading and the official notice was being posted. Bu Liang could not respond clearly to his interrogation, and the discovery of blood on his teeth and gums further aggravated his plight: it caused an immediate commotion, and a bunch of local residents came up and surrounded him, shouting, "If this man is not the murderer, who else could it be?"

Allowing him no time to defend himself, they tied him up and dragged him to the court. Some of his acquaintances standing in front of the yamen remarked: "He is a rascal who has never been up to any good. Little wonder that he has committed such a crime."

The magistrate seated himself upon the dais[25] and ordered Bu Liang brought in. As he began his interrogation, he could hear only mumblings that were completely incomprehensible. The magistrate had a lictor slap

Bu Liang twice on the mouth and ordered him to stick out his tongue, which he found had been partly bitten off, with fresh traces of blood still evident.

"What is the name of this cur?" the magistrate asked the residential co-ordinators.

A person who hated him told the officer his name and also outlined his past crimes, which included rape, fraud, robbery, and blackmail.

"It is obvious," said the magistrate, "that this felon tried to rape the young nun. He first murdered the old nun when she opened the gate for him, and then sexually assaulted the novice, who retaliated by biting off his tongue. In a fury, this cur killed her. Can he possibly deny it?"

Bu Liang, upon hearing this charge, gestured with both his hands and feet, trying to signal that he wished a brush and a piece of paper so that he could write a statement in his defense. Yet his inability to articulate even a syllable greatly provoked the magistrate.

"You sly ruffian!" he shouted. "You can expect no paper and brush from me!"

He then turned to the lictor[26] and said, "Given his inability to say a word and the lack of the lethal weapon as material evidence, it seems unlikely that we will have a confession. Select a heavy bamboo rod and flog him a hundred strokes until he meets his end!"[27]

A dandy leading a life of dalliance among women, Bu Liang certainly could not long endure such heavy torture. Having received no more than fifty strikes, he perished. The magistrate, after ordering the local co-ordinators to have His corpse claimed by his relatives and arrange cremation for the nuns, filed a document, in which he made the following comment:

> Bu Liang, where is your tongue?[28] I know how you lost it. Young nun, who could withstand the temptation of your lovely neck? That is why it ended up broken. Needless to say, this is a rape-murder case, serious enough to put the convict to death. This is a record for future reference.

Thus the district magistrate solved the case. But no more of this.

Licentiate Jia and his wife were delighted as they heard street-gossip about the court desicion. No one knew that Madam Wu had been raped and that her husband was the one who had killed the nuns. This vengeance, carried out successfully without destroying his wife's good reputation, should be attributed to the Licentiate's acumen as well as to the revelation he had received from the Boddhisatva. Now the couple loved each other even more than before: one admiring her husband for his courage and the other appreciating his wife's faithfulness.

People of later times came to discover the truth. Some remarked that for all his ingenuity and for the success of his subtle way of taking revenge, his wife had after all been raped. Although no one outside their family might have known the secret, the wife herself must have suffered from her trauma. Her misfortune arose simply because she did not exercise sufficient caution in dealing with a nun, and this should be a good lesson for all virtuous women.

A good flower withers and loses its scent,
For it has exposed itself to an alluring light.
Remember this important piece of advice:
Women should stay home and not go outside.

One Woman and Two Monks[1]

A beauty may incur a motive for murder,
As a monk tends to be incited by erotica;
A hungry devil of lust is a real Raksasa,
He may spill the blood of a visitor.

Our story goes that in Lin'an[2] there was a Provincial Graduate[3] named Zheng who lived and studied at the Temple of Felicity and had a room of his own, which, located at its northwestern corner, was called Clear Cloud Domicile. Guangming, the handsome and generous abbot, loved to make friends with officials and scholars. Since the temple was well supported and Guangming himself was rich from family resources, scholars enjoyed being with him. Zheng was a lodger staying there for the longest time and was also his bosom friend. Though he had been invited to all the exquisitely furnished rooms and serenely secluded quarters, he had never been granted admittance to one small abode, which was situated in the depths of exclusivity and remained closed all the time. Guangming was rarely seen going to that place, and each time he came out from it he was careful to lock the door behind him. No one else had ever entered it, and Zheng, in spite of his intimacy with the monk, was no exception. He thought that it was the treasure-house of the chapel, and like everyone else, took care to keep away from it as well as he could.

One day Guangming was in that abode when the hall bell rang sonorously, announcing the arrival of a high-ranking official and his family. Guangming had to rush out to welcome his patrons. Zheng, taking a stroll by himself at the time, happened to pass by the lodge and discovered that its door had been left ajar. "This structure has always been closed and never have I had a chance to see the inside," he said to himself. "I wonder why it is open today?"

He let himself in.

Taking a look around, he found that the room was finely floored, elegantly furnished, and well decorated, though nothing in it was extraordinary, and nothing was precious enough to be worth hiding away. "These monks are eccentric," he thought. "There is actually no secret about this room. I don't understand why Guangming takes the trouble to keep the door locked all the time."

While looking around, he noticed that above a small bed there was a tent hook, and on it hung a purple sandalwood fish with a tiny mallet.[4] The fish was so smooth and shaped with such refinement that it aroused his interest. He took it down, held it in his hand and scrutinized it, meanwhile randomly striking the fish with the mallet a couple of times. Suddenly, a bell sounded from beneath the floor, and then behind the bed a small floor-board opened and a young, beautiful woman emerged. She was so astonished at the sight of Zheng that she drew back at once. Zheng, too, was shocked, for he recognized that the woman was his own cousin.

The secret entrance had been ingeniously designed. Its cover could be raised along the joint to serve as a trap-door, but closed it looked exactly like ordinary flooring. Only from below could it be lifted and no one was able to remove it from above. In fact, a clap on the fish was a signal, upon hearing which, anyone inside could ring the bell and come out. Beneath the floor was a cellar with its own window and an exit which led to the kitchen through a covert tunnel. This underground place was so well-hidden that even Heaven would not have known of its existence.

"No wonder that the bald knave kept the door perpetually locked," Zheng reflected. "Now that I have discovered his secret, it is very likely that he will punish me." In a flurry, he reinstalled the fish and rushed out. No sooner, however, had he crossed the threshold than he bumped headlong into Guangming, who was startled to find that the door had been left unlocked. Zheng's rather jittery expression and his purple-red face could not but give rise to suspicion. Looking ahead, the monk saw the wooden fish still swinging to and fro from the hook. He knew that his secret had been discovered.

"Have you seen anything just now?" he asked.

"Oh no, nothing," Zheng replied.

"Please come in with me and sit for a moment!" said Guangming, grabbing Zheng's arm and dragging him back into the room. He then bolted the door behind him and drew out a sword from the head of the bed. "Although we are close friends," he muttered, "I can't forgive you for what you have done today. I shall do whatever I can in order to save myself from discovery and execution. You have only yourself to blame for entering this house, mistakenly or not. Now it is time to end your life. Do not blame me!"

Zheng began to weep. "It was unfortunately my own fault to fall into this fiery pit," he whined. "Since I cannot be pardoned, and there is no way to escape death, I beg you to grant me some wine so I might dull my senses and feel no pain when you cut off my head. I have been with you for so long, you should show some mercy on me!"

Given their lengthy friendship, Guangming found it hard to reject his pitiful plea. Taking his sword with him, he locked the door from the outside and went to the kitchen; and after having fetched a jug of wine, poured him a large bowl.

"I can't drink without food," said Zheng. "Could you please give me something simple to eat?"

While Guangming complied once again, going to the kitchen in search of food, Zheng tried every possible means to escape, but without success. He then began to search for something which could be used as a weapon. There was, however, neither a stick nor a brick in the room; all the objects he could lay his hands on were too flimsy to serve his purpose.

Suddenly an idea dawned on him as he cast his eye upon the large wine jug. He tore a piece of cloth from his gown and stuffed it into its mouth. The jug, with the wine it contained, weighed about six or seven pounds. With the jug in his hand, he concealed himself behind the door, and when Guangming re-entered, struck him hard on his shaved head. The monk nearly collapsed from the blow. Before he could raise his hands to protect himself, he received another two blows to the top of his head, which made him collapse completely. Zheng then kept hitting his head with the jug as if he were beating laundry, until Guangming's skull cracked. He died immediately.

Seeing that he was dead, Zheng locked the corpse inside and fled. No one had yet noticed anything amiss when he went rushing to the yamen to report the foul play to the county magistrate. Without delay, the magistrate dispatched an officer and a troop of soldiers to the site of the crime. They surrounded the lodge before breaking in. Guangming was still stretched out on the floor, his head smashed and rivulets of blood everywhere. However, the woman was nowhere in evidence.

"I know how to make her appear," Zheng volunteered, a smile playing on his face.

He took the wooden fish from the hook and struck it twice. As expected, a ring of the bell sounded and then the floor-board opened and a woman surfaced. The officer shouted and seized the trap-door before she could retreat and shut it. Then they all leapt into the secret entrance.

Down below was a cellar, and on one side of its tiled walls was a window facing a small stone-walled courtyard. This place, obscure to outsiders, sheltered five or six women. They were brought out one by one, and under interrogation, confessed that they had been abducted from their villages by the monks. Zheng's cousin had been tricked into entering the abode while she was in the temple burning incense and praying for pregnancy. The two bearers of her sedan-chair had been besotted, so they had no inkling of where she was. When her family charged them with abduction, they, as suspects, were both thrown into jail. Guangming's highly-placed social connections and his careful concealment of the woman enabled him to go scot-free. Who would have thought that Zheng's cousin would have been found in this very abbey? All the monks involved in the crime were sentenced to death by the county magistrate.

Gentle reader, monks receive alms from their patrons and have no worry about their food and clothing. Their rooms are clean and their beds are comfortable. Sleeping in their beds with nothing else to distract them makes them think of no more than their groins. Despite the possession of a few young novices as their catamites, their desires are unslaked. As the saying goes, "No matter how many steamed-buns you eat, you still need a proper meal."[5] Women, moreover, love to burn incense and pray to the Buddha, and will therefore frequent monasteries. After spying a beauteous female visitor, it was hard for monks not to dream of her as they sleep alone at night. That is why they will try every possible means to seduce a woman. Seduction itself is a horrible moral transgression; yet monks are capable of behaviours even more heinous. As a poem puts it:

> Not a wicked man is not a monk,
> And not a monk is not wicked;
> Of all the wicked monks,
> The baldest is most wicked.

In search of sexual gratification, monks will resort to any evil, even arson or murder. The abbot of Lin'an, whose story I have just related, is a typical example. Since he was on good terms with Zheng, he could have requested him not to leak the secret, or he could have begged him or offered him some bribes. Why should he have tried to kill him, only to bring about his own death? Obviously, the law of Heaven could not tolerate an iniquity like this.

To reveal the inhuman brutality of the clergy, I shall now tell you another tale, a story of a monk whose wickedness is exceptional.

> Rape and murder go hand in hand,
> And even more dangerous is jealousy.
> If as male lovers they do not disband,
> How can we warn against debauchery?

Our story goes that in Wenchuan county in Chengdu prefecture, Sichuan province, there lived a farmer named Jing Qing. His wife, née Du, was fair of form, sexy, and voluptuous. She thought her husband too coarse to be her equal, and would each day pick a quarrel with him.

One day, over a trivial dispute, she felt such anger that she returned to her parents' home, where she stayed for nearly ten days. Her family comforted her and she finally relented and decided to go back. There was only about a mile between the two households, and being familiar with the route, she usually went and returned unescorted. It so happened that on her way back that day it began to rain cats and dogs. Du did not bring an umbrella with her, nor was she able to find a shelter in this barren region. Just at that moment, she heard a bell ringing in the distance. She looked up and saw a temple looming large at the end of a small pass. She made a detour to the temple, intending to seek refuge there until the downpour ceased.

This monastery, isolated in the wilderness, was called the Temple of the Zen Pacific, and there resided ten monks. In the house of the forecourt lived three monks; the old master with his two young disciples. The Old Monk, named Dajue, was the supervisor of the house, and one of the disciples, Zhiyuan, was a handsome and amiable youth whom the Old Monk loved dearly. The other disciple, Huiguang, was only a boy, about eleven years old. Though in his late fifties, the Old Monk was as lustful as a young man. Every night he would share his bed with Zhiyuan, and would embrace him, regaling him with talk of sexual congress with women. When he was sufficiently aroused, he would satisfy his desire upon his young partner; its lewdness is beyond description.

On that day, both the master and the disciple were standing at the doorway when they saw a beauteous woman rush in to take shelter from the rain. Her arrival aroused their desire just as a mouse before a cat. The Old Monk winked at the younger one, saying, "A Boddhisattva Guanyin[6] is entering! Go welcome her."

Zhiyuan, assuming a jocular air, approached Du. "Hello, young lady!" he said. "I suppose you are coming here to take shelter from the rain?"

"Oh yes," Du replied. "It's raining heavily and I seek refuge for a short while."

"But the rain seems unlikely to stop soon," said Zhiyuan, smiling. "Since there is no place for you to sit here, nor is it polite of me to leave you outside, I suggest that you enter our humble abode and tarry with a cup of tea until the skies clear."

If Du had been a "decent" woman, she would have refused this invitation and would have chosen to remain outside so that she might leave when the rain ceased. Women should most carefully avoid the private quarters of monks. Who would have thought that Du was a hussy exceedingly fond of sexual adventures? Observing that Zhiyuan was a light-complexioned and clean-shaven young man, very adept and graceful in conversation, she found herself taking a fancy to him.

"The rain will keep me here for some time anyway," she thought. "To have a seat inside is certainly much better than standing here. I might as well do as he suggests." She then followed Zhiyuan into the temple.

Seeing the woman coming in, the Old Monk instantly slipped back into their domicile and opened his bedroom to await his guest. Zhiyuan and Du winked at each other as they walked toward the living quarters. After entering the house and taking their seats, they had the boy monk, Huiguang, serve tea. Zhiyuan chose a fine bowl from the tea tray, and tucking up his sleeve, presented it to Du, who received it with both hands, and in the meantime cast a glance upon him. The more she looked at him, the more she found him handsome and attractive. As she grew infatuated, she accidentally brushed the bowl with her sleeve, which was thus soaked.

"You have wet your sleeve," said Zhiyuan. "You may, if you wish, go to the inner room and dry it on the brazier."

This suggestion of his revealed clearly to her his real purpose. But to go into his bedroom was precisely what she wanted. Instead of rejecting his invitation, she asked him where the room was in which she could find the heater. Zhiyuan led her to his master's bedroom, for he knew that the Old Monk was already inside waiting for her and that he must give way to him first. When Du entered the room, Zhiyuan pointed to the brazier, saying, "You may dry your sleeve on it. There is still some fire." He then backed out.

Du felt rather confused to see him reluctant to enter. "Is he not brave enough to make love with me?" she wondered. Just as she stretched out her hand to dry her sleeve, the Old Monk jumped out from behind the bed and seized her with his hands. Du squealed like a pig being slaughtered.

"There is nobody around," said the Old Monk. "It's no use screaming here. You came into my room and you have no one but yourself to blame!"

Du strove to escape, yet the clever Young Monk had already bolted the door from the outside. The Old Monk, firming his hold on her body, rammed his penis recklessly against her from inside his pants. Du yielded after some coy resistance.

"Where is Young Master?" she asked. "I was not expecting you!"

The Old Monk grinned. "You want my disciple, do you? He is my bedmate. Let me finish our business first and I shall allow him to accommodate you."

"I am infatuated with that handsome young novice," Du mused, "but have now unfortunately fallen into the hands of this ancient fogey and have no way of getting rid of him. If I permit him to have his way with me, he will certainly allow me to share his disciple." She then reluctantly submitted to him, letting him carry her to the bed and engage her in the work of clouds and rain.

> One at the height of his passion dashes madly to fight,
> The other is lethargic, reluctant her partner to satisfy.
> One feels lucky to taste the fruit without much ado,
> The other by wrongly offering her flower makes herself a fool.
> One is so fervent as to gasp like fire-fanning bellows,
> The other is listless as a sack that blood and bone holds.
> For all the tasteless rashness they have undergone,
> This momentary enjoyment is a love affair on every account.

Though highly passionate, the Old Monk was not a man with sexual stamina. Quite a bit of his sperm had leaked as he hugged Du, and the real engagement lasted for only a short while before he spent. Du had initially been very impatient with him. Now her discontent turned to ill-feeling. She rose and tied her skirt, grumbling, "You worthless old idiot! Aren't you ashamed? What have you been so desperate for?"

Knowing that he had left her unsatisfied, the Old Monk felt rather dejected. He called out to Zhiyuan to open the door for him, and Zhiyuan, unlatching it, stepped in and asked, "Was it good?"

"What an experienced woman!" said the Old Monk. "It is just that today I wasn't skillful enough and left her somewhat disappointed."

"I can work her up," said Zhiyuan.

He rushed into the room, and closing the door behind him, turned and embraced her. "My darling one," he cooed, "I am sorry that I let you suffer at his hands."

"You enticed me into this room," Du complained, "only to expose me to rape by that old fool!"

"He is my master and I had no choice," said Zhiyuan. "Could you let me do something to compensate you?" He took her to him, attempting to carry her to the bed.

Since her experience with the Old Monk had been so insipid, Du assumed a deep cast of seriousness. "Such a shameless pair!" she cursed. "One has just finished and the other immediately to take his turn!"

"What my master did to you was simply a prelude," Zhiyuan said.

"But you and I are about the same age and we mustn't squander this golden opportunity!" With this he dropped to his knees before her.

Du raised him up. "I complained only about that old fogey," she said. "In fact, I love you."

Seizing this chance, Zhiyuan took her into his arms and planted a deep kiss on her mouth. He then carried her to the bed and engaged her at once in copulation, which, in comparison with the previous session, was indeed very different:

122

> He meets the beauty like a starving tiger devouring a lamb,
> As a thirsty dragon seeks water, so is she crazed for the young man.
> Lustful, the village wench cavorts wild and promiscuous,
> Experienced, the Buddha man conquers the lecherous.
> One thrusts hard and the other strives to receive him,
> Both of them vie to be triumphant, with equal enthusiasm.
> Although her gate is thrust wide open by the old master,
> From the "Boddhisattva," the young novice obtains more water.

Zhiyuan was in the prime of his life, virile and brimming with energy. Du, attracted by his masculine beauty, also experienced great sexual passion. They copulated nearly a full hour before coming to a stop. Du revelled in total satisfaction.

"I have heard that monks are skillful," she said. "That incompetent old fogey is an embarrassment to all of you. But you are really a great lover and I would like to sleep with you tonight!"

"I am overjoyed that you like me," said Zhiyuan. "I wonder if it would be a problem for you to stay here overnight? May I ask where you are from?"

"My maiden name is Du," she said, "and I have married into the Jing family living in a nearby village. The other day my husband and I had cross words and I went back to my parents', where I stayed several days. Today I was on my way home when it began raining. I came in to take shelter from the rain and it so happened that I encountered you. My husband knows nothing of my return. Since he keeps no contact with my parents, nobody knows I am here. It should be fine for me to remain for a few days."

"Excellent!" Zhiyuan exclaimed. "Tonight we can revel the entire night in pleasure! The only thing I am worried about is that my master might wish to share the fun with us."

"Oh no," said Du, "I can't stand that old fogey!"

"But he is the head of the house and it is not polite to exclude him," said Zhiyuan. "Anyway, you can finish him off quickly."

"How can three persons have sex together?" Du protested. "That's very embarrassing!"

"The Old Monk may be lecherous," said Zhiyuan, "but his sexual abilities are limited. We may, from both sides, throw ourselves into an all-out assault, and it will take only one of us, either you or me, to dispose of him. Then we may forget him and make love only to each other."

They conversed congenially and kept talking for a long while, unaware that the Old Monk was standing just outside. Hearing the ceaseless creaking of their bed, the Old Monk regretted that he had finished too soon to enjoy the greatest of pleasures while being inside her. As jealousy of their indulgence in sensual delight arose in him, he became impatient for them to come to completion and finally, unable to bear them any longer, broke into the room. Seeing their bodies entwined and their tongues enwrapped, he was greatly irritated.

"She did not treat me the way she is treating him," he thought. "In broad daylight," he then screamed at Zhiyuan, "don't you feel ashamed to shut yourself in the bedroom to sleep? Now that we have had a taste, we should consider a long-term plan."

Responding to his master's complaint, Zhiyuan said, "Master, I should tell you that we may indeed look forward to a long intimacy."

"How can that be possible?" asked the Old Monk.

"Because the young lady is going to stay here tonight," Zhiyuan told him.

The Old Monk broke into a broad grin. "We will not let her go so soon," he said.

"If we were to force her to remain, she might lay charges," Zhiyuan warned him. "Now that she has offered to stay of her own accord, we shall not be involved in trouble."

"Where does she live?" asked the Old Monk.

The disciple repeated what Du had told him, which made his master rapt with joy. He scurried off to prepare supper, and before long the meal was laid out and the three of them sat around the table, eating. Du refused to drink no matter how the Old Monk urged her, but while she rejected him with a variety of excuses, she neverless imbibed all the wine Zhiyuan poured her. She ogled him, flattering this handsome young man with her intimate gaze. The Old Monk, by applying some teasing words, would occasionally find a moment to cut into their tender conversation, but he could hardly arouse Du's interest; what he said was therefore largely ignored. He was somewhat conscious that he was an unwelcome person. Still, he begrudged giving her up like a dog that begrudges giving up a hot greasy plate in the middle of licking it.

After supper the three of them did sleep together. Du put her arms around Zhiyuan's neck the moment they crawled into bed, paying no attention to his master. The Old Monk had ejaculated during the day and was unable to achieve erection. Thinking that their intercourse might help stimulate his own sexual desire, he decided to let them begin. Their ecstatic moans, accompanied by the lubricious sounds of sex, indeed excited him. In a fervour, he started to savour her charms here and there, and then threw one arm around her and with the other pulled her to his bosom. His caress of her vagina, now filled up by Zhiyuan's member, aroused him so much that his own penis, urged on by his hand, became semi-hard. He tried to dislodge his disciple and take his place, but Zhiyuan was just reaching the summit of his ecstasy and was unwilling to give way to him. Meanwhile, with both her arms, Du clutched the Young Monk tightly, protecting him from being pushed away.

"Master, I can't stop," Zhiyuan cried. "If you can't hold back, please just mount my rear and satisfy yourself!"

"No," said the Old Monk. "It's ridiculous to eat everyday fare when delicious game-fare is laid out before me."

Clutching himself to them, he finally forced his disciple to stand down. Du was piqued. When the Old Monk began to thrust forward into her, she, out of resentment, deliberately wriggled her hips twice. The Old Monk had long been in a frenzy of lust; no longer able to contain himself, he spent his force immediately. He then came crashing down, gasping horribly for breath.

"Was it worth the bother?" Du sneered.

He felt too ashamed to answer. Without a word, he turned to the other side of the bed to sleep, leaving them to rally their guns and flags for another battle. Both being young, Zhiyuan and Du were capable of long bouts of love-making. A short nap was sufficient to recover their energy and a new round ensued at once. Jealous as he was, the Old Monk could do nothing but swallow his envious saliva. That night saw him make many a clumsy, lewd spectacle of himself.

At daybreak Du rose. After washing and dressing, she said to Zhiyuan, "I am leaving now!"

"Yesterday you said you could easily stay here for a few days," Zhiyuan reminded her. "This temple is out-of-the-way and no one knows you are here. You and I have just started our intimate relations, so how can you be so hard-hearted as to part with me? I can't understand what has made you change your mind."

"It is not that I wish to leave you," Du whispered in his ear. "I simply can't put up with that old fogey and his disgusting harassment. If you want me to stay, you must agree to one condition: he mustn't sleep with us in the same bed!"

"I doubt that my master will agree on this point," Zhiyuan murmured.

"Fine if he disagrees," said Du. "Then I shall take my leave!"

Her determination left the Young Monk with no alternative. He had to go to the Old Monk to talk the matter over with him. "The young woman is going to leave," he reported. "What shall we do?"

"You two are intimate," said the Old Monk. "Why does she wish to go so soon?"

"She is from a respectable family," said Zhiyuan, "and feels ashamed to sleep with two men in one bed. That's the reason she is unwilling to remain. In my opinion, we'd better install another bed in the opposite room, so that I might sleep with her alone for one night. After I have persuaded her to stay for a few more days, I can surely find you an opportunity. Let's not share her together until she knows you better. If we fail to comply with her, she will definitely depart, which, of course, is not good for either of us."

Zhiyuan's reasoning reminded the Old Monk of their *menage à trois* the previous night. "The threesome made me oversexed and I behaved like a nuisance," the Old Monk reflected. "Obviously, that is not a satisfying way for making love. If she leaves, what will I gain? It would be better to let them sleep without me, and in that way I might later get a chance to have her alone in my bedroom for a whole night. Why should I take the trouble to stick to them in one bed, only to ask for her rebuffs?"

"Well," he then said to Zhiyuan, "your plan has its merits. As long as she stays, we shall both benefit. That consideration aside, you are, after all, my loverboy. I will not object even if it's only for your own interest."

Though agreeable in words, the Old Monk was actually very jealous in his mind. Unable, however, to formulate a better idea, he had to compromise temporarily. When Zhiyuan told Du that they had been permitted to sleep in a separate room, she was so delighted that she decided not to leave. She eagerly anticipated the coming of the night.

That evening the Old Monk said, "Tonight I shall sleep alone to husband my strength and you two may enjoy yourselves for the whole night. Make sure to persuade her to remain for a longer time and tomorrow I shall take my turn."

"No problem," said Zhiyuan. "Tonight I will do my best to ensnare her. If the three of us were to share a bed as we did last night, the result could be no more than the ruin of the whole arrangement. We ourselves might feel a lack of satisfaction and she would leave without doubt.

Please wait until I have talked her around, and then I can ensure that you will have a night alone with her. I shall guarantee that you will then be satisfied."

"This is exactly what my lover should do for me," said the Old Monk.

That night Zhiyuan and Du slept in a separate room. With the door closed, they were carefree, amusing themselves merrily and without constraint.

Let us now return to the Old Monk, who, afraid of losing the woman, slept alone in his own room that night, just as Zhiyuan had suggested. No woman accompanied him, nor his own disciple who had previously been his constant bedmate. Being alone, he felt desolate. To make things worse, visions of the young lovers cavorting in bed kept appearing before his eyes, preventing him from sleeping a wink. He pounded the bed with his fists and turned his pillow upside down, tossing and turning restlessly through the entire night.

The next morning he arose and grumbled to his disciple, "You two shared great pleasure, but do you know how terribly you made me suffer?"

"Isn't it true that we had no other means to keep her here?" Zhiyuan returned.

"But tonight she must be mine for the whole night!" said the Old Monk.

Zhiyuan dared not disobey him. He urged Du to join him when night fell. Du, however, refused to comply. "Don't you remember what I told you when you begged me to stay? Why are you insisting again that I sleep with that loathsome old fool?"

"He is the head of this household," Zhiyuan insisted.

"So what?" Du retorted. "I am not his wife so why should I fear him? If you press me once again, I shall disappear in a flash!"

Zhiyuan knew that she would not give in and had to go back to the Old Monk. "She is shy and can't convince herself to come to your room," he said. "Master, could you go to hers instead?"

Taking his advice, the Old Monk groped his way into the opposite bedchamber where Du slept. Du had already been in bed, awaiting the return of Zhiyuan. When the Old Monk sidled up to her bed and threw himself upon her, she mistook him for the Young Monk and embraced him at once, her deep kiss sending shivers throughout his entire body. It was only after intercourse had begun that she discovered that he was not the man she had been expecting.

"You old fool!" she cursed. "Can you never stop harassing me?"

The Old Monk, however, paid not the slightest heed. He instead began thrusting furiously, determined to arouse and satisfy her. However, he overexerted himself and soon gasped for breath. Du had just begun to enjoy his strokes, and now realized the imminence of his ejaculation and the end of the battle. She felt so frustrated that she turned her body around and pushed him, with all her might, off the bed. The Old Monk fell to the floor, his semen shooting wide of its mark and forming a sticky mess on the edge of the bed and his own thighs.

"What a venomous shrew!" he thought, staggering to his feet and trudging back to his room, his heart full of resentment.

No sooner had he made his exit than Zhiyuan returned to fill in the gap. Her lust inflamed by the Old Monk, Du was more than delighted that the Young Monk had come back in time. Without even allowing herself time for a word, she clasped him at once and an erotic melee ensued, bustling with exciting noises.

The Old Monk, now back in his own quarters, remained sullen. "I have been ousted," he thought, "and they are indulging themselves in pleasure! Why not go listen to what they are doing?" He then retraced his steps back to their sleeping chamber. He had hardly got there when his ears were assailed by their lewd cries and the bouncing of the bed, so loud that it sounded as if the earth were shaking.

"The bitch has been playing favourites!" he muttered between his teeth, his fists clenched. "If she had shown me a little affection, I, too, could have experienced some pleasure. Now that the two of them wish to make merry only with each other, I shall do whatever I can tomorrow to break them up!"

Despondent, he retired to his room. When he awoke the next morning, he felt an itching and sore sensation in his genitals, and his urine, as he relieved himself, came dripping out with difficulty. This dysfunction, known as "turbid water" illness,[7] obviously resulted from his incomplete ejaculation the previous night. It could have been avoided had Du not thrown him down from her bed.

"How greatly has that vicious woman made me suffer!" he said to himself bitterly.

When Du arose the next morning, the Old Monk, brazen-faced, once again sought to engage her in light conversation. Du was indifferent, offering no response to his flirtations. Galled by her snubs, the Old Monk was further infuriated as he saw her whispering in his disciple's ear, giggling heartily all the while.

That evening Zhiyuan said to Du, "To spare you trouble, I shall go warm his bed first. I shall see to it that he is used up and without stamina."

"Please do it quickly," Du bade him. "I will be waiting for you in bed."

Zhiyuan went into his master's room. "For the last two nights," he said as ingratiatingly as he could, "I failed to keep you company. Tonight, please allow me to share your bed so that I might atone for my guilt."

"Why should I eat leftovers when there is a fresh young chick at home?" the Old Monk bellowed. "Bring her to me. I must sleep with her now!"

"But she will not listen to me," said Zhiyuan. "You must go yourself and beg her in person."

"I'll see if she dare refuse!" said the Old Monk spitefully.

He stole into the kitchen and took a knife before heading toward her room. "If she confronts me again, I shall finish her off!" he deliberated.

Du, hearing footsteps approaching her bed, took it for granted that Zhiyuan was returning from his errand. She thought that all this time spent in his master's bedroom should have sufficed to complete his task. "Elder Brother," she called, "please secure the door! I don't want that old fogey to come rape me."

Hearing these words, the Old Monk fumed. He shouted in a wrathful voice, "Yes, this old fogey must sleep with you tonight!" He then reached out, and with one savage pull, dragged her half-way off the bed.

Seeing him bear down on her in a menancing rage, Du cried, "Why are you being so violent? You can never force me into submission!" She struggled, clinging firmly to the bed. As the Old Monk continued to tug at her, she screamed, "Even if you murder me, I would never sleep with you!"

"You dare resist!" the Old Monk burst out in anger. "I'll give you a stab and kill you!"

He seized her by the throat, and in a fit of rage, was so forceful that he choked the life out of her. Du twitched twice and died.

Zhiyuan had been lying in bed, waiting for the Old Monk to return. When he heard shrieks and strange noises from the opposite room, he was not certain what was happening. He rushed out, only to run straight into his master, who, knife in hand, was just stepping out from Du's bedchamber.

"I have killed that bitch!" he told his disciple.

Zhiyuan was shocked. "You really did that?"

"Yes, I am not joking!" said the Old Monk. "Why should I allow the two of you to enjoy yourselves without me?"

Zhiyuan fetched a candle and entered the room, and the scene of Du's corpse affected him enormously. "Master," he groaned, "I could never conceive of the notion that you would commit such an act!"

"She refused to comply," said the Old Monk, "and I was so provoked that I lost control of myself. Now that I have killed her, it is no use blaming me any more. What we should do right now is bury her as quickly as we can, and afterwards, I will find you another woman, a good one, all right?"

Despite his distress, Zhiyuan had no choice but to take a shovel and go to the backyard to bury the corpse. "If I had known that this would happen," he murmured, shedding tears in secret, "I would have allowed her to leave earlier. How could I have thought that she would be slain for no reason at all!"

The Old Monk, fearing that Zhiyuan might resent him, did all he could to soothe him. The truth was thus covered up. Huiguang, after all, was a mere boy. Curious as he was about the sudden disappearance of the woman, he made no attempt to look into the matter. Other people did not even know that a murder had taken place. But let's say no more of this.

Our story continues that two or three days had passed since Du left her parents' house. Her parents, not knowing whether or not the couple had reconciled, sent someone to inquire after their daughter. Meanwhile someone from the Jing household went to the Dus' intending to take the young wife back home. Both messengers failed to find her. The Jings accused the Dus of having remarried their daughter by taking advantage of her bad conjugal relationship with her husband, and the Dus countered that this was exactly the reason for an intentional murder on the part of their in-laws. Since both the parties blamed the other, unable to reconcile the charges, they formally filed their allegations and brought the case to the county authority.

The magistrate was absent at the time and the acting officer was the Captain of the Guard named Lin Daling. A native of Fujian province, Lin was only a graduate of the National Academy,[8] but nevertheless, he was a very capable, discerning judge. He ordered the plaintiffs of both families brought to the court for interrogation.

"Your Honour," said Jing Qing, "I, a humble man, often quarreled with my wife and not long ago she felt so wronged that she returned to her parents' home. My father-in-law, out of considerations of his own, has concealed his daughter somewhere and has no intention of returning her to me. This should not be permitted in law!"

"It is true," said Old Du, "that our daughter returned to stay with us for a few days because of their squabble. Three days ago, however, my wife and I persuaded her to go back to her husband. We believe that they quarreled again for some unknown reason and in the end our daughter was murdered. In spite of this, the Jings have accused us of tucking her away. I beg Your Honour to make a fair judgment." With this he wept, tears coursing down his face like raindrops.

From his appearance Judge Lin could discern that Jing Qing was an honest farmer rather than a malicious murderer. "Why couldn't you get along as husband and wife?" he asked him.

"My wife thought I was too coarse a match for her," Jing Qing replied. "This is the reason why she so often picked quarrels with me."

"What is your wife's appearance?" Judge Lin asked.

"She is fairly comely," said Jing Qing.

Judge Lin nodded and then turned to Old Du. "Your daughter must have considered her marriage a mismatch," he said. "Since she disliked her husband, you and your wife, out of parental feelings toward her, might possibly have taken her side. It is not unlikely, therefore, that you have remarried her into another family. Things like this are not unprecendented."

"Our house lies not far from our son-in-law's," Old Du defended. "How could we hide the truth if we had remarried our daughter? Can you believe that we would conceal her in some remote region where she would be unable to come back home for a visit? If she, indeed, had been remarried, sooner or later the world would discover her new husband. We would never dare do such a thing. It is obvious that the Jings have murdered her, and that is why she is nowhere to be found."

The judge pondered over their arguments for some time. "Neither of your suppositions is well-grounded," he said. "I believe that something unforeseen must have occurred to her as she made her way home. Since she probably had an accident midway and there was no one to help her, neither of you has been informed. This court is now adjourned until the matter has been further investigated."

He then issued a "missing" circular and bade his constables to search for Du in every possible place. Quite a long time passed and yet their investigations were still fruitless.

Let us now turn to a youth called Yu who worked for the county jurisdiction as an entrance guard. He was twenty years old, effeminate, and clever. The people of Fujian province are extremely fond of male love[9] and so, too, was Judge Lin, who doted immensely upon his gatekeeper. Yu, feeling secure as Lin's favourite, would sometimes engage in illicit practices, and on one occasion, was so careless as to be caught on the spot. In spite of all his attempts to cover his misconduct, Judge Lin could not openly violate the principles of justice. He thought that the only way to save Yu was to let him perform a meritorious service, thereby to atone for his wrongdoings. He then secretly summoned him to his office.

"Your transgressions are grave and I must dismiss you," he said. "If I pardon you, I would be subject to criticisim. So for the time being, you are fired, and I shall post a notice on the wall lest my colleagues complain about me."

The guard, upon hearing this discipline, kowtowed to his supervisor, apologizing for the trouble he had caused. "But," the judge went on to say, "you should not think that it is the end of your career. Actually I have conceived a way of saving you. The case of the missing woman is still pending and we have yet to discover the real cause of her disappearance. I would like you to investigate the matter for me in secret. You may pass yourself off as a man expelled from the yamen, and search in every possible location between the two households, whether town or village, Daoist shrine or Buddhist monastery. If you do find where she is, I shall not only reinstate you, but also reward you handsomely. Then, no one can raise any babble of criticism against me."

Yu had no choice but to follow the judge's instrucitons. He rushed here and there and stopped at every place he thought might provide him with the information he needed. His appearance resembling a page, he would not incur an iota of suspicion even when he put his nose into private business. But in spite of his diligence and care, he learned nothing.

One day he spied a group of idlers sitting together, gossiping. He sidled up to eavesdrop on their conversation. One of them noticed him as he looked up. "Look," he said in a low voice to his companions, "what a nice-looking youth!"

"There is a young monk at the Temple of the Zen Pacific who is also stunningly handsome," another one remarked. "But his master, a lecherous old monk, is a terribly devious rascal."

Yu feigned that he had heard nothing, and strolled off. "Is this young monk really as beautiful as they said?" he wondered. "Perhaps I should pay a visit and find out for myself."

Yu, in fact, was a homosexual, and the prospect of seeing a handsome youth greatly excited him. As he was uncertain how to get there, he asked directions along the way, and upon entering the temple gate, found an unusually beautiful disciple seated on the threshold of their living quarters. "That must be him," he thought.

Zhiyuan, at the sight of a comely young man, also felt a surge of passion. He scrambled to his feet and greeted him, "Elder Brother, what brings you to our humble place?"

"I came here just to amuse myself," Yu replied.

He was so stricken by Zhiyuan's good looks that upon being invited to tea he joyfully entered their house. The Old Monk, who at the time was inside, burst into a broad smile as he saw his disciple bring in an attractive visitor. He asked Yu's name and where he lived.

"I was previously an entrance guard at the yamen," Yu told him. "For some minor mistakes I was discharged and now have no fixed place to stay. This is why I came here."

The Old Monk was delighted to learn of his situation. "Our small house can accommodate you," he said. "If you wish to stay here just for a few days, it should be all right."

Ingratiating themselves, the Old Monk and his disciple plied their guest with wine and tea. After gobbling down two bowls of liquor, the Old Monk became rather tipsy. He dragged Yu into his bedroom, and stripping his pants off, sodomized him. Unlike the fussy village wench who had not seen much of the world, Yu was experienced, capable of tolerating even a man like this old codger. This made the Old Monk feel very happy.

Gentle reader take note. Men whose sexual stamina is weak are particularly fond of male love. Do you know why? Because male love cannot be merged into natural union. Since the person who takes the passive role receives little pleasure and wishes only to finish the intercourse rather than obtain gratification, the penetrator is free to do whatever he likes without having to concern himself whether his penis is hard enough or his ejaculation is too quick. In the case of having sex with a woman, he must take care to please her. If he spends at midpoint and she has not yet been satisfied, she will certainly grow furious, which will land him in a miserable state. Making male love, however, is much simpler, and you can find joy in your own way. That is why the Old Monk felt on this occasion a sense of contentment.

When they finished, Zhiyuan said to his master, "I brought Elder Brother in, but you anticipated me by taking him first. Tonight he must accompany me!"

"As you wish, as you wish," said the Old Monk, beaming.

Yu was himself eager to remain, so that night he and Zhiyuan slept together in the same bed.

> Both young men are an equal match,
> Taking turns a good time they catch;
> To have sex, Zhiyuan is the first one,
> Yet he offers his partner the same fun.

The two beautiful youths, satiated after taking turns in anal delight, fell into a sleepy embrace. The next morning the pesky Old Monk sought once again to drag Yu to his bedroom for intercourse. Zhiyuan, mindful of the previous incident with Du, felt quite jealous this time.

"In all fairness," he said disgruntled, "Elder Brother should be my companion and you have no right to take him away from me!"

"Why?" asked the Old Monk.

"You have me all day long to work off your lust," said Zhiyuan, "but whom can I go at to relieve myself?[10] Not long ago I found someone, but my enjoyment of pleasure had hardly started when you interposed and ended it. Elder Brother tarries here simply because of my invitation, and I think it is reasonable that I demand that he stay with me!"

Though taking offense at his disciple's recalcitrant attitude, the Old Monk dared not confront him in a direct way. He pursed his lips, very unhappy. Yu was observant. That night he brought up the topic again as he and Zhiyuan reached the ecstatic height of their coupling.

133

"You said something was 'ended' some time ago. What did you mean?" he asked.

Zhiyuan, in his sexual excitement, spoke without thought: "Not long ago we had a woman from a nearby village and were in the middle of sex in a threesome when the old ignoramus, with such jealousy I could never imagine, abruptly ended all our relations. I still burn with regret as I recall what has happened."

"Where is the woman now?" asked Yu. "Why not fetch her here to join us?"

Zhiyuan heaved a sigh. "Where can I find her?" he said.

Yu intuited that there was more to it than what he had been told, so he continued his interrogation. But the Young Monk refused to disclose any further information concerning the woman's whereabouts. Yu had to drop the subject.

The next day when there were no other people around, he asked the Boy Monk in a low voice, "Is it true that a woman stayed here some time ago?"

"Yes," the Boy Monk answered.

"How long did she stay?" Yu asked.

"Only for a few days," said the Boy Monk.

"Then where did she go?" Yu asked.

"I didn't actually witness her departure," said the Boy Monk. "She just one night suddenly disappeared."

"What did she do when she was here?" Yu pressed.

"I have no idea," said the Boy Monk. "I know only that she passed two nights with the Old Master and the Young Master and then was seen no more. Since her disappearance my two masters have frequently quarreled, but I hardly understood what they argued about."

In spite of the vagueness of the boy's responses, Yu had none-theless got some ideas of what had really occurred to the woman. Yet he pretended that he had noticed nothing unusual and spoke to the master and the disciple, "I have been here for two days now, and today I would like to go out for a walk."

"Don't abandon us for good," said the Old Monk.

"He won't," said Zhiyuan, winking at Yu with a smile. "He may perhaps leave you, but how could he part with me?"

Yu returned his wink, saying, "I will be back shortly."

He then left the temple, making his way directly to the yamen. He reported to Lord Lin what Zhiyuan and the Boy Monk had told him. Lord Lin nodded and said, "So that is it! Judging from their information, the woman must have been murdered by that malicious Old Monk. If she had escaped the temple, she should have been home within three days. Where else could she have gone, do you suppose? No wonder that half a year has passed and no trace of her has been found."

He bade the guard to keep the secret. The next morning Lord Lin rose early and set out in his sedan for the temple, accompanied by a bevy of retainers. At his bidding, one of them in front of the procession went announcing his arrival: "Lord Lin had a dream last night and is coming to your temple to offer incense!"

All the monks were at once gathered together to receive him. Descending from his palanquin, Lord Lin entered the monastery to burn incense. On completion of his prayers, the abbot served him tea, with the other monks standing in line on either side. Lord Lin stepped down from the platform. He looked up while descending, as if he were listening to a voice high above. He kept looking up for some moments and then suddenly bowed to Heaven, saying, "Your servant now knows the truth of the matter."

He then raised his head and bowed once again, saying, "Your servant now knows the man."

He then rushed down the stairs, shouting, "Where are the constables? Hurry up and catch the murderer for me!" The constables snapped to attention ready for duty. Lord Lin quickly darted a glance at the monks and noticed that in spite of their astonishment, they stood in rapt attention showing no trepidation at all, except for an elderly priest who was stupefied, his face pale and his teeth chattering. Lord Lin pointed at him with his finger, ordering him to be bound up.

"Do you see?" he spoke to them. "Heaven has revealed to me that this old monk, whose name is Dajue, was the murderer of the woman of the Jing family." He then turned to the Old Monk and shouted, "Confess now to the crime you have committed!"

All the other monks, though unaware of the murder, were aghast that

Lord Lin, who had never before set foot in their temple, knew that the Old Monk was called Dajue. "It is obvious that he has received some divine instructions from Heaven," they thought. Little did they know that it was the guard Yu who had provided him this intelligence beforehand.

The Old Monk had been caught off guard by this unanticipated raid. What made him more frightened was the revelation of the power from Heaven. Paralysed with panic, he kowtowed over and over again, incapable of uttering a single word. Lord Lin ordered the constables to place him in squeezers,[11] which, eventually, forced him to confess everything: how he and Zhiyuan had had sex with the woman and how he had become jealous of her intimacy with his disciple and had finally murdered her. Zhiyuan was then put to torture. Being a delicate youth fearful of the pain of the squeezers, he confessed even before the ropes began to tighten: "My master killed her," he screeched, "and her corpse is buried in the backyard."

Lord Lin then had the constables accompany the two monks to the courtyard, where, after having dug into the ground, they did discover the corpse of a woman, her neck broken and her body covered in blood.

The two criminals were then taken to the yamen, where Lord Lin recorded their confessions. The death penalty was meted out for Dajue for his rape and murder, and Zhiyuan was sentenced to a three-year term of imprisonment for his involvement in seduction and homicide without turning in his accomplice, with the condition that he must return to secular life and perform servitude after his release. After the two families Jing and Du were summoned to claim the corpse for burial, the case was finally closed. Yu was not only rewarded profusely, but reinstated as well. When the news of the monk's lechery and murder spread, people in the county all praised Lord Lin as a wonder-judge. The verdicts of the court were later comfirmed by the superior official, and the Old Monk was executed after the autumn equinox. There was jubilation in the area as the news passed from one person to another, and today, the legend of Lin, how perceptive he was, how he received assistance from Heaven and used magical powers to solve the puzzling case, is still widely circulated in Sichuan province.

> The village wench is picky in the choice of her partner,
> The hungry devil of lust is heartless as a contender.
> Willing to offer his rear courtyard[12] is Yu the guard,
> And in making Heaven work Judge Lin is a fine actor.

The Wife Swappers[1]

The man, in hand, with a Hook of Wu,[2]
Ready to chop a horde of enemies into pieces;
But to a flower[3] he will yield to the mood,
However tempered out of iron his heart is.

Behold! Those heroes Xiang Ji and Liu Ji[4]
Were causing all to fret when they angered;
Yet in the arms of the women Yu and Qi,[5]
Even they were willing to be conquered.

This lyric, composed long ago by a person of virtue, indicates that men are most concerned with sex. It does not matter if they are heroes or a cold-blooded murderers, their mortal coil[6] will go soft once they see an alluring woman. Look at the Hegemon-King of Western Chu and Gaozu the founding emperor of the Han.[7] How valiant they were in fighting to rule the land under heaven![8] However, one begrudged parting with his concubine Yu even before committing suicide,[9] and the other, in spite of his royal drunkenness, was reluctant to make his consort Qi discontented.[10] If men like them were unable to hold back from making sentimental spectacles of themselves, how, then, can ordinary people who are not their equals?

A romantic youth, passionate and highly predisposed to sexual enjoyment, will find it hard to keep his mind focused. Yet sex is something indirectly related to the moral merits of the nether world.[11] Men keeping away from the wives and daughters of others and respecting their chastity have mysteriously been recompensed for their goodness with divine benefaction. Some won the highest places in the examinations, some gained important positions with handsome emoluments, and some fathered eminent sons. There is no need to recount these stories, for most of them can be found in the biographies of dynastic histories. As for those who indulged themselves in sex and conceived ruses for the seduction and violation of good women, they either died an untimely death, or lost their official posts, or brought disaster to their own wives and daughters. There are none who have not received their just desserts.

Here is a case in point. In the last year of the Chunxi reign of the Song dynasty, there was in Shuzhou a Licentiate named Liu Yaoju, whom people called by his style: Tangqing. Tangqing's father held an official post in Pingjiang prefecture and Tangqing lived there with his parents.[12] In the fall of that year the Provincial Examination was to be held,[13] and taking advantage of his father's position, Tangqing chartered a boat and left for Xiuzhou to take the examination.

The boat set sail.

Looking back toward the stern, Tangqing was startled to find that the rudder was in the hand of a beautiful young girl, about the age of sixteen or seventeen. Her hair cascading gracefully at the temples and a coquettish tenderness shining in her eyes, she looked unusually attractive in spite of her plain clothes and light makeup. Standing on the stern, she could be compared to a picture of a slanting crabapple reflected on the surface of water.

Tangqing grew infatuated and was not contented just to gaze at her. Watching the proceedings on the boat, he found that she was the boatman's daughter. "There are shining pearls in the old oysters as the saying goes," he murmured to himself in admiration, "and this is indeed true!"

He would have struck up a light conversation with her if he had not feared that her father, who, also sailing the boat at the stern, might see through his motives. He pretended to be disinterested, avoiding looking toward the stern directly. But once in a while he would steal a glance at the girl, and with each glimpse, was struck more by her beauty and charm. He was about to act on his impulses when an idea presented itself.

Complaining that the craft was too heavy and slow and that he might be late for the examination, he urged the boatman to go ashore to tow the vessel. The boatman was an elderly man with a son and a daughter, and both of them were his helpers. The son, Sanguanbao, was actually on the bank towing it at the time. When his father was sent to join him, only the daughter was left at the helm.

Now Tangqing, being alone on the deck, felt comfortable enough for flirtation. He started, in a routine manner, with some casual questions, of which he asked at least ten, but received replies only once or twice. The girl was very charming in the way she responded, and Tangqing kept winking at her as she was speaking. She either shunned his stare shyly or assumed a solemn cast to stop his flirtations. However, when Tangqing averted his eyes, paying no more attention to her, she would tease him with some sarcastic comments, giggling behind his back and squinting stealthily at him. It was obvious that she pretended to be unperturbed before his gaze yet tried to incite him covertly. To resist seductiveness like this was certainly not easy, and Tangqing felt as if his soul was being swept away.

It was the moment, he decided, to advance. He swung open his suitcase, took out a fine, white, silk handkerchief, and twisted into it a walnut as a love knot. He then tossed it to her. The girl saw that something was thrown to her, but feigned that she did not, and continued sculling without showing a trace of emotion on her face. Fearing that she might indeed have failed to notice the handkerchief, Tangqing repeatedly winked at her and with his hand motioned for her to hide it. However, she stood there exhibiting no reaction at all, as though she were wholly unaware of what he was doing. Seeing her father coil up the rope and prepare to come back aboard, Tangqing became even more anxious, gesturing frantically with both hands and feet. Still, the girl remained as motionless as before. Tangqing felt at a loss as to how to handle the situation and regretted bitterly his folly. He wished only that he could reach out a long arm to get his handkerchief back.

Now the old man was back on the boat. Tangqing's face blushed red and a cold sweat dripped from his body. He was so embarrassed that he desired nothing more than to find for himself a place to hide. Just at that moment, he noticed that the girl lightly stretched out her foot to the handkerchief, drew it back with the tip of her shoe, and covered it under the bottom of her skirt. She then stooped down to pick it up and hid it away in her sleeve. Then she raised her head and gazed out upon the water, a smile playing on her face. Tangqing, after having undergone so much anxiety, was very grateful for her concealing his handkerchief at this critical moment. A sense that she was even more lovely than before welled up in him.

They began to take an interest in each other. The next day Tangqing once again sent her father ashore by using the same pretext. When both father and son were away towing the boat, he, brazen-faced, spoke to the girl to express his gratitude: "Thank you very much for your kindness to me yesterday. Without it, I could never again be able to face your family."

"I thought you to be bold," the girl replied with a grin, "but actually you are just a coward."

"You are both beautiful and clever," said Tangqing. "You should find yourself a good husband who is worthy of you. What a pity it is that a colourful phoenix should be confined to a hen-house by mistake!"

"I am afraid you are not quite right," said the girl. "A beautiful woman usually has an unfortunate life, and this has been so ever since time immemorial. I am not the only one who suffers this fate. We are all predestined; how can I complain about it?"

Tangqing greatly admired her sagacity. Now that they were congenial in conversation, a few of feet distance seemed unable to separate them.

One in the cabin and the other on the stern, they began to flash amorous glances at one another. Yet despite their growing intimacy, they were incapable of anything more substantial than verbal communication, for the boatman on the bank could see them as he looked over his shoulder.

After their arrival at Xiuzhou, Tangqing continued to remain on the boat instead of looking for lodgings. His mind was on the girl even when he was sitting for the examination. No sooner had he received the question sheet than he began to write, and he wrote with such an astonishing speed that he finished his essay at one go. He left the examination hall ahead of time, heading toward the boat without delay.

Having nothing to do on board, the boatman and his son went to town to shop, leaving the daughter on watch. Seeing her alone, Tangqing was beside himself with joy. He jumped hastily onto the boat.

"Where are your father and brother?" he asked.

"They are shopping in town," she said.

"I would like to speak with you," said Tangqing. He went to unfasten the mooring rope. "May I trouble you to move the boat to a quiet place?"

The girl understood his purpose and propelled the vessel to a spot well away from prying eyes. Tangqing leapt onto the stern and drew her to him.

"I am in the prime of life and haven't yet married," he said. "Should I happen to be the man you desire, I would propose that we make a life-long union."

"I am no beauty," said the girl. "Although it has long been my wish to marry a gentleman of your stature, how dare a straggly, undernourished vine entertain the lofty hope of climbing a stately pine? You are destined for an official career, and I doubt that you will be interested in a humble woman like myself once you have succeeded. I can't accept your proposal, and beseech you to conduct yourself properly!"

Her seriousness elicited both Tangqing's sympathy and strong sexual feelings. Yet he knew that it was too soon to push her. As he grew impetuous, he patted her on the shoulder and said, "Please don't be so concerned with gains and losses. For the last two days I was out of my mind because of you and was barely able to control myself. I longed to approach you and be with you. Today, thank Heaven, we have been granted a fine opportunity. Only you and I are here, and we can do whatever we like to fulfill our desire. I had no expectation that you would refuse me. I feel dejected. What use is the life of a man whose hopes are dashed? When you concealed the handkerchief for me, I was filled with gratitude. Now that I can't unite with you, I would rather sacrifice my life to repay your kindness."

He made as if to plunge into the river. The girl quickly seized him, and grabbing his gown cried, "Don't be hasty! Let's discuss it first."

Tangqing spun around at once and pulled her into his arms.

"There is no need for further words!" he said.

He carried her into the cabin and they got onto his bed together. The pleasure they experienced, like the discovery of a treasure, was far more exciting than they had expected.

After they had finished, the girl rose, fixed her dishevelled hair, and brushed down Tangqing's clothes for him, saying, "I consider it my honour that you love me, and therefore offered you my body regardless of shame so as not to let you down. Although our carnal pleasure is momentary, my affection for you is and will be as firm as gold and stone. Please let this impaired flower flow no more with water in vain!"

"I am very delighted that I have won your precious love," Tangqing replied, "which, I swear, I will never abandon. The examination results will soon come out; if I pass, I will marry you in a proper ceremony and have you live in a golden house."

Both of them, for a while, basked in loving affection and joy. Finally the girl said, "I am afraid that my father will come back soon."

She moved the boat to where it had been previously anchored. Tangqing deliberately disembarked and did not return until after her father was back aboard. The liaison that had occurred between them thus went undiscovered. But:

> A secret affair discreditable,
> Is to God's lightning eye discernible.

Tangqing's father was in Pingjiang, anticipating good news from his son. One night he had a dream. He saw two yellow-robed men approach him with a sheet of paper in their hands, announcing, "The results of the examination have been posted on the heavenly gate[14] and your son has received the highest recommendation."[15] However, the paper they were holding was suddenly snatched by a passer-by. "Liu Yaoju," this mysterious stranger said, "can't be recommended this time due to his misbehaviour." His father was so startled as to awaken himself suddenly, only to find that it was a dream.

"This dream is strange," he reflected. Though he knew nothing of what Tangqing had done, the words he had heard in the dream filled him with apprehension about his son's possible failure.

His worries came true. When the results of the Xiuzhou examination district came out, Tangqing was indeed absent from the list of recommended candidates.[16] At first he had been highly praised by the invigilator who suggested that he be awarded first place. But another examiner, impressed with a different paper, proposed to downgrade him to second place.[17] The invigilator was unwilling to concede.

"I would rather fail him than see him receive only the second place," he said. "I am sure he will achieve first place if he retries the examination the next time. I don't wish to see him unfairly ranked." Indignant, he placed Tangqing on the failure list.

Tangqing waited on the boat while people hustled and bustled about, reporting the news of success. No one, however, came to him; his boat was quiet. He sighed, realizing that there was no hope for him. The girl standing on the stern was disappointed too, tears spilling out of her eyes. Tangqing consoled her when there was no one around, and then taking their boat, went back home.

When he arrived and reported in to his parents, his father related his dream to him. "Since I had that dream," he said, "I knew you wouldn't succeed. But I wonder what dishonest things you did that affected your marks?"

"I did nothing dishonest," Tangqing said.

In his heart, however, he was very astonished. "How could this be true?" he murmured to himself, not without suspicion. It was not until much later that he heard the rumour that he could have had the highest recommendation but for his moral discredit. He felt deeply chagrined.

Still he longed for the girl. After receiving the highest recom-mendation in the next examination, he, recalling his promise, mounted a search for the girl everywhere, but without success, for she had been drifting along the river and nobody knew where she was. For the remainder of his life, no matter that he had eventually passed the State Examination, Tangqing mourned her loss bitterly.

Gentle reader, you have now seen how Tangqing was punished for his misdemeanour. He was forced to try the Provincial Examination twice, and was never allowed a single chance for a reunion with the woman he loved. The girl was not predestined to be his wife, and that is why the retribution he received exceeded the norm. I must here offer a piece of advice to all men in the world: Do not rashly seduce good women! How well the ancients have said:

> If I defile not another's wife,
> He will not defile mine;
> But if I defile another's wife,
> In turn, he will do so to mine.

Now I shall tell you another tale of retribution, a story of how a man wished to seduce his friend's wife, only in the end to have his own wife seduced by the friend.

During the Yuan dynasty, there lived in the Yuanshang district of Mianzhou prefecture[18] a young man by the name of Yi Rong. He was a scion of a distinguished family and his ancestor had once held the position of the Censor of Embroidered-Garments.[19] His wife, surnamed Di, was very beautiful, enjoying a reputation as the most dazzling creature in the entire city.

It was local custom that women were permitted to go on outings, and wealthy households were much inclined to show off their decorative wives. If a man married a beauteous woman, he might not only boast of her so much as to spread her fame far and wide, but also take her along with him and let her appear on public occasions. In flowery mornings or on moonlit evenings, lords and ladies would gather together, and would, in the hubbub of jostling crowds, exchange intimate touches. No one would pay the slightest attention to the improper conduct of others.

On their way to their homes at night, men would find amusement making comments on the females they had seen, and would rate them one by one. Discussing a pretty woman, they would become loud and frivolous, with little care whether her husband might overhear their words. When their conversation did reach him, the husband would take it as praise for his wife and would therefore feel pleased and happy. Even though he might hear something unpleasant about himself, he would not take offence. This practice became ever more prevalent during the Zhiyuan and the Zhizheng reigns.[20]

Having Di the ravishing beauty as his wife, Yi was certainly very proud to go out in her company, to parade her charm and grace. Wherever they went, he would hear people's adulation of her. His friends and acquaintances would tease him or compliment him for being married to so gorgeous a woman. Even strangers, upon learning that he was Di's husband, would introduce themselves to him, and would flatter him or ply him with food and drink.

As a man so fortunate in his marriage, Yi was well received wherever he went. He never bothered to carry money with him, for there was certainly someone who would treat him and offer him wine and meat. It was, therefore, a common occurrence that he returned home full and tipsy.

There were, however, few men in the district who did not harbour the depraved intention of seducing his wife. Since Yi was from a distinguished family and a formidable man himself, no one dared to lay a finger on him for any reason. They, of course, were envious, but except for some furtive stares or verbal flirtations, they could make no approaches to Di. An ancient proverb says it well:

> An exposed hoard solicits robbers,
> An alluring face entices rapists.

Being such a stunning beauty living in such an era, how could Di preserve her chastity? Inevitably she became involved in an affair. Without coincidences there would have been no story. It so happened that at that time a man called Hu Sui living on the same street also had an exceedingly beautiful wife by the surname of Men, who was only slightly inferior to Di. So comely was she that no one else but Di could compare to her.

Hu was a libertine. Having an uncommonly pretty wife, he still felt that she was not enough for him, and was covetous of the more attractive beauty, Di. On the other hand, Yi was deeply infatuated with Men. Upon first sighting her, he even began to think of seducing her and making her his own woman. Over time, this fantasy of his had grown into a most obsessive desire.

With deceitful intentions on their minds, the two men began to forge a friendship. As their intimacy grew, they even considered the possibility of sharing their wives with each other. While Hu was rather crafty, Yi was of a straightforward disposition and would sometimes unintentionally betray his interest in Men in front of her husband. Hu knew how to exploit Yi's weakness. He often tricked him into speaking his mind openly and kept him from backsliding. Yi thought that his friend was easy-going and he could achieve his goal without much difficulty. Never had he suspected that Hu intended to seduce Di but did not want him to see through his real intentions.

One day Yi said to Di, "Everyone praises you for your beauty, but to be honest, Hu's wife is not at all inferior. How could I find a way to get her? We live but once. If I have both of you, I shall die contented."

"You and Hu are such good friends," said Di. "Why not speak to him frankly?"

"I have already hinted to him my intention," said Yi, "and it seemed that he took no offense. However, I find it hard to bring the matter up bluntly. If you act as my go-between, then things could possibly be arranged. But I am afraid that you might be jealous."

"I am not a jealous woman," said Di. "I have never failed to help you whenever I could. But this matter is different. It concerns a woman who is usually confined to her boudoir. How could you reach her and lay your hands on her? Unless we all become friends and Hu allows you to see his wife and you do the same for him, inviting the couple over to our home, I don't think I can create an opportunity for you to carry out your plan."

"My good wife," Yi exclaimed, "you are absolutely right!"

From that time on, Yi became more hospitable to Hu and often invited him over for drinks. Hu's wife Men usually came with her husband, and Yi would assign Di to keep her company. To amuse Hu and also to arouse Men, Yi would engage high-class courtesans and rakes to cavort with them in their orgies. When the time came for carnal pleasures, Di would take Men into the secluded part of the room, where they could, unobserved, peek out from behind the screen. The lewdness of the activities they watched would ignite the flames of lust even in a woman of stone, and one of the voyeurs, who, seeing their two husbands, with seductive thoughts on their minds, vying with each other to arouse their beautiful wives, indeed responded.

Which of the women do you suppose it was? It was Di. Though Men was observing the same scene, she was, after all, a guest, and did not feel at ease in someone else's residence. Di, in her own home, could abandon herself to the wanton enjoyment of the racy panorama. As a handsome man, Hu was superior to Yi not only in appearance but also in temperament and the art of love. Di was totally enraptured by him. From time to time she would expose herself from behind the screen, ogling him. She also paid extra attention to the supply of wine and food, without showing the slightest sign of fatigue on her face. Yi was pleased with his wife's capability as his helpmate, little perceiving that she harboured her own purposes.

"How rare it is to find two bosom friends who both have such beautiful wives," Yi slurred to Hu, drunk.

"Oh, my ugly crone can hardly be compared to your lady," said Hu, modestly. "Her beauty is sheer perfection."

"In my humble opinion, they are about the same," said Yi. "It is just that we don't have much fun sticking only to our own woman. Now that we are in high spirits, why not exchange our wives so that we may taste a different flavour?"

These were precisely the words Hu had been longing to hear. But duplicitous as ever, he replied, "You may esteem my ill-favoured crone, but how could I sully your paragon of a wife with anything indecent? My ethical principles bar me from any such act."

"Man, we are drunk! Listen to what we are talking about!" Yi grumbled, breaking out in laughter. With that, they both laughed and the party soon broke up.

Tipsy, Yi staggered into the inner room. "Would you agree to a trade of wives between Hu and myself?" he mumbled to Di, lifting her chin with his hands and staring into her eyes.

"You silly turtle!"[21] Di cursed him unctuously. "You are a man of a good family. Don't you feel ashamed to take someone else's woman at the expense of your own wife's body? You have some nerve to ask me this!"

"Well," said Yi, "we are all good friends and this will be for our mutual amusement. You should not take it so seriously."

"I can help you only from behind the screen," said Di. "I will never involve myself in what you suggest."

"I am just joking," Yi laughed. "Do you think I would really trade you for that inferior woman? I only want to seduce her. That's all."

"For that you must be patient," Di told him. "If you keep Hu happy and well-entertained, it's not unlikely that he will go crazy and offer you his wife the way you wish."

"How perceptive you are!" Yi exclaimed. "This is indeed good advice, my understanding mother!" He hugged her, and then they retired to their chamber for the night. But no more of this.

Our story continues that Di, who had grown enamoured of Hu, began to fear that her bad-natured husband might cause trouble for her. "He said those insane words simply out of his excitement at the prospect of seducing Men," she mused. "If I really do as he has suggested, he would doubtless give me the cold-shoulder afterwards, and put me in a difficult situation. This, certainly, would be very unfavourable to me. I must conceive a plan that will allow me to do as I wish behind his back and enjoy pleasure to my heart's content."

One day Hu came to visit Yi and was invited for dinner. This time the two men were alone and there were no other guests accompanying them. Di, as usual, served them from behind the screen. She signalled Hu to keep his wits about him, and he took her warning in tacit understanding, sipping only a small mouthful of wine each time while coaxing Yi into gulping down several bowls.

"My worthy brother," he said, "you have always loved me, treating me even more graciously than my own kith and kin. You condescend to consider my ugly crone and she admires you just as highly. In fact, I have discussed the matter with her and she has kind of agreed. As long as you continue to take care of me and entertain me with lavish banquets and a hundred courtesans, I shall exert all my efforts to ensure that your wish is fulfilled."

"If you present me only one opportunity," said Yi, "I will be more than willing to treat you a thousand times!"

Excited by their conversation, Yi went on a drinking spree, draining big bowls one after another. Hu kept egging him on with obsequious words until the latter became dead drunk. Taking advantage of having to help him to bed, Hu entered the inner part of the room, where, behind the screen, Di was standing. Instead of avoiding him, she reached out quietly to support her husband. Seeing that Yi still remained unconscious, Hu leaned over to plant a kiss on Di's face. Di, in return, stroked his leg with the tip of her foot. She then summoned her maids Yanxue and Qingyun to carry their master into the bedroom. Now left to themselves behind the screen, Hu instantly took Di to his arms, and she turned to fall into his embrace.

147

"You don't know how much I have been yearning for you," he cajoled in a coquettish voice, anxious to begin their lovemaking. "If today I am allowed to enjoy the heavenly pleasure, it would be the greatest stroke of fortune in my three lives!"[22]

"I love you, too," said Di. "So no more words!"

She removed her pants and reclined on a lounge chair placed in the middle of the room. Then she raised her legs, making herself ready for doing the work of clouds and rain. How ironic it was that Yi, who desired to seduce Hu's wife, should be the first one to become a cuckold! Truly:

> Chasing a friend's wife he leaves his woman neglected,
> But behind his back a tryst is secretly inaugurated.
> As selling dumplings in order to noodles purchase,
> Whoever else would be so silly to make such a mistake?

No stranger to pleasure, Hu was an expert in the art of love. By bringing into play all his skills, he offered Di the most overwhelming sexual delights she had ever experienced. Di felt total satisfaction.

She warned Hu at the end of their play, "Never let my husband know of this!"

"My good Sister-in-Law," said Hu, "I thank you for the pleasure you have afforded me. But didn't you know that your husband has long since promised that I could enjoy your favours? I don't think he will care even if he learns of our dalliance."

"My husband has been lusting after your beautiful wife," said Di, "and that's why he gave you such an irresponsible promise. He may be lecherous and intemperate in sex, but he is also very hot-tempered. You must never get on his bad side. What we should do right now is to conceive a plan that will ensure our pursuit of long-term intimacy in secret without his knowledge."

"What plan, then, will accomplish this purpose?" Hu asked.

"The weaknesses of my husband are women and wine," Di told him. "Whenever you find a courtesan of highest renown, take him to her and urge him to stay in the brothel overnight. We can then indulge ourselves in pleasure throughout the night."

"Marvellous!" Hu said. "Since he is desirous of ravishing my wife and has promised me a myriad of 'treatments' at brothels, I shall take advantage of his offer and have a good courtesan detain him. I am certain he will be loath to leave her. The only problem is how to supply him with sufficient money for his cathouse expenses?"

"Don't worry about that," said Di. "Just leave it to me."

"My good Sister-in-Law," Hu exclaimed, "if you can solve the problem of costs, I will surely do everything I can to keep you happy and satisfied!"

Things thus settled, they parted.

In fact, Hu's family, unlike Yi's, was in a rather straightened situation. That explained why Yi, with his generous provision of wine and delicacies, had been able to establish a close camaraderie with him. But never had Yi expected that his fawning guest would turn out to get the upper hand! His squandering of money on banquets and the enjoyment of sex gradually exhausted his adequate family resources. Now Di had her lover, causing their finances to deteriorate further, for she not only often urged her husband to seek pleasures outside, but invited Hu over to her expensive dinners that contained numerous savory dishes. Their daily expenses were huge; however, in her state of satiation, Di cared not a whit.

There came a time at last when Yi fell into financial difficulties. Urged by his wife and Hu, he had to sell off some family property at a loss. Di deducted a portion of the proceeds from the sale and saved it for her own adulterous purposes. Hu continued to seek out well-known courtesans for Yi to visit, and with wine and food prepared for his enjoyment, Yi would usually stay in the pleasure quarters for days on end.

To prolong his sojourn there, Di would send him money and items she had hidden away as subsidies for his overspending, and meanwhile, she and Hu, in the absence of her husband, would indulge their sensual natures as much as they could. Yi thought his wife was generous and became ever more wanton and dissipated.

Occasionally he would return home for a few days. Seeing the complaisance in his wife which was completely devoid of discontentment or jealousy, Yi felt grateful. Even in his dreams he extolled Di as a "good woman."

One day Di was preparing wine and fruit for Hu when Yi happened to come back. He noticed the food on the table and asked, "For whom are you making this feast?"

"For you," Di replied. "I knew you would return today, so I have made some dishes for you. To alleviate your boredom, I have also had a maid send for Hu to join you."

Hearing these words, Yi exclaimed, "No one but my wife knows me so well!"

Before long, Hu arrived. Being happy to drink with him, Yi babbled about brothels and prostitutes, and occasionally would also mention Men as he grew excited.

"How can you still be interested in my ugly wife after dallying with so many courtesans?" Hu asked. "Well, if you still find her alluring, I shall do whatever I can to arrange an assignation for you."

Yi was full of gratitude, to be sure. It never occurred to him that Hu was only paying him lip service. By enticing him to the pleasure quarters and getting him drunk day and night, he had virtually deprived him of time to seduce Men. In the meantime, he himself was growing more and more intimate with Di, letting not even one single night slip by without sharing the same bed with her.

Now Yi was back home, obviously presenting an obstacle for their rendezvous. It became imperative to free themselves from this inconvenience. Hu had a special recipe for brewing a type of liquor, which he gave to Di. Anyone who drank ten cups[23] of this formulated alcohol would fall into a drunken slumber. When this privately-concocted liquor was ready for use, Yi was no longer a threat to them even in his own home, for he would collapse after a few cups. While Yi was lying insensible, Hu would emerge and change the concoction to a safe drink for Di and himself, and then they would drink and talk, and engage in sensual pleasure all evening. Yi, however, remained ignorant.

One day he returned home while Di and Hu were in the midst of a meal. Though Hu managed to conceal himself without being discovered, Di did not have time to clear away the cups and plates which were scattered all over the table. Naturally, this gave rise to Yi's interrogation.

"A relative dropped by and I asked him to stay for dinner," Di explained. "Since he is not much of a drinker, he has slipped away for fear that you might force him to quaff a few cups and he might not be able to endure it."

Yi dropped the subject without further questions. He had taken for granted what Di had said earlier about her unwillingness to involve herself in wife-swapping, and never since then had he doubted her virtue. He trusted her even more when Hu did his utmost to fawn on him and keep him company in his philandering and drinking. Indeed, it was hard for Yi, a careless man, not to be deceived. Both Hu and Di were adept and shrewd, and moreover, they had the maids to aid them as their accomplices. They could even gloss over the traces their mistress and her lover had unwittingly left. Little wonder that Yi was so stubborn in taking Hu the seducer as his best friend and the unfaithful Di as his chaste wife. As time wore on, more and more of his neighbours learned of his cuckoldry. They mocked him by composing a doggerel verse to the deviant tune of "Sheep on the Mountain Slope":[24]

> The place of breeze and moon[25]
> No man is unwilling to frequent.
> Yet with such a lovely wife,
> You should feel content.
> What is the point of visiting courtesans,
> Only to leave your lady-love free to pay your retributive debt?
> You seek to hold another woman with one single hand,
> Yet your own wife tries with both her hands a betraying attempt!
> While she has obtained what she needs,
> Have you ever had a chance for your own date?
> Cutting a cat's tail to prepare for the cat's meal,
> You deserve to have wasted your abundant wealth away.
> Alas! your over-indulgence in the love of flowers
> Has cost you money and made you unfortunate.
> Alas! engaging in a debauched life,
> You can never expect a decent life to elongate!

It was not long before Yi's befuddled life of wine and sex caused him to fall sick. He took to his bed and stayed home all day long. With his constant presence, Hu felt too uncomfortable to visit Di, and decided not to see her again. One day Di had somebody pass a message to him: "My husband is bedridden, and besides, the maids are on my side and will help me cover things up. Please feel free to come visit me."

Her encouragement finally dispelled Hu's doubts. He resumed his visits and called on Di whenever the mood struck, as if Yi were not at home. On one occasion, he was so careless because of his old habit that he strolled right past Yi's bed and was seen by him.

"How is it that Mr. Hu was walking out from inside?" Yi asked.

"Where is Mr. Hu?" said Di and her two maids in chorus. "We saw nobody."

"I did see a man," said Yi. "But you all claim that no one was there.

Is it that I am so sick that my vision has become blurred and what I saw was a mere ghost?"

"Perhaps not a ghost," said Di. "Since you have become so obsessed with his wife, it is not unlikely that when you opened your foggy eyes in delirium, you might have seen an illusion."

The next day Di told Hu of this incident.

"Well, you may concoct some nonsense like this to deceive him," he said, "but I doubt that it will work for long. After his recovery, he will no doubt discern the truth and will then be suspicious of us. Since he thought that he might have seen a ghost, I'd better show him a real ghost to convince him that he was indeed befuddled, lest he become distrustful."

"Are you serious?" said Di, smiling. "How could you find a real ghost?"

"I will hide myself tonight in a rear room when it turns dark," Hu explained. "In any case, I would like to take advantage of the opportunity to make love with you. Tomorrow morning I will emerge disguising myself as a monster. Isn't this plan a killing of two birds with one stone?"

That night Di arranged for Hu to stay in another room, and bade the two maids to wait upon their master at his bedside. Saying that she was exhausted from caring for him and must lay her head in a different chamber, she left her husband and joined Hu for the entire night. The next morning Hu daubed his face with indigo and dyed his beard red. He also wrapped his feet in cotton pads so that he could walk so lightly as to be imperceptible. When he was informed that Yi was half-awake, he darted out directly in front of his bed. Yi, after all, was a sick person. He cried out in frightened astonishment as he caught sight of the strange figure. "Ghost! Ghost!" He dove beneath his quilt, trembling without cease.

Di rushed to his bedside, asking, "Why such a fuss?"

"I told you that what I saw yesterday could have been a ghost," he whimpered, "and today I did see a ghost. I fear that my condition bodes ill rather than well and you should hurry to send an exorcist to save me."

Because of this shock, Yi became more seriously ill. Feeling very sad, Di had to send for a Buddhist master. At that time, there dwelt, thirty miles away from Yuanshang district, a Zen adept styled Sitting Consciousness, who, known also by the name "Empty Valley," was of a moral integrity unequalled within the surrounding mountains. With rich gifts Yi invited him to their residence, and then had a confessional altar built for the purpose of supplicating the protection of the Buddha. The Zen adept did not rise on time the day he started his trance; it was not until late afternoon that he finally woke up.

"Do you have an ancestor who served as the Censor of Embroidered-Garments?" he asked.

"Yes, my late grandfather," Yi replied.

"And among your acquaintances, is there a man by the surname of Hu?"

"Yes, he is my close friend," said Yi.

Di was startled to hear them mention the name of her lover. With a guilty conscience, she began to eavesdrop on their conversation.

"What I saw in my trance was very strange," said the adept.

"May I know the details?" Yi asked.

"At the beginning, I saw your ancestor, the Censor of Embroidered-Garments, bringing a suit against Hu before the God of Earth[26] for the ruining of his grandson's life. The God of Earth, who is not high enough in rank to judge a case of this kind, suggested to your grandfather: 'Today the North Dipper and the South Dipper are going to descend at the foot of Mount Yusi[27] and you should go there to appeal to them. I am sure you will be given a hearing.' Your grandfather then invited me to go with him. After reaching the mountain, we saw two ancients seated face to face, one in a rosy garment and the other in green, playing chess. Your grandfather kowtowed to them and then lodged his complaint. However, they paid him no heed at all. In spite of their disregard, your grandfather continued until they finished the game.

"Then they said to him, 'Fortune, happiness, disaster, and licentiousness are all governed by heavenly laws. You are a Confucian scholar and should be able to understand that trouble is usually caused by oneself, not by someone else, and hence there is no purpose in seeking redress from us. Your grandson has failed in his filial duties and should rightly receive the death penalty. But given your status as an eminent Confucian scholar and the gravity of discontinuing your family line, he will be spared. As for Hu, a seducer and an instigator of evil, his retribution will be meted out either in this world or in the next. Please return home, for Hu will assuredly be punished. You need not resent him, nor is it necessary for you to appeal to us.' Having so said, they turned to me and went on, 'You are fortunate to lay your eyes on us. Since you are now a witness, you must relate what you have seen to make people know that fortune and disaster never befall anyone without reason.' Then both men disappeared. This is what I saw in my trance. I am very surprised to learn that you have an ancestor who was a Censor of Embroidered-Garments and a friend surnamed Hu!"

Di was thunderstruck, standing motionless with a feeling of loss. Yet Yi had not yet realized that his wife was also involved. He thought that his grandfather's complaint was directed only against Hu for his instigation of debauchery and squandering of his family property. So as soon as he learned that he could be spared, he felt instantly relieved and his illness began to improve.

In the meantime, Di fell sick from fretting too much about her lover. When Yi had completely recovered in the next few days, Hu came down with an indisposition. At the outset it was merely pain at his waist, but after a week or so, he suddenly experienced a serious ulcer-attack. His physician concluded that this disease, caused by over-indulgence in wine and sex, had resulted in the exhaustion of the internal fluids and therefore there was not much hope for a cure.

Hu's critical condition brought Yi to his bedside every day. As a family friend, Yi felt no scruple about entering their bedchamber to make inquiries. Men, looking after her husband at his sickbed, was at the beginning embarrassed with Yi being there, her manner rather unnatural. In time, however, her appreciation of his financial assistance led her into conversation with him, and still later, she even began to regard him with fondness. Yi had long admired her, and this state of affairs offered him a golden opportunity for seduction. When their passion reached a high pitch, they made love behind Hu's back. Now, finally, Yi's long-standing wish had been fulfilled and his cuckoldry compensated. Truly:

> Measure for measure,
> Heaven is fair.
> A long patient contact
> Leads to this affair.

After their first intimacy, they adhered to each other just as Di and Hu had in the early days of their love. Knowing that Hu's days were numbered and that his health could not be restored, they swore not only to love each other, but to remain, like mountain and sea, a devoted couple to their ripe old age.

"My wife is not jealous," Yi told Men. "The other day she proposed that I take you to my home and she would help me seduce you. After we get married, we may live together and the three of us may enjoy mutual pleasures. Isn't it wonderful!"

Men responded with a cold smile. "She is so willing to help others, so she certainly knows how to help herself!"

"Help herself?" Yi was confused.

"She has for a long time been sleeping with my husband," Men said. "My husband often stayed out overnight and was actually in your bed when you were away from home. Did you know nothing of this?"

Now, finally, Yi had awakened from his dream and sobered up from his inebriation. He realized that he had been deceived. "No wonder that in his trance the Zen adept saw my grandfather accusing Hu of having ruined my life," he thought. "My seduction of his wife must be his karmic retribution."

"In fact," he said, "I saw your husband one day going out from our house, but I was tricked into believing that it was an hallucination. If you hadn't told me the truth, I would still have been kept in the dark."

"But when you return home," said Men, "please don't reveal to your wife what I have told you, to spare me her opprobrium."

"Now that I have you, I will make no issue of it," Yi replied. "Actually, there is little point in making a scene as your husband lies dying."

He then quietly left Men and went back home, saying not a word to Di. A few days later Hu died; Yi went to offer his condolences. When he returned home, he found his wife weeping. She missed her lover and was overwhelmed with grief. Being now a conscious observer, Yi certainly understood the real reason for her tears.

"Where are your tears coming from?" he asked, with a cold smile.

There was no response.

"I have already discovered your secret," he said. "It is no longer necessary to hide it from me."

Di's face turned liverish blue. Springing to her defense, she blurted out, "What do you know and what do I hide from you? I am sighing and weeping simply because you have lost a good friend!"

"Don't justify yourself!" said Yi. "When I was out overnight, did he sleep in his own house and did you sleep alone? And who was the man I saw from my sickbed a few days ago? You sigh and shed your tears simply because you have lost your own lover!"

He had hit home. Di no longer dared to defend herself and retreated into silence and melancholy. Hu was on her mind every moment, appearing whenever she closed her eyes. As her depression grew deeper and deeper, she finally fell sick and lost her appetite for food. She died soon afterwards. Half a year later, with arrangements by a matchmaker, Yi formally took Men as his wife, and they lived in concord and mutual love. Recalling the words of the Zen adept about fortune and disaster, Yi awoke fully to the power of karma.

He said to Men, "I was attracted to you and sought to seduce you, only to have had my own wife first seduced by Hu. This is the just come-uppance for my sexual licence. Hu and my wife committed adultery behind my back; both are now gone and have left you to me. These are the just desserts for their sexual dissipation. Anyone who wishes to indulge in illicit sex should learn a lesson from our case. The Zen master has already revealed to me the power of karma in all its fullness, and I shall henceforth follow his precepts. Although there is little remaining of the patrimony of my family, we can still make do with what we have, if we keep to a simple and decent life."

He then formally took the Zen adept as his teacher and began to abide by the Five Commandments like a Buddhist monk.[28] Not only did he himself keep away from sexual promiscuity, but he also ensured that his wife did not go out seeking pleasure. As a testimony to the infallibility of karma, their story gradually spread throughout the Han-Mian region, where the local people, urged by the Zen adept, finally changed their customs.

> In the Jiang-Han region
> Women tend to be licentious;
> Unbounded by cultural tradition,
> Men are equally lecherous.
> Seeing two beautiful wives,
> Both husbands prepare to seduce;
> The most swift-of-foot, however
> Is first to seize the goose.
>
> He urges his rival to go whoring,
> While he takes the abandoned wife.
> Yet his own untimely death,
> Leaves his estate to the man still alive.
>
> This worldly retribution,
> Takes place without mistake;
> So pray you take my advice:
> Let your desire not lead you astray!

The Elopement of a Nun[1]

It is not wine that is intoxicating,
> But the drinker who lets himself be inebriated;
It is not a woman who is alluring,
> But the spectator who makes himself fascinated.
If you are crazed for someone
> Not predestined for you in your three incarnations,
You must use the sword of wisdom
> To cut off your evil intentions.

As we know, most marriages are predetermined by the three incarnations. No matter how capable a man may be in spending money like water and using every conceivable stratagem to achieve his goal, it is not unlikely that his endeavours will come to naught in the end. By contrast, someone may be penniless, like Sima Xiangru who had nothing but bare walls in his home,[2] yet he still can have his wish fulfilled when Fate favours him. He can make the acquaintance of the woman he wishes to marry, and without much difficulty, be betrothed to her through the help of a matchmaker. Astonishingly, he can even seduce an apparently unattainable woman who knows nothing of him, is of a different type, and comes from a different class, and make her his wife. As the old saying goes:

> Destiny in marriage has been decided
> On the Peach Feast in a previous life.[3]

It is obvious that marriage is no small matter. That is why chivalrous men who performed incredible feats to bring difficult couples together, like Kunlun Knave,[4] Yellow-Shirt Gallant,[5] and Aide Xu,[6] have become so popular that their legends have been handed down from ancient times to the present. An ordinary man, after having spied a beautiful woman, will scheme to have a secret assignation with her, and once entangled in love, will desire further to possess her through the bonds of matrimony. Strange things will therefore occur and unsavoury plots will arise, which, in spite of facilitating some momentary enjoyment, will soon bring stigma to the woman's family, and eventually, when caught in adultery, will cause his own death without even a burial place.

"Story-teller," you may argue, "according to what you have said, how could you explain the fact that someone starts with an illicit liaison but receives a positive result? And how could you account for the phenomenon that someone engages in seduction yet escapes without punishment? Why do these people not all die a disgraceful death?"

Gentle reader, there is something of which you may perhaps be unaware. Things as trivial as the mouthful of water you drink and the morsel of food you eat are all predestined. Country flowers and wild grasses[7] would not offer themselves to your touch but for your predestined lot, to say nothing of the formal union between you and your wife. With the assistance of co-operative karma from a previous life, an adulterer may work out a happy marriage, and if previous karma has been repaid, even a ravisher is able to escape alive. That is why in this world we find such fortunate men as you have just mentioned, and they are evidently different from those who cling to their lust with tenacity, only to have themselves destroyed at last.

Now I shall tell you the story of how a man, disguised as a woman, engaged in seduction and met his untimely death.

In the town of Suzhou prefecture there lived a distinguished squire who owned an extremely large manor. Located right next to his manor was the Nunnery of Merits and Virtues which the squire had built. Five young nuns lived there, and the most outstanding of them was the nun by the surname of Wang. Nun Wang, who came from a different area, was not only beautiful but romantically inclined. Though the youngest, about the age of twenty, she, on the recommendation of the squire, had been commissioned to the convent management.

Indeed, Nun Wang was exceptionally competent. First, she was very fluent in her speech and could discourse on any topic, whether it was about yellow and white[8] or east and west. Visiting official households was her expertise, and never had she failed to carry out a congenial conversation with their womenfolk. Secondly, she was suave, self-effacing, and perceptive, capable of adapting herself to others and playing up to them. Thirdly, she was well-versed in writing and dexterous at embroidery.

Because of her remarkable mastery of composition and needle-work, the females of wealthy households would engage her to tutor them in their homes, or would go to the nunnery to receive her instruction and guidance. These students aside, she had a daily stream of patrons who came either to pray for the conception of a son or to perform Buddhist rites for protecting themselves from misfortune. Sometimes she would go door-to-door herself, inviting the women she called upon, whether they were of rich families or from villages, to gather together at her nunnery.

The sanctuary, with seventeen meditation rooms all furnished with beds and bedclothes, was large enough to provide visitor accommodations, and not a single day passed that did not see women coming and going. Some of them would stay overnight or for several days on end, while others, after their first visit, would never return again. No male dared to enter the nunnery, for the squire had posted a placard prohibiting any men from amusing themselves within the premises of the holy place. Even members of the squire's own family, for fear of arousing suspicion and offending the Buddha, would not bother their wives and daughters while they were inside the chapel. Such heedful cautiousness helped the nunnery attract more and more female pilgrims.

Let us have no more of this tedious explanation. Our story goes that a judicial officer of Changzhou sub-prefecture, whose surname was Yuan, was accompanying an Investigating Censor from the Censorate[9] on his inspection tour. When they arrived in Suzhou, the Censor decided to look into the performance of the prefectural administration, and this left his colleague with no choice but to seek spacious lodgings for himself due to the hot weather and the inconvenience of being too close to his superior during his investigation. With the arrangement made by the district yamen, the judicial officer then moved into the manor of the distinguished squire.

One day at dusk, the judicial officer was ambling in the garden when he saw a small tower. Inspired by the thought that the height of the building would enable him to survey the entire neighbourhood, he ascended the stairs, and after having reached the top floor, found himself inside a room, which, judging from the dust and cobwebs everywhere, had obviously seen no visitors for a long time. But with a gentle breeze blowing in from the outside, it was a pleasant spot to enjoy the evening's coolness. This was exactly what the judicial officer was looking for, and he stood before the window, a long while passing unnoticed.

Looking to one side, he found that at a little distance there was another small storeyed building, inside which some five young women seemed to be cavorting with a beautiful nun. He shrank back at once so as not to be seen by them, and then carefully peeked out from behind the window. The nun was now hugging one of her companions, and shortly afterwards, turned to another one. Putting her arm around her shoulders, she pressed her face to hers, and kissed her on the lips.

"Strange!" the judicial officer murmured after having watched for some time, shaking his head. "If she really is a nun, why does she behave in such a manner? There must be something dubious about this."

Full of suspicion, he summoned a functionary the next day.

"Do you know the temple here and what name it goes by?" he inquired.

"That is the Nunnery of Merits and Virtues and it belongs to the squire," the functionary replied.

"Who lives there, monks or nuns?" the judicial officer asked.

"Only five nuns," said the functionary.

"Are there any penitents who go there to see monks?" asked the judicial officer.

"This nunnery is under the surveillance of the squire," said the functionary. "No man dares to enter it, not to mention monks. Most of the patrons are women from official households in the local area and they visit it every day."

The judicial officer felt rather puzzled. When the district magistrate arrived for a courtesy call, he told the magistrate about what he had seen the previous evening, and the latter suggested that he take some constables to raid the nunnery. Taking his advice, the judicial officer set out in his sedan at once. After having the cloister besieged on all sides, he entered. But he found, as the nuns came hurrying out to greet him, that there were only four and the one he had seen the previous day was not present.

"So far as I know," he spoke, "five nuns live in this temple. Why is one missing?"

"Our supervisor happens to be out," they said.

"You have a small tower," the judicial officer went on. "I wonder how I can enter?"

They all prevaricated. "Our premises contain only a few structures," they said, "and we know nothing about the small tower you are referring to."

"Nonsense!" the judicial officer shouted.

But when he searched the entire convent, not even neglecting the sleeping chambers, he could not find the entrance to that building.

"That is strange!" he said to himself.

He ordered a novice taken into a room and there he asked her some random questions. After she was released, the other three nuns were brought in for interrogation.

"You dare deceive me!" he yelled in a wrathful voice. "The novice has just confessed to me that you have a storeyed building and yet you have the nerve to bluff about it! You cunning and wicked liars! I shall have the lictor put a finger squeezer on you all!"

The nuns, out of fright, hastened to confess. "Yes, we do have a storeyed building, and you may enter it through the door hidden by wallpaper behind the bed."

"Such being the case, why did you just now lie to me?" the judicial officer demanded.

"We would have told you the truth," said the nuns, "but for some ladies and maidens being inside."

The judicial officer ordered them to open the secret door, and bringing with him four or five constables, went in. They passed through a zigzag tunnel, and on reaching the stairs, clearly heard laughter and voices overhead. They came to a stop.

"You go up!" said the judicial officer to his assistants. "If you find the nun there, arrest her and bring her downstairs!"

Obeying his order, the constables charged up at once. Three women and two young girls were sitting at a table drinking with a nun, and they were so shocked at the sight of the constables that they scattered in all directions trying to conceal themselves. Together the constables rushed forward, and with little trouble, laid their hands on the arms and legs of the delicate nun and dragged her roughly downstairs. After determining from her where she slept, the judicial officer had her room searched immediately. Nineteen silk damask handkerchiefs were ferreted out, each having hymenal blood on it. Also found was a register that recorded the dates and the names of the women who had sojourned in the nunnery overnight. Details were provided in smaller characters, such as:

"So and so first came on a certain day."
"So and so came upon recommendation."
"So and so had hymenal blood."
"So and so had no hymenal blood."

The judicial officer, after reading the register, became so furious that his hair nearly stood on end. He ordered all the nuns arrested and taken to the yamen. The female clients were all struck dumb with what was happening to the nuns. Not knowing the real cause of their arrest, they scurried out of the temple, hired sedans, and rushed back home.

Upon his return to the office, the judicial officer had the nuns put to torture. However, they maintained that they had not fallen foul of the law. Their refusal to reveal the truth left him with no recourse but to summon a midwife to make a physical examination of each of the suspects. When he was informed that they were indeed female, he found himself at his wit's end about coping with the matter.

He brooded: "If this is indeed the case, how can we account for the handkerchiefs and the register?"

He called the midwife to a private room and asked her in a low voice, "Are you sure that you saw nothing suspicious?"

"Well, only the younger nun is a little different from ordinary women," she replied. "But I saw no male endowment on her."

In a flash, the judicial officer was enlightened. "I have heard of the art of penis contraction," he said to himself. "That nun, physically different, must in fact be a male. I know of a method that can reveal her true colours."

He instructed the midwife to smear oil on the nun's privates and then to let a dog lick them. Allured by the fragrant odour, the dog thrust out its long tongue and began to lick her. A dog's tongue is very hot; its continuous lapping rendered the young woman intolerably itchy. As shivers ran through her body, her "rod," thick and stiff, suddenly popped out from below, making the midwife and the other four nuns cover their faces in no time.[10]

The judicial officer flew into a rage.

"You sly ruffian!" he roared. "Even the death penalty would be too good for you!"

In order to get a confession, he ordered the lictor to beat him forty strokes with the heavy bamboo and apply the squeezers. Under the torture, the false nun finally confessed:

"Originally I was a local itinerant monk and have looked feminine ever since my childhood. In a deserted place I learned from my master how to obtain female essence and how to contract my penis, the skills of which enabled me to sleep with ten women in a single night. I practised the disciplines of the White Lotus Cult[11] and often involved myself in sexual orgies.

"When I first arrived at this convent for a visit, all the nuns, out of hospitality, invited me to stay. I told them that I could transform myself into a female by withdrawing my genitals, and was thereafter entrusted with the supervision of the nunnery. Most of the supplicants I received were ladies and maidens from gentry families, and when they came, I would entice them to that building to share my sleeping accommodations. They had no idea that I was a man until after I had let out my contracted object. Since their passions had been aroused, they were usually willing to allow me, of their own accord, to make love to them. Some of them were principled. Using lustful spells, however, I could mesmerize them and then have coitus with them all the same. I would not let them rise until I had reached completion. That is why some visitors, after their first overnight stay, would never come back again. The majority, however, consented to share my bed willingly and some even wished to continue our liaisons forever. Never did I anticipate that my true gender would be exposed by Your Honour. I plead guilty."

He was in the midst of his confession when the squire, who had been advised by his wife and daughters that "our nuns have been taken to the yamen," had someone submit a letter on his behalf pleading for clemency. Infuriated, the judicial officer disdained to even pen a reply. He simply wrapped up the handkerchiefs and the register in a packet and had them sent to him. When the squire saw the things, he felt such deep shame that he gave up his efforts to defend his protégées. The judicial officer then wrote the following verdict:

> According to our investigation, the criminal Wang has been found to be a sly fugitive from the area of Three Wus.[12] He advocated the White Lotus Cult for the purpose of deceiving simple believers and donned red makeup with the intention of passing himself off as a female. He was previously a monk studying under a shaman-sorcerer, and later he metamorphosed himself into a Boddhisattva and secreted pretty women in his golden house. When he meditated in bed, moving his jade-like fingers and pressing his tender hands together, who could tell whether he was a friar or a novice? As he lay on an embroidered couch with his golden lotus removed, who knew if he was a man or a woman? A stork perches on the nest of a phoenix and it is likely that they will have congress; as a snake slithers into the dragon's cave, no one is able to prevent them from doing the work of clouds and rain. The bright moon, unknowing, shed its light on the pale boudoir, and as a result, revealed that the celibate was not alone. The clear breeze unintentionally blew into the rich family, and consequently, showed that the ascetic had company. Destroy his abode and burn his books! Eradicate all traces of him forever! Lay open his heart and gouge out his eyes! Let them be compensation for his crime![13]

163

With the proclamation having thus been made, he ordered the lictor to subject the convict to various instruments of torture. As fragile as pastry dough, the monk was not able to bear the pain and died on the spot. The other four nuns, after receiving thirty strokes each, were all officially sold. The nunnery was then demolished and the corpse of the monk was thrown into its Guanyin Pond.

When the news spread, people went in swarms to the nunnery to take a look at him. The sight of the monk's unusually large penis, seven or eight inches in length like that of a donkey, made them laugh up their sleeves. "No wonder women were so crazed for him!" they remarked. Upon hearing of his death, several of the ladies who had been intimate with him hanged themselves.

This monk, having indulged his seductive ways for years, died without even a burial place. If he had considered that this was not an appropriate way to live his life and had repented earlier and changed his mind, he might perhaps have chosen to lead a secular life. He might then have taken a wife and lived to a ripe old age. In this way, he might have become one of those fortunate men in the category of "seducers who escape without being punished," as you have mentioned.

But ordinarily, men cannot control themselves once they have gone so far. Having had one taste, they will, against their good conscience, follow the same pattern until they ruin themselves. There is hardly a single one among them who does not perish in the end. Indeed:

> Good will be rewarded with good and evil with evil,
> Sooner or later each will receive what he deserves.

So much for the story of the disguised monk. Let me now relate to you the tale of a young woman who camouflaged herself as a monk, yet had a happy outcome.

During the Hongxi reign,[14] there lived outside the Eastern Gate of the capital of Huzhou prefecture a certain Yang family. The master of the house had long been dead and the mother lived alone with her son and daughter. The daughter, eleven or twelve years old, was as beautiful as a flower and was of great intelligence. Sad to say, however, she had suffered indispositions from her early childhood. Mother Yang, who was in a state of constant worry for her daughter's health, was willing to do anything as long as it would improve her condition.

One day, mother and daughter were embroidering together when they saw a nun coming to visit them. Mother Yang rose cheerfully to receive her, and found that she was the abbess of the Green Duckweed Nunnery in Hangzhou. The nun, in fact, was a glib talker, and as an advocate of sexual enjoyment, was frequently involved in indecent activities with the co-operation of her two young novices. She was a family friend of the Yangs and called on them regularly. On that day she was making a special trip to pay a visit to Mother Yang, bringing for her a small packet of southern dates, a bottle of autumn tea, a plate of almonds, and a plate of walnuts.

After a brief chat, she set her eyes on the daughter. What did she look like?

> Lithe and graceful in bearing,
> And with a figure well-formed and charming;

As white as a pear flower with raindrops,
And as tender as a peach bud in gentle wind.
At light pace she tripped about,
Revealing under her skirt her new bamboo sprouts.[15]
With timidity she opened her tiny red mouth,
Looking as if she wished to speak out.
Should Feng Zhi[16] be able to contain his desire,
Lu nan[17] would surely be excited and run wild.

165

"How old is she?" the nun asked, after having examined the girl closely.

"Twelve," Mother Yang replied. "She is clever and can do all kinds of work. It's just that she is delicate and often falls prey to this illness or to that disease, making me feel rather worried. How I wish I could take her illness upon myself!"

"Ma'am, have you prayed to the Buddhas and the Bodhisattvas to seek their help?" asked the nun.

Mother Yang sighed.

"What haven't I tried?" she said. "But my prayers have not been much consolation to her, nor have been my supplications to Heaven. Is it that some unlucky star has intruded into her life? And is there some way that we can get rid of it?"

"It must have come with her birth," said the nun. "Could you please tell me her eight characters[18] so that I might foretell her future?"

Mother Yang was happily surprised. "I didn't know that you had the ability to foretell the future!" She then told her the hour, date, month, and year of her daughter's birth.

The nun pretended to make calculations for some while.

"The fate of your daughter portends well," she claimed, "if she lives apart from you."

"I love her and cannot bear to part with her," said the mother. "But since I wish her to grow up healthy and sound, I am afraid I must do as you suggest. The only way for her to live away from me is to find a family that will consent to adopt her as their own child. This task is certainly not easy and cannot be accomplished in a short period of time."

"Has your daughter ever accepted her betrothal present?" the nun asked.

"Not yet," replied Mother Yang.

"It is the fate of your daughter to live by herself," the nun told her. "Engagement can only lead to further deterioration of her health. My prediction tallies with her destiny, and if she does as I suggest, not only will her health be good, but her life-span will be extended, too. But given your unwillingness to separate from her, I am reluctant to make this point clearer to you."

"I will release her provided it is really good for her health," Mother Yang expressed her partial agreement.

"Good!" The nun seized the opportunity quickly. "Then I would suggest that you permit her to join the Buddhist order. When she is far removed from the turmoil of the world, she will be able to avert disaster, and good fortune will therefore befall her. This is the best solution for her."

"Your advice is most sensible and I thank the Buddha for your suggestion," Mother Yang said. "Although I am very unwilling to give her up, the prospect of serious illness and the loss of her life leave me with no choice. Since you know me, thanks to our lot in previous incarnations, I wonder if you could favour us by accepting my little daughter as your disciple?"

"Your daughter is a star of felicity," said the nun. "I would make a wager that even the Buddha and the Boddhisattvas would rejoice in her membership in our sanctuary. I would certainly, if it were not for my own incompetence, take her as my disciple, and that would be the greatest honour for me. But to be frank with you, I fear I am not worthy of the responsibility."

"You are being too modest!" said Mother Yang. "I wish only that you devote some of your time to her care. I can then set my mind at rest."

"Ma'am, I hope you are not doubting me!" said the nun. "Your daughter is so precious a girl, how would I dare to neglect her? Although our humble nunnery is not wealthy, owing to the patronage of our clients, we are not short of food and clothing. So you needn't worry about these things."

"Then," said Mother Yang, "shall I just select a date and send her to your place?"

Tears flowed down from her face as she looked through the calendar. The nun soothed her, and the date was finally set. Mother Yang invited her guest to stay for two days, then hired a boat and bade her daughter go to the temple with the nun. Mother and daughter cried on each other's shoulders as they parted. Finally, the daughter said farewell to her mother, and left with the abbess for her new home, where she was introduced to the other nuns and formally accepted the prioress as her mentor. On a carefully chosen day she took her tonsure and was baptized Jingguan as her religious name. From that day onward, the daughter of the Yangs began a new life as a nun in the Green Duckweed Nunnery. Who should bear the blame for this folly but her own mother?

Although her body is weak and frail,
Wuchang[19] has no right to drag her away.
Sending her to the Gateway of the Void
Simply leaves her to decide her own fate.

Do you know why the nun exhorted Mother Yang to enrol her daughter in the convent? It was because she relied on her young beautiful novices, who were educated to work in the manner of prostitutes, to engage in illicit business for her. Since the daughter of the Yangs was attractive and her mother only wished her to grow up in good health, the nun had been confident that she would be able to talk the woman into taking her advice. Fortune-telling was no more than a charade by which to lure the mother to make a wrong decision.

The daughter of the Yangs was only twelve years old at that time and had not yet attained the age of puberty. That was why she had made no objection to her mother's decision. Had she been only a few years older, she would probably have chosen death rather than obey her.

After her ordination, Jingguan would, sometimes with the abbess and sometimes by herself, return home to see her mother. She made her visit several times each year. Previously the mother had doted immensely upon her daughter, and her frequent illnesses used to fill her with great anxiety and gloom. Now she had been away. She might still be sick from time to time, yet being away from home, she saved her mother a great deal of anxiety. Since her regular visits and healthier looks brought her mother much comfort, Jingguan never again mentioned the recurrence of her old chronic disease, lest her mother be disturbed. This made her mother feel vindicated that she was right to consign her daughter to a monastic life in a Buddhist temple. She was therefore no longer worried about her daughter's health.

Our story forks at this point.

In Huzhou, there lived on Yellow Sand Street a licentiate whose double-character surname was Wenren[20] and whose personal name was Jia. Originally a native of Shaoxing, Wenren moved with his family to Huzhou because his grandfather was employed as a private tutor for a household in Wucheng county. Being a seventeen-year-old, he resembled Pan An[21] and was as talented as Zijian.[22] He lived with his forty-year-old mother and had yet to marry due to his straitened family circumstances.

His handsome features, refined and charismatic, as well as his knowledge and experience, won him popularity, and none of his friends failed to respect him. They loved him so much that they were often willing to give him financial aid. Whenever they hosted a party or embarked on an excursion,

Wenren would invariably be among those invited. His absence from their gatherings would greatly disappoint them.

One day, in the middle of the first month (February) when the plum-flowers were in bloom, a friend of Wenren, having hired a boat, invited him to go touring with him. Their plan was to find some amusement in Hangzhou and then to stop by the Western Brook to enjoy the vewing of plum blossoms. After taking leave of his mother who had agreed to his travel, Wenren set off with his friend. It took them only a day to reach their destination.

"Perhaps," his friend suggested, "we should first see the plum-flowers at the Western Brook, and tomorrow we can visit the town." He then bade the boatman to go to the Western Brook, and an hour later they arrived.

The boat had hardly come to anchor when Wenren and his friend disembarked. They climbed the bank, followed by their servants who were carrying the containers of wine on their shoulders.

After about a quarter of a mile, they came upon a grove, its fir trees being so large that no one could get his arms around them. Behind the woods, there loomed a hard-to-see temple, surrounded by a painted wall. Its south-facing double gate was slightly open, and a brook flowed at its front. Deeply fascinated by this tranquil site, they tarried, surveying the scene at leisure. Since the gate was not entirely closed, they could see somebody inside spying on them.

"What a serene temple!" exclaimed Wenren's friend. "Do you think we should enter to ask for a cup of tea?"

"We'd better take advantage of the daylight to enjoy the plum-blossoms first," said Wenren. "On our return, we should have time to drop in here."

"Okay!" his friend agreed.

They strode along, and upon reaching the retreat, were captivated by its beautiful vista.

> Shreds of silver rain fall everywhere,
> And shards of jade are piled layer on layer.
> Gentle breezes waft a fragrant smell,
> More delightful than Jia Wu's aromatic water.[23]
> The whiteness is so luminescent in the sunlight,
> Even Xishi's[24] garments couldn't be that bright.
> With dragon-like trunks defying ice and frost,
> The romantic youths the uneven shadows invite.
> A minstrel can't stop his singing and writing,
> And a scholar feels loath to quit his drinking.

After disporting themselves for a while, they directed their servants to bring them the wine jugs. They drank until it was late and there was little wine left. Rather tipsy, they headed back to their boat.

As the darkness grew, they felt the need to hasten and had no time to stop at the temple. They passed the night on their boat and disembarked the next morning at the Pine Wood Dock. But let us say no more of this.

Our story goes that the temple Wenren and his friend had seen was none other than the Green Duckweed Nunnery, the place where the daughter of the Yangs was leading her monastic life. By that time Jingguan had turned sixteen and had grown into a peerless beauty, demure and graceful. Her charming looks were a great allurement to male visitors, who would either fix their gaze upon her or tease her provocatively. While her fellow nuns, wreathed in smiles, would make up to those libertines and receive them with flirtaciousness, Jingguan would remain aloof, never joining them in their frivolity. She, not tempted at all by what they did, would do no more than just look on impassively. Even their erotic activities, which she detected from time to time, were not bewitching to her, and she would usually pretend that she saw nothing at all. Most of the time she simply shut herself in her own room, practising meditation, reading the classics, or writing poems. Rarely did she go out.

It so happened that on the very day Wenren and his friend were looking around, she came out to take a stroll. Looking through the opening of the gate, she saw a remarkably refined youth whose appearance differed greatly from the ordinary men of the world she had seen. She stared at him until she obtained a close look. Still, this was not sufficient. How she wished, on their departure, that she could follow them to take one more look!

She languished, and returned to her room, feeling dejected. "He is so beautiful, looking as if he were an immortal descended from Heaven," she thought. "If I could make his acquaintance and marry him, I am sure we would be able to live a happy life. What a mistake I have made in taking the holy orders!" She sighed, tears welling into her eyes. Truly:

> The mute who eats a rhizome of goldthread
> Cannot complain to others about its bitterness.

Gentle reader take note. Men and women who wish to become a monk or a nun must reach the stage in which the four elements are not present.[25] That is to say, they must purge their desires and be down-to-earth in their determination to join the Buddhist clergy. Only when they are cleansed and with no desires, and are resolute to cultivate themselves day and night in earnest according to the religious doctrines, will they succeed in attaining enlightenment. Nowadays it is too often the practice that parents rashly send their young children into the gateway of the void, little realizing that it is easy to begin but difficult to persist, especially when their children have grown up and experienced the awakening of love. After they have tasted sexual passions, even though they may still be able to contain themselves, they will feel that it is religious obligation that forces them to do so. That is the reason why those who loath to resign themselves to the rules and regulations would often go so far as to desecrate the meditation rooms and Buddha-halls. Indeed, this is precisely the meaning of a proverb: "You begin with a search for happiness, yet finish enmeshed in crime." So, pray, take my advice: Do not send your sons and daughters on that path!

Let us have no more of this digression. Our story resumes that another four months had passed after Wenren returned home from Hangzhou. That year the Provincial Examination was to be held,[26] and the Touring Provincial Commissioner for Education[27] had recommended Wenren as the highest qualified candidate. Though it now was the sixth month, the weather had not yet turned hot. Wenren packed his belongings and got ready to leave for Hangzhou, where his aunt, the widow of the late Secretary Huang,[28] lived. He planned to stay at her manor and sequester himself in a quiet room to concentrate on his studies. The date of departure set, Wenren received some money for traveling from his friends. After having made arrangements for his mother, he hired a boat and set off, bringing with him a bag of books and his page Ah Si.

As they were passing through the Eastern Gate, a young monk on the bank called out to them with a distinct Huzhou accent, "Is this boat going to Hangzhou?"

"Yes, indeed," answered the boatman. "I am taking a gentleman to the city for the examination."

"Could you take me along as well?" the monk inquired. "I will pay the fare."

"What, sir, is the purpose of your journey?" asked the boatman.

"I am a priest at the Soul-Veiled Monastery,"[29] said the monk. "I returned here to visit my family and am now going back."

"I can't make this decision myself," said the boatman. "I must ask the gentleman."

Ah Si, having heard their conversation, popped his head out from the prow. "You pesky bald donkey!" he shouted. "My master is on his way to take the Provincial Examination and wishes a smooth beginning, not an unexpected baldhead like you who can bring him nothing but bad luck.

If you want to go, then just go with us, or I shall pour a pot of water over you to clean up your 'cock!'"[30]

Do you know the joke about this "cock" pun? In the past people mocking monks said, "The head of a monk is not a head for governing but a head to subvert the government!" *Luan* (subvert) and *luan* (cock) are homophones. Wenren had once used this pun as a swearword while poking fun at his friends, and that was how Ah Si had picked it up. He was now using it to cast aspersions on the monk.

"I was just inquiring and had no intention of offending you," said the monk. "Why shout and yell at me like this?"

At this moment Wenren pushed open the window.[31] Before his eyes appeared a comely and handsome young priest. "He said he was from the Soul-Veiled Monastery," Wenren reflected. "That monastery is situated in a scenic setting, surrounded by lofty mountains and limpid waters. If I allow him on our boat, I shall be able to make his acquaintance, and later on may perhaps put up in that temple."

"Don't be impolite!" he chided his servant. "Let this priest board if he wishes to go to Hangzhou with us."

Fate, it seemed, came to his assistance. The boatman had no sooner received approval than he managed to drag the boat to the shore. The monk got on the boat, and was greatly taken aback as he caught sight of Wenren. He stared at him for a while.

"I have never seen such a beautiful monk before," thought Wenren. "He appears so effeminate that I nearly mistook him for a girl. If he were indeed a female, what a beauty he would be! What a pity that he is a man!"

After they had exchanged greetings with each other, Wenren led the monk into the cabin. The boat, now with the aid of a favourable wind, proceeded very fast with its sail unfurled, as if it were flying. Inside the cabin Wenren and the monk took their seats. They asked each other's name and found that they both came from the same area and spoke the same local dialect. The conversation, therefore, became quite congenial. The monk, with his alluring eyes, looked Wenren up and down. From the way he spoke, Wenren could tell that he was a cultivated youth rather than a rustic friar.

The intense heat of the summer was oppressive, and Wenren suggested to his companion that he remove his gown if he wished.

"Never mind," said the monk. "I am feeling fine." Then he added, "Sir, if you would be more comfortable without your clothes, please feel free."

They dined as evening descended. After the meal, Wenren politely proposed to the monk that he bathe first, but the monk declined. Wenren then went to take his own bath. Feeling tired, he then tumbled into bed immediately. As Ah Si retired on the prow and both the master and the servant drifted down the tides of sleep, the monk blew out the light, undressed, and crawled into Wenren's bed to sleep. However, he was unable to fall asleep. He tossed and turned and sighed frequently. As soon as Wenren was in a sound slumber, he sat up quietly, and with his hand, began to feel Wenren's body. Who would have thought that the place he was touching was none other than where Wenren's erect object was located. He nudged at it until his bedmate woke up. Perceiving him straighten his back, the monk quickly removed his hand and lay down beside him.

In fact, Wenren had been aware of what was being done to him. "I had no idea that this monk would be such a lecher!" he thought. "As so handsome a youth, he must have fallen prey to his master's lust and must have experienced the ways of male love before. I might as well do it with him! Why not have a try, with such delicious meat readily displayed before my mouth?"

Wenren, after all, was a young man vulnerable to temptations. He rolled over to the other side of the bed, and with his face pressed against the monk's, stretched out his hand to caress him. The monk, whose body was curled up, made no sound at all, pretending that he was unconscious. Wenren then let his hand fondle its way down until it reached the monk's breasts, which felt like two soft buns.

"He is not fat," thought Wenren. "How does he possess such buxom tits?"

As he moved downward to his rear-courtyard flower,[32] the monk, startled, instantly turned over to lie on his back, forcing Wenren to make a frontal assault on him. Wenren felt with his hand all the way to the monk's crotch, and found that there was no male organ and that in its place was only a bun-shaped mound. This time it was he who was taken aback.

"Astonishing!" he burst out.

After a pause he asked, "What on earth are you? Tell me! I want you to tell me the truth!"

"Please don't shout, sir," the monk implored. "To tell you the truth, I am a nun, and I disguised myself as a monk simply to avoid unwanted solicitations on the road."

"Well, well," said Wenren, "this being the case, it means that we are destined to sleep together. Sure enough, I won't let you go tonight." Not allowing himself further questioning, he rolled atop her at once.

"Sir, I beg you to have mercy," the nun entreated. "I am still a virgin with my maidenhead intact. Please treat me gently."

Inflamed beyond control, Wenren pulled her thighs apart and thrust hard into her, paying no heed to her imploring. But for this tender flower of a girl, the discomfort was indeed too great. At the height of his passion, Wenren hurriedly applied some spittle to her vulva, yet it still took her a while to be able to engulf him completely. She clenched her teeth enduring the pain, and before long the clouds dispersed and the rain came down.[33]

"I was so lucky to meet you," said Wenren. "If this is not a dream, I would like you to inform me of your residence so I may contact you later."

"I am the daughter of the Yangs," she told him, "and my family live right outside the Eastern Gate of the capital of Huzhou. It was my mother's fault that I entered the Buddhist order, and now I live in the Green Duckweed Nunnery at the Western Brook, where everyone calls me Jingguan. Since my enrollment in the nunnery, I have seen only rustic visitors or villagers not worth a second look. In the first month of this year when I was strolling in the courtyard of our convent, I happened to catch a glimpse of you standing outside the wall looking around. You appeared so handsome that I felt I had fallen for you at first sight. I have been pining for you ever since and today fortune so favoured me that I was able not only to meet you once again but to share your bed in bliss! Since this was exactly what I wished to occur, I submitted to you without rejection. But I am not a licentious nun. I hope that you won't treat me as a companion good only for a momentary encounter. I entreat you, sir, to consider taking me as your spouse."

"Are your father and grandfather still living?" Wenren asked.

"My father has long been dead," she replied, "but my mother is still alive, and she lives with my elder brother. It was she that I was visiting yesterday, and you may imagine how shocked I was to meet you again. Sir, may I inquire as to your marital status?"

"I haven't yet married," Wenren replied. "It was really a stroke of luck to make your acquaintance, a beautiful girl of my age! I think we are a good match; besides, you are the daughter of a gentry family in my own prefecture, and for this reason alone, I have the duty to disengage you from the nunnery. We must have a thorough discussion to plan for our future."

"I have offered you my body, so you know I won't be of two minds," said Jingguan. "But today we are busy and probably can't conceive a method for my escape. Our small nunnery is not far from the city and is very peaceful. You might wish to lodge there first to make preparations for the examination, and meals will be provided, at no cost to you, by our workers. In this way we shall be able to see each other every day, and later, when a chance presents itself, we may proceed to further steps. What do you think?"

"Your idea seems good," said Wenren. "But I am afraid that the other nuns might raise objections."

"We have but a single matron," Jingguan told him. "She is nearly forty years old and very lecherous. Two of my fellow nuns, about twenty, also lack decency, and I have seen them in carnal behaviour with male visitors. But none of their associates were as handsome as you are and I have no doubt that they will be smitten once they lay their eyes upon you. You might make their acquaintances first so that later on you will be able to take advantage of it. They will be only too happy to have you stay at our nunnery; it's almost impossible that they will drive you out."

Wenren was excited. "You are right!" he said. "In that case, I shall send my servant back home when we reach the Pine Wood Dock tomorrow morning, and shall accompany you to your nunnery." With this, he embraced her. As they became aroused, they made love again. Truly:

> Never in his life has he entered a flowery mine,[34]
> Once in there he feels thrilled right to his spine.
> Is he now in a dream or is he wide awake?
> In the dark he gazes wide-eyed for a long time.

After they had finished, they heard morning roosters crowing loudly. Jingguan, fearful of discovery, quickly arose and donned her clothes. Before long, the boatman also arose, and started to sail his vessel. Ah Si was the last one to tumble out of bed. He prepared water for his master and combed his hair for him. Then they ate breakfast together. The boat glided through the pass before it became too crowded.

"Where shall we stop?" Ah Si inquired. "We'd better ask permission from the Huangs for a place to stay."

"Don't be so anxious!" said Wenren. "This young priest has informed me that his monastery has some unoccupied rooms, and we are now going to the Pine Wood Dock."

Upon their arrival, Wenren declared that he and the "monk" would travel on to the Soul-Veiled Monastery. He hired a porter to convey the baggage, and then instructed Ah Si: "You go back home with the boat and tell the Serene Lady[35] that I am fine and she needn't worry herself. I will stay at this priest's temple studying until the examination is over.

Then I will return home. It is not necessary for her to dispatch somebody to inquire after me."

As soon as Ah Si had left, Wenren hired two sedan-chairs to take himself and the "monk" to the Green Duckweed Nunnery. The porter, who had beforehand been directed where to go, reached the nunnery about the same time as they did. Wenren paid him and the sedan carriers, and then let Jingguan usher him into the courtyard.

"This gentleman," Jingguan announced, "wishes to take lodging at our convent to prepare for the Provincial Examination."

All the nuns grinned the moment they saw Wenren, greeting him warmly. The more they observed of him, the more fascinating he seemed. They invited him to tea with eagerness, and then cleaned a room for him and helped him put away his baggage. After supper, Wenren took a bath, and it goes without saying that the abbess was the first one to claim the privilege of amorous delights. Her lovemaking with him, as enthusiastic as one can imagine, lasted for the whole night.

After that first night, the rivalry between the two young novices to be Wenren's bedmate began, and they took turns accompanying him at night. Jingguan ignroed their rivalry, letting them indulge their enjoyment as much as they desired. They were, of course, very grateful to her.

Having spent a month of intemperance at the nunnery, Wenren finally collapsed, no longer able to perform in sexual bouts. The nuns, with ginseng soup and *xiangru* juice,[36] nourished him, and with lychee and lotus seeds, fed him, trying almost everything that was good for his recovery. Wenren had never before enjoyed such solicitous treatment.

Time passed quickly. Soon the Thread-needle Day[37] had gone and the Ullambhana Festival[38] on the fifteenth of the seventh month was approaching. On that day, feasts were to be prepared in each household for the delivery of spirits, and it had long been a tradition in Hangzhou that religious services would be commissioned and the lakeshore would be decorated with lanterns.

As early as the twelfth day of the seventh month, a wealthy family had somebody send for the abbess, requesting from her the recitation of sutras and the performance of religious rites for them. The abbess agreed.

"Since we are going to that house," the two novices said, "and will be there for three days from the thirteenth to the fifteenth, someone should remain here to take care of Mr. Wenren. Really it would be lucky to spend time alone with him!"

They both wished to stay. Jingguan just kept silent.

"For a sacrosanct activity of this kind, I must go in person," said the abbess. "Since it was Jingguan who introduced Mr. Wenren to our nunnery and since both of you have already spent much time with him, I suppose that it is fair to let Jingguan remain here to keep him company."

The two young nuns made no objection. "Well, the decision is reasonable," they said.

Jingguan, to be sure, was delighted. She saw them to the gate as they, in the company of their odd-job workers, bringing their packed religious accoutrements and suitcases departed for that household.

"This is not a place for us to stay," she said to Wenren when she came back. "Have you had any idea how to escape? In view of the approaching examination, it is especially important to you. If you are reluctant to leave, your failure in the examination might be inevitable, and you might even die from over-indulgence."

"I know," said Wenren. "I have consorted with them simply because I can't bear to part from you. You must be aware that I harbour no serious intentions toward them."

"My fondest wish," said Jingguan, "was to elope with you after we met on the boat. But if I had done so, the abbess would surely have tracked me down and that would have caused great trouble to my family. Now that you have been here for some time and they have all been intimate with you, I might flee with you by taking advantage of their absence. They are very afraid of having their scandal exposed, so I doubt they will dare to chase you."

"This matter needs to be handled cautiously," said Wenren. "I am a licentiate, and besides, my mother is still living. If you are to escape and hide in my house, she will certainly be surprised, and, as a result, may reject you. On the other hand, your nunnery may pursue you, and when their search involves the local yamen, my future career may be ruined. Moreover, what do you think would happen to you should you be caught? That's not the way the thing should be done. I suggest that you await the completion of the examination. If I pass, our betrothal won't be difficult at that time."

"Even your success in the Provincial Examination wouldn't give you sufficient reason for marrying a nun," Jingguan objected. "And what if you fail? How would you deal with that scenario? This is certainly not a good plan, believe me. Since my entry into the nunnery, I have often copied sutras and prayers for my patrons and have been handsomely paid. Now with about a hundred taels of silver I have saved, I can afford to leave this place and put up in some lodgings elsewhere until your examination is finished. Then we can go to your home together. What do you think?"

Wenren pondered her suggestion for a while.

"Not a bad idea," he said. "My widowed aunt of the Huang family lives in the city. As a devout Buddhist, she maintains a small nunnery in her residence where incense burns day and night. The old nun taking care of the incense and the like is my wet nurse. Perhaps I should tell my aunt about our situation, and then take you to her home nunnery and ask permission for my wet nurse to look after you. Since my aunt is the widow of an official, her place is safe from prying. You could live there, letting your hair grow, and after the examination, I will marry you with a proper ceremony. Isn't this a reasonable plan? Whether the result of the examination turns out to be good or bad, you can continue your sojourn there until your hair grows long enough for you to leave. Then we can go wherever we want."

177

"Marvellous!" Jingguan exclaimed. "Hasten now to your aunt's place, for in three days they will return and this plan will be foiled."

Wenren sped off to the city at once, and upon his arrival, went to see his aunt immediately. After an exchange of greetings, his aunt said, "I have long been expecting you. Why didn't you come until today? Is it that you have found other accommodation?"

"I should tell you, my dear aunt," said Wenren, "that an unforeseen event took place as I looked for accommodations. Today I came especially to seek your help."

"What is the matter?" she inquired.

Wenren then fabricated a story. "My late tutor, Master Yang had a daughter, and our acquaintance can be traced back to our childhood. Abducted by a nun, however, she later disappeared and nobody knew where she was. When I was trying to find a quiet place for myself, I, by pure chance, ran across her in the Green Duckweed Nunnery at the Western Brook. She has now grown into a beautiful woman. She is disenchanted with the monastic life, and due, perhaps to our predestined fate, even wishes to marry me. She is my former teacher's daughter and I feel obliged to disengage her from her current situation. But I have a problem: my examination is near, and with her tonsured head, I can't bring her to my home, nor does time permit me to sue the nunnery for their abduction. Since you, dear aunt, have a home chapel and my wet nurse is its caretaker, may I bring her here to stay for a short period of time? Even her discovery by her abbess would result in nothing serious, for she still is within the confines of a Buddhist temple. If nobody comes after her, I would like to marry her after the examination is over. I really wish your assistance in helping me save her."

"You have found yourself a Chen Miaochang,"[39] said his aunt, laughing, "so you came to me for help? In view of her as the daughter of your former teacher, I shouldn't blame you for your proposal. However, since you intend to marry her, it would be better for her not to stay in my nunnery. You are both young, and when you visit her, you might desecrate my holy place. There is, in my house, a quiet room, which, with some cleaning and tidying, may be good enough to accommodate her. She may live there letting her hair grow. I will bid my maid look after her and you may visit her as often as you wish. When there is no one around in the evening, you may ask your wet nurse to keep her company. Is this arrangement good enough for you?"

178

"My dear aunt, you have given us a second life!" Wenren exclaimed with gratitude. "I will fetch her here right away."

He took his leave and hired a sedan, bidding the bearers to take him to the Green Duckweed Nunnery. He had no sooner arrived than he told Jingguan what his aunt had arranged for them, and Jingguan was rapt with joy. She took all her personal belongings and packed them up immediately.

"At this time I want *only* you to hide away," said Wenren. "On their return, I shall turn back lest they become suspicious of me. My baggage is better left here for the time being."

"Are you not yet ready to sever your ties with them?" Jingguan was confused.

"This is entirely for your good," said Wenren, "and I have no intention of renewing my relations with them. All I desire is to assist you to escape without leaving the slightest trace, like a cicada sloughing its skin. If they learn that I am involved in your leaving, their litigation against me may be inevitable. Now there is not much time left for me. What if I am incriminated in a lawsuit, unable to take the examination?"

"I usually go unaccompanied when I visit my home," Jingguan said. "If they ask you, you may hem and haw, saying that you happened to be away and did not see me leave. They will therefore assume that I have returned home and will look no further into the matter. By the time they have discovered the truth, you will probably have finished the examination and we can elope together. Since you are not a resident of this prefecture, where can they search for you? In case you are caught, you need only say that their charges against you are all trumped up."

The two of them had thus conceived their scheme.

Jingguan mounted the sedan, and Wenren, after having closed the gate of the nunnery, followed behind her. Before long they arrived at the residence of his aunt, who, upon seeing Jingguan, found a girl of light complexion, her head cleanly-shaved and her cheeks resembling peach flowers, so delicate that even a puff of wind might break them. She was deeply impressed by her beauty.

"No wonder my nephew fancies you!" she said with a smile. "You may stay in the inner quarters where outsiders are not allowed to enter, so you don't have to worry about strangers."

She then turned to Wenren. "When you are here, you may share the room with her," she said. "But I strongly suggest that you find lodging for yourself somewhere else. They might pursue her; and if they do discover that she is with you, you shall be in trouble. Moreover, you are soon to take the examination and you must apply yourself to your studies."

"Yes, my dear aunt," Wenren answered. "I will ration my visits."

With permission for Jingguan to reside at the house, Wenren that night nestled in her chamber. The next morning he departed and went seeking a lodging for himself elsewhere. But no more of this.

Our story continues that three days later, the nuns of the Green Duckweed Nunnery returned after completing their religious services. To their surprise, they found that the gate was unlatched. They entered and saw not a soul.

"Where did they go?" they wondered. In fact, it was Wenren, not Jingguan, who was their concern. They quickly dashed to his room first, and felt much relieved at the sight of his baggage and books which still remained where they had been before. Jingguan, however, was nowhere to be seen. Her room was pristine, and they could not conjecture where she was. They were wondering what steps to take next when Wenren emerged.

"Here he is! Here he is!" they cried, with beaming smiles.

The abbess embraced Wenren at once, and without taking even a moment to inquire about Jingguan, said, "For three days we have been separate and I have been missing you badly! I can't wait any longer and must now drag you to my room for a bit of sport."

Ignoring the burning lust which was also obvious in her two young nuns, she slid into her chamber with Wenren and was serviced the best way she could ever dream of. She felt extremely satisfied.

"Since you have been here with Jingguan, do you know where she is?" the abbess asked after their lovemaking was complete.

"Yesterday I went to the city and was there for the whole day," said Wenren. "Because I was unable to return when it was late, I spent the night at a friend's house. I have just come back and was not even aware that she was missing."

"Perhaps she felt lonely in your absence and returned to Huzhou to see her mother," said the nuns. "Anyway, she had you all to herself for three days and must have enjoyed all kinds of pleasure. It should be our turn now; let's not be too concerned with her for the moment."

As they desired nothing but the pleasures of Wenren's company, none of them cared much about Jingguan's disappearance. Restlessness, however, was perceivable in their partner. Having consorted with them for three days or so, Wenren told them that it was time for him to leave and find a place closer to the venue of the examination. Without a reason to deter him, they had to let him go. Wenren packed up his baggage, feeling happy that he was finally able to free himself from their grip.

"Please make time to come back for a visit!" the nuns pleaded over and over.

Wenren promised he would, and then bade them farewell. Several more days elapsed and there was still no sign of Jingguan's return nor any tidings about her. Being very worried, the abbess dispatched someone to Mother Yang's to ascertain whether she was there, only to discover that she had not returned home recently.

The news was shocking. Fearing that the mother might come looking for her daughter, the abbess did not dare to uncover the truth and could only search for Jingguan in secret.

After his departure, Wenren never again came back for a visit, which could not but give rise to the abbess' suspicion. How she wished that she could question him! Since she had no inkling of where he lodged, there was nothing she could do but wait. Still she nursed the hope that he would return after the examination.

Now the three tests[40] were all over. The abbess bore the lapse of another few days, yet her hope of seeing him was once again dashed. In fact, Wenren did very well in the examination; after which, he proceeded immediately to his aunt's home to see Jingguan, completely oblivious to the women at the Green Duckweed Nunnery.

Now, finally, the nuns realized that there was no hope at all of reuniting with him.

"How lucky we were to meet such a heartless man!" the abbess and her two novices said peevishly. "It is not unlikely that he masterminded the abduction of Jingguan. How else can we account for her sudden disappearance?"

They would have charged him with kidnapping had they not feared that this might cause some calamity to themselves due to their involvement in the dubious relations. The possibility of going to the examination locale to search for him, or of locating where he lived in Huzhou so as to cause trouble at his home, was then carefully considered, but no agreement was reached, since they were, after all, women, unable to make a decisive move by themselves.

A neat coincidence occurred at this moment. While they were in the midst of discussion, there came an impatient knock on the gate.

"Is it that Wenren is back?" they wondered. Rushing out, they saw a large palanquin, along with three or four small sedans, stationed in front of the entrance.

"Her Ladyship has arrived!" the person who had been knocking on the gate announced.

The abbess, upon recognizing her guest as a patron from a southern district, hurriedly expressed a warm welcome. The lady descended from her carriage, and escorted by three or four maidservants who had quickly stepped down from their sedans before her, entered the convent. After a formal exchange of greetings with the abbess, the lady took her seat and was entertained with tea. She then dismissed her servants, bidding them return to the boat to await her. She told them that she would not be back with them until about noon.

Once they were gone, the lady went into the abbess's room and said, "My husband passed away three years ago and since then I haven't visited your establishment."

"What a great honour it is to have Your Ladyship revisiting our humble place," said the abbess. "I presume that now your mourning period is over and you have come here to burn incense?"

"Precisely," said the lady.

"The autumn weather is so pleasant that I hope you will find time to enjoy it," said the abbess.

The lady heaved a sigh. "I have not the spirit for that," she said.

The abbess could tell that her guest had something on her mind, so she deliberately spoke in a provocative way, "Your husband is gone and you must be suffering from loneliness?"

The lady rose to close the door.

"I have always regarded you as my confidante," she said, "and I hope you won't mind if I tell you of a private matter. You say I am lonely; in fact, I have been in widowhood for only three years! Why am I feeling so jittery? You nuns lead a celibate life, and I wonder how do you while away your time?"

"You think we are celibate?" the abbess laughed. "To be honest, we have patrons to keep us company from time to time, and that alleviates our boredom to a great extent. How could we otherwise endure such a desolate life?"

"Do you have company now?" the lady asked.

"Yes, I did have a lover recently, a young licentiate who lodged here to prepare for the Provincial Examination," the abbess told her. "He left only the other day but has not yet returned. We were just now discussing how to conduct a search for him when you arrived."

"You'd better forget him," said the lady, "for I have a proposition for you. Oblige me without reserve and I shall guarantee that you will be happy that you did so."

"What is this, then?" the abbess inquired.

The lady related the whole story. "A few days ago," she said, "when I went to pray in the Monastery of Luminosity and Felicity, I came upon an extremely handsome young monk, who, not yet tonsured, was in my sleeping chamber when I was preparing to retire. To be frank with you, I was aroused at the sight of him due to my years of abstinence. He served my tea, and as a lad in his teens, did not even try to keep a decent distance from me. His mouth was so soft and his tongue so tender and alluring, he seemed surpassingly lovely. I grew so infatuated that I lost control of myself. I dismissed my servants and swept him into my bed to test him on his potential for intercourse. Who would have thought that this errand boy was a veteran womanizer, whose object was even larger and harder than a grown male's. My mind was wholly fixed on him and I could not bear to part with him. After deliberation for the whole night, I decided to take him to my home. Given my status as a widow, however, I must guard against busybodies in order to protect my reputation. To live in a state of constant caution, dodging about here and there to avoid this person and that fellow, would prevent my attainment of happiness. For this reason, I came here to seek your help.

"I would like to bring him here and have his head shaved. Since his facial features are very delicate, it would be no problem to pass him off as a nun. My plan is this: I will first return to my home, and you may later bring him to my residence under the pretext of seeking sanctuary. I will let you live in my home convent to be in charge of the conversion of all the womenfolk in my household. With your assistance in this way, I shall be able to revel in real pleasure and even Heaven wouldn't know the truth. Now that I have explained my purpose in making this special trip, I hope you will not reject my request. If you agree to do what I ask, you will be entitled to some benefit for your participation. I am certain that with this young man in your hands, you will even forget your own lover, no matter how you love him."

"Indeed, this is an intriguing proposition!" said the abbess. "My only concern is that you might be jealous of me should I share your pleasures."

"It is I who ask for your help," said the lady, "so your imaginary fear is utterly groundless. After your arrival, I may even request your sharing of my bedchamber lest people become suspicious. Is this not an excellent arrangement?"

"My dear friend," said the abbess, "if you arrange things the way you have suggested, I shall certainly accompany you even though I may risk my own life. Of the three nuns in my care, one went missing some days ago. I may take your young man as my lost disciple, and no one, I believe, will doubt his identity. But how can you manage to get him here, I wonder?"

"I have instructed him to meet me at this nunnery," the lady told her, "and he promised to do so without divulging the secret to his master. He should be arriving soon."

They were in the midst of conversation when a nun knocked on the door, reporting, "There is a young man outside inquiring about the lady."

"That must be him," the lady said. "Please hasten to invite him in."

From inside she could see a lad rush into the courtyard and the two young nuns, all smiles, greeting him. She nodded to him, motioning him to enter. The abbess, who had received a deep bow from him the moment he stepped in, looked him up and down without blinking her eyes. The lady seized his hand and dragged him closer to the nun.

"Now you do believe what I have told you?" she said.

"I am dazzled," said the abbess. "The charms of this young man make me weak-kneed and limp."

The lady burst into laughter. Embarrassed, the abbess went into the kitchen to prepare vegetarian food, and there she told her two disciples about her new commission.

"How fortunate for you!" they said, biting at their fingernails.

"Yes," said the abbess. "So it is very likely that I shall go to her place."

"You are going to abandon us for the sake of your own pleasure!" grumbled the two disciples.

The abbess comforted them. "This is a godsend for me," she said. "But here all by yourselves, you will find enjoyment too."

She poked fun at them for a while before returning to the reception room. The lady was holding her lover in a close embrace as the nun came in. She released him at once, fished out from her portmanteau a package containing ten taels of silver, and handed it to the abbess.

"This is the payment for our arrangement," she said. "I shall leave my young man here with you as I take the boat home. I hope that within the next ten days you will both arrive. Don't be late!" She gave some instructions to the youth before heading for the dining hall for her vegetarian meal. After lunch, she departed in her sedan. The abbess saw her off, then closed the gate behind her.

Slipping back in, she once again cast her gaze upon the lad, feeling as if she had plucked a shining pearl from the darkness. She drew him into her embrace and kissed him, and meanwhile, caressed and kneaded his object with her hand until his passion was aroused. As his penis engorged, she stripped her clothes off and took him into herself. It took only a short session with him to set her atingle all over.

"You belong to both of us, me and the lady," said the abbess, "and I can enjoy the privilege of being alone with you for only a few nights."

184

Their love-making over, the abbess fetched a razor and shaved his head. Looking at him closely, she could not help laughing. "Now you indeed look like Jingguan!" she remarked. "Since you will have a name-in-religion while you are there, allow me just to call you by that name."

That night they slept together. The two novices, lustful as they were, could do nothing but swallow their envious saliva. The next day, having packed up her personal belongings, the abbess hired a boat and set off for the southern district, accompanied by the young man.

"You are to remain here," she enjoined her two disciples before departure. "Upon arrival, I shall send you a message if everything is fine. If I decide not to return, you may break up and go back to your own homes. If someone from the Yang family inquires about Jingguan, you may say that she went with me to a household in the south."

The two young nuns, only too eager to see the abbess leave so that they could dissolve, replied in chorus, "No problem, no problem."

The abbess and the youth, after disembarking, passed themselves off as sisters in front of people; at night, they shared their bed just like husband and wife. A few days later, they reached their destination, and claiming to be nuns, were both invited to stay in the lady's home convent. A summons from the lady to her bedchamber was not infrequent, and sometimes both of them would sleep with their mistress simultaneously. The nun introduced the lady to her repertoire of lovemaking skills, and they were so unrestrained in their sexual play that it seemed as if nothing in their *menage à trois* was superfluous and the only body part which could not be brought into play was one of their heads.

The youth, however, was no match for these two middle-aged bawds. After living with them for a couple of years, he finally fell sick and died. The lady, inconsolable, soon succumbed in her turn. The family then began to find fault with the nun and even dragged her into court, accusing her of the theft of money and household goods. The nun was finally convicted and imprisoned. She died in jail. All this, of course, occurred much later.

Let us now resume our story. After the departure of the abbess, no one from the Green Duckweed Nunnery looked further into the disappearance of Jingguan. Living in the manor-house, she felt safe and secure. When the results of the examination came out, Wenren found that he had been awarded first place in the Classics Test. Overjoyed, he first reported the good news to his aunt and then went to Jingguan's room, where he dallied pleasantly with her in private. In the days following, he spent the daytime in the city engaging in social activities for new graduates, and returned to his fiancée in the evening.

Meanwhile, he sent somebody to check out the situation for him at the Green Duckweed Nunnery, and was informed that the abbess had decamped for parts unknown and the two young nuns had returned to their homes, leaving the site locked up and deserted. He told Jingguan this happy news, and both of them were filled with relief, feeling as if a great weight on their minds had suddenly lifted.

Now, with all his business in the city finished, Wenren decided to go back to Huzhou. He went first to consult with his aunt. "Jingguan's hair is still short," he said. "I cannot marry her now, nor is it wise to take her to my home immediately. My dear aunt, could you please continue to harbour her here until the time I leave for the State Examination?"[41]

Once again he obtained her permission.

Jingguan cautioned him before he took leave of her: "You must not tell my mother about our relationship. It was she who sent me to the nunnery. If I suddenly return to the secular life, she will be shocked. Please keep our secret until my hair has grown long enough to be able to go back with you. Then she will have no choice but to accept the status quo."

"Good advice," said Wenren.

He took his leave, and on his arrival home, bowed deeply before his mother. But he told her nothing of Jingguan. At the end of the tenth month he set out for the State Examination, and stopping by at his aunt's on the way to the capital, found that Jingguan's hair had reached her shoulders and was barely long enough to be combed into a coil.[42] He wanted to bring her along with him, but his aunt argued strongly against it.

"In my opinion," she said, "this young woman is virtuous and will be a good match for you. If you intend to marry her, you must not travel with her now, for this will be seen as improper behaviour for her. I suggest that you leave her here, and by the time you pass the examination and come back, her hair will be long and I can tell people that she is my adopted daughter and is returning to Huzhou for her wedding. Does this seem a reasonable arrangment for you?"

Wenren found it hard to contradict her sensible advice. He reluctantly parted with Jingguan and traveled by himself to the capital. As expected, he passed the State Examination, and in the Palace Test was awarded second place. On the New State Graduates list printed by the Board of Rites, there was a special notation beside his name indicating that he was "engaged to Miss Yang." The Board of Rites wrote him a note of permission to the effect that by the decree of the emperor, he would be granted funds and gifts for his wedding ceremony. Wenren returned at speed to his home, and after bowing to his mother, explained to her that he had come home for the celebration of his wedding.

"But you haven't been engaged yet," said his mother. "Who is your fiancée?"

"When I lived in Hangzhou," Wenren replied, "my aunt promised me that she would permit me to marry her adopted daughter. I should have told you earlier."

"Her adopted daughter?" his mother became even more confused. "Why have I never heard of her?"

"Mother, you will soon make her acquaintance," said Wenren.

He selected an auspicious day, and after having a boat decorated with flowers and brocades, set out for Hangzhou, with hired musicians beating drums and playing trumpets on board all the way there. Upon arriving at the Huang mansion, he bowed low to his aunt and told her that he had received imperial permission to return for the wedding. His aunt was greatly delighted.

"Now you see that my advice is wise," she said. "How glorious you are today!"

Wenren then hurried to Jingguan's quarters. They described to each other how painful their separation had been. Jingguan, now dressed as a bride, told Wenren that she had been treated most kindly by Lady Huang and had formally taken her as her adoptive mother.

Lady Huang arranged hairpins and flowers in Jingguan's hair and personally escorted her to the decorated sedan. On board the boat, she found herself surrounded by colourful candles lit for them on this special day. Truly:

> Behind the crimson gauze bed curtain they are newlyweds,
> Under the brocade quilt they can but produce familiar objects.

When they reached home, they bowed in obeisance before Wenren's mother, who was deeply impressed by her daughter-in-law's good countenance. Remarking on her Huzhou accent, she said, "You are from Hangzhou, but you speak Huzhou dialect." It wasn't until Wenren explained that the bride was originally a native of Huzhou but had been sent to a nunnery in Hangzhou that his mother finally understood.

The next day, accompanied by Wenren, Jingguan went back to her own home. Wenren had a servant present his invitation cards, one to his mother-in-law and one to his brother-in-law. Mother Yang could only think that there must be some mistake and adamantly refused to take them. Jingguan had no choice but to appear in person.

"Mother!" she called.

Surprised to see a young lady dressed in a phoenix hat and a rosy cape,[43] Mother Yang hurriedly rose to her feet to greet her, although she had not yet recognized her.

"Mother," said Jingguan, "it is I, your daughter from the Green Duckweed Nunnery!"

The voice sounded familiar. Upon closer examination, Mother Yang finally recognized her. She now had hair and was dressed differently; only careful scrutiny enabled her to make out who she was.

"I have neither seen nor heard from you for a year or so," said the mother. "I was informed that you had accompanied the abbess to a household in the south, and have been missing you ever since! I worried even more when I sent a man to check on the nunnery earlier this year and was told that it was deserted. How have you come to your present state?"

The daughter related to her how she had met Wenren on the boat the previous year and how Wenren obtained imperial permission for their marriage: the whole story from the very beginning to the end. Mother Yang was so delighted that she stomped on the floor several times.

So excited was she as she conversed with her daughter that she was reluctant to stop and had her son invite Wenren to enter. A graduate from a government school, the son had learned the etiquette of receiving guests. Cupping one hand in the other before his chest, he saluted his brother-in-law, and then, after ushering him into the house, stood aside with his sister, making a space for Wenren to bow low to the mother. Mother Yang felt as if she were in dreamland.

"If I had known that you would have such a day," she said, "I would never have sent you to the nunnery."

"If you hadn't," said the daughter, "how could I have become what I am today?"

Wenren invited Mother Yang to his house, to enjoy the wedding banquet. With clamorous music to accompany them, they feasted and drank until after midnight.

Later, Wenren suffered disappointment from several setbacks in his official career, and only attained a measure of prosperity after reaching

THE ELOPEMENT OF A NUN

the age of fifty. He then retired from his post and his wife, the daughter of the Yangs, was officially granted the title "Respectful Lady."[44] They both lived to a ripe old age in the countryside.

Wenren once met a skilled physiognomist and inquired of him why he had suffered reverses and frustrations in his career. The physiognomist replied that they constituted retribution for his earlier sexual indulgence. Wenren was then filled with regret for his premarital promiscuity and often warned young men not to lodge in nunneries.

This has been a story about a woman who started out in life with an illicit affair but ended in a happy state. Had it not been for her predestined fate, how might we account for such an unusual destiny in marriage?

> There is no marriage which depends not on Heaven,
> But people, alas, are doubtful and stubborn!
> If a marriage destiny can be changed by human will,
> Why seek a mystic missionary to make wonders happen?

In the Inner Quarters[1]

Money is spent to teach your women to sing and dance;
You are, however, to leave them to another man.
This is but what will happen to you after you die,
Yet even worse is your retribution when you're still alive.

There is not a rich man in the world who does not have a bevy of concubines in his home. He is proud of being flanked by girls from Yan and ladies from Zhao[2] and entertained by rows of beauties singing and dancing before him. Does he know, however, that men and women are roughly equal in their sexual capacity? One man alone is hardly capable of intercourse with several women, and moreover, rich men are generally middle-aged and their flowery concubines are usually much younger. How can the limited sexual energy of one man satisfy a whole party of female partners in bed? This explains why their inner quarters are either filled with bitterness or notorious for scandalous liaisons.

Some men of wealth may be very strict with their family regimes. But however rigorous they are, and however well their compounds are girdled by bronze walls and guarded by a patrolling gate keeper, who, a bell in hand, watched so vigilantly that not even water can find a fissure to seep in, they are able only to confine the bodies of their women, not their minds. Treating them simply as good-for-nothings, their women are loath to share their real passions, and will, instead, take each and every advantage to carry on illicit liaisons behind their backs. If you have racked your brains and spent your money, only to buy detestation from your sweethearts, do you think your efforts are worthwhile?

Consider how Red Whisk[3] abandoned her Duke of Yue[4] and Red Silk[5] fled from her high-ranking official! Incidents of this kind, too numerous to be recounted, may occur while you are still living. After you die, both your withered flowers and your tender buds, like monkeys escaping when a tree crashes down, will scatter and become another man's concubines. There is hardly one out of a thousand who will refuse to remarry as Guan Panpan did.[6] After all, such things will not affect you too much until after your death and you may therefore disregard them. Being a rich man, you may think that you should be concerned only with the present and enjoy life to the fullest. As an observer, however, I cannot but worry about your situation.

In the Song dynasty, there lived in the capital a scholar who was now returning from a journey. When evening began to descend, he passed the rear courtyard of a certain residence, noticing that there was a breach in the wall low enough for him to jump over.

Tipsy, the scholar vaulted the gap and found himself inside a huge garden, where flowers and trees were everywhere and small paths crisscrossed the ground. He looked around, fascinated. Thinking that the scene must be worth exploring further, he strolled along the stone-paved trails, and after several twists and turns, gradually penetrated deeper. There was no one around, and he took time to enjoy the landscape while wandering about at ease.

It grew dark now. He began to turn back, but forgot the way he had come. He was in the midst of recalling when, abruptly, he saw a red gauze lantern appear in the distance. "It must be some guests of the family coming for a visit," he thought.

The scholar was flustered, and the way leading to the exit became even more elusive. He decided to hide himself somewhere temporarily. On the left side of the path was a small pavilion, in front of which was a grotto made of Lake Tai stones,[7] its opening covered by a small felt blanket.

"What an excellent hideout!" he exclaimed. "If I conceal myself in there, no one will discover me!"

He rushed to the cave and was about to pull up the flap to enter when, all of a sudden, a man darted out from inside. The scholar was greatly startled. Setting his eyes upon this fugitive, he found that he was a very beautiful youth. But he could not conceive why he was hiding inside. This beautiful young man, assuming that somebody was following on his heels, was panic-stricken. He scurried off and soon disappeared into the darkness.

"I am so sorry," said the scholar to himself, "but I must take refuge in here for the moment."

He squatted uncomfortably in the cave, with no doubt that it was a safe place. Nevertheless, as the saying goes, "Events are unpredictable and enemies are bound to meet on a narrow road." To his great surprise, he found that the red gauze lantern was also advancing toward the pavilion. Watching from the darkness of the grotto, which made the lantern and its surroundings even brighter, he caught sight of about ten young women outside, all in beautiful attire, and all coquettish, frivolous, and seductively charming. He peered in fascination, having no expectation that this bevy of women would swarm to the cave, and reaching out their hands, lift the felt blanket. All of them, to be sure, were taken aback as they found a stranger inside.

"Why is this gentleman not the one we are expecting?" they said, looking at each other in great confusion. A mature woman among them seized the lantern and cast its light upon the scholar.

"This one is not bad!" she said, after having taken a close look at him.

With her delicate hand she seized him by the hand and pulled him out of the cave. Submissively the scholar let her lead him and did not even dare to ask her where they were going. Yet he was certain that nothing untoward could possibly occur.

He was ushered into their boudoir where a feast of wine and delicacies had been laid out. Each of the beauties vied to entertain him, as if they wished to win in a *liubo* game.[8] They began by exchanging cups with him, and then proceeded to encircle his neck with their arms, stroking his face, and kissing him on the mouth. A few cups of wine were sufficient to render them bubbling with lewd excitement, and finally, without observing further proprieties, they forced him onto the bed.

Some of them, having crawled inside the bed curtain, busied themselves with the removal of their clothes, while others were active around his waist. With no idea how to take turns, they had to start with whoever was closest to him. The moment he ejaculated, they used their tongues to clean his body and fondled his organ until he was brought once again to erection. Fortunately, he was a young man capable of releasing twice more his "string-of-beads" arrows.[9] However, without even so much as a minute's recuperation between such strenuous bouts, even a man of iron could hardly endure. He felt sick and tired. Yet the women did not disperse until about the fifth watch.[10] By that time the scholar was utterly depleted, his whole body listless and numb, and his limbs too weak to support him.

The mature woman assisted him into a large chest, which she directed two or three maids carry away. Once they were outside the compound, the maids turned the chest over to release him, and then went hurrying back, closing the gate behind them.

Day now broke. Fearing that he might be seen and be involved in trouble, the scholar plucked up his strength and dragged himself back home. He made no mention of his adventure to anyone.

A few days later when he had been nursed back to health, he revisited the mansion. He inquired about the identity of the owner whose compound was surrounded by the wall with a breach, and was informed that it was the Grand Preceptor Cai Jing's residence.[11] This discovery so astonished him that for a long while he remained tongue-tied, his body covered with a cold sweat. He never again dared to go near that neighbourhood.

193

IN THE INNER QUARTERS

Gentle reader, you can imagine how powerful Cai Jing the Grand Preceptor was and how strict his orders. But lo and behold, what sort of things his concubines did behind his back! One male "guest" was frightened away, and another arrived and replaced him. They gave free rein to sensual pleasures as if there were no one around. Why did the Grand Preceptor not subject them to discipline in order to put a stop to their extramarital affairs? It was simply because he had too many concubines to take care of.

Among the four notorious officials, Gao, Tong, Yang, and Cai,[12] of the Northern Song dynasty, Yang Jian,[13] the Commander-in-Chief of the Imperial Guard, who was almost as powerful as Cai the Grand Preceptor, also suffered a similar scandal, which later became public and turned him into a laughing stock. If you are not yet tired, gentle reader, I shall relate to you this story in detail.

> Pretty women in the harem are for sex crazed,
> For they hardly get their rain and dew[14] sufficient.
> Now with the Terrace Villa as a place of tryst,
> To make love to King Xiang[15] they are too impatient.

Our story goes that in the Song dynasty, the Commander Yang Jian, a very high official who was a lecher and also an evildoer, was in the emperor's good graces. He had so many concubines that no one but Cai the Grand Preceptor could compare with him.

One day the Commander decided to visit his ancestors' graves in Zhengzhou. He took along with him a bevy of senior wives as well as their maids, leaving at home all the other women who were either too old or too young to serve him, or too delicate to endure inclement weather, or indisposed for feminine reasons. The total number of those who remained, including maids and wet nurses, amounted to fifty or sixty.

The Commander was, by nature, a suspicious man. To prevent his concubines from leaving their quarters, he had all the passageways between the middle gate and outer gate locked and sealed with paper strips containing the date written in red ink. On the wall of the veranda inside the middle gate, he had a hole made, with a rotating tray installed so that food prepared outside could be swivelled in. An old housekeeper surnamed Li was entrusted with surveillance, and a guard, whom no one dared to look in the face, was hired to patrol, beating a drum and clappers every night from evening to daybreak.

Among those left behind, there were some dazzling beauties such as Madam Beautiful Moon, Madam Jade, Sister Smile, and Aunt Flower, and they were all the Commander's favourite concubines. Since they were sequestered in the inner quarters and had only maids to keep them company, they found the days long and the nights endless. To while away their tedious hours they could do no more than play mahjong, flower-collecting games,[16] kickball, or play on the swings.[17] Though these diversions were hardly satisfying, daytime was, in any case, easier to while away. Much more unendurable were the lonely nights.

Madam Jade had previously been the wife of a jade carver in Chang'an.[18] As a clever and attractive woman, she had been well known in the capital and had engaged in several extramarital affairs.

195

The Commander had once chanced to see her, and taking advantage of his power, seized her and made her his seventh lady. He loved her dearly and called her "Jade," for he said she looked as beautiful as a jade carving. This name obviously also implied her origins.

Compared to her female peers in the household, Madam Jade was unmatched both in intelligence and licentiousness. She dreamed of seducing young men even when the Commander was at home, and now that he was away, how could she not burn with lust, confined with nothing to do all day long?

The Commander had a retainer,[19] whose surname was Ren and whose style was Junyong. Though he had failed in the Civil Service Examinations, his calligraphy was good, and he was also competent at secretarial work such as the composition of letters and invitations.

As a young man of about thirty, Ren Junyong was rather handsome. He had been the Commander's catamite when he was in his teens wearing his hair in two topknots.[20] What with his rear courtyard relationship,[21] and with his sense of humour and docile disposition, he had won the Commander's favour, dwelling as a constant hanger-on at his manor. In view of the inconvenience he might cause getting on and off the carriages in the company of a train of women, Ren Junyong was bidden to remain home instead of taking the trip. He lived, as usual, in a studio right outside the compound.

Ren Junyong had a very close friend, a childhood classmate named Fang Wude, whom he would call on for a chat and a drink whenever he had spare time. Since the Commander was gone to visit the graves and there was little work for him to do, he now had more time at his disposal. He would, during the day, invite his friend to stroll around the streets, and at night they would stay in the licenced quarters together, or he would return to his studio to sleep. But no more of this.

Our story continues that Madam Jade, with the Commander being away, found the nights too lonely to bear. She bade Rosy Cloud, her most intimate personal maid, to share her bed. To give vent to her suppressed desires, she talked to the maid about lovemaking, and when she became aroused, took out her paraphernalia and had her maid strap a dildo[22] around her waist to couple with her, as if the maid were her male lover. Rosy Cloud did as she had been instructed, making her mistress moan with pleasure and wriggle her nether parts enthusiastically.

"Is this dildo as pleasurable as a real man?" Rosy Cloud asked, quite excited.

"It is only for fun and can't really satisfy our sexual appetite," said the mistress. "The feel of a real man is of course much better."

"Since a real man is so good," said Rosy Cloud, "isn't it regrettable that a man who lives here is left unused?"

"You mean Ren Junyong?" asked Madam Jade.

"Yes," said Rosy Cloud.

"He is our Commander's most favoured guest," said Madam Jade, "and is indeed very handsome. We often feel a surge of passion as we peek at his fine looks from our rooms."

"How fine it would be if we could manage to entice him into our compound!" Rosy Cloud suggested.

"He may be available," said Madam Jade, "but the wall is so high I don't think he can scale it, unless he has two wings."

"We certainly need some special devices," said Rosy Cloud. "Or it is indeed impossible."

"I might be able to conceive a method," said Madam Jade.

"Just beyond the wall of our rear courtyard is where he lives," Rosy Cloud told her. "Maybe we should rise early tomorrow morning and go out into the back yard to see if we can do something there. Ma'am, you really should devise a plan so that he can enter and we can both of us enjoy some recreation together."

Madam Jade laughed. "I haven't secured him yet and you are already looking forward to sharing the prize with me!" she said, chidingly.

"It is hardly fair to have him all to yourself," Rosy Cloud returned. "Since we are both interested in him, why not help each other?"

"You are right," Madam Jade agreed.

There was no further conversation that night.

With the coming of day, they rose, and after washing and dressing, opened the door and went out into the garden. They plucked flowers to adorn their hair while making their way toward the wall facing the outer house.

Soon they reached a swing suspended at the end of long ropes hanging down from a tree. Madam Jade broke into a broad smile. "Aha," she said, "that may be very useful!" She then sighted a ladder, used for trimming trees, leaning against a Lake Tai stone. "Look! Look!" she called to her maid. "With rope and a ladder, we don't have to worry about the wall anymore."

"Have you had an idea?" asked Rosy Cloud.

"Yes," said Madam Jade, "but let's get closer to the wall that faces his studio. I should like to survey there first before telling you what I am thinking."

Rosy Cloud led her mistress to two umbrella trees. "His studio is on the other side of the wall," she said, motioning her mistress to look in that direction. "He must be alone now."

Madam Jade looked in that direction, thinking for a while. "Things look pretty good," she said. "We can smuggle him in through here tonight without much difficulty."

"How shall we do it?" asked Rosy Cloud.

"We shall quietly fetch the ladder and lean it against this umbrella tree," Madam Jade told her. "You will use the ladder to reach a higher bough and call out to him, and he should be able to hear you."

"To climb from our side and make him hear me won't be difficult at all," said Rosy Cloud. "The problem is how he can climb the wall from his side."

"I will bind up some planks, one foot apart, with the rope of the swing," said Madam Jade. "Rolled up, these planks will appear to be only a bundle of firewood; but spread, they can function as a rope ladder. After you have arranged a time with him, you climb the tree and affix the rope to a solid branch. Make sure that it holds fast before throwing it over the wall to his side. With this ladder in place, we shall be able to admit an entire army of men, not to mention just one person."

"Why," Rosy Cloud exclaimed, "this is indeed a clever idea! Let us hasten to fashion it now!"

Gleefully, she went trotting back to their quarters and fetched about ten small planks, which she handed over to her mistress. Madam Jade had her unfasten the rope from the swing, and then bound these planks herself to ensure that they would be sufficiently safe and secure.

"Now get the wooden ladder and place it against the tree," she said. "Once you are up there, you should be able to see whether you can convey a message to him. If you don't see him around, climb down the ladder and go to his house to set a time with him."

Rosy Cloud did as she had been told. Petite in stature, she was quite agile, and it took her only a few minutes to reach a top bough. As she craned her neck looking around, she saw none other than Ren Junyong himself returning home from a place where he and his friend Fang Wude had just spent the night. He was about to step into his studio when Rosy Cloud called out to him, with a grin, "Aren't you Mr. Ren?"

Hearing somebody speaking and chuckling on the wall, Ren Junyong looked upward and saw a young girl with two buns on her head.[23] He recognized that it was Rosy Cloud. As a young man in his prime, he felt a sudden arousal.

"Dear sister, what did you say?" he asked.

Rosy Cloud intended to excite him. "Sir, you are returning in the early morning, so you must have spent the night away, I suppose?"

"Yes, I did," Ren Junyong admitted. "It's agonizing to sleep alone."

"Look," said Rosy Cloud, "who inside the walls is not sleeping alone? Why not enter so we all may have company?"

"But I have no wings," said Ren Junyong. "How can I fly over?"

"If you really wish to join us, you need no wings," Rosy Cloud told him, "for I might be able to arrange it."

Ren Junyong bowed in gratitude toward the top of the wall. "Many, many thanks to you, Sister. I would appreciate it if you could enlighten me how you may help me."

"Wait a while," said Rosy Cloud. "Let me consult with my lady first. I will tell you the result this evening." She then quickly descended from the tree.

Although he had undertood every word she said, Ren Junyong still felt quite puzzled. "Which of the ladies is willing to grant me such an opportunity and how can I enter the compound?" he mused. "Anyway, I should be patient and wait until I receive her further message this evening." He then looked forward to the setting of the sun. Truly:

> A three-legged bird appears for no reason
> In the round sun that radiates and glistens
> But how can I obtain a Houyi bow[24]
> To shoot it down, making it no longer glow?

We should, for the time being, leave him awaiting the coming of the evening. Our story turns to Madam Jade, who, after having heard every word of their conversation, returned excitedly to her room before Rosy Cloud could seek her instructions. Presently, Rosy Cloud was also back.

"Tonight you won't be alone," she said to her mistress.

"Well," said Madam Jade, "he is a young man and may perhaps change his mind. Such things are not unlikely."

"But he looked so anxious that it seemed as if he wanted to fly over the wall," said Rosy Cloud. "When I told him that I could help him, he kept thanking me for the invitation. I myself see nothing which he should be afraid of. Let's just make preparations for amusement tonight!"

Madam Jade, to be sure, was very delighted. A lyric to the tune of "The Moon Over the Western River" describes the scene as follows:

> The bed is covered with exotic brocades,
> And incense is kindled in the burner.
> Fruits and confections are set on the table,
> Together with fragrant tea and liquor.
>
> Like a horse-ape long trapped in a pitfall,
> She is now of the mandarin duck covetous.
> With bait to entice this handsome man,
> She is sure to have a marvellous time.

Now it was dark. The mistress and her maid were again back in the garden. Rosy Cloud, after reaching the ladder, climbed the tree as she had done that morning and coughed loudly a couple of times. Ren Junyong had frequently popped his head out from his window since nightfall, and was looking around when he heard her signals. He raised his head and saw the maid perched on a high branch.

"Oh, my kind sister!" he cried, too impatient to wait any longer. "I have been looking upward for so long that I have almost worn out my eyes. Please be quick to let me in."

"Wait a moment," said Rosy Cloud. "I will be back with you shortly."

She hastily descended the ladder and reported to her mistress: "He has been waiting anxiously for a long time."

"Then hasten to admit him," said Madam Jade.

Rosy Cloud fetched the rope ladder, and carrying it under her arm, worked her way up the tree. She fastened the rope to a high bough and then shouted: "Watch out!" tossing the ladder over the wall. It reached to the ground.

Seeing the ladder, Ren Junyong was rapt with joy. He tentatively stepped on the planks and found them sturdy enough. He then held the ropes with his hands and started to ascend, step by step, toward the top of the wall.

Rosy Cloud hastened down the ladder and shouted, "He is coming! He is coming!"

Madam Jade felt somewhat embarrassed. She retreated to a Lake Tai stone some distance away and seated herself on it to await her "guest." By now, Ren Junyong had succeeded in climbing over the wall. He jumped off the ladder and enfolded the maid in his embrace the moment he landed on the ground.

"Sister mine," he cried, "you are my benefactor. You are the creator of my greatest happiness!"

"Phooey! You shameless swine!" Rosy Cloud spat at him. "Don't be so greedy! Go report to the lady first!"

"Which lady?" asked Ren Junyong.

"The seventh lady, Madam Jade," Rosy Cloud told him.

"You mean the beauty so famous here in our capital?" Ren Junyong was surprised.

"Who else would you expect to meet if it were not her?" said Rosy Cloud.

"I dare not see her," Ren Junyong murmured.

Rosy Cloud yelped. "She is the one who desired you and devised this plan to get you in. What is there to be afraid of?"

"I am afraid that I might not live up to her expectations," said Ren Junyong.

"Don't be so modest!" Rosy Cloud snorted. "It must be fate that is favouring you. I only hope that you won't forget me once you have made her acquaintance."

"This you needn't worry about," said Ren Junyong. "I certainly won't forget you, and will return your kindness to me with equal favour."

Speaking as they walked, they soon found themselves in front of Madam Jade. In a high-pitched voice, Rosy Cloud announced, "Here is Mr. Ren!"

Ren Junyong, all smiles, bowed low to the lady. "My fair lady," he said, "I could never have dreamed that a man so insignificant as myself would be permitted to meet you today. You condescend to offer me so glorious an opportunity, and I can only attribute this honour to some merit gained in my former existence."

Madam Jade replied, "Though a humble woman remaining in her inner quarters most of the time, I have been fortunate enough, due to the banquets our Commander invited us to attend, to catch a glimpse of your handsomeness long ago. I have long been pining for you, and now that the Commander's absence has left me alone, I have made a point of inviting you so that we could have a chat. I would be greatly honoured should my invitation not be denied."

"For me, nothing would be more difficult than to reject the favour of Your Ladyship," said Ren Junyong. "But I fear that I might cause serious trouble if the Commander discovers the truth."

"The Commander is careless," said Madam Jade. "And moreover, he has no eyes in the back of his head. Since the way you entered was safe and no one knows you are here, there is nothing to worry about. Sir, please come with me to my bedchamber!"

She bade Rosy Cloud lead the way, and she and Ren Junyong, arm in arm, walked behind her. Ren Junyong was so excited that it was as though his soul had flown beyond the sky. He thought nothing of the consequences as he let himself be conducted into her room.

It now was completely dark and silence reigned over the rest of the household. When delicacies and wine had been quietly laid out by Rosy Cloud, the lady and her guest, sitting face to face, began to drink, while at the same time conversing in sweet and tender voices and interchanging glances. After three cups of wine, their passions were aflame and they embraced each other. The pleasure they enjoyed in bed afterwards is beyond description.

> As a lonely guest living in his master's outer house,
> He ascends today to the top of Mount Penglai.[25]
> The savour of this first encounter is surely different,
> Like a meeting of the Shepherd and his Weaving Maid.[26]

When the clouds had dispersed and the rain had come down,[27] Ren Junyong said, "I heard of your reputation long ago. But never did I dream that I might today share your bed! The benefaction you have granted me is as high as the sky and as large as the earth. I am afraid I might not be able to repay you."

"I have always yearned for a romantic affair," Madam Jade replied. "But with our Commander's strict surveillance, I have been unable to fulfill my wish. The entertainments we have day and night do not really satisfy me, and my days would certainly have drained away without pleasure had I not conceived this method to allow your entry. I wish to extend our intimate relationship as long as possible, and I would not complain even though I may die from overindulgence."

"Just to be permitted near your jade body is a stroke of great fortune," said Ren Junyong, "not to mention that you have graced me by filling me with your rain and dew, and fulfilled my wishes by merging your body into mine. Even if this affair should cost me my life, I would have no regrets."

They talked on and on carelessly, unaware of the approaching dawn until the maid appeared at the bedside urging Ren Junyong to depart.

"You have been enjoying yourself for the whole night and you should feel satisfied!" she said. "If you don't get up now, just when do you expect to leave?"

Ren Junyong rose in a hurry and donned his clothes. Madam Jade held his hand, very reluctant to part with him. She did not release him until after she had begged him twice to return. Rosy Cloud, following the instruction of her mistress, escorted Ren Junyong to the wall, where he made his exit via the rope ladder the same way he had entered. That evening he climbed over the wall into the compound once again. Truly:

> In the morning he leaves,
> In the evening he arrives.
> He goes not by the street,
> He does things in secret.

Rosy Cloud, after their tryst continued in this fashion for several nights, was allowed to participate, and the three of them then made love together in the same bed.

Happy and satisfied, Madam Jade would sometimes betray herself as she, absent-minded, carried on conversations with her female companions. At the beginning they did not pay much attention to what she said. But gradually they noticed that there was something unusual in her manner and began to have suspicions. Some of them purposely remained alert at night, and eventually overheard strange noises issuing from her bedroom. They were all women burning with sexual passions and eager to find some excuse so that they could also derive benefit from the troubled waters.[28] However, none of them was able to obtain a shred of reliable evidence.

One day they were in high spirits, intending to play on the swing. When they got to the spot where the swing had been hanging, they found that its rope was missing. Madam Jade and Rosy Cloud kept silent.

Ren Junyong, on the first two days of his rendezvous, had unfastened the rope ladder and hidden it away when he went out, lest it be seen by anyone on the street. As time wore on, however, he was no longer so cautious. Knowing that he would use it in the evening anyway, he simply left it where it was. So now the rope ladder, even while he was out, remained there, hanging from the tree over the wall. It was discovered before Madam Jade and Rosy Cloud could tuck it away.

"Isn't this the rope for the swing?" the ladies asked of each other. "Why is it tied to this tree and thrown out to the other side of the wall?"

Sister Smile was the youngest among them and also the most agile. Noticing a wooden ladder leaning against the tree, she leaped onto it and scrambled up, and soon reached a high bough. While she was tugging the rope back in, all those standing below were taken aback, for they found that the rope had some planks attached to it.

"How strange!" they exclaimed. "Someone must have entered and exited over the wall!"

Madam Jade blushed, and for a long while, could not utter a word.

"Obviously," said Madam Beautiful Moon, "someone among us must have had an affair with someone from outside. We must report it to Steward Li and ask him to investigate. When our Commander returns, he can be informed of what has happened."

As she spoke, she cast a meaningful glance at Madam Jade, who, in her predicament, could do nothing but remain silent, her eyes downcast.

By now Aunt Flower had intuited who the guilty party might be. "Madam Jade, why are you so silent?" she asked with a smile. "It seems that you have something on your mind. You should tell us what it is so that we may help you."

Rosy Cloud realized that there was no point in prevarication. "If we keep the matter secret," she said to her mistress, "they will surely make a scene, which will force us to give him up even if we are unwilling. Please tell them the truth so that we may continue to live on good terms."

All clapped their hands and said, "Well said, Rosy Cloud! There is no point in deceiving us."

Madam Jade then told them, from beginning to end, the whole story of their seduction of Ren Junyong, the retainer who lived in the studio outside the wall.

"Good sister!" said Madam Beautiful Moon. "How could you do such a thing behind our backs!"

"Please don't mention it any more!" said Sister Smile. "Now that we all know what has happened, we should perhaps consider sharing the pleasure together."

"Some may wish to do so," Madam Beautiful Moon deliberately protested, "but others probably will not. How could you make such a suggestion?"

"Even if we don't," said Aunt Flower, "we are all sisters and have a duty to help each other."

"You are absolutely right, Aunt Flower!" exclaimed Sister Smile. With this, they all laughed and drifted away.

Madam Beautiful Moon, who was very close to Madam Jade, had actually been titillated by the discovery of the liaison. She intended to share the fun with her boon companion, and it was only because of the presence of the other concubines that she had assumed a puritanical cast.

She went into the boudoir of Madam Jade after they had dispersed.

"Is he coming this evening, Sister?" she asked.

"Why should he not?" said Madam Jade. "To be frank with you, he visits every night, and it is unlikely that he will fail to come tonight."

"When he comes, you will still keep him all to yourself?" Madam Beautiful Moon asked.

"Sister," said Madam Jade, "you said yourself that you wouldn't take part in such activities."

"Well, I was not being honest when I said that," Madam Beautiful Moon explained. "In fact, I would also like to join the fun, should you permit me."

"Certainly I am willing to accommodate you, if that's what you want," Madam Jade replied. "Tonight I shall send him to your room when he arrives."

"But I don't even know him," said Madam Beautiful Moon. "I would feel most embarrassed if he comes directly to my chamber. I only wish to be your helper."

Madam Jade smirked. "I hardly need a helper, you know," she said.

"I tend to be timid at the beginning," murmured Madam Beautiful Moon. "So perhaps I shall take your place in your bedroom? Please just keep it secret until he and I become familiar with each other."

"Such being the case, you simply need to hide yourself somewhere first," Madam Jade told her. "After he gets into bed and removes his clothes, I will extinguish the light and let you replace me."

"Sister, are you sure you will really do me this favour?" asked Madam Beautiful Moon.

"Of course!" said Madam Jade.

They had thus made their arrangements. That evening Rosy Cloud was once again dispatched to the back yard, to put the rope ladder back in its place so Ren Junyong could climb in. Madam Jade, upon his arrival, sent him to bed immediately. She then blew out the light, quietly led her friend out from her hiding-place, and pushed her toward him.

By that time Madam Beautiful Moon had become very aroused both because of the endearments she had heard them exchange with each other and because of Ren Junyong's handsome features, which, as he walked in, she had glimpsed from the dark corner behind the lamp. She was in such a frenzy of impatience as she was approaching the bed that her eyes flared with lustful fire. She felt she could not wait a moment longer.

In the darkness she felt no shame and swiftly slipped under the quilt. Ren Junyong, who had been waiting in bed for some time already, mistook her for the familiar Madam Jade and scrambled upon her body immediately,

204

starting to enter without even allowing her time for a single word. Burning with lust, Madam Beautiful Moon did her best to receive him. Now Ren Junyong was deep inside her. He found that the texture of her body was somehow different, and also noticed that the way she made love was rather affected. Her unusual reticence gave rise to his further suspicion.

"My dear heart," he whispered in a tender voice, "why don't you speak tonight?"

There was no response. As he continued to nudge her with his questions, Madam Beautiful Moon simply held her breath and let out not even a single breathing sound. Ren Junyong was bewildered. He grew impatient, and finally stopped moving his body, murmuring, "Strange! Strange!"

Madam Jade, who was standing at the bedside while Ren Junyong made his interrogation, could not help but break into giggles. She whipped aside the bed curtain and struck him a firm blow. "You knave!" she scolded. "You are getting what you desire, so why be so curious? Listen, it's Madam Beautiful Moon who is now in my bed. You are most fortunate to have her to sleep with you, a lady who is ten times better than I am!"

His hunch confirmed, Ren Junyong said, "Please accept my deepest apologies, for I was unaware that it was another fine lady who deigned to offer me, an insignificant man, such a special favour. I beg you to forgive me for taking these liberties without bowing to you and making your acquaintance first."

"You need not speak so gently," Madam Beautiful Moon spoke at last. "Now that you know who I am, your curiosity should be satisfied."

Thrilled to hear her sweet voice, Ren Junyong once again resumed his assault, this time even more vigorously. Soon Madam Beautiful Moon reached her climax.

"Oh, my kind sister," she cried, "I am dying! I thank you so much for allowing me to take part in such pleasure!" With this, her female essence flowed out and her limbs and body went limp.

Being greatly aroused, Madam Jade could not help stripping off her own clothes and leaping onto the bed to join them. Fortunately, she found that Ren Junyong's "flag-and-gun"[29] was still standing. Her passion slaked, Madam Beautiful Moon quickly loosened her hold and pushed Ren Junyong toward his hostess. Ren Junyong mounted her at once and another bout started. Truly:

> Kissing green and hugging red are most exciting
> On Mount Wu[30] enveloped by clouds and rain.

The romantic aroma that butterfly is stealing,
Shuttling from east to west simply for a change.

But let us say no more of their love-making in a *menage à trois*. Our story proceeds with Sister Smile and Aunt Flower who, after learning of Madam Jade's adulterous activities, planned to intercept Ren Junyong on his evening visit. They intended to involve Madam Beautiful Moon in their seduction so they might share their pleasures together. After the evening meal they went to her quarters. Finding her absent, they became suspicious and hurried to Madam Jade's room to ascertain whether she was there. At that time Rosy Cloud happened to be standing outside the door.

"Is Madam Beautiful Moon with your mistress?" they inquired.

"Yeah, she is in there," the maid replied, giggling. "She is now in my lady's bed."

"Are they sleeping together?" they asked. "That will be inconvenient when he comes."

"What inconvenience?" said Rosy Cloud. "The three of them have already been in bed together and have not yet found anything inconvenient."

Both Sister Smile and Aunt Flower were stunned. "You mean that the man is already inside?"

"Yeah," said Rosy Cloud. "By now he may well have become tired of 'in and out!'"

"What a hypocritical prude!" Sister Smile blurted. "This very morning she opposed my suggestion, but now she has made herself first to claim the prize!"

"Is it not always loose women who appear most prudish?" Aunt Flower remarked.

"Go make a scene!" said Sister Smile. "We shall see if they dare to reject us!"

"Oh, no!" Aunt Flower dissuaded her. "The man must be exhausted after dealing with the two of them; I don't believe he will have much energy left for us."

She then whispered in Sister Smile's ear, "Let us be patient today, and tomorrow we shall make our preparations early and entice him into our quarters. I am sure he will let us have our way with him." With that they returned to their own rooms. Nothing happened during the rest of the night.

The next morning, after Ren Junyong had taken his leave, Rosy Cloud came to the bedside, reporting to her mistress that Sister Smile and Aunt

206

Flower had been searching for Madam Beautiful Moon the previous night.

"Did they know that I was here?" Madam Beautiful Moon immediately asked.

"Certainly!" said Rosy Cloud.

Madam Beautiful Moon was struck dumb with surprise. "What should I do?" she murmured. "They must have had a good chuckle behind my back!"

"The best way," said Madam Jade, "is to coax these two dames to join us, so that we don't have to remain on guard against each other. Nor will it be necessary for Ren Junyong to leave in the morning and come back in the evening. He may stay here all day long and we can take turns sleeping with him. Is this not a fine strategem?"

"Your suggestion is appropriate," said Madam Beautiful Moon. "It is just that I feel too embarrassed to raise the matter with them."

"Do not fret, Sister," Madam Jade comforted her. "You need say nothing at all today. If they don't ask you about last night, well and good; if they do, I shall take the opportunity to involve them in our scheme."

Madam Beautiful Moon felt a sense of relief. Because of the sensual activity she had enjoyed during the night, she was exhausted and did not rise until noon. Though relaxed and satisfied, she was nonetheless very much on guard against the other two women, fearing that they might ridicule her. Who would have thought that while she did her best to avoid them, Sister Smile and Aunt Flower, harbouring their own intrigue, did not mention a word about her in her presence, as if nothing had happened the previous day.

That evening, after careful deliberation, Sister Smile and Aunt Flower went out into the garden to await the arrival of Ren Junyong. They concealed themselves in a hidden spot near the tree, and before long saw him scale the wall and descend the ladder. No sooner had he adjusted his cap and brushed down his gown and began to stride toward his destination, than Sister Smile darted out.

"Hatl!" she shouted. "What are you, a male, doing in this domain of women?"

At that very moment, Aunt Flower also charged out. She caught hold of Ren Junyong's clothes and screamed, "Thief! Thief!"

Ren Junyong was shocked. He defended himself in a garbled explanation, "It's ... it's ... it's ... the two ladies inside who ... who ... have invited me in. Sisters, please don't scream so loudly."

"Are you Mr. Ren?" asked Sister Smile.

"Yes, yes," he repied immediately. "This insignificant man is indeed Ren Junyong, not a counterfeit."

"So it is you who has cunningly seduced our two ladies!" said Aunt Flower. "You know this is a horrible crime. Do you wish it made public or shall we settle it privately?"

"I was invited by the ladies," Ren Junyong whined, defending himself. "Otherwise how could I have been so bold as to climb into your compound? I am certainly unwilling to make it public. I prefer that it be settled privately."

"To make it public would mean that we would hand you over to Steward Li and let the Commander mete out punishment to you when he returns," said Sister Smile. "However, if you wish to settle it privately, you must follow us quietly to our quarters, not to theirs, and allow us to punish you."

Ren Junyong broke into a broad smile.

"I trust you won't treat me too harshly, will you?" he said. "Okay, I shall go with you."

They tiptoed to Sister Smile's boudoir, and there Aunt Flower joined them in the bed. They tossed and turned, like clouds and rain raging in a fury, like mandarin ducks in heat in their conjugal felicity. But let us say no more of this.

Our story goes on that Madam Jade and Madam Beautiful Moon, failing to see Ren Junyong enter that evening, sent Rosy Cloud to the back yard to give him a signal. Carrying a lantern, Rosy Cloud went into the garden, and by its light, observed that the rope ladder had been moved to the inner side of the wall. She knew that he must be in the compound already, for every time he came in, he was very careful to pull the ladder inside lest somebody see it from the street and follow on his heels.

She reported back to the two ladies. "Mr. Ren is inside the compound! Since he is not here, he must be somewhere else."

Madam Jade pondered for a while.

"Someone must have kidnapped him!" she declared, laughing.

"He must be in the bedroom of one of those two vixens," said Madam Beautiful Moon.

Rosy Cloud was sent off once again, this time on a detective mission. She rushed first to Aunt Flower's quarters and found the room locked and quiet, and then headed for Sister Smile's, where she heard laughter and squeaks from the bed inside her chamber. She knew that they must be in the midst of intercourse and was very jealous. She sped back at once.

"He is indeed in their chamber," she reported. "If we hasten over there right now, we can catch them in the act."

"Wait a moment," said Madam Beautiful Moon. "Since they did not disturb us last night, we have no reason to trouble them now. For the sake

FROM LING MENGCHU'S *Two Slaps*

of our sisterhood, let's not take such an initiative."

"I am just planning to trick them into collusion," said Madam Jade. "Who would have thought that they have pre-empted me, carrying on with him already! This is exactly what I was hoping for. In order to teach them a lesson and compel them to collaborate with us, our best course is to cut off his way out tomorrow morning instead of creating a disturbance tonight."

"But how shall we accomplish this?" asked Madam Beautiful Moon.

"Well, what we need to do is just have Rosy Cloud unfasten the rope ladder and stow it away," said Madam Jade. "Without the rope ladder, he certainly can't leave. Then we shall see how the two of them can hush the matter up."

"Brilliant! Brilliant!" Rosy Cloud exclaimed. "We're the ones who fashioned the ladder and enticed him inside, and now they have seized the prize from under our very noses! Isn't that ridiculous?"

She seized the lantern and ran back into the garden in a huff. With alacrity she climbed the tree, undid the rope, and then coiled the ladder into a bundle and carried it back to the room.

"Here you are!" she said, presenting it to her mistress.

"Put it away somewhere," Madam Jade bade her. "Since there is little we can do tonight, let's go to sleep now." The two ladies then retired to their own bedrooms, feeling very lonely indeed. Truly:

> The jade hourglass marks the same time,
> Yet night is long in one room and short in another.

Embracing Ren Junyong, Sister Smile and Aunt Flower spent a tempestuous night. When day dawned, they urged him to rise and depart, and bade him to return again in the evening. Then they went out of the house together, with Ren Junyong walking in front and Sister Smile and Aunt Flower following in his wake, their hair dishevelled and their faces unwashed. Reaching the tree, Ren Junyong climbed the ladder as usual, but this time there was no rope ladder awaiting him. He could not jump from the high wall, and had to descend the tree again.

"The rope ladder has disappeared!" he said. "I think it must have been taken away by the other two ladies. Last night I failed to visit them and they might have somehow caught wind of my whereabouts and deliberately put me in this awkward situation. Could you please find another rope to let me out?"

"I would happily do so," said Sister Smile, "if you tell me where to find a thick enough rope to lift you up and let you down."

"Then it seems that I have no alternative but to go to them and make my apologies," he said. "Perhaps that way I can solve the problem."

"But that would cause us great embarrassment," said Aunt Flower.

As the three of them hesitated about what to do next, they saw Madam Jade and Madam Beautiful Moon, accompanied by Rosy Cloud, rush into the garden. "You may carry on your secret activities," they said, laughing and clapping their hands, "but can you make him fly over the wall?"

"Somebody did things this way before us, and we just followed suit!" returned Sister Smile.

"No bickering!" said Aunt Flower. "We should have helped each other as we agreed at the beginning. Since you abandoned us and monopolized all his attention, we, on the spur of the moment, decided to have our own fun without your knowledge. Let us now drop the matter. I beg you to bring out the ladder and let him go."

"Is it necessary?" asked Madam Jade, smiling. "Now that we all know him and have been intimate with him, we might as well allow him to stay here. It won't hurt any one of us, will it? So why not indulge ourselves and be happy together for awhile?"

All of them broke into smiles.

"Wonderful idea! Wonderful idea!" they exclaimed. "Nothing could be better than your suggestion!"

Clasping Ren Junyong's arm, Madam Jade, together with her companions, returned to their living quarters. From that moment onward, Ren Junyong remained inside the compound day and night. This morning he sat shoulder to shoulder between the two Madams, his thighs stretched out on top of theirs, and that evening he lay in bed in the arms of Sister and Aunt. The endless sexual indulgence eventually depleted his energy and he grew exhausted, desirous of nothing but a respite from them so that he could recuperate for a few days. Yet this was no longer his own decision, and his request, to be sure, was not granted. To husband his strength, the ladies used their private savings to purchase nutritious foodstuffs for him, and also pooled their funds to offer a large bribe to Steward Li lest he betray them.

Ren Junyong, in a haze of sexual abandon, was unaware that he had exceeded the bounds of pleasure. But:

> One should not be fully satisfied,
> Nor enjoy excessive complacency.
> As extreme fortune begets sorrow,
> So will he end in woeful misery.

Happy and contented, Ren Junyong passed over a month in the inner quarters until one day the servants working outside reported that the Commander was returning. The concubines, all in their sleepy or drunken state, did not take their words seriously. To their surprise, however, the Commander arrived in no time, and all of a sudden, the gates of the mansion were thrown wide open. Panicky and in great confusion, they bade their maids to escort Ren Junyong to the rear courtyard. The maids urged him to get out as quickly as possible, and once Ren Junyong had mounted the wall, they removed the ladder immediately.

"Go! Be quick about it!" they shouted at him, and then, in a rush, hurried back.

In the mad haste of flight, Ren Junyong did not notice that the rope ladder had not been replaced until he reached the top of the wall. Now he could neither climb down the other side nor return to the courtyard, since the wooden ladder had already been removed.

"I shall be in serious trouble if somebody catches sight of me," he thought. He considered jumping down, yet since he was extremely enervated and his limbs were weak and aching, he failed to muster enough courage. After wrestling for awhile, he found he could do nothing but sit trembling atop the wall, like

> A goat that butts into a fence
> Gets stuck in the predicament.

"Enemies are bound to meet on a narrow road," as the old saying goes. Immediately upon his arrival, the Commander proceeded to sniff around the compound to check if there was anything suspicious. Entering the rear courtyard, he raised his eyes and caught sight of a man sitting high on the wall. A shiver of fear ran down Ren Junyong's spine as he, looking down from above, recognized that it was the Commander. Since there was no escape, he could do no more than bend down to the best of his ability. This is what is called "a rabbit covers its face," that is, hiding his countenance without concealing the body.

The Commander was shrewd enough to know that nothing related to the inner quarters – but a clandestine affair – could bring a man up to the top of the wall. Given the possible implication of his concubines, which would surely become a scandal if leaked out, he deliberately spoke in a loud voice, "The wall is so high that I don't believe a mere mortal could climb it. The man up there must be possessed by evil spirits. Let us fetch a ladder to get him down so that we may interrogate him."

The servants standing nearby rushed to bring a ladder, and then helped Ren Junyong to get down step by step. Ren Junyong, having heard what the Commander had said, swiftly conceived a plan to extricate himself from the blunder he had made. He pretended to be in a befuddled state and unaware of what was happening to him as he allowed himself be dragged to his master.

"Isn't this Ren Junyong?" asked the Commander, looking at him closely. "Why does he look like this? He must be possessed by demons!"

Ren Junyong made no reply, his eyes remaining closed. The Commander then had somebody go to the Temple of Godly Happiness to fetch a Taoist exorcist. Who would dare to disobey his order? So it was only a short while before an adept arrived, and the Commander instructed him to make an examination of his retainer.

"He is indeed possessed by evil spirits," said the adept mysteriously. With sword in hand,[31] he then chanted some incantations and sprayed a mouthful of water onto Ren Junyong's face.

"Now," he intoned, "he should recover."

Ren Junyong, as expected, did open his eyes. "How did I come to be here?" he asked.

"Do you remember how you came into this place?" the Commander asked him.

Upon hearing this, Ren Junyong quickly fabricated a story. "Last night as I sat alone in my studio, I entered a trance-like state. I saw five generals approach me, all wearing splendid uniforms and flowery hats. They demanded that I accompany them to the Palace of Heaven to copy out some documents. Thinking that their appearance was odd, I refused. They then ordered their elfish retinue to arrest me and I was carried high into the air. Fortunately, I was able to grasp a tree bough. I cried out desperately, 'I am Commander Yang's guest and you cannot treat me in such an impolite way!' Hearing your name, the elves loosened their hold so I fell to the ground and lost consciousness. Who would have thought that I would now be before you! Commander, when did you return and what is this place?"

"You were just now atop the wall," the bystanders told him. "The Commander found that you have been possessed by spirits and had somebody help you down. Now you are in the rear courtyard."

"According to what he said," the Commander inquired of the priest, "what kind of spirits do you think possessed him?"

"In terms of his description," the adept replied, "they must have been Wutong Spirits.[32] These spirits are hidden hereabouts and frequently cause disturbances when they are begging for food. I shall give him a small paper amulet and he may place it on the wall of his room. Prepare some beef, pork, and mutton, as well as wine and fruit. After he has composed himself, everything should return to normal."

The Commander ordered the servants on duty to prepare the sacrifices as had been instructed. After the adept had left, Ren Junyong was carried back to his studio to rest. "How lucky I was to survive this crisis," he thought.

Since his sexual over-indulgence had weakened him greatly, Ren Junyong, on the pretext that his health had been strained by the so-called spirit possession, confined himself to his bed for recuperation over the next ten days. He was, after all, a young man, and soon became much better. When he was well, he went into the compound to pay a visit to the Commander.

"Commander," he said, "if you had not engaged the priest to rescue me, I would have been unable to resist the demons and would probably have lost my life."

"I am glad that you have recovered," said the Commander, happily. "I have been away from you for a long time, and today should take the opportunity of your recovery to treat you to wine and food. Let's drink as much as we wish!"

At his bidding, beverages and delicacies were promptly served. They drank while playing a riddle-solving game,[33] immersed in a state of euphoria. Ren Junyong acted with decorum, trying his utmost to flatter his master. Once he purposely mentioned the incident of his "possession," attempting to find out what the Commander really thought.

"I feel regret that I left you alone in your studio while I was away, and I am definitely the one who should take the blame for your falling prey to demons," the Commander said, soothing him as much as he could.

Ren Junyong was secretly delighted. "It seems that the truth has not leaked out," he said to himself. "But how, I wonder, can I meet those beauties again? Perhaps I can see them only in my dreams for the rest of my life."

Visions of them often emerged before him as he slept alone at night in his quiet room, and he felt awash with relief at the thought of his lucky avoidance of the Commander's suspicion. The Commander, however, was a shrewd man. The moment he had seen his retainer on the wall, his intuition told him that something must have happened. Later, his discovery of the rope ladder, which, due to Madam Jade's neglect, had been stored in the closet of her chamber since that night, further comfirmed the questions in his mind. He believed that this was what they had used to entice men into the compound and therefore had Rosy Cloud flogged.

Under torture, Rosy Cloud confessed everything. The Commander then cross-examined the others until he knew everything inside out. Still he feigned ignorance, treating his retainer as well as he had treated him before, sometimes even better. Truly:

> He harbours a sword in his bosom,
> And conceals a dagger behind his smile.
> Yet tantalizing the tiger's mouth,
> How can the man escape alive?

One day the Commander invited Ren Junyong to drink with him. He took him into an inner study, where they imbibed with great conviviality for a long while. Two courtesans entertained them with songs and took turns urging Ren Junyong to drain his cup. Observing these beauteous singing girls, Ren Junyong could not prevent himself from thinking of the women in the inner quarters with whom he had enjoyed very pleasurable relations. He began to feel depressed and quaffed more and more liquor until he fell into a stupor.

The Commander then rose and left the study. When the courtesans followed, only Ren Junyong remained, lying passed out in his chair. Suddenly four or five brawny men strode in and tied him up before he could utter a word. So inebriated was Ren Junyong that he was not conscious of what was happening to him. He babbled incoherently as he was lifted onto a couch, his life, as one of the stalwarts quickly drew out his sharp knife, being already like:

> The moon over the mountains at the fifth watch,
> Or a lamp to be burnt out at the third watch.

Gentle reader, you should know that homicide was not an unknown occurrance in Commander Yang's household, and moreover, the crime committed by Ren Junyong could very well warrant the penalty of death. But why did the Commander take the trouble to invite him to his inner study and entertain him with food and wine if execution were his aim? The reason was that the Commander was going to destroy him only partially. The punishment to be meted out to his retainer was not a customary one.

Knife in hand, one of the strong men quickly ripped off Ren Junyong's pants, and gripping his genitals with his left hand, used his right to slice them off deftly. He then picked up the twin testicles and threw them away.

"*Ai-ya!*" Ren Junyong burst out of his dream.

The pain was so unbearable that he fell into a dead faint. Quickly, the assailants took out a healing styptic salve and applied it to the wound, and then released him from his bonds and swiftly departed, closing the door behind them.

Who were these strong men? They were professional castrators employed by the palace. The Commander, though very angry with Ren Junyong for debauching his women, decided, in view of his former service as a good-humoured companion, not to kill him, but to have him castrated. That he had ushered him into the inner study where the deed was to be performed was simply to protect him from exposure to wind. A newly castrated male is very vulnerable to cold air, and this explains why "to go to the silkworm house,"[34] a phrase used by the ancients, alludes to this penalty.

The Commander instructed his servants to attend to Ren Junyong with minute care to make sure that no further harm would be done to him. Attention, he said, should especially be paid to his daily diet and the like. Ren Junyong suffered such excruciating pain that he could have died many a time but for the exceptional care he received. Although he realized that his outrageous castration was a direct result of the Commander's detection of his liaisons, where could he go to lodge a complaint? There was nothing he could do but swallow his humiliation.[35]

Fortunately, he survived. Ten days later he could, with difficulty, arise from his bed. He bade a servant to pour him a basin of water, and washing his face, saw a few wisps of beard fall from his chin into the water. He hastened to fetch a mirror, which, upon closer examination, revealed that he now looked exactly like a eunuch. He then moved his eyes downward to the site of the wound below his belly, where the organ he had once used for intercourse was located. There now remained only a large scar. Running his fingers along the scar, he cried, his tears trickling down like rain.

> In the past he was happy, surrounded by flowers,
> Today seated by himself, he is sorrowful.
> He realizes now that women and luxurious living
> Are only for those whose good fate is predestined.

After Ren Junyong's castration, the Commander became very hospitable toward him, greeting him with a smile whenever he saw him. Now that his retainer had lost his genitals, he had nothing more to guard against. He would even invite him into the inner quarters and let him sit among his womenfolk to drink and play games with them.

Ren Junyong had now simply become a joke, an object that could only provide the women with amusement. At the beginning, those like Madam Jade and Madam Beautiful Moon who had had intimate relations with him would speak of their love affairs of bygone days, full of compassion and sorrow. But, after all, Ren Junyong was no longer a man capable of producing his snake[36] for them to play with. He was, in their eyes, totally useless, good to look at, but of no use any more.

"When the Commander returned," said Ren Junyong to his erstwhile lovers, "I thought that my hopes of seeing you again would be dashed forever. I had no expectation that I would still be able to get together with you from time to time. It is only that I have been transformed into a cripple, wholly useless to you. How tragic it is! How very tragic!"

He now spent most of time with the concubines in the inner quarters, rarely venturing out. Being a eunuch, with his voice changed and his beard gone, he felt acutely embarrassed to meet anyone he knew on the street. He even lost contact with his closest friend Fang Wude, whom he had not seen for almost half a year. Fang, in fact, had once visited the Commander's residence to inquire after Ren. But in accordance with the instructions they received, the household staff told him that his friend had died.

One day the Commander and his concubines went visiting the Temple of Serving the Country,[37] and Ren Junyong was bidden to join the excursion. While he was strolling about by himself in the Great Mercy Hall, he chanced to bump into his friend. What with his changed facial features and the news about his death, Fang Wude was not quite certain that the person he saw was Ren Junyong, though he appeared very familiar. He turned away after a momentary hesitation.

Ren Junyong, however, recognized him. "Wude! Wude!" he called. "Why are you avoiding me?"

Fang knew then that it was indeed his friend. He rushed back to greet him, and Ren Junyong, holding his hands, could not help wailing and sobbing.

"I regret deeply that I haven't seen you in so long," said Fang. "Has something unfortunate happened to you?"

"Yes," Ren Junyong replied, "but it is impossible to explain to you in a few words." He then related the entire story to him, and after finishing it, was practically drowned in tears. "A short-lived pleasure has brought me such misfortune!" he cried.

"You indulged yourself to excess and that is why you were punished," said Fang Wude. "But it is all over now, and you must not be overwhelmed with remorse. Visit your friends as often as you can, and a happy life is still within your grasp."

"I am far too ashamed to see them," said Ren Junyong. "I would feel contented if I could but manage to drag myself through my remaining days of humiliation."

Fang Wude expressed his sympathy and then took leave of him. He later learned that Ren Junyong died of depression in the Commander's residence. This was the retribution for his illicit sexual liaisons, and Fang Wude, whenever he encountered a young man in search of romantic adventures, would admonish him by telling the story of his friend.

Gentle reader take note. Sanguine youths are not the only ones who should exercise caution in matters of sex. The rules are the same for men of an older age. In spite of his cruel revenge, the Commander Yang Jian suffered, after all, the disgrace of the debauchery of his women and his own cuckoldry. Is this not a lesson for all wealthy men who have kept or aspire to keep a harem of beauties at home?

> Odd is the carnal object hanging down below,
> Which some cannot tolerate but others like to fondle.
> Here is a piece of advice for all the lecherous to learn:
> Let not your body be held hostage by your tiny organ.

Another poem which mocks the Commander Yang:

> You had his genitals cut off to eliminate his desires,
> Yet he can still dally with your concubines.
> As a palace girl needs a eunuch for consultation,
> Who can prevent her from flirtation?

Notes on Stories

Fatal Seduction

[1] The original title of this story (story 6 of *Slapping the Table in Amazement*) is: "With an Extraordinary Wine Nun Zhao Inebriated the Flower / Using an Unusually Clever Stratagem Licentiate Jia Avenged the Humiliation."

[2] *Nigu* (nun), *daogu* (shamaness), and *guagu* (soothsayer) are called "three kinds of aunts," and *yapo* (slave broker), *meipo* (go-between), *shipo* (sorceress), *qianpo* (procuress), *yaopo* (female quack), and *wenpo* (midwife) are called "six types of crones."

[3] Zhang Liang and Chen Ping helped Liu Bang defeat Xiang Yu and establish the Han Dynasty. Liu Bang would have been killed by Xiang Yu but for Zhang Liang's information and advice. Chen Ping was very poor when he was young. He married a girl who had married five times before, but each time her husband had died immediately. When rumour had it that Chen Ping carried on in secret with his brother's wife and accepted money from various generals, Liu Bang's suspicions were aroused. He summoned Wei Wuzi, who had first recommended Chen Ping to him, and began to berate him. But Wei replied, "I recommended the man because of his ability. But now Your Majesty questions me on his behaviour! Even the most shining examples of chaste and loyal behaviour would be of no help in deciding our fate in battle, so why should Your Majesty trouble about such questions?" Liu Bang then pardoned Chen Ping. Later Chen Ping devised six ingenious strategies for Liu Bang.

[4] Sui He (fl. late 3 – early 2 centuries BC) was renowned as a skillful speaker. During the Chu-Han War Liu Bang dispatched him as an envoy to the residence of Qing Bu, the King of Jiujiang, telling him, "If you can persuade Qing Bu to raise an army and revolt against Chu, Xiang Yu will be bound to halt his advance and attack him. If I can get Xiang Yu to delay for a few months, I will surely be able to seize control of the empire!" Sui He went and pleaded with Qing Bu, who as a result revolted against Chu. Lu Jia (c. 228 – c. 140 BC) was also famous as a rhetorician and was one of Liu Bang's trusted advisors, serving time and again as an envoy to the various nobles.

[5] "Di" in the original text is "*Dishi.*" "*Shi,*" when it follows a woman's maiden name in the old times, usually indicates that the woman in question is married. Since Ling Mengchu in his stories often used "*shi*" for married women regardless of their social status, it is usually omitted in the translation.

[6] "Lady" is an honourific title granted to wives of rank 3a and higher officials.

[7] Traditional Chinese men's garments did not have pockets, and men usually put small objects inside their sleeves, which, Venetian in style, were long, but not wide, and open at the wrist.

[8]   Theoretically speaking, a string of cash (*yiguan*) was equal to a thousand coins (*yiqian wen*), and a thousand coins were equal to a tael of silver (*yiliang yinzi*). In fact, however, the exchange rate differed from time to time and also from place to place. For example, during the years from the Chongning reign to the Xuanhe reign (1102–1125), a tael of silver could be exchanged for 1,250 coins, and in Zhejiang province, was only worth 250 coins.

[9]   Su Qin (fl. early 3rd century BC) was an itinerant politician, who travelled from court to court of the Six States during the Warring-State period, persuading their rulers to adopt his strategies. Zhang Yi was also a politician working with his mouth and tongue.

[10] "Six ingenious stratagems" refers to the schemes employed by Chen Ping.

219

[11] The Board of Personnel was the department in charge of the supervision of officials, taking care of matters such as their appointment and dismissal, promotion and demotion, etc. The central administration of the Tang dynasty consists of *sansheng* (three departments): *Zhongshu sheng* (the Secretariat), *Menxia sheng* (the Chancellry), and *Shangshu sheng* (the Department of State Affairs). Under the Department of State Affairs there were *liubu* (six boards): *libu* (Board of Personnel), *hubu* (Board of Revenue), *libu* (Board of Rites), *bingbu* (Board of War), *xingbu* (Board of Justice), and *gongbu* (Board of Work).

[12] According to van Gulik, the "clouds" can be explained as "the ova and vaginal secretions of woman" and the "rain" as "the emission of semen of the man." See *Sexual Life in Ancient China*, p. 39.

[13] "Pumen pin" (The Universal Gateway) is the 25th chapter in *Lotus Sutra*.

[14] There are three Chinese versions of *Lotus Sutra*, respectively translated by Kumarajiva (*Jiumo Luoshi*), Dharmaraksa (*Zhu Fahu*), and Jnanagnpta (*Shena quduo*). As far as the *ji* (verse form) of "Pumeng ping" is concerned, Kumarajiva and Dharmaraksa's versions differ greatly (Jnanagnpta's version does not even have the verses).

[15] Wuzhou is the modern Jinhua County in Zhejiang province.

[16] *Xiucai* (literally, "cultivated talent") was in the Ming-Qing times an unofficial reference to *shengyuan* (students in governmental schools) who were qualified to participate in the Provincial Examination (*xiangshi*) in the Civil Service Examination sequence. They were a distinguished class representing the advanced citizenry of their particular town, given seats of honour at the conventions of the magistrates, and could enjoy a great many civil privileges. All *xiucai* (or *sheng yuan*), were enrolled in prefectural or county schools and subjected to instruction, periodic reviewing tests, and the discipline of school officials. They were exempt from corvée duty and were entitled to free board and a monthly stipend of a whole *shi* (Chinese bushel).

[17] Guanyin (or Guanshiyin), sometimes translated as "the Goddess of Mercy," literally means Boddhisattva Perceiver of Sound. Guanyin is the most widely revered bodhisattva, Buddha-to-be, in East Asia, especially in the Tiantai, Tantric, and Meditation Schools.

[18] Bu Liang is a punning name that suggests the words "*bu liang*," meaning "not good."

[19] A slightly changed form of the colloquial expression "a toad wants to eat the flesh of a swan," which is usually used to mock people who have a vain hope.

[20] This colloquial expression means "doing something bad to a person when s/he is drunk."

[21] Nunneries (*anyuan*) were smaller and more private in comparison with monasteries (*si*), and since there were so many in the Ming, they were usually exempt from the regulations governing monasteries. This is perhaps the reason why Ling admonishes women to avoid "nunneries" only.

[22] "The Mantra for the Purification of the Mouth" contains fourteen words: "*xiu li xiu li, mo ke xiu li, xiu xiu li sa po ke.*" "The Mantra for the Protection of the God of Earth" contains eighteen words: "*nan wu san man duo, mu tuo nan an, du lu du lu, di wei sa po ke.*"

[23] This idiom is usually used in a derogatory sense, meaning "too greedy."

[24] "The golden bird" (*jinniao*), or sometimes "the golden crow" (*jinwu*), is usually used as a metonymy referring to the sun. "The jade hare" (*yutu*) is a metaphor for the moon, because the legend goes that there is a white hare in the moon.

[25] The magistrate was the official in charge of the entire administration of the district under his jurisdiction, whose duty it was to collect taxes, register births, deaths and marriages, keep up to date the land registration, and maintain the peace. He was also the presiding judge of the local tribunal, responsible for the punishment of criminals and hearing all civil and criminal cases. Since the magistrate supervised practically every phase of the daily life of the people, he was referred to as the "Father-and-Mother Official" (*fumu guan*).

[26] The magistrate, while presiding over the court, was usually assisted by the personnel of the tribunal, such as secretaries, constables, coroner, the warden of the jail, lictor and guards. The lictor in Chinese is "*zaoli*" (literally, the runner wearing a black uniform), because in accordance with the stipulation, the staff of yamen must wear black uniforms, and hence the name.

[27] Theoretically, this was illegal. It was stipulated in the first years of the Hongwu reign (1368–1399) that the punishment of 50 strokes with the light bamboo should be decided by the county (*xian*) magistrate, the punishment of 80 strokes with the heavy bamboo, by the magistrate of the sub-prefecture, and the punishment of 100 strokes with the heavy bamboo, by the prefect. Matthew Ricci pointed out, however, that in spite of the seemingly lenient penal codes, many were illegally put to death by magistrates, due to a fixed and ancient custom of the country permitting a magistrate, without any legal process or judgement, to subject a person to flogging when it might please him to do so.

[28] In the original text, it is "*wu she*" (my tongue), not "your tongue." Obviously "*wu*" (my) was a slip of pen, and in order to make the sentence understandable, it has been corrected.

One Woman and Two Monks

[1] The original title of this story (story 26 of *Slapping the Table in Amazement*)

is: "A Village Woman Lost her Life in Sexual Entanglements / The Judge Solved the Case by Using Heavenly Revelations."

[2]   Lin'an is modern Hangzhou in Zhejiang Province.

[3]   A Provincial Graduate (*juren*) in Ming-Qing times was the official designation granted to a successful candidate in a Provincial Examination (*xiangshi*), entitling him to proceed further in the Civil Service Recruitment Examination sequence. Literally he was "offered up," in the sense that he was also available for immediate appointment. But after the early Ming no one could expect this status alone to lead to an eminent career.

[4]   This sort of wooden fish is a skull-shaped musical instrument upon which monks beat time with a mallet when chanting.

221

[5]   This colloquial expression perhaps reflected the dining custom only in the Wu area (the Lower Yangzi valley). "Steamed bun" as a general term refers to both "stuffed steam bun" and "steam bun without stuffing." In the Lower Yangzi areas, steamed buns are usually eaten as a snack. The main food, in present days as in Ming-Qing times, has been rice.

[6]   "A Boddhisattva Guanyin" refers to Du. Guanyin is the model of Chinese beauty. To say a lady or a young girl is a "Guanyin" is a compliment to her beauty.

[7]   Urethritis.

[8]   The National Academy (*Taixue*) or (*guozi jian*) was the highest institution of learning in the Ming dynasty. It was first established in Nanjing in the Hongwu reign (1368) (originally it was called *guozi xue*) and later in the Yongle reign (1403) another one was founded in Beijing. In the Ming dynasty, officials were selected (1) from the Civil Service Examinations, (2) from the National Academies, (3) from recommendations (*jianju*), and (4) from applications (*quanxuan*). Talented and capable officials were usually the ones who graduated from the National Academies. However, they could only hold positions in prefectures (*fu*) and counties (*xian*) as rank 6 or lower officials. Ling was rather dissatisfied that the Civil Service Examinations system had become the only prestigious way of selecting officials in the late Ming. That is why in this story the transitional phrase *suiran* (though), which has been translated as "nevertheless," is used.

[9]   "Male love" (*nanfeng*) was very popular in late Ming times. Fujianese were especially fond of male same-sex relations. In Fujian province, men of different classes, noble and humble alike, would seek partners of similar social status. The older one was called "*qixiong*" (elder bond brother) and the younger one was called "*qidi*" (younger bond brother). When the elder brother visited the younger brother's house, the younger brother's parents would treat him as if he were their son-in-law. The elder brother was obliged to take financial responsibility for the younger brother's living and marriage expenses. An affectionate couple slept together like husband and wife even when they were over thirty.

[10] This is because the old monk always plays an active role and Zhiyuan is always his passive (submissive) partner. In Ming China, the man who was senior in age or position usually played the active role in male same-sex intercourse, that is, he usually engaged in the penile penetration of his junior partner.

[11] To those who had committed serious crimes such as robbery or who had been sentenced to death, the judge could apply the *tinggun* (cudgel), *jiagun* (squeezers), or *laotie* (branding iron). Squeezers as an instrument of torture, which began to be used in court when Song Lizong was on the throne (r. 1225–1264), were made of wooden sticks and ropes, and could squeeze thighs as well as fingers.

[12] "Rear courtyard" (*houting*) or "rear-courtyard flower" (*houting hua*) is a euphemism for anus.

The Wife Swappers

[1] The original title of this story (story 32 of *Slapping the Table in Amazement*) is: "Hu Fulfilled his Lustful Desire through Simulated Swapping / The Buddhist Adept in his Trance Predicted his Retribution."

[2] Hook of Wu (*Wugou*) was a curved sword made in the area of Wu.

[3] A metaphor for beautiful women.

[4] Xiang Ji (232–202 BC), styled Yu, was born into a noble family in the State of Chu. After Chen She and Wu Guang had arisen in rebellion against the Qin court, Xiang Yu and his uncle began their uprising. Later Xiang Yu defeated the main forces of the Qin and proclaimed him the Hegemon King of Western Chu (*xichu bawang*). He ruled nine provinces. In what the historians call the "Chu-Han War," which lasted about four years, he and Liu Bang fought to rule the country, and he was finally defeated by Liu Bang in 202 BC.

[5] Yu (Yu ji) and Qi (Qi furen) were respectively Xiang Yu and Liu Bang's favourite concubines.

[6] The literal translation should be "sack of flesh and blood."

[7] Liu Bang was the King of Han (*Han Wang*) instead of the emperor of the whole country when he was fighting with Xiang Yu. But his personal name was tabooed in the Han dynasty and writers of later ages were accustomed to addressing him by his posthumous title Gaozu, even though this was sometimes anachronistic from the narrative point of view, as it is here.

[8] "The land under heaven" (*tianxia*) refers to China, not to the world.

[9] This refers to the moving scene before Xiang Yu died. For details, see *Shi ji* (Record of Grand Historian), *juan* 7.

[10] This refers to the following episode. The emperor (Liu Bang) wished to remove the heir apparent (his son by Empress Lu) and set up Ruyi, the king of Zhao, his son by Lady Qi, in his place. Many of the high ministers had strongly advised him against this. Zhang Liang told Empress Lü that probably only four old men whom the emperor had not succeeded in attracting to his court might be able to make the emperor change his mind. With Zhang Liang's arrangement, a banquet was held and wine set out in the palace. The heir apparent waited upon the emperor and the four old men who accompanied him. The emperor then called Lady Qi to his side, saying, "I have hoped to change the heir apparent, but these four men have come to his aid." Lady Qi wept. The emperor sang, "The great swan soars aloft, / In one swoop a thousand miles. / He has spread his giant wings / And spans the four seas.

/ He who spans the four seas – / Ah, what can we do? / Though we bear stringed arrows to down him, / Whereto should we aim them?" He sang the song through several times and rose and left the banquet. See Watson, *Records of the Grand Historian of China: Han Dynasty I*, pp. 109–112.

[11] Moral merits of the nether world is a literal translation of "*yinde*" (meaning, do something good secretly), a term which is related to the concept of Buddhist karma.

[12] Here the original text is: "Tangqing also held an official post in Pingjiang." This, obviously, is, a slip of pen, which has been corrected according to its source material.

[13] The Provincial Examination was held every three years.

[14] "Heavenly gate" (*tianmen*) refers to the gate of the compound where the provincial government was located, not the gate of the imperial palace in which the "son of heaven" (*tianzi*) resided. The result of the Provincial Examination was first brought out on a large placard, which the examination officials placed outside the government compound, in full public view. Then the governor-general of the province sent to each prefecture the names of the successful candidates who had passed the examinations and the prefect passed the news down to the district magistrate, who in turn informed the man himself. The fact that the examination officials were sent "by imperial commission" (*qinchai*) as the emperor's deputies probably explains the employment of the term "heavenly gate," which obviously implies that the result of the examination was posted on behalf of the emperor as if it had been done by the emperor himself.

[15] "Recommendation" means recommendation for the State Examination. This is another way of saying that the man passed the Provincial Examination.

[16] "*Juren*" (who passed the Provincial Examinations) literally means "recommended men" (for taking the State Examinations).

[17] Usually the papers were read twice by two examiners. They first passed through the hands of the associate examiners, who had to do the grading in designated places and were forbidden to carry a paper anywhere else on their own initiative. They used blue ink for their remarks and decided in general upon passes and failures. When they wrote "mediocre" on the cover, or "without merit," the paper failed. When the paper was considered to be "excellent in style and content," they wrote "recommended" on the cover and then the paper was delivered to the chief and deputy examiners, who usually read only those recommended papers, although they were free to have other answer sheets brought to them.

[18] Mianzhou is the modern Hanyang county in Hubei province.

[19] The Censor of Embroidered-Garments as an imperially-ordered assignment was first set by Wudi of the Han. In the Yuan dynasty, the Censor of Embroidered-Garments was a rank 2a official.

[20] Zhiyuan and Zhizheng reigns, which were both the reign names of the last Emperor Shundi of the Yuan dynasty, correspond to the years 1335 – 1367. In *Chuke pai'an jingqi*, collated and annotated by Wang Gulu, "Zhiyuan and Zhizheng reigns" is "*Da Yuan Zhizheng chao*" (the Zhizheng reign of

223

the Great Yuan dynasty), which corresponds to the years 1341 – 1367. But the Shangyoutang edition collated by Li Tianyi is perhaps more trustworthy so far as this point is concerned, because it is confirmed by the source material upon which Ling Mengchu's story is based.

[21] The turtle, because of its long neck and pointed head which resembles a man's penis, is sometimes used as a term of vulgar abuse, implying that the person who is cursed has indulged in some unnatural vices (for instance, incest or pseudo-incest). It can also denote "a man who connives at (or derives profit from) his wife's fornication," or a man who is unwittingly deceived by his wife.

[22] The three lives (in sanskrit, "trayo-dhvanah") are the previous life, this life, and the future life.

[23] In China the genteel classes in the past used very small cups for drinking.

[24] "Sheep on the Mountain Slope" (shanpo yang) is a tune from sanqu (lyric-song). The orthodox form of "Sheep on the Mountain Slope" contains 41 words. Its prosody and tones are as follows: four seven, three, seven, one three, and one three; – – x |, – – x |, x – x | – –|, | – –, | – – x – x | – –|, x | – – x, –, x – x, –, x | x. But the "Sheep on the Mountain Slope" in this story has 131 words and its prosody is completely different. Although chenzi (inserted words) are allowed in qu they could never be as many as 90 words for such a short qu as "Sheep on the Mountain Slope." Maybe this is the reason why the author, an experienced hand in writing sanqü, called it a deviant tune (taidiao) of "Sheep on the Mountain Slope." Since Sui Shusen's Quan Yuan Sanqu (A Complete Collection of the Songs of the Yuan Dynasty) and some other source books do not contain any of the deviant forms of "Sheep on the Mountain Slope," this sanqu verse was perhaps entirely Ling Mengchu's own invention.

[25] A euphemism for brothel.

[26] The God of Earth was a deity protecting a certain local area.

[27] Mount Yusi, originally called Qunyu feng, was in the southeast of Xiajiang county, Jiangxi province.

[28] The five precepts of Buddhism are: (1) slay not, (2) steal not, (3) lust not, (4) be not light in conversation, and (5) drink not intoxicants nor eat meat.

The Elopement of a Nun

[1] The original title of this story (story 34 of Slapping the Table in Amazement I) is: "Wenren Engaged in Illicit Sexual Bouts in the Green Duckweed Nunnery / Nun Jingguan Appeared in Splendor at Yellow Sand Street."

[2] Sima Xiangru (179 – 117 BC) was a poet in the Han dynasty. Because of his talent in writing prose-poems, he was appointed by Emperor Wu as a high-ranking official in his court. But Xiangru had been poor before he occupied that distinguished position. At Linqiong in the province of Shu where he lived, there were a number of rich men at that time, and one of them was called Zhuo Wangsun, whose household included 800 servants and slaves. Zhuo Wangsun had a daughter named Zhuo Wenjun, who was fond of music and had only recently been widowed. One day Zhuo Wangsun gave

a party for Xiangru and on that occasion Xiangru played the lute. Wenjun had already heard of his reputation as a gifted poet and as a handsome man, and when she saw him drinking and playing in her own home, she felt an instant love for him. That night Wenjun ran away from home and joined him, and the two of them eloped to Chengdu, where they took up residence in Xiangru's house, four bare walls with nothing inside.

[3] Peach Feast (*pantao hui*) refers to the magnificent dinner party held by the mythological figure, the Queen Mother of the West, at Jasper Lake in the Kunlun Mountains.

[4] For the story of Kunlun Knave, see Note 4 of "In the Inner Quarter."

[5] Yellow-Shirt Gallant (Huangshan Ke) was a man who brought the unfaithful husband Li to his abandoned wife Jade (Huo Xiaoyu) for a reunion. Li was a young scholar from a good family, upon whom senior scholars looked as an outstanding literary star. Through a match-maker he made the acquaintance of Jade, the youngest daughter of Prince Huo, who, after the prince's death, had been driven out of the family and had thus become a courtesan. Jade admired Li's talent, and not caring at all that he was a poor literatus, co-habited with him for two years. When Li came first in the Civil Service Examination and was appointed secretaty-general of Zheng county, Jade begged him not to abandon her and Li promised that he would not. At this time, however, Li's parents had arranged a marriage for him and he had no choice but to accept it. So he never returned to Jade. Jade fell ill from sorrow. When the news reached her that Li was back in the capital, Jade entreated her friends to help her get together with her old lover. A handsome man, splendidly dressed in yellow shirt, learned of her situation, and one day stepped forward and bowed to Li as the latter was viewing peonies in a temple, saying, "Is your name Li? I have long been an admirer of you and have hoped to make your acquaintance; today I am so fortunate as to encounter you. My humble home is not far, and I will have musicians to entertain you. I only hope that you will favour me with a visit." When Li was conducted to Jade's house, the Yellow-Shirt Gallant pushed him through the gate and bolted it, calling out to Jade, "Here is Master Li!"

[6] Aide Xu (Xu Yuhou, i.e., Xu Jun) was a man who helped Lady Liu (Liushi) escape from General Shazhali's residence to reunite with her husband Han Xu. For details, see *Tangren Xiaoshuo* (Stories of the Tang Dynasty), "Liushi zhuan" (Story of Lady Liu).

[7] "Country flowers and wild grasses" (*xianhua yecao*) is a metaphor for frivolous women whom men tend to pick for sexual adventures.

[8] Literally, "yellow" and "white" refer to gold and silver respectively, or to the making of the pills of immortality from gold or silver. So "talking on yellow and white" can also be explained as "talking on finance and alchemy," interesting topics for women of rich families.

[9] The Censorate (*ducha yuan*, or *chayuan*) was a surveillance organ of the Ming central government, consisting of 2 Censors-in-Chief (*du yushi*), 2 Vice Censors-in-Chief (*fudu yushi*), and 4 Assistant Censors-in-Chief (*qiandu yushi*).

[10] "Nun" Wang is perhaps a hermaphrodite, i.e., a bisexual person who can

be a "man" for women and a "woman" for men. This condition was
documented in earlier times. In the Jin dynasty, according to Shen Defu
(1578 – 1642), there was a person living in the capital who had both male
and female sexual organs, and was capable of having sex with men and
women. Shen Defu also tells us that in Ming times a mistress of a gentry
family in Changshu county could change into a man, and she changed her
gender semimonthly. When she was not a woman, her husband avoided her
and she would have sex with her maids. It was said that her "shaft" was
even more virile than that of a man and her intercourse with her maids could
last for a whole night. Professor He Qinglian, an orthopaedist who has been
called the "father of sex transformation" in China, claimed that there are
at least seven different types of gender. That is, in addition to normal male
and female, there are another five kinds of people: (1) pseudo-man, who has
ovaries, a womb, cervix, and "penis;" (2) pseudo-woman, who has a cervix
and hidden testicles, but has no ovaries nor womb; (3) hermaphrodite, who
has testicles, ovaries, sperm, menses, a penis, and cervix; (4) neutral person,
who has no testicles, nor ovaries; (5) transsexual person, who tends to
change into a woman if he is a man or a man if she is a woman.

[11] The White Lotus Cult (*bailian jiao*) was a religious movement characterized
by a belief in the imminent advent of a saviour called Maitreya (*mi-le*) and
a tendency to rebel against the state. It had originally been very close to the
lay Buddhism propagated by the Pure Land tradition, but in the late Yuan,
Han Shantong, who founded the White Lotus Society (*bailian hui*) and
proclaimed that "the empire was in great disorder, Maitreya Buddha shall
descend to be reborn and the king of light shall appear in this world," rose
in Maitreyaist uprising and finally overthrew the Yuan dynasty. In the late
imperial period, the White Lotus Cult was prohibited by the government,
and its believers were usually persecuted and killed.

[12] In this story, "Three Wus" is simply a name for the Lower Yangtze region.

[13] This passage, with the change of only two or three words, was taken from
a *wenyan* story. See Tan Zhengbi, ed., *Sanyan Liangpai ziliao* (Source
Materials of Three Words and Two Slaps), p. 734.

[14] Hongxi was the era-name of Emperor Renzong of the Ming dynasty (r.
1425), who reigned from 1425 – 1426.

[15] "New bamboo sprouts" refer to her newly-bound feet. For the custom of
footbinding in traditional China, see Howard Levy, *Chinese Footbinding:
the History of a Curious Erotic Custom.*

[16] Feng Zhi was a virtuous and filial man living in the time when Emperor
Jingzong of the Tang was on the throne (r. 825 – 826). When he was young
and lived by himself, a fairy (Shangyuan Furen) descended to visit him at
night. Feng Zhi rejected her, but the fairy kept visiting him once a week,
and appeared to him four times altogether. Feng Zhi, however, remained
unmoved by her seduction from the beginning to the end.

[17] Lu Nan also refers to a man who is sexually continent. The source of this
allusion comes from Mao's explanation of the two lines of a poem in *Shijing*
(Book of Poetry): "In the state of Lu there was a man living alone by himself.

226

His neighbour happened to be a lonely widow. One night, a violent storm damaged her house and she came rushing over to the man's house to take refuge. The man, however, refused to open the door. The woman then spoke to him through a window, 'Why did you not open the door and let me in?' The man replied, 'Man should not live with a woman who is not related to him until after he is sixty. That is how I have been taught. You are a young lady and I am a young man, so I can't let you stay in my house.'"

[18] "Eight-characters" (*bazi* or *zao*) in Chinese fortune-telling refer to one's birth hour, date, month, and year. In pre-modern China, time was designated by Heavenly Stems (*tiangan*) and Earthly Branches (*dizhi*), so all the time units, no matter whether it was hour, date, month, or year, were expressed by two characters, one from the Heavenly Stems and the other from the Earthly Branches. The Chinese astrologist tells people's fortunes on the basis of the relationships of the "*wuxing*" (five elements, i.e., metal, wood, water, fire, and earth) manifested by the conbination of his or her eight characters.

[19] Wuchang was originally a Buddhist term, meaning that everything in the world, including life and death, is not constant. Later, however, it gradually became the name of a ghost, whose job it was to drag the living person into the nether world.

[20] Since "*Wenren*" is close to "Min-Ling" in Wu dialectal pronunciation, it may be regarded as a pun, which suggests that the hero with this surname could be a member of either the Min or Ling family. So it is very likely that this story is, to some extent, autobiographical, or, at least, related to a family member or relative of the author.

[21] Pan An was the famous Jin poet Pan Yue (247–300), and Anren was his style ("An" is a short form for "Anren"). Pan Yue was a very handsome man. When he was young he liked to travel, and often walked along the main boulevard of Luoyang, playing his musical instrument as he went. Women who saw him would surround him and throw fruit and presents to him. It was thus a common occurence that he would return home with a cart fully loaded with gifts.

[22] Zijian was the poet Cao Zhi (192–232) and Zijian was his style. Cao Zhi was the son of Cao Cao, the founder of the Wei Kingdom in the Three Kingdom period. Cao Cao and his two sons, Cao Pi (the eldest son) and Cao Zhi (the younger son) were all "great poets" in the Jian'an period, and Cao Zhi was "especially talented" among them.

[23] Jia Wu's aromatic water refers to the precious perfume paid as a tribute to the Jin court by the Western Regions (i.e., the regions west of Yumenguan, including parts of Central Asia). Since its scent could last a month after it was applied, the emperor regarded it as a rare treasure and bestowed it only on Jia Chong and another high ranking official. Jia Wu was Jia Chong's daughter. She stole the perfume from her father and gave it to her lover Han Shou. Han Shou's colleagues smelled the unusual fragrance when they were together and told Jia Chong about it. Jia Chong then knew that his daughter was carrying on secretly with this man. As a result, Jia Chong had to marry his daughter to him.

[24] Xishi was a well-known beauty in the state of Yue in the Spring and Autumn

227

period. She is also known as Xianshi, or Xizi.

[25] The four elements (*sida*) is a Buddhist term, referring to earth, water, air (or wind), and fire. Buddhism considers the four elements as the essential materials in the world, but it also maintains that the four elements come from emptiness and are insubstantial. Thus, everything composed of the four elements is no more than a transient phenomenon.

[26] The Provincial Examination (*xiangshi*) was held only on the Chinese cyclical years of Zi, Wu, Mao, and You, that is, it was held every three years.

[27] "The Touring Provincial Commissioner for Education" in the original text is "*daojian*," a phrase which, judging from the context, seems a slip of pen for "*daotai*."

[28] Secretary (*zhushi*) was an official of rank 6a in the Ming dynasty, usually in charge of a bureau (*si*) or a section of a Board (*bu*) or any other agency in the central government.

[29] The Soul-Veiled Monastery (*Lingyin Si*) is located at the foot of Mount Lingyin in Hangzhou. It faces Feilai Peak, with the Cold Spring (*Lengquan*) flowing in front of it.

[30] "Subverting head" (*luandai tou*) and "head of the penis" (*luandai tou*) are homophonous in Chinese, and the latter in the Wu dialect is always used as obscene language.

[31] A passenger boat (*kechuan*) in olden times usually had windows on both sides of the cabin. Feng Zikai (1898 – 1974?), a modern cartoonist and essayist, has given a detailed description of the layout of the passenger boat: "The passenger boat is a special kind of boat in the region of rivers and lakes where we live. There, rivers extend in all directions and people brought up in these areas would rather take a boat than walk, even if the place they are going to visit is only about a mile away. The passenger boat is tastefully designed and well furnished. It consists of three parts: prow, cabin, and stern, all divided by wooden partitions. The stern is where the boatman works and it is also the place for cooking. The cabin is for passenger(s) to sit and sleep. And the prow is usually filled with articles of daily use. In the cabin one can find a bed, a small table, and windows on both sides. Below the windows is a fixed plank for sitting. The small table is usually placed at the corner of the cabin, with three short legs standing on the sitting-board and one long leg on the floor. If there are four people drinking together, the three short legs can be lengthened and the table can therefore be put in the middle. The table is square, about two feet on each side, on which people can also play mahjong. On the walls of the cabin hang framed pictures or calligraphic works. Thus it looks like a small living room. This kind of boat can even be compared to '*huachuan*' (the gaily painted pleasure-boat)." See *Feng Zikai Juan* (The Works of Feng Zikai), p. 98.

[32] For "rear-courtyard flower," see Note 19 for "One Woman and Two Monks."

[33] "The clouds have dispersed and the rain has come down" (*yunshou yusan*) is a common euphemistic way of saying that sexual intercourse has come to completion.

[34] "Flowery mine" (*huaguan*) refers to a woman's vagina.

[35] "Serene Lady" (*anren*) was an honourific title awarded to wives of rank 6a or 6b officials in the Ming.

[36] Xiangru juice is a Chinese herbal tonic, especially good for edema and halitosis.

[37] Thread-needle Day was the seventh day of the seventh month in the Chinese lunar calendar. On that night women would place melons and fruits in the courtyard and would, by threading a seven-holed needle, beg Weaving Maid, who was to meet Shepherd Boy that night, to bestow wisdom and skill on them.

[38] "Ullambhana" means "rescuing persons in dire straits." The Ullambhana Festival was on the fifteenth day of the seventh month. It is said that on that day Mulian offered to Buddha various kinds of food and five kinds of fruit (peach, plum, apricot, chestnut, and date), in the hope of rescuing his mother from the hungry ghosts, who were hanging her by her feet, ready to devour her. Since the Six Dynasties, the fifteenth of the seventh month had always been a day for common people to redeem lost souls. On that day monks and nuns would be hired and people would make offerings and say prayers.

229

[39] Chen Miaochang is the heroine in Gao Lian's play *Yuzan ji* (The Jade Hairpin). This play was later completely rewritten by Ling Mengchu.

[40] The Provincial Examination consisted of three tests. The first test started on the ninth day of the eighth month, and there was an interval of three days between each test. The first test examined the student's knowledge of the Classics and the examinee had to answer three questions, two for the Five Classics, and one for the Four Books. Thus, the first test was also known as the "Classics Test" and the person who won first place in this Classics Test was called "*jingkui*." The second test was essay writing and the examinee had to write an argumentative essay on a given topic. The third test was an essay question on current affairs and the examinee was expected to contribute his opinions on government policy. If the student passed all these three tests, he would be eligible to take the final tests, i.e., the tests on (1) riding, (2) shooting, (3) calligraphy, (4) math, and (5) law.

[41] The State Examination (*huishi*) was also held every three years, though not in the same years as the Provincial Examination. It occurred in the following years, that is, in the Chinese cyclical years of Chen, Xu, Chou, and Wei. It also consisted of three tests, and the first test started from the ninth day of the second month, with an interval of three days between each test. Those who successfully passed the Provincial Examination were eligible to participate in a State Examination in the capital, and those who passed the State Examination would soon reassemble for the Palace Examination (*tingshi* or *dianshi*), conducted by the emperor himself on the first day of the third month, in which the State Graduates were ranked by merit into three groups (*jia*).

[42] "Coil" (*ji*) in the Chinese text is "*bin*" (hair on the temples). Obviously this is a slip of pen.

[43] In Ming China only women from noble families were permitted to wear the phoenix cap and rosy cape (*fengguan xiapei*). Women of non-noble lineage, however, could also wear them for their wedding ceremony. The cap had a

phoenix decoration made of gold with jade on it.

[44] "Respectful Lady" (*gongren*) was an honourific title awarded to wives of rank 4 officials and of low-ranking nobles in the Ming.

In the Inner Quaters

[1] The original title of this story (story 34 of *Slapping the Table in Amazement, Second Collection*) is: "Ren Junyong Gave Rein to his Sexual Indulgence in the Inner Quarters / Commander Yang Found Amusement in Gelding his Retainer."

[2] "Girls from Yan" (*yanji*) and "ladies from Zhao" (*zhaonu*) refer to beautiful concubines. It is said that in ancient times women from the State of Yan and the State of Zhao were the most beautiful.

[3] Red Whisk is a fictional character in Du Guangting's "Qiuranke Zhuan" (The Man with a Curly Beard). For her story, see *Tang Song chuanqi ji* (Collection of Tang-Song Romances); for the English translation, see *Tang Dynasty Stories*.

[4] Yang Su, because of his military merits, had been enfeoffed Duke of Yue before he became Councillor. For his biography, see Wei Zheng, *Sui shu* (History of the Sui Dynasty), *juan* 48.

[5] Red Silk, which means a girl wearing a red silk dress, is also a fictional character in a Tang story. For details, see "Kunlun nu" (Kunlun Knave) by Pei Xing, in *Taiping Guangji* (Works Widely Collected during the Taiping Reign), *juan* 194.

[6] Guan Panpan was originally a courtesan in Xuzhou, who later married the minister Zhang Jianfeng, becoming one of his concubines. After Zhang died, she secluded herself in his residence for about ten years, refusing to remarry. When the poet Bai Juyi wrote a verse mocking her way of living, she starved herself and died.

[7] The stone produced in Lake Tai (*Taihu*) in Jiangsu province is well-known for its use in rockeries and garden decoration.

[8] *Liubo* or *liuzhuan* was a game played with twelve pieces on a board resembling the plate of the Han sundial. The moves were determined by throwing six sticks (*zhu*) divided into two sides. Each piece was marked with one of the four animals symbolizing the directions of space. There seems to have been a central belt, like the Milky Way in later systems, and when a piece landed there it was promoted to a "leading piece" with greater powers.

[9] A euphemism for ejaculation.

[10] "Fifth watch" (*wugeng*) is daybreak. In pre-modern China, the night was divided into five sections: *jiaye* (the first section of night, roughly 8 pm – 10 pm), *yiye* (the second section, roughly 10 pm – 12 pm), *bingye* (the third section, roughly 12 pm – 2 am), *dingye* (the fourth section, roughly 2 am – 4 am), and *shuye* (the fifth section, roughly 4 am – 6 am).

[11] Cai Jing (1047 – 1126) was a native of Fujian Province. He obtained his *jinshi* degree when he was only 24 years old, and later became the most powerful minister at the court of Emperor Huizong (r. 1101 – 1126). Among the official posts he assumed were Left Grand Councillor, Grand Academician

of the Hall for Veneration of Governance, Grand Preceptor, and Minister of Personnel. It was not until the capital was in imminent danger and the emperor abdicated in favour of his son Qinzong that Cai Jing was ousted and exiled to the south. He died on the way to Tanzhou. In popular literature Cai Jing is usually referred to as Grand Preceptor Cai, because the Grand Preceptor was one of *Sanshi* (*three preceptors*) who, from antiquity to the Song times, had been officially considered as the 3 paramount aides to the ruler and held the highest possible ranks in officialdom.

[12] Gao = Gao Qiu (? – 1126), Tong = Tong Guan (1054 – 1126), Yang = Yang Jian (? – 1121) and Cai = Cai Jing, are all historical figures, notoriously known as the four evil ministers.

[13] Yang Jian, as a historical figure, was a eunuch.

[14] "Rain and dew" is a euphemism for semen.

[15] This allusion comes from a story told by Song Yu (3rd century BC) to King Xiang of Chu (r. 298 – 265 BC) about a tryst between the Goddess of Witch's Mountain (or Mount Wu) and his father King Huai (r. 328 – 299 BC) in the prose preface to "Gaotang fu" (Rhapsody on Gaotang), which has been traditionally attributed to Song Yu (a poet who was regarded as a follower of Qu Yuan). More probably it was a Han work dating from the first century BC.

[16] "The flower-collecting game" (*Dou baicao*) is an ancient game for women. In it, the players could make wagers by matching the names, or comparing the quality, of the flowers they collected.

[17] "Kickball" (*cuju*) is an old Chinese football game. It was a popular outdoor sport for both men and women.

[18] Chang'an, now in the northwest of Chang'an county, Shanxi province, was in Chinese history the capital of several dynasties. But "Chang'an" can also be used as a common name, referring to any place where an emperor stayed (*xingzai*).

[19] In ancient China aristocrats and high-ranking officials kept retainers in the fashion of Lord Mengchang (d. 279 BC), a member of the ruling house of the State of Qi during the Warring States period (475 – 221 BC). Lord Mengchang was famous for his patronage of large numbers of retainers. He recruited guests and retainers from feudal lords, even welcoming those who had committed an offence, setting aside his own income to care for them.

[20] "Wearing one's hair in a topknot" (*zongjiao*) is a common expression in Chinese literature for childhood. A Chinese boy usually wore the tufts of his hair in two topknots until the age of sixteen when he began to keep his hair long, in preparation for the capping ceremony at the age of twenty.

[21] A euphemism for male same-sex relationships.

[22] A dildo in Chinese is usually called "Mr. Horn" (*guo xiansheng*). According to van Gulik, the dildo, or the "double olisbos," to use his term, was a short-ribbed stick made of wood or ivory, with two silk bands attached to the middle. See *Sexual Life in Ancient China*, p. 163.

[23] In the Ming, an unmarried girl wore her hair in two buns, and hence the term "*shuanhuan nuzi*," which implies that the girl in question, usually a teenager, was unmarried.

[24] Hou Yi is the famous archer of Chinese legend. It is said that in the time of Yao there were ten suns scorching all vegetation. Yao ordered Hou Yi to shoot down nine of them and Hou Yi successfully did so.

[25] Mount Penglai is the legendary mountain where immortals lived. According to *Sanhai Jing* (Book of Mountains and Seas), Mount Penglai is in the sea. Guo Pu says that "on the top of the mountain there is a gold-jade palace of immortals, where all birds and animals are white, looking as if they were clouds."

[26] The Weaving Maid (the star Vega) crosses the Milky way to meet her lover the Shepherd (the star Altair) once a year on the night of the seventh day of the seventh month.

[27] A euphemism referring to the end of sexual intercourse.

[28] "Troubled waters" (*hunshui*) is an elliptical form of the idiom *hunshui moyu* (to fish in troubled waters), meaning "to gain benefit by taking advantage of a chaotic situation."

[29] A euphemism for penis.

[30] Mount Wu, sometimes translated as "Witch's Mountain," is located on the border between the provinces of Sichuan and Hubei, its shape resembling the Chinese character "*wu*." Mount Wu in literary works often alludes to the place where men and women meet each other for a tryst.

[31] For Daoist priests, the sword was an indispensable weapon, which could be used to kill demons or drive away evil spirits, and help those who possessed it become immortal.

[32] The Wutong Spirits (*Wutong shen*) or (*Wulang shen*) are seen as five men. One legend has it that they were deified soldiers who died for the establishment of the Ming dynasty, and because soldiers are interested in women, Wutong Spirits were prone to seduce young girls. Wutong Spirits are not always harmful, and more often they simply play tricks on men.

[33] This is a game played by people while they are drinking. Participants would hold some small object like a coin, a chess-piece, or a melon seed in his fist and let the other guess what it was. The loser had to drink a cup of wine as a forfeit.

[34] In Ancient China, kings and feudal lords usually had their own mulberry trees and a house for rearing silkworms. The house, which they called *canshi* (silkworm house), was built near a river, ten cubits in height, with the surrounding walls topped with thorns and the gate locked from the outside. Since silkworms need warm conditions, the house was kept warm and well insulated, with a fire burning in it all the time. A newly castrated man also needs a warm and well-insulated room after the surgery, and that is why going to the silkworm house can also mean "to be castrated."

[35] Although castration was formally abolished in the Sui dynasty (589–618 AD) and was not recorded in the penal codes of later dynasties, it seems that emperors and high-ranking officials of the Ming still continued this practice often at will.

[36] Slang for penis.

[37] The Temple of Serving the Country (*Xiangguo si*) was located at the centre of Kaifeng, Henan province.

Selected Bibliography

This bibliography includes only those cited or mentioned in the text and notes, but some materials of minor importance and items unavailable or not extant are usually omitted. For the Chinese books published before twentieth century, the names of the publishers which are unknown are left out.

Principal Editions of Ling Mengchu's Two Slaps

The present translation is based on the Shangyou tang 尚友堂 edition collated by 李田意 , but Wang Gulu's 王古魯 annotated edition was often consulted when the translation was undertaken.

1. *Chuke pai'an jingqi* 初刻拍案驚奇. Collated and annotated by Wang Gulu 王古魯. Beijing: Renmin wenxue chuban she, 1957. *Erke pai'an jingqi* 二刻拍案驚奇. Collated and annotated by Wang Gulu 王古魯. Beijing: Renmin wenxue chuban she, 1957.

2. *Pai'an jingqi* 拍案驚奇. Collated by Li Tianyi 李田意. Hong Kong: Youlian chuban gongsi, 1986. *Erke pai'an jingqi* 二刻拍案驚奇. Collated by Li Tainyi 李田意. Hong Kong: Youlian chuban gongsi, 1986.

Below are the major works of Ling Mengchu, or edited by him, which are listed in in *Houzhou fuzhi* 湖州府誌 and *Wucheng xianzhi* 烏程縣誌, with a few extra titles suplemented by Ye Dejun 葉德鈞, Wang Gulu 王古魯 and Shi Changyu's 石昌渝:

"Beishu fu" 北輸賦;
"Daishan ji" 戴山記;
"Daishan shi" 戴山詩;
"Dangzhi houlu" 蕩櫛後錄;
Dongpo chanxi ji 東坡禪喜集;
Dongpo shuzhuan 東坡書傳;
Guoce gai 國策概.;
Guomen ji 國門集;
Guomen ji yiji 國門集乙集;
Heping xuanshi 合評選詩;
Hou hanshu zuanping 後漢書纂評;
"Huoni gong" 惑溺供;
Jiaokou shice 剿寇十策;
Jibian dudan 己編蠹斷;
Jijiangzhai shiwen 雞講齋詩文;
"Juedi baochou" 掘地報仇;
"Juejiao juzi shu" 絕交擧子書;
"Liu Bolun" 劉伯倫;
"Mang zepai" 莽擇配;
"Mouhu yinyuan" 驀忽姻緣;
Nanyin sanlai 南音三籟;
Ni Si Shi Han yitong buping 倪思史漢異同補評;
"Ni Zhengping" 倪正平;
"Qiaohe shan" 喬和杉;

Qulu 曲律;

Shanding Songshi buyi 删定宋詩(史)補遺;

Shengong shishuo 沈公詩說;

Shengmen chuanshi dizhong 聖門傳詩嫡冢;

Shijing renwu kao 詩經人物考;

Shiliuguo chunqiu shanzheng 十六國春秋刪正;

"Zhushan fu" 杼山賦;

"Songgongming nao yuanxiao" 宋公明鬧元宵;

Su Huang chidu 蘇黃尺牘;

Tanqu za zha 譚曲雜札;

"Taohua zhuang" 桃花莊;

Tao Jingjie ji 陶靖節集;

Wusao hebian 吳騷合編;

Xuan fu 選賦;

"Xuehe ji" 雪荷記;

Yan shi yi 言詩翼;

Yan Zhu ou 燕筑謳;

Zuozhuan hezheng 左傳盒證.

Works in Chinese

Ban Zhao 班昭. *Nujie* 女誡, in *Nu sishu* 女四書. Shanghai: Jiangzuo shulin, 1887.

Bao Zunxin 包遵信. "Ming-Qing zhiji shehui sichao he wenyi fuxing" 明清之際社會思潮和文藝復興, *Zhongwi wenhua bijiao yanjiu* 中外文化比較研究. Beijing: Sanlian shudian, 1988.

———. "Wanxia yu shuguang" 晚霞與曙光, *Pipan yu qimeng* 批判與啓蒙. Taipei: Lianjing chuban shiye gongsi, 1989.

Boping xianzhi 博平縣誌. 1831 edition.

Cai Guoliang 蔡國梁. *Ming qing xiaoshuo tanyou* 明清小說探幽. Hangzhou: Zhejiang wenyi chuban she, 1985.

Cai Meibiao 蔡美彪, et al. *Zhongguo tonghsi* 中國通史. Beijing: Renmin chubanshe, 1978.

Chen Cuiying 陳翠英. *Shiqing xiaoshuo zhi jiazhiguan tantao* 世情小說之價值觀探討. Taipei: National Taiwan University Press, 1996.

Chen Dongyuan 陳東遠. *Zhongguo funu shenghuo shi* 中國婦女生活史. Shanghai: Commercial Press, 1937.

Chen Duo 陳多. "Ling Mengchu" 凌濛初, in *Zhongguo gudai xiqujia pingzhuan* 中國古代戲曲家評傳. Zhengzhou: Zhongzhou guji chuban she, 1992.

Chen Hao 陳灝, ed. *Liji jishuo* 禮記集說. Taipei: Shijie shuju, 1962.

Chen Jiru 陳繼儒. *Chongzhen songjiang xianzhi* 崇禎松江縣誌. Beijing: Shumu wenxian chuban she, 1990.

Chen Lizhi 陳智麗. "Rujia wenhua yu xiandai hua: Tu Weiming jiaoshou fangtan" 儒家文化與現代化: 杜維明教授訪談, *Renmin ribao* 人民日報, overseas edition, July 16, 1998.

Chen Sen 陳森. *Pinhua baojian* 品花寶鑑. Shanghai: Guji chubanshe, 1984.

Chen Shidao 陳師道. *Houshan shihua* 後山詩話, in Ouyang Xiu 歐陽修, *Liuyi jushi shihua* 六一居士詩話. Shanghai: Commercial Press, 1937.

Chen Shou 陳壽. *Sanguo zhi* 三國誌. Beijing: Zhonghua shuju, 1973.

Chu Renhuo 褚人獲. *Jianhu guangji* 堅瓠廣集, in *Biji xiaoshuo daguan* 筆記小說大觀. Yangzhou: Jiangsu guangling guji keyin she, 1984.

Dai Qingxiang 戴欽祥. *Zhongguo gudai fuzhuang shi* 中國古代服裝史. Taipei: Commercial Press, 1994.

Dao'an 道安. *Guang hongming ji* 廣弘明集.

Deng, Siyu 鄧嗣禹. *Zhongguo kaoshi zhidu shi* 中國考試制度史. Taipei: Xuesheng shuju, 1967.

Dharmaraksa 竺法護, trans. *Miaofa lianhua jing* 妙法蓮華經, in J. Takakusu & K. Watanabe, eds., *Dazhengzang* 大正藏, vol. 9. Tokyo: Society for the Publication of the TaishoTripitaka, 1924.

Di'an Sanren 狄岸散人. *Yu Jiao Li* 玉嬌李, in *Ming-Qing yanqing xiaoshuo daguan* 明清言情小說大觀, vol. 2. Beijing: Huaxia chuban she, 1993.

Ding Fubao 丁福保, ed. *Foxue da cidian* 佛學大辭與. Shanghai: Yinyue shuchu, 1939.

_____, annot. *Yulan peng jing jianzhu* 盂蘭盆經箋注. Shanghai: Yixue shuju, 1918.

Ding Yaokang 丁耀亢. *Xu Jin Ping Mei* 續金瓶梅, in *Jin Ping Mei xushu sanzhong* 金瓶梅續書三種. Jinan: Qilu shushe, 1988.

Dong Guoyan 董國炎. *Dangzi, rouqing, tongxin: Mingdai xiaoshuo sichao* 蕩子，柔情，童心：明代小說思潮. Taiyuan: Beiyuan wenyi chuban she, 1992.

Dong Kang 董康, ed. *Quhai zongmu ti yao* 曲海總目提要. Tianjin: Guji chuban she, 1992.

Dongxuan Zi 洞玄子, in *Mishu shizhong* 秘書十種. Manually copied out by Yiyu Anzhu 吟月庵主.

Du Guangting 杜光庭. "Qiuran ke zhuan" 蛛髯客傳, in Wang Piqiang 汪畔彊, *Tangre xiaoshuo* 唐人小說. Hong Kong: Zhonghua shuju, 1987.

Du Wan 杜綰. *Yunlin shipu* 雲林石譜. Shanghai: Commercial Press, 1936.

Du You 杜佑. *Tongdian* 通典. Beijing: Zhonghua shuju, 1988.

Duan Chengshi 段成式, comp. *Youyang zazu* 酉陽雜俎. Beijing: Zhonghua shuju, 1981.

Fan Lian 范濂. *Yunjian jumu chao* 雲間據目鈔, in *Biji xiaoshuo daguan* 筆記小說大觀, vol. 6. Yangzhou: Jiangsu guji chuban she, 1984.

Fan Shuzhi 樊樹志. *Ming-Qing Jiangnan shizhen tanwei* 明清江南市鎮探微. Shanghai: Fudan University Press, 1994.

Fang Ruhao 方汝浩. *Chanzhen houshi* 禪真後史, in Hou Zhongyi 侯忠義, et al., eds., *Mingdai xiaoshuo jikan* 明代小說輯刊. Chengdu: Bashu shushe, 1993.

Fang Xuanling 房玄齡, et al. *Jin shu* 晉書. Beijing: zhonghua shuju, 1974.

Feng Baoshan 馮保善. "Ling Mengchu jiaoyou xintan" 凌濛初交遊新探, in *Ming-Qing xiaoshuo janjiu* 明清小說研究, no. 1, 1995.

Feng Menglong 馮夢龍, ed. "Hao Daqing yihen yuanyang tao" 赧大卿遺恨鴛鴦絛, in *Xingshi hengyan* 醒世恒言. Beijing: Renmin wenxue chuban she, 1990.

_____, ed. "Qian Sheren tishi yanzi lou" 錢舍人題詩燕子樓, in *Jingshi tongyan* 警世通言. Beijing: Renmin wenxue chuban she, 1990.

_____, ed. "Shi Runze Tanque yuyou" 施潤澤灘闕遇友, in *Xingshi hengyan* 醒世恒言. Beijing: Renmin wenxue chuban she, 1990.

_____, ed. *Shange* 山歌, in *Feng Menglong quanji* 馮夢龍全集. Shanghai: Guji chuban she, 1993.

_____, ed. *Taixia xinzou* 太霞新奏, in *Feng Menglong quanji* 馮夢龍全集. Shanghai: Guji chuban she, 1993.

Feng Yu-lan 馮友蘭. Cong Li Zhi shuoqi" 從李贄說起, in *Zhongguo zhexue shi lunwen erji* 中國哲學史二集. Shanghai: Shanghai renmin chuban she, 1962.

Fengyuexuan Ruxuanzi 風月軒入玄子. *Langshi qiguan* 浪史奇觀, in *Zhongguo guyan xiping congkan* 中國古艷稀品叢刊, 5th series.

Feng Zikai 豐子愷. *Feng Zikai juan* 豐子愷卷. Xi'an: Taibai wenyi chuban she, 1996.

Foguang da cidian 佛光大辭典. Taiwan: Foguang chuban she, 1988.

Furong 芙蓉主人. *Ci pozi zhuan* 痴婆子傳. Taipei: Guoji shuandi chuban she, 1994.

Fu Weilin 傅維麟. *Mingshu* 明書. Shanghai: Shangwu yinshu guan, 1936.

Fu Yiling 傅衣凌. "Cong yipian shiliao kan shiqi shiji Zhongguo haishang maoyi xingzhi" 從一篇史料看十七世紀海上貿易性質, in Fu Yiling, *Ming Qing shehui jingji shi lunwen ji* 明清社會經濟史論文集. Beijing: Renmin wenxue chuban she, 1982.

Gan Bao 干寶. *Soushen ji* 搜神記. Shanghai: Commercial Press, 1937.

Gao Tingzhen 高廷珍, et al. *Donglin shuyuan zhi* 東林書院志. Taipei: Guangwen shuju, 1968.

Gao Zecheng 高則誠. *Dengcao heshang* 燈草和尚. Taipei: Shuangdi guoji chuban, 1994.

Gusu zhi 姑蘇志. Taipei: Commercial Press, 1980 (reprint).

Gu Yingtai 谷應泰. *Mingshi jishi benmo* 明史記事本末. Taipei: Sanmin shuju, 1963.

Gu Yanwu 顧炎武. *Rizhi lu jishi* 日知錄集釋. Taipei: Shijie shuju, 1962.

———. *Tianxia junguo libing shu* 天下郡國利病書. 1879 edition.

Gui Youguang 歸有光. "Shu Zhang zhennu sishi" 書張貞女死事; "Zhang zhennu yushi" 張貞女獄事, in *Gui Zhengchuan ji* 歸震川集. Taipei: Shijie shuju, 1963.

Guo Qijia 郭齊家. *Zhongguo dudai de xuexiao he shuyuan* 中國古代的學校和書院. Beijing: Kexue jishu chuban she, 1995.

Han Dacheng 韓大城. *Mingdai chengshi yanjiu* 明代城市研究. Beijing: Zhongguo renmin daxue chuban she, 1991.

Hejian fuzhi 河間府志. 1981 (reprint).

He Liangjun 何良俊. *Siyou zhai congshuo* 四友齋叢說. Beijing: Zhonghua shuju, 1959.

He Manzi 何滿子. *Zhongguo aiqing yu liangxing guanxi* 中國愛情與兩性關係. Hong Kong: Commercial Press, 1994.

He Qiaoyuan 何喬遠. *Mingshan cang* 名山藏. Taipei: Chengwen chuban she, 1969.

Hong Pian 洪楩, ed. "Wenjing yuanyang hui" 刎頸鴛鴦會, in *Qingping shantang huaben* 清平山堂話本. Shanghai: Guji chuban she, 1990.

Hong Pimo 洪丕謨. *Zhongguo gudai suanming shu* 中國古代算命術. Shanghai: Renmin chuban she, 1989.

Hou Wailu 笑外廬. *Zhongguo sixiang tongshi* 中國思想通史. Beijing: Renmin wenxue chuban she, 1958.

———. *Zhongguo shiqishiji sixiang shi* 中國十七世紀思想史. Beijing: Renmin chuban she, 1962.

———, et al, eds. *Song Ming lixue shi* 宋明理學史. Beijing: Renmin chuban she, 1987.

Hu Guang 胡廣, et al., eds. *Sishu daquan* 四書大全. Taipei: Commercial Press, 1976.

———, et al, eds. *Xingli daquan* 性理大全. Taipei: Commercial Press, 1974.

———. *Taizong shilu* 太宗實錄, in Academia Sinica, ed., *Ming shilu* 明實錄. Taipei: 1966.

Hu Shiying 胡忠瑩. *Huaben xiaoshuo gailun* 話本小說概論. Beijing: Zhonghua shuju, 1980.

Hu Yinglin 胡應麟. *Shaoshi shanfang bicong* 少室山房筆叢. Taipei: Shijie shuju, 1963.

Huang Dawei 黃達維. "Zongxu" 總序, in *Zhongguo lidai jinhui xiaoshuo jicui* 中國歷代禁毀小說集粹. Taipei: Shuangdi guoji chuban she, 1994.

Huang Tsung-hsi 黃宗羲. *Mingru xue'an* 明儒學案. Beijing: Zhonghua shuju, 1985.

Huang, Ray 黃仁宇. "Cong *Sanyan* kan wan Ming shangren" 從三言看晚明商人, in Ray Huang, *Fangkuan lishi de shijie* 放寬歷史的視界. Taiwan: Yunchen wenhua shiye youxian gongsi, 1991.

Huang Yiming 黃意明. *Zhongguo fuzhou* 中國符咒. Hong Kong: Zhonghua shuju, 1991.

Huzhou fuzhi 湖州府志. 1874 edition. Taipei: Chengwen chuban she, 1970 (reprint).

Ji Yun & Yong Rong 紀昀, 永瑢, et al., eds. *Siku quanshu zongmu titao* 四庫全書總目提要. Shanghai: Commercial Press, 1939.

Jiading xianzhi 嘉定縣誌.

Jiangxi Yeren 江西野人. *Yiqing zhen* 怡情陣. Taipei: Guoji shuandi chuban she, 1994.

Jiangzuo Shui'an 江左誰菴. *Zui chunfeng* 醉春風. Taipei: Shuangdi guoji chuban, 1994.

Jinmu Sanren 金木散人. *Guzhang juechen* 鼓掌絕塵. Shanghai: Guji chuban she, 1990.

Jnanagnpta 奢那崛多, trans. *Lianhua jing* 蓮華經, in Takakusu & Watanabe, eds., *Da zheng zang* 大正藏. Tokyo: Society for the publication of the Taisho Tripitaka, 1924.

Kong Lingjing 孔令鏡, ed. *Zhongguo xiaoshuo shiliao* 中國小說史料. Shanghai: Shanghai gudian wenxue chuban she, 1957.

Kumarajiva 鳩摩羅什, trans. *Miaofa lianhua jing* 妙法蓮華經 (Saddharma pundarida sutra), in *Da zheng zang* 大正藏. Tokyo: Society for the publication of the Taisho Tripitaka, 1924.

Lang Ying 郎瑛. *Qixiu leigao* 七修類稿. Taipei: Shijie shuju, 1963.

Li Dongyang 李東陽, et al., eds. *Da Ming huidian* 大明會典. Taipei: Zhongwen shuju, 1963.

Li Fang 李昉, et al., comp. *Taiping guangji* 太平廣記. 1846 edition.

_____. *Taiping yulan* 太平御覽. 1828 edition.

Li Houji 李厚基. "Guanyu *Erpai* de zuozhe Ling Mengchu" 關於二拍的作者凌濛初, *Guangming ribao* 光明日報, May 4, 1958.

Li Mengsheng 李夢生. *Zhongguo jinhui xiaoshuo baihua* 中國禁毀小說百話. Shanghai: Guji chuban she, 1994.

Li Shizhen 李時珍. *Bencao gangmu* 本草綱目. Taipei: Dingwen shuju, 1973.

Li Tiaoyuan 李調元. *Nanyue biji* 南越筆記. 1881 edition.

Li Tien-yi 李田意. "Chongyin *Erke pai'an jingqi* yuankan ben xu" 重印二刻拍案驚奇原刊本序, in *Erke pai'an jingqi* 二刻拍案驚奇. Hong Kong: Youlian chuban youxian gongsi, 1986.

Li Xu 李詡. *Jie'an laoren manbi* 戒菴老人漫筆. Beijing: Zhonghua shuju, 1982.

Li Zehou 李澤厚. "Song-Ming lixue pianlun" 宋明理學片論, *Zhongguo gudai sixiangshi lun* 中國古代思想史論. Beijing: Renmin chuban she, 1986.

Li Zhi 李贄. "Cangshu shiji liezhuan zongmu qianlun" 藏書世紀列傳總目前論, in *Cangshu* 藏書. Taipei: Xuesheng shuju, 1986.

_____. "Deye ruchen houlun" 德業儒臣後論, in *Cangshu* 藏書. Taipei: Xuesheng shuju, 1986.

Lin Chen 林辰. *Mingmo xiaoshuo shulu* 明末小說述錄. Shenyang: Chunfeng wenyi chuban she, 1982.

_____. "*Erkepai'an jingqi* xiaoyin" 二刻拍案驚奇小引, in *Erke pai'an jingqi* 二刻拍案驚奇. Shanghai: Guji chuban she, 1983.

Ling Mengchu 凌濛初. "*Pai'an jingqi* fanli" 拍案驚奇凡例, in *Pai'an jingqi* 拍案驚奇. Hong Kong: Youlian chuban gongsi, 1986.

_____. "*Pai'an jingqi* xu" 拍案驚奇序, in *Pai'an jingqi* 拍案驚奇. Hong Kong: Youlian chuban gongsi, 1986.

_____. "Xibie" 惜別, in Feng Menglong, ed., *Taixia xinzou* 太霞新奏. *Feng Menglong quanji* 馮夢龍全集. Shanghai: guji chuban she, 1993.

Ling Xuan 伶玄. "Feiyan waizhuan" 飛燕外傳, in Gu Yuanqing 顧元慶, ed. *Gushi wenfang xiaoshuo* 顧氏文房小說. Shanghai: Hanfenlou, 1925.

Liu Bendong 劉本棟. "*Pai'an jingqi* kaozheng" 拍案驚奇考證, in *Ling Mengchu yu Erpai* 凌濛初與二拍. Taipei: Tianyi chuban she, 1982.

Liu Chen 劉辰. *Guochu shiji* 國初事跡. Shanghai: Bo gu zhai, 1920.

Liu Dalin 劉達臨. *Zhonguo gudai xingwenhua* 中國古代性文化. Yinchuan: Ningxia renmin chubanshe, 1993.

Liu, Shide 劉世德, et al, eds. *Zhongguo gudian xiaoshuo baike quanshu*
中國古典小說百科全書. Beijing: Zhongguo gudian xiaoshuo baike quanshu chuban she,
1993.

Liu Tingji 劉廷璣. *Zaiyuan zazhi* 在園雜誌. Taipei: Yonghe zhen wenhui chuban she, 1969.

Liu Yongcheng 劉永成. "Lun zhongguo ziben zhuyi mengya de lishi tiaojian"
論中國資本主義萌芽的歷史條件, in Nanjing Daxue lishixi, ed., *Ming-Qing ziben zhuyi
mengya yanjiu lunwen ji* 明清資本主義萌芽研究論文集. Shanghai: Shanghai renmin chuban
she, 1981.

Liu Zifu 劉再復. *Shengming jingshen yu wenxue daolu* 生命精神與文學道路. Taiwan: Fenyun
shidai chuban gongsi, 1989.

Liu Zongyuan 柳宗元. "Hejian fu zhuan" 河間婦傳, in *Liu Zongyuan sanwen
quanji* 柳宗元散文全集. Beijing: Jinri Zhongguo chuban she, 1996.

Lu Rong 陸容. *Shuyuan zaji* 菽園雜記. Shanghai: Commercial Press, 1936.

Lu Shuxiang 呂叔湘. "Wenyan he baihua" 文言和白話, in *Lu Shuxiang wenji* 呂叔湘文集, vol.
4. Beijing: Commercial Press, 1990.

Lu Tiancheng 呂天成. *Xiuta yeshi* 繡榻野史. Taipei: Shuandi guoji chuban she, 1994.

Lu Xun 魯迅. *Zhongguo xiaoshuo shilue* 中國小說史略, in *Lu Xun quanji*, vol. 9. Beijing:
Renmin wenxue chuban she, 1989.

_____, ed. *Tang-Song chuanqi ji* 唐宋傳奇集, in *Lu Xun quanji* 魯迅全集. Beijing: Renmin
wenxue chuban she, 1973.

Lu Yunlong 陸雲龍. *Sanke pai'an jingqi* 三刻拍案驚奇. Beijing: Beijing University Press, 1987.

Luo Kanglie 羅康烈. *Bei xiaoling wenzipu* 北小令文字譜. Hong Kong: Longmeng shudian,
1962.

Luo Shubao 羅樹寶. *Zhongguo gudai yinshua shi* 中國古代印刷史. Beijing: Yinshua shi, 1993.

Luo Zhufeng 羅竹風, comp. *Hanyu da cidian* 漢語大辭典. Shanghai: Cishu chubanshe, 1986.

Ma Duanlin 馬端臨. *Wenxian tongkao* 文獻通考. Shanghai: Tushu jicheng chu, 1899.

Ma Meixin 馬美信. "Wan Ming wenxue chutan" 晚明文學初探, in *Zhongguo shoupiwenxue
boshi xuewi lunwen xuanji* 中國首批文學博士學位論文選集. Jinan: Shandong University
Press, 1987.

Mao Heng 毛亨, ed. *Maoshi zhengyi* 毛詩正義. Hong Kong: Zhonghua shuju, 1964.

Mao Qiling 毛奇齡. *Ming Wuzong waiji* 明武宗外紀. Taipei: Guangwen shuju, 1964.

Mengyuan lao 孟元老. *Dongjing menghua lu zhu* 東京夢華錄注. Annotated by Deng
Zhicheng 鄧之誠. Taipei: Shijie shuju, 1963.

"Nianyu guanyin" 碾玉觀音, in *Jingben tongsu xiaoshuo* 京本通俗小說. Shanghai:
Commercial Press, 1939.

Zhenze xianzhi 震澤縣志. 1893 edition. Taipei: Chengwen chuban she, 1975 (reprint).

Ouyang Daifa 歐陽代發. *Huaben xiaoshuo shi* 話本小說史. Wuhan: Wuhan chuban she, 1994.

Pei Xing 裴鉶. "Kunlun nu" 昆侖奴, in Li Fang 李昉, et al., comps, *Taiping guangji* 太平廣記,
vol. 194. 1846 edition.

Peng Xinwei 彭信威. *Zhongguo huobi shi* 中國貨幣史. Shanghai: Qunlian chubanshe, 1954.

Pi Xirui 皮錫瑞. *Jingxue lishi* 經學歷史. Taipei: Heluo tushu chuban she, 1974.

Qian Mu 錢穆. *Song Mong lixue gailun* 宋明理學概述. Taipei: Zhonghua wenhua chuban shiye
weiyuan hui, 1953.

Qian Yong 錢泳. *Luyuan conghua* 履園叢話. Taipei: Wenhai chuban she, 1981.

Ren Jiyu 任繼愈, et al., eds. *Zhongguo daojiao shi* 中國道教史. Shanghai: Shanghai renmin
chuban she, 1990.

Ren Na 任訥. *Sanqu gailun* 散曲概論. Shanghai: Zhonghua shuju, 1931.

Rong Zhaozu 容肇祖. *Li Zhuowu ping zhuan* 李卓吾評傳. Shanghai: Commercial Press, 1937.

_____. *Mingdai sixiang shi* 明代思想史. Shanghai: Kaiming shudian, 1941.

Ruan Kuesheng 元藝生. *Chayu kehua* 茶余客話. Taipei: Shijie shuju, 1963.

Shen Congwen 沈從文. *Zhongguo gudai fushi yanjia* 中國古代服飾研究. Hong Kong: Commercial Press, 1981.

Shen Chaoyang 沈朝陽. *Huang Ming Jia-Long liangchao wenjian ji* 皇明嘉隆兩朝聞見記. Taipei: Xuesheng shuju, 1969.

Shen Defu 沈德符. *Bizhou xuan shenyu* 敝帚軒剩語. Shanghai: Commercial Press, 1939.

_____. *Wanli yehuo bian* 萬歷野獲編. 1869 edition.

Shen Jianshi 沈兼士. *Zhongguo kaoshi zhidu shi* 中國考試制度史. Taipei: Xuesheng shuju, 1960.

Shi Changyu 石昌渝. "Ling Mengchu" 凌濛初, in 劉世德, et al., eds., *Zhongguo gudian xiaoshuo baike quanshu* 中國古典小說百科全書. Beijing: Zhongguo gudian xiaoshuo baike quanshu chuban she, 1993.

Shi Kekuan 施克寬. *Zhongguo huanguan mishi* 中國宦官秘史. Beijing: Baowen tang shudian: 1988.

Sima Qian 司馬遷. *Shi ji* 史記. Beijing: Zhonghua shuju, 1974.

Song Lian 宋濂, et al., eds. *Yuanshi* 元史. Beijing: Zhonghua shuju, 1976.

Song Ruohua 宋若莘, "Nu Lunyu" 女論語, in *Nu sishu* 女四書. Shanghai: Jiangzuo shulin, 1887.

Song Yingxing 宋應星. *Taigong kaiwu* 天工開物. Hong Kong: Zhonghua shuju, 1978.

Song Yu 宋玉. "Gaotang fu" 高唐賦, in Xiao Tong 蕭統, comp., *Wenxue* 文選. Shanghai: Commercial Press, 1960.

Sunu jing 素女經, in Ye Dehui 葉德輝, ed., *Shuangmei ying'an congkan* 雙梅景闇叢刊. Changsha, 1907.

Sui Shusen 隋樹森, comp. *Quan Yuan sanqu* 全元散曲. Beijing: Zhonghua shuju, 1964.

_____. *Yuanqu xuan waibian* 元曲選外編. Beijing: Zhonghua shuju, 1959.

Sun Kaidi 孫楷第. "Sanyang Erpai yuanliu kao" 三言二拍源流考, *Cangzhou ji* 滄州集. Beijing: Zhonghua shuju, 1965.

_____. *Zhongguo tongsu xiaoshuo shumu* 中國通俗小說書目. Beijing: Zuojia chubanshe, 1957.

Tan Qixiang 譚騏驤, ed. *Zhongguo lishi ditu ji* 中國歷史地圖集. Beijing: Zhongguo ditu chuban she, 1982.

Tan Zhengbi 譚正璧. *Sanyan liangpai ziliao* 三言兩拍資料. Shanghai: Guji chubanshe, 1981.

Tang Gang & Nan Bingwen 湯綱, 南炳文. *Mingshi* 明史. Shanghai: Shanghai renmin chuban she, 1985.

Tang Xianzu 湯顯祖. *Tang xianzu ji* 湯顯祖集. Edited & collated by Xu Shuofang 徐朔方. Beijing: Zhonghua shuju, 1962.

Tang Yin 唐寅, ed. *Sengni niehai* 僧尼孽海, in *Zhongguo guyan xipin congkan* 中國古艷稀品叢刊.

Tang Yuyuan 唐宇元. "Cheng-Zhu lixue heshi chengwei tongzhi jieji de tongzhi sixiang" 程朱理學何時成為統治階級的統治思想, *Zhongguo shi yanjiu* 中國史研究, no. 1, 1989.

Tian Rucheng 田汝成. *Xihu youlan zhiyu* 西湖遊覽志餘. Taipei: Shijie shuju, 1963.

Tianfang Daoren 天方道人. *Xinghua tian* 杏花天, in *Zhongguo guyan xiping congkan* 中國古艷稀品叢刊.

Tu Wei-ming 杜維明. *Xiandai jingshen yu rujia chuantong* 現代精神與儒家傳統. Taipei: Lianjing chuban shiye gongsi, 1996.

Tuo-tuo 脫脫, et al., comps. *Songshi* 宋史. Beijing: Zhonghua shuju, 1977.

Wang Ao 王鏊. *Zhenze changyu* 震澤長語, in Shen Yunlong 沈雲龍, ed., *Ming-Qing shiliao huibian I* 明清史料匯編I. Taipei: Wenhai chuban she, 1967.

Wang Chunyu 王春瑜. *Ming Qing shi sanlun* 明清史散論. Shanghai: Dongfang chuban zhongxin, 1996.

Wang Gulu 王古魯. "Baihai yishao lu" 稗海一勺錄, in Wang Gulu, ed. and annot., *Chuke pai'an jingqi* 初刻拍案驚奇. Hong Kong: Gudian wenxue cheban she, 1976.

———. "Benshu de jieshao" 本書的介紹, in Zhang Peiheng 張培恒, ed., *Erke pai'an jingqi* 二刻拍案驚奇. Shanghai: Guji chuban she, 1983.

Wang Guowei 王國維. *Song Yuan xiqu kao* 宋元戲曲考. Taipei: Yiwen yinshu guan, 1964.

Wang Hongtai 王鴻泰. *Sanyan Liangpai de jingshen shi yanjiu* 三言兩拍的精神史研究. Taipei: Taiwan National University, 1997.

Wang Lina 王麗娜. "*Sanyan Erpai* yu *Jingu qiguan* haiwai cangben, waiwen fanyi ji yanjiu zhuzuo" 三言二拍與今古奇觀海外藏本及研究著作, *Zhonghuawenshi luncong* 中華文史論叢. Shanghai: Shanghai guji chuban she, vol. 29, 1984.

Wang Piqiang 汪辟疆, ed. *Tangren xiaoshuo* 唐人小說. Hong Kong: Zhonghua shuju, 1987.

Wang Qi 王圻. *Sancai tuhui* 三才圖繪. Taipei: Chengwen chuban she, 1970.

Wang, Qi 王琦. *Yupu zaji* 寓圃雜記. Beijing: Zhonghua shuju, 1962.

Wang Shizhen 王世貞, ed. *Yanyi bian* 艷異編. Shanghai: guji chuban she, 1990.

Wang Shunu 王書奴 中國娼妓史. *Zh8ngguo changji shi* 中國娼妓史. Shanghai: Shenghuo shudian, 1935.

Wang Tianyou 王天有. *Wan Ming Donglin Dang yi* 晚明東林黨議. Shanghai: Guji chuban she, 1991.

Wang Yinglin 王應麟. *Sanzi jing* 三字經, in Song Hong 宋洪, et al., comps., *Mengxue quanshu* 蒙學全書. Changchun: Jilin wenshi chuban she, 1996.

Wang Zhizhong 王枝忠. *Gudian xiaoshuo kaolun* 古典小說考論. Yinchuan: Ningxia renmin chubanshe, 1992.

Weixing Shiguan Zhaizhu 唯性史觀齋主. *Zhongguo tongxing lian mishi* 中國同性戀秘史. Hong Kong: Yuzhou chuban she, 1961.

Wei Yingwu 韋應物. *Wei Suzhou ji* 韋蘇州集. Sahnghai: Shanghai guji chuban she, 1993.

Wei Zheng 魏徵. *Sui shu* 隋書. Beijing: Zhonghua shuju, 1973.

Wucheng xianzhi 烏程縣誌. 1881 edition.

Wu, Han 吳晗. "Wan Ming shihuan jieji de shenghuo" 晚明士宦階級的生活, in *Wu Han wenji* 吳晗文集, Li Hua 李華, et al., eds. Beijing: Beijing chuban she, 1988.

———. *Zhu Yuanzhang zhuan* 朱元璋傳, in *Wu Han wenji* 吳晗文集. Beijing: Beijingchuban she, 1988.

Wujiang xianzhi 吳江縣誌. 1747 edition. Taipei: Chengwen chuban she, 1975 (reprint).

Wu Weiye 吳偉業. *Suikou jilue* 綏寇紀略. Taipei: Guangwen shuju, 1968.

Wu Yue 吳越, trans. "Guanyu mingmo baihua xiaoshuo de zuozhe he duzhe" 關於明末白話小說的作者和讀者, in *Ming-Qing xiaoshuo yanjiu* 明清小說研究, no. 2, 1988.

Wu Ze 吳澤. *Rujiao pantu Li Zhuowu* 儒教叛徒李卓吾. Shanghai: Shanghai huaxia shudian, 1947.

Wu Zimu 吳自牧. *Mengliang lu* 夢梁錄. Hangzhou: Zhejiang renmin chuban she, 1980.

Xizhou Sheng 西周生. *Xingshi yinyuan zhuan* 醒世姻緣傳. Shanghai: Guji chuban she, 1981.

Xizihu Fuxi Jiaozhu 西子湖伏羲教主. *Cu hulu* 醋葫蘆. in Hou Zhongyi 侯忠義, et al., eds. *Mingdai xiaoshu jikan* 明代小說輯刊. Chengdu: Bashu shushe, 1993.

Xia Xie 夏燮. *Ming tongjian* 明通鑒. Beijing: Zhonghua shuju, 1980.

Xiaomingxiong 小明雄. *Zhongguo tongxing xing'ai shilu* 中國同性性愛史錄. Hong Kong: Fenhong sanjiao chuban she, 1984.

Xiaoxiao Sheng 笑笑生. *Jin Ping Mei cihua* 金瓶梅詞話. Collated by Mei Jie 梅節. Hong Kong: Xinghai wenhua chuban youxian gongsi, 1987.

Xiao Xinqiao 蕭欣橋. "Guanyu huaben dingyi de sikao" 關於話本定義的思考, *Ming-Qing xiaoshuo yanjiu* 明清小代研究, no. 1, 1990.

Xiao Yaotian 蕭遙天. *Zhongguo renming de yanjiu* 中國人名的研究. Beijing: Guoji wenhua chuban gongsi, 1987.

Xie Boyang 謝伯陽, comp. *Quan Ming sanqu* 全明散曲. Jinan: Qilu shushe, 1993.

Xie Zhaozhe 謝肇淛. *Wu zazu* 五雜俎. Beijing: Zhonghua shuju, 1959.

Xu Changling 徐昌齡. *Ruyi jun zhuan* 如意君傳. Taipei: Shuandi guoji chuban she, 1994.

Xu Dixin 許滌新, et al. *Zhongguo ziben zhuyi de mengya* 中國資本主義的萌芽. Beijing: Renmin chubanshe, 1985.

Xu Guangqi 徐光啓. *Nongzheng quanshu* 農政全書. Shanghai: Guji chuban she, 1979

Xu Ke 徐珂, ed. *Qingbai leichao* 清稗類鈔. Shanghai: Commercial Press, 1917.

Xu Jian 徐堅, ed. *Chuxue ji* 初學記. Beijing: Zhonghua shuju, 1980.

Xu Zhuoyun 許倬雲, et al, eds. *Zhongguo tushuwenshi lunji* 中國圖書文史論集. Beijing: Xiandai chuban she, 1992.

Yan Gengwang 嚴耕望. "Tangren duo dushu shansi" 唐人多讀書山寺, in *Dalu zazhi* 大陸雜誌, vol. 2, no. 4, 1951.

Yan Wenyu 嚴文郁. *Zhongguo shuji jianshi* 中國書籍簡史. Taipei: Shangwu yinshu guan, 1992.

Yang Bojun 楊伯峻, annot. *Chunqiu Zuozhuan zhu* 春秋左傳注. Beijing: Zhonghua shuju, 1981.

Yao Lingxi 姚靈犀. "Si wuxie xiaoji" 思無邪小記, in *Zhongguo guyan xipin congkan* 中國古艷稀品叢刊, 7th series.

Yao Siren 姚思仁, ed. *Da Ming lu fulu zhushi* 大明律附例注釋. Beijing: Beining Daxue chuban she, 1993.

Yao Zhiyin 姚之駰. *Yuan Ming shilei chao* 元明事類鈔. Shanghai: Commercial Press,1935.

Ye Dejun 葉德鈞. "Ling Mengchu shiji xinian" 凌濛初事跡繫年, *Xiaoshuo xiqu congkao* 小說戲曲叢考. Beijing: Zhonghua shuju, 1979.

Ye Sheng 葉盛. *Shuidong riji* 水東日記. Taipei: Xuesheng shuju, 1965.

You Guo'en 游國恩, et al. *Zhongguo wenxue shi* 中國文學史. Hong Kong: Zhongguo tushu kanxingshe, 1986.

Yufang mijue 玉房秘訣, in Ye Dehui 葉德輝, ed., *Shuangmei ying'an congkan* 雙梅景闇叢刊. Changsha: 1907.

Yu Jideng 余繼登. *Diangu jiwen* 典故記聞. Beijing: Zhonghua shuju, 1981.

Yuan Hongdao 袁宏道. *Jietuo ji* 解脫集, in *Yuan Hongdao ji jianjiao* 袁宏道集箋校. Shanghai: Guji chuban she, 1981.

Yuan Ke 袁珂. *Zhongguo shenhua chuanshuo* 中國神話傳說. Beijing: Zhongguo mianjian wenyi chuban she, 1984.

_____, annot. *Shanhai jing* 山海經. Chengdu: Bashu chuban she, 1992.

Yuan Zhongdao 袁中道. *Youju shilu* 游居柿錄, in *Kexue zhai ji* 珂雪齋集. Shanghai: Guji chuban she, 1989.

Yue Hengjun 樂蘅軍. *Songdai huaben yanjiu* 宋代話本研究. Taipei: Guoli Taiwan Daxue wenxue yuan, 1969.

Zang Lihe 臧勵龢. *Zhongguo gujin diming da cidian* 中國古今地名大辭典. Hong Kong: Commercial Press, 1982.

Zeng Yongyi 曾永義. *Ming zaju gailun* 明雜劇概論. Taipei: Taipei jiaxin jijin hui, 1967.

Zhang Bing 張兵. *Ling Mengchu yu Erpai* 凌濛初與二拍. Shengyang: Liaoning jiaoyu chuban she, 1993.

Zhang Dai 張岱. *Tao'an mengyi* 陶庵夢憶. Shanghai: Shijie shuju, 1947.

Zhang Han 張瀚. *Songchuang mengyu* 松窗夢語. Beijing: Zhonghua shuju, 1985.

Zhang He 張荷. *Wu Yue wenhua* 吳越文化. Shenyang: Liaoning jiaoyu chuban she, 1991.

Zhang Huixin 張惠信. *Zhongguo yinding* 中國銀錠. Taipei: Taipei xian zhonghe shi, 1988.

Zhang Liwen 張立文. "Luelun Song Ming lixue" 略論宋明理學, *Lun Song Ming lixue* 論宋明理學, ed., Zhongguo zhexueshi xuegui 中國哲學史學會. Hangzhou: Zhejiang renmin chuban she, 1981.

Zhang Peiheng 章培恒. "Jiaodian shuoming" 校點說明, in Zhang Peiheng, ed., *Erke pai'an jingqi* 二刻拍案驚奇. Shanghai: Guji chuban she, 1983.

Zhang Qiyun 張其昀, comp. *Zhongwen da ciadian* 中文大辭典. Taipei: Zhongguo wenhua xueyuan chubanbu, 1967.

Zhang Tingyu 張廷玉, ed. *Mingshi* 明史. Beijing: Zhonghua shuju, 1974.

Zhang Xie 張燮. *Dongxi yang kao* 東西洋考. Shanghai: Shangwu yinshu guan, 1936.

Zhang Xiumin 張秀民. "Mingdai Nanjing de yinshu" 明代南京的印書, in *Zhang Xiumin yinshua shi lunwen ji* 張秀民印刷史論文集. Beijing: Yingshua gongye chuban she, 1988.

Zhao Ye 趙燁. *Wu Yue chunqiu* 吳越春秋. Shanghai: Commercial Press, 1937.

Zhao Yi 趙翼. *Gaiyu congkao* 陔餘叢考. Taipei: Shijie shuju, 1965.

_____. *Nian'er shi zhaji* 廿二史箚記. Taipei: Shijie shuju, 1962.

Zheng Longcai 鄭龍采. "Biejia Chucheng go muzhi ming" 別駕初成公墓誌銘, in Zhou Shaoling 周紹良, "Quhai congshi" 曲海叢拾. *Xuelin manbu* 學林漫步, no. 5, 1982.

Zhenze xianzhi 震澤縣誌. 1893 edition. Taipei: Chengwen chuban she, 1970 (reprint).

Zheng Zhenduo 鄭振鐸. *Chatu ben zhongguo wenxue shi* 插圖本中國文學史. Beijing: Renmin wenxue chuban she, 1982.

_____. "Ming-Qing erdai de pinghua ji" 明清二代的平話集, in Zheng Zhenduo, *Zhongguo wenxue lunji* 中國文學論集. Hong Kong: Gangqing chuban she, 1979.

Zhou Xibao 周錫保. *Zhongguo gudai fuzhuang shi* 中國古代服裝史. Beijing: 1984.

Zhu Guozhen 朱國禎. *Yongchuan xiaopin* 涌幢小品, in *Biji xhiaoshuo daguan* 筆記小說大觀, vol. 7. Yangzhou: Jinangsu guli chuban she, 1978.

Zhu Xi 朱熹. *Zhu Wengong wenji* 朱文公文集. *Siku congkan* 四庫叢刊 edition.

_____. *Zhu Zi yulei* 朱子語類. Compiled by Li Jingde 黎靖德. Taipei: Zhengzhong shuju, 1982.

_____, ed. *Henan Chengshi yishu* 河南程氏遺書. Shanghai: Commercial Press, 1939.

_____, ed. *Sishu jizhu* 四書集注. Taipei: Xuehai chuban she, 1984.

Zhu Yilu 朱義祿. *Rujia lixiang rege yu Zhongguo wenhua* 儒家理想人格與中國文化. Shenyang: Liaoning jiaoyu chuban she, 1995.

Zui Xihu Xinyue Zhuren 醉西湖心月主人. *Bian er chai* 弁而釵. Collated by Xiao Xiangkai 蕭相愷, in Hou Zhongyi 侯忠義, et al., eds., *Ming dai xiaoshuo jikan* 明代小說輯刊. Chengdu: Bashu shushe, 1993.

_____. *Yichun xiangzhi* 宜春香質. Collated by Xiao Xiangkai 蕭相愷, in Hou Zhongyi 侯忠義, et al., eds., *Mingdai xiaoshuo jikan* 明代小說輯刊. Chengdu: Bashu shushe, 1993.

Works in Western Languages

Althusser, Louis. *For Marx*. New York: Pantheon, 1969.

Anonymous. *My Secret Life*. Introduction by G. Legman. New York: Grove Press, 1966.

Ball, Dyer J. *Things Chinese, or: Notes Connected with China*. Hong Kong: Kelly & Walsh, 1903.

Benjamin, Walter. "The Author as Producer," in *Illuminations*. Harcourt Brace & World, 1968.

_____. "The Work of Art in the Age of Mechanical Reproduction," in David H. Richter, ed.,

The Critical Tradition: Classical Texts and Contemporary Trends. New York: St. Martin's Press, 1989.

Beurdeley, Michel, et al. *The Clouds and the Rain: The Art of Love in China.* Switzwerland: Office du Livre, 1969.

Birch, Cyril, trans. *Stories from a Ming Collection: Translations of Chinese Short Stories Published in the Seventeenth Century.* New York: Grove Press, 1958.

Booth, Wayne. *The Rhetoric of Fiction.* Chicago: University of Chicago Press, 1961.

Boxer, Charles Ralph, trans. & ed. *South China in the Sixteenth Century.* London, 1953.

Brecher, Edward. *The Sex Researcher.* Boston: Little Brown, 1969.

Chan, Albert. *The Glory and Fall of the Ming Dynasty.* Norman: University of Oklahoma Press, 1982.

Chan, Wing-tsit. *Religious Trends in Modern China.* New York: Octagon Books, 1969.

Chang, Chun-shu & Shelley Chang. *Crisis and Transformation in Seventeenth-Century China.* Ann Arbor: University of Michigan Press, 1992.

Charney, Maurice. *Sexual Fiction.* London: Metheun, 1981.

Ching, Julia. *To Acquire Wisdom: The Way of Wang Yangming.* New York: Columbia University Press, 1976.

Cleland, John. *Fanny Hill: Memoirs of a Woman of Pleasure.* Ontario: Fitzhenry & Whiteside, 1989.

de Bary, Wm. Theodore. "Individualism and Humanitarianism in Late Ming Thought," *in Self and Society in Ming Thought.* New York: Columbia University Press, 1970.

de Beauvoir, Simone. "Shall We Burn de Sade?" in Austryn Wainhouse & Richard Seaver, comp. & trans., *The Marquis de Sade.* New York: Grove Press, 1953.

Dennerline, Jerry. The Chia-Ting Loyalists: Confucian Leadership and Social Change in Seventeenth-Century China. New Haven: Yale University Press, 1981.

Djiang, Chu & Jane Djiang, trans. *Compilation of Anecdotes of Sung Personalities.* Taipei: St. John University Press, 1989.

Duberman, Martin, et al., eds. *Hidden From History: Reclaiming the Gay and Lesbian Past.* New York: Meridian, 1990.

Eberhard, Wolfram. *The Local Cultures of South and East China.* Translated by Alide Eberhard. Leiden: E. J. Brill, 1968.

Ebrey, Buckley Patricia. *The Inner Quarters: Marriage and Lives of the Chinese Women in the Sung.* Berkeley: University of California Press, 1993.

_____, et al, ed. *Marriage and Inequality in Chinese Society.* Berkeley: University of California Press, 1991.

Egerton, Clement, trans. *The Golden Lotus.* London: Routledge & Kegan Paul Ltd, 1957.

Ellis, Havelock. *Psychology of Sex.* London: W. Heineman, 1948.

Elvin, Mark. *The Pattern of the Chinese Past.* Stanford: Stanford University Press, 1973.

Eye Weekly, April 16, 1998, p. 39.

Fairbank, John K. *The Great Chinese Revolution: 1800-1985.* New York: Harper & Row, 1986.

_____. *United States and China.* Cambridge: Harvard University Press, 1983.

Feng, Yu-lan. *A History of Chinese Philosophy.* Translated by Derk Bodde. Princeton: Princeton University Press, 1953.

Gagnon, John & William Simon. *Sexual Deviance.* New York: Harper & Row, 1967.

Gallaghar, Louis, trans. *China in the Sixteenth Century: The Journal of Mattew Ricci.* New York: Random House, 1953.

Greenberg, David F. *The Construction of Homosexuality.* Chicago: University of Chicago, 1988.

Gulik, Robert van. *Sexual Life in Ancient China.* Leiden: E. J. Brill, 1974

_____. *Erotic Colour Prints of the Ming Period*. Tokyo: privately published, 1951.

Haar, B. J. Ter. *The White Lotus Teachings in Chinese Religious History*. Leiden: E. J. Brill, 1992.

Hanan, Patrick. *The Chinese Vernacular Story*. Cambridge: Harvard University Press, 1981.

_____. "The Sourses of *Jin Ping Mei*," in *Asian Major*, vol. 10, 1962.

_____, trans. *The Carnal Prayer Mat*. New York: Ballantine Books, 1990.

_____, trans., *A Tower for the Summer Heat*. New York: Ballentine Books, 1992.

Hawkes, David, trans. *The Story of the Stone*, vol. I. Penguine, 1973.

Hinsch, Bret. *Passions of the Cut Sleeve: The Male Homosexual Tradition in China*. Berkeley: University of California Press, 1990.

Ho, Ping-ti. *The Ladder of Success in Imperial China: Aspects of Social Mobility*. New York: Columbia University Press, 1962.

Hsia, C. T. *The Classic Chinese Novel*. Bloomington: Indiana University Press, 1980.

Hu, Lenny. "Indigenous Intertextuality and Ye Shengtao's *Wenyan* Stories," unpublished paper.

_____, trans. *The Embroidered Couch*. Arsenal Pulp Press, 2001.

Hu, Shi. *The Chinese Renaissance*. New York: Paragon Book Reprint Corp, 1963

Huang, Martin W. *Literati and Self-Re/Presentation: Autobiographical Sensibility in the Eighteenth-Century Chinese Novel*. Stanford: Stanford University Press, 1995.

Hucker, Charles. *A Dictionary of Official Titles in Imperial China*. Stanford: Stanford University, 1985.

_____. *The Censorial System of Ming China*. Stanford: Stanford University Press, 1966.

Hunt, Morton. *Sexual Behavior in 1970s*. Chicago: Playboy Press, 1974.

Hurvitz, Leon, trans. *Scripture of the Lotus Blossom of the Fine Dharma*. New York: Columbia University Press, 1976.

Kao, Karl S. "*Bao* and *Baoying*: Narrative Causality and External Motivations in Chinese Fiction," in *Chinese Literature: Essays, Articles and Reviews*, 1989.

_____. "Introdiction," in *The Classical Chinese Tales of Supernatural and Fantastic*. Bloomington: Indiana University Press, 1985.

Kronhausen, Eberhard & Phyllis. *Pornography and the Law: the Psychology of Erotic Realism and Pornography*. New York: Ballentine Books, 1959.

Legge, James, trans. *Confucian Analects, The Great Learning and the Doctrine of the Mean*. New York: Dover Publications, 1971.

Li, Tien-yi. "The Original Edition of *Po'an ching-ch'i*," in Li Tien-yi, ed., *Pai'an jingqi*, vol. 2. Hong Kong: Youlian chuban gongsi, 1986.

Li, Zehou. "Some Thoughts on Ming-Qing Neo-Confucianism," *Chu Hsi and Neo-Confucianism*. Ed. By Wing-tsit Chan. Honolulu: University of Hawaii Press, 1986.

Liang, Fangzhong. *The Single Whip Method of Taxation in China*. Translated by Wang Yu-chuan (partial translation of Liang's *Yitiao bian fa*). Cambridge: Harvard University Press, 1956.

Lin, Yutang. *My Country and My People*. New York: Reynal & Hitchcock, 1935.

_____. *The Gay Genius: the Life and Time of Su Tungpo*. London: William Heinemann Ltd, 1948.

Liu, James T. C. "How did a Neo-Confucian School Become the State Orthodoxy?" *Philosophy East and West*, 1973.

Liu, Shih-chi. "Some Reflections on Urbanization and the Historical Development of Market Towns in the Lower Langtze Region, ca 1500-1900," *The American Asian Review*, Spring, 1984.

Lu Xun. *A Brief Hisotry of Chinese Fiction*. Translated by Yang Hsien-yi and Gladys Yang. Beijing: Foreign Languages Press, 1976.

Lynn, Richard, trans. *The Classic of Changes*. New York: Columbia University, 1994.

Macherey, Pierre. *A Theory of Literary Production*. Boston: Routledge & Kegan Paul, 1978.

Mair, Victor. "Buddhism and the Rise of the Written Vernacular in East Asia: The Making of National Languages," in *Journal of Asian Studies*, vol. 53, 1994.

Marx, Karl. *A Contribution to the Critique of Political Economy*. London: Lawrence & Wishart, 1971.

Maspero, Henri. *Taoism and Chinese Religion*. Translated by Frank A. Kierman, Jr. Amherst: The University of Massachusetts Press, 1981.

Mather, Richard B., trans. *A New Account of Tales of the World*. Minneapolis: University of Minnesota Press, 1976.

McMahon, Keith. *Causality and Containment in Seventeenth-Century Chinese Fiction*. Leiden: E.J. Brill, 1988.

_____. *Misers, Shrews and Polymamists: Sexuality and Male-FemaleRelations in Eighteenth Century Chinese Fiction*. Duke University Press, 1995.

Meskill, John. *Gentlemanly Interests*. Ann Arbor: University of Michigan Press, 1996.

Mills, Janes, ed. *Bloomsbury Guide to Erotic Literature*. London: Bloomsbury, 1993.

Montrose, Louis A. "Professing the Renaissance: The Poetics and Politics of Culture," in Aram Veeser, ed., *The New Historicism*. New York: Routledtge, 1989.

Ng, Vivien. "Homosexuality and the State in Late Imperial China," in Martin Duberman, et al., eds., *Hidden from History: Reclaiming the Gay and Lesbian Past*. New York: Meridian, 1990.

Nienhauser, William, ed. *The Grand Scribe's Records*. Bloomington: Indiana University Press, 1994.

Overmyer, Daniel. *Folk Buddhist Religions: Dissenting Sects in Late Traditional China*. Cambridge: Harvard University Press, 1976.

Owen, Stephen, ed. *Anthology of Chinese Literature*. New York: W. W. Norton & Company, 1996.

Plaks, Andrew. "The Problem of Incest in *Jin Ping Mei* and *Honglou Meng*," *Paradoxes of Traditional Chinese Literature*. Edited by Eva Hung. Hong Kong: Chinese University of Hong Kong Press, 1994.

Prusek, Jaroslav. *Chinese History and Literature*. Prague: Academia, 1970.

Radtke, Kurt. *Poetry of the Yuan*. Canberra: Australian National University, 1984.

Rawski, Evelyn. *Agricultural Change and the Peasant Economy of South China*. Cambridge: Harvard University Press, 1972.

_____. "Economic and Social Foundations of Late Imperial Culture," *Popular Culture in Late Imperial China*. Edited by Evelyn Rawski, et al. Berkeley: University of California Press, 1986.

Rolston, David. *Traditional Chinese Fiction and Fiction Commentary*. Stanford: Stanford University Press, 1997.

Roy, David, trans. *The Plum in the Golden Vase*. Princeton: Princeton University Press, 1992.

Schafer, Edward. *Pacing the Void: T'ang Approaches to the Stars*. Berkeley: University of California Press, 1977.

Schlepp, Wayne. *San-ch'u: Its Technique and Imagery*. Madison: The University of Wisconsin Press, 1970.

Scott, John, trans. *The Lecherous Academician and Other Tales by Master Ling Mengche*. London: Deutsch, 1973.

Shirohauer, Conrad, trans. *China's Examination Hell: The Civil Service Examinations of Imperial China* by Ichisada Miyazaki. New York: Weatherhill, 1976.

Siegel, Lee. "De Sade's Daughters," *Atlantic Monthly*, Feb., 1997.

Skinner, William. "Regional Urbanization in Nineteenth-Century China," in William Skinner, ed., *The City in Late Imperial China*. Stanford: Stanford UniversityPress, 1977.

Struve, Lynn. *The Southern Ming*. New Haven: Yale University Press, 1984.

Polo, Marco. *The Travels of Marco Polo*. London: J. M. Dent & Sons Ltd, 1927.

Tien, Ju-kang. *Male Anxiety and Female Chastity: A Comparative Study of EthicalValues in Ming-Qing China*. Leiden: E. J. Brill, 1988.

Tsien, Tsuen-hsuin. *Paper and Printing*, in Joseph Needham, ed., *Science and Civilizationin China*, vol. 5, part 1. Cambridge University Press, 1985.

Tu, Wei-ming. *Neo-Confucian Thought in Action: Wang Yang-ming's Youth*. Berkeley: University of California Press, 1976.

Vassi, Marco. *Saline Solution*. New York: Masquerade Books, Inc., 1997.

Veeser, Aram, ed. *The New Historicism*. New York: Routledge & Kegan Paul, 1989.

Vitiello, Giovanni. "The Dragon's Whim: Ming and Qing Homoerotic Tales from the Cut Sleeve," *T'oung Pao*, vol. lxxviii, 1992.

Watson, Burton, trans. *Records of Grand Historian of China: Han Dynasty I*. New York: Columbia University Press, 1993.

Watt, Ian. *The Rise of the Novel*. Berkeley: University of California Press, 1957.

Weber, Max. *The Protestant Ethics and the Spirit of Capitalism*, trans., Talcott Parsons. New York: Charles Scribner's Sons, 1958.

Widmer, Ellen & Kang-i Sun Chang, eds. *Writing Women in China*. Stanford: Stanford University Press, 1997.

Wile, Douglas. *Art of the Bedchamber: The Chinese Sexual Yoga Classics*. Albany: State University of New York Press, 1992.

Williams, Raymond. *Marxism and Literature*. Oxford: Oxford University Press, 1978.

Wu, Yenna. *The Chinese Virago*. Cambridge: Harvard University Press, 1997.

_____. "The Invention of Marital Hierachy: Shrewish Wives and henpeched Husbands in Seventeenth-Century Chinese Literature," *Harvard Journal of Asiastic Studies*, vol. 48, 1988.

Yang, Lien-sheng. *Money and Credit in China: A Short History*. Cambridge: Harvard University Press, 1971.

_____. "The Concept of 'Pao' as a Basis for Social Relations in China," in John K. Fairbank, ed., *Chinese Thought and Institution*. Chicago: The University of Chicago Press, 1957.

Yang, Hsien-yi & Gladys Yang, trans. *The Courtesan's Jewel Box*. Beijing: Foreign Languages Press, 1981.

Yusushi, Oki. "Women in Feng Menglong's 'Mountain Song,'" in Ellen Widmar & Kang-i Sun Chang, eds., *Writing Women in Late Imperial China*. Stanford: Stanford University Press, 1997.

Glossary
Of Names, Titles, and Terms

Introduction

anren 安人

baihua 白話

Bai Kun 白昆

baoying 報應

bi 屄

bimo yadao 筆墨雅道

bingchen 丙辰

Bizhouzhai ji 蔽帚齋集

butian jieming dan 補天接命丹

caizhan zhi shu 採陰之術

caizi jiaren xiaoshuo 才子佳人小説

caizi yin 才子淫

Cao Zhi 曹植

Changle 長樂

Changshu 常熟

Cheng Hao 程灝

Chenghua 成化

Cheng Yi 程頤

Chengzu 成祖

Chongzhen 崇禎

chuanqi 傳奇

Chunqiu zuozhuan pingzhu ceyi
    春秋左傳評注測義

chunyao 春藥

ci 詞

Daming fuzhi 大名府誌

dangzi yin 蕩子淫

di 翟

dianruan daofeng 顛鸞倒鳳

diben 底本

Dishi 狄氏

Donglin dang 東林黨

duiyu 對語

Erpai 二拍

fanli 凡例

fanshang 犯上

Fan Wenzhong (Fan Zhongyan) 范文正
    (范仲淹)

Feng Mengzhen 馮夢貞

fubang 副榜

fugong 副貢

Fule yuan 富樂院

fuxue sheng 附學生

Gao Lian 高濂

Gaomintang shi 高密堂詩

Geng Dingli 耿定理

Geng Dingxiang 耿定向

gengzi 庚子

gongguo ge 功過格

Gongyi 恭懿

goulan 勾欄

Gu Kexue 顧可學

Gu Xiancheng 顧憲城

Guozi jian 國子監

guose 國色

hanhua weiguan feng he yu
    含花未貫風和雨

hanlin 翰林

Hanshu pinglin 漢書評林

Han Shantong 韓山童

Hangzhou 杭州

hejin 合卺

Hequ zhi 河渠誌

He Tengjiao 何騰蛟

He Xinyin 何心隱

hongqian wan 紅鉛丸

Hongwu 洪武
houting 後庭
houting hua 後庭花
huaben 話本
Huang Tingjian 黃庭堅
hui 回
Hu Shi 胡適
Jiji zhenjing 既濟真經
Jikongguan zhuren 即空觀主人
Jiajing 嘉靖
jiao 教
jiashen 甲申
Jianghuai 江淮
jiaofeng 交鋒
Jigu ge 汲古閣
Jiling guo 吉零國
jinshi 進士
Jin tong can Tang 金統殘唐
jinyiwei baihu 錦衣衛百戶
Jingnan zhi yi 靖難之役
jingshe 精舍
jiancan xunyu 間參訓諭
Jiandeng xinhua 剪燈新話
jianmin 賤民
Jiaxing 嘉興
jieyuan 嗟怨
Jinghuan xiangu (Madam Fairy)
　　警幻仙姑
Jujintang 聚錦堂
juren 舉人
jushi 居士
juan 卷
junyan 君言
kanguan (kanguan tingshuo)
　　看官 (看官聽說)
Kangxi 康熙
Kuaixuetang ji 快雪堂集
Kuaixuetang riji 快雪堂日記
li 理
Libu 禮部
Lidai diwang xingshi
　　tongpu 歷代帝王姓氏統譜

Ling Bo 凌波
Ling Bo'an 凌波岸
Ling Chucheng 凌初成
Ling Dizhi 凌迪知
Ling Runchu 凌潤初
Ling Shijiu 凌十九
Lingshi zongpu 凌氏宗譜
Ling Xuanfang (Ling Yuanfang) 凌玄房
　　(凌元房)
Ling Yueyan 凌約言
Ling Yuzhi 凌遇知
Ling Zhanchu 凌湛初
Ling Zhen 凌震
Ling Zhilong 凌稚隆
Linhao 臨濠
Linqing 臨清
Li Wenzhong 李文忠
lixue 理學
liyi fenshu 理一分殊
Li Zicheng 李自成
lienu 烈女
linshan sheng 廩膳生
Liu Ji 劉基
luan 亂
luandaitou 亂代頭
Luo Rufang 羅汝芳
Ma Lian 馬廉
maocai yideng 茂才異等
Mao Jin 毛晉
Masuda Wataru 增田涉
Miaoniang 妙娘
Min 閩
Minggong leichao 名公類鈔
Min Qiji 閔齊及
Mulan ci 木蘭辭
Naide weng 耐得翁
nanfeng 男風
nanfeng yidu 男風一度
nanxing 男形
neijiao 內交
ni huaben 擬話本
nizuo 擬作

Pan An (Pan Anren) 潘安 (潘安仁)
Pan Jinlian 潘金蓮
pianwei 篇尾
pianwen 駢文
pinxiao 品簫
qing 情
Qingchi fanzheng daoren 情痴反正道人
Qingyuan dang 慶元黨
qingjia 卿家
qiqiang 旗槍
qiushi fang 秋石方
qu 曲
rouju 肉具
ruhua 入話
sangangwuchang 三綱五常
sanjiao 三教
sanqu 散曲
Sanyan 三言
Shanfeitang 壇飛堂
Shangyou tang 尚友堂
se 色
Shen Duanming 沈端明
Shengze zhen 盛澤鎮
Sheshen zhong miaofang 舍身眾妙方
Shen Su liangfang 沈蘇良方
Shenzong 神宗
shengyuan 生員
shenxu jiao 滇恤膠
shi 詩
shi 實
shi'e 十惡
Shiji pinglin 史記評林
shi yan zhi 詩言志
shizhen 市鎮
Shizong 世宗
shuohua de 說話的
shufang 書坊
sijia 私家
Songjiang 松江
Suihang 隨航
suoyang zhi shu 縮陽之術
Suzhou 蘇州

Taihu 太湖
Tao Shiling 陶奭齡
Tao Zhongwen 陶仲文
tiao 糶
Tongrentang 同人堂
Tongwentang 同文堂
touhui 頭回
Toyoda Minoru 豐田穰
tuoyang 脫陽
wasi (wazi, washe) 瓦肆 (瓦子, 瓦舍)
waifu 外婦
waijiao 外交
Wang Gen 王艮
Wang Ke 汪客
Wang Shizhen 王世貞
Wang Ting 王梃
Wang Yangming 王陽明
Wanli 萬歷
Wanxing tongpu 萬姓統譜
Wujing zhengyi 五經正義
Weijin 魏晉
Wenren 閩人
Wen Ruoxu 文若虛
Wenxiutang 文秀堂
wenyan 文言
wenyuan caifeng 文鴛彩鳳
Wen Zhengming 文徵明
Wu 吳
Wu Zetian 武則天
Wuzong 武宗
xianliang fangzheng 賢良方正
xiaoling 小令
xiaozi 小子
Xiaozong 孝宗
xieshi 寫實
xieyi 寫意
Xindiao wanqu changchun
新調萬曲長春
Xingmeng 醒夢
xionghuang yin 凶慌淫
Xiuzhou 秀州
xu 盧

249

Xuande 宣德
Xue Aocao 薛敖曹
Xue Fangshan 薛方山
Xuzhou 徐州
yangdao 陽道
Yang Jian 楊戩
yangju 陽具
yangwu 陽物
yi 矣
yiren 宜人
yishishi yue 異史氏曰
yiwei wenre,bian buzuguan
　　一為文人，便不足觀
yinhui xiaoshuo 淫穢小說
yinyang 陰陽
Yizhen 倚枕
Yongle 永樂
youshi weizheng 有詩為証
yu 欲

Yuchuang 雨窗
Yue 越
Yueyanglou ji 岳陽樓記
yunshou yusan 雲縮雨散
yunyu 雲雨
Yuzan ji 玉簪記
zengguang sheng 增廣生
Zhang Juzheng 張居正
Zhang Xianzhong 張獻忠
Zheng Chenggong 鄭成功
Zhengde 正德
zhenghua 正話
zhi 之
Zhuo Tian 卓田
Zhu Di 朱棣
Zhu Yunwen 朱允文
Zhu Yuanzhang 朱元璋
Zijian 子建

Stories

anyuan 庵院
Bai Juyi 白居易
bailian hui 白蓮會
bailian jiao 白蓮教
Baiyi jing 白衣經
baojia 保甲
bazi 八字
bin 贇
Bu Liang 卜良
buliang 不良
Cai Jing 蔡京
canshi 蠶室
Cao Pi 曹丕
Cao Zhi 曹植
Chang'an 長安
Chen Miaochang 陳妙常
Chen Ping 陳平
chenzi 櫬字

chi 笞
chisha mantou, dangbude fan 吃煞饅頭，
　　當不得飯
Chu Huaiwang 楚懷王
Chu Xiangwang 楚襄王
cuju 蹴鞠
cuohe shan 撮合山
daodao ling 叨叨令
daogu 道姑
daojian 道間
daotai 道台
Daxue 大學
Da Yuan zhizheng chao 大元至正朝
Deng Yubin 鄧玉賓
dianshi 殿試
dizhi 地支
Dongjing 東京
ducha yuan 都察院

Du You 杜佑
du yushi 都御史
fangzhang baozheng 坊長保正
fengguan xiapei 鳳冠霞帔
Feng Zhi 封陟
fumu guan 父母官
fuzhi 符紙
Gao Qiu 高逑
Gaozu benji 高祖本記
gongbu 工部
gongjian 貢監
gongren 恭人
guagu 卦姑
guan 官
guan 冠
guanke (menke) 館客 (門客)
Guan Panpan 關盼盼
Guanyin (Guanshiyin) 觀音 (觀世音)
gui 龜
guo xiansheng (jiao xiansheng) 郭先生 (
角先生)
Han Changli 韓昌黎
hanlin yuan 翰林院
Han wang 漢王
hao 號
He Qinglian 何清漣
Hongfu 紅拂
hongxi 洪熙
Hongxiao 紅綃
Hou Yi 后羿
huachuan 畫船
huaguan 花關
Huai shui 淮水
Huangshan ke 黃衫客
Huanzhe 宦者
huazhen 花陣
hubu 戶部
Huiji 會稽
hunshui (hunshui moyu)
混水 (混水摸魚)
Huo Xiaoyu 霍小玉
ji 醫

ji 偈
jia 甲
Jia Chong 賈充
Jia Wu 賈午
jian'an 建安
Jingdi 景帝
jishou 稽首
jiagun 夾棍
jianju 薦舉
jiaye (yiye, bingye, dingye, shuye)
甲夜 (乙夜, 丙夜, 丁夜, 戊夜)
jingkui 經魁
jinniao (jinwu, junwu) 金烏 (金烏, 俊烏)
jujian 舉監
Kaifeng 開封
laihamo xiangchi tian'e
rou 癩蛤蟆想吃天鵝肉
laotie 烙鐵
libu 吏部
Li ji 禮記
lijian 例監
Ling Shu (Lin Qinnan) 林紓 (林琴南)
Lingyin shan 靈隱山
liu 流
Liu Bang (Liu Ji) 劉邦 (劉季)
liubo (liuzhuan) 六博 (六轉)
liubu 六部
Liuhou shijia 留侯世家
Liushi zhuan 柳氏傳
Liu Xiang 劉向
Lu Jia 陸賈
Lu nan 魯男
ma bailiu 馬佰六
meiyan er 媚眼兒
Mengchang jun 孟嘗君
Menxia sheng 門下省
mianling 緬鈴
Mianzhou 沔州
Mi-le 彌勒
Mulian 目蓮
nanfeng 南風

nanwu sanman duo, mutuo nan'an,
南無三滿哆, 母馱喃唵,
dulu dulu, ddiwei sapo ke
度嚕度嚕, 地尾薩婆呵
nigu 尼姑
niangzi 娘子
meipo 媒婆
pantao hui 蟠桃會
Pan Yue 潘岳
Penglai shan 蓬萊山
Pumen pin 普門品
Qi furen 戚夫人
qixiong (qidi) 契兄 (契弟)
qianpo 虔婆
quanxuan 銓選
Qunyu feng 羣玉峰
Qu Yuan 屈原
Renzong 仁宗
sangu liupo 三姑六婆
sanhun qipo 三魂七魄
sansheng 三省
sanshi 三師
sanwu 三吳
shanpo yang 山坡羊
Shangshu sheng 尚書省
Shangyuan furen 上元夫人
Shaoxing 紹興
Shazhali 沙吒利
sheng 生
Shen Kuo 沈括
shi 士
shi 氏
shipo 師婆
shi yushi 侍御史
Shu 蜀
shuhuang daobai 數黃道白
shumi yuan 樞密院
si 死
si 寺
sichou zhi fu 絲綢之府
sida 四大
sikong 司空

Sima Xiangru (Changqing)
司馬相如 (長卿)
situ 司徒
Su Qin 蘇秦
Sui He 隨何
taibao 太保
taifu 太傅
taishi 太師
taiwei 太尉
taixue 太學
tiangan 天干
tianmen 天門
tinggun 梃棍
tingshi 廷試
ti duxue daotai 提督學道台
Tong Guan 童貫
tu 徒
wanmin 萬緡
Wei Zhongxian 魏忠賢
wenpo 穩婆
Wuchang 無常
Wudi 武帝
wugeng 五更
wugou 吳鉤
Wushan 巫山
wushe 吾舌
Wutong shen (Wulang shen)
五通神 (五郎神)
wuxing 五行
Wuzhou 婺州
Xiangguo si 相國寺
xiangru yin 香薷飲
xiangshi 鄉試
xianhua yecao 閒花野草
Xichu bawang 西楚霸王
xiaoyi 小衣
Xiang Yu (Xiang Ji) 項羽 (項籍)
xingbu 刑部
Xingfa 刑法
Xinhua jun jiedu shi 新化軍節度使
Xishi (Xianshi, Xizi) 西施 (先施, 西子)
xiucai 秀才

xiuli, xiuli, mokexiuli, xiuxiuli, sa po ke
  俺利，修利，摩柯俺利，俺俺利，
  薩婆呵
xiuyi yushi 繡衣御史
Xi wangmu 西王母
Xu yuhou 許虞侯
yapo 牙婆
yangfeng 陽鋒
yanji 燕姬
Yang Su 楊素
Yang Wenhui 楊文會
yaopo 藥婆
yiguan 一貫
yiliang yinzi 一兩銀子
yiqian wen 一千文
yin 淫
yinde 陰德
yufei 于飛
Yu ji 虞姬
yulu 雨露

yushi tai 御史臺
yushi zhongcheng 御史中丞
Yusi feng 玉筍峰
yutu 玉兔
zan 拶
zao 造
zaoli 皂隸
Zhang Liang 張良
Zhang Yi 張儀
zhang 杖
Zhang Jianfeng 張建封
zhaonu 趙女
Zhengzhou 鄭州
Zhiyuan 至元
Zhizheng 至正
zhu 箸
Zhuo Wangsun 卓王孫
Zhuo Wenjun 卓文君
zi 字
Zixu fu 子虛賦

Acknowledgments

Teachers and friends whom I wish to thank for reading the manuscript and giving me kind advice or incisive comments for revisions are numerous. Among them I am particularly indebted to C. T. Hsia of Columbia University, Patrick Hanan of Harvard University, Richard J. Lynn of the University of Toronto, Karl. S. Kao of Hong University of Science and Technology, Sharon Yamamoto of the University of Hawaii Press, Tim Iles, Martin Hunter, and Steve Duncan.

And I also wish to thank Robert Hegel of Washington University in St Louis, Wendy Larson of the University of Oregon, Wayne Schlepp of the University of Toronto, Gary Carter, David Daomin Zhou, Mark Zhu, Andrew Yang, and Emily Andrew for their encouragement, support, kindness, or help, and graduate students of my comparative literature seminar whom I taught last year as a visiting professor at Hebei University for their critiques of the translation, which, though immature sometimes, were, too, invaluable.

My greatest gratitude goes to my mentor R.W.L. Guisso of the University Toronto. From the days I was his Ph.D student to the present, he has spent much time offering me his insights and suggestions on issues related to sexuality, women's studies, and Chinese history, and directing me to improve my English style by polishing my translated stories one by one. If this book has merit, I should first ascribe them to his magnanimous contribution.

I am very grateful to the Robart's Library and the Cheng Yu-Tung East Asian Library of the University of Toronto. Without their excellent facility and the very helpful services the staff provided, I can hardly imagine that I would have been able to finish this project.

To the late Zhang Yi (1900-1987), President of Fudan University (from 1943-1950) and the translator of Shakespeare's *Henry VI*, and to Professor George McWhirter of the Department of Creative Writing of the University of British Columbia, my appreciation is profound. The former taught me how to render English into Chinese when I was a college student in Shanghai, while the latter gave me his generous guidance, in my years of graduate studies at UBC, in translating Chinese into English. I wouldn't have dared to attempt the translation of Ling Mengchu's stories but for the necessary training I received there.

Thanks are also due to the editor Linda Field for her careful editing and proofreading, and to the publisher Brian Lam, as well as Blaine Kyllo and Robert Ballantyne, who, most encouraging even before the manuscript was submitted, guided the process of making this book with admirable professionalism and enthusiasm.

Lastly, I wish to thank my wife who patiently endured the less pleasant aspects of authorship and gave me the strong support I needed.

L.L.H.

About the Translators

Lenny Hu, translator of Lü Tiancheng's *The Embroidered Couch* (Arsenal Pulp Press), Philip Roth's *Goodbye, Columbus*, and numerous other literary works, was born in China and received his higher education in North America. He has taught at universities both in China and Canada, including, most recently, the University of Toronto. Currently he is working on the translation of late Ming erotica.

R.W.L. Guisso, a historian of Chinese history and a scholar of Chinese women studies, is the author of two books, *Wu Tse-t'ien and Politics of Legitimation in T'ang China* and *First Emperor of China*. He has also edited a number of volumes on such subjects as the history of women in East Asia and has recently completed a volume on the contributions of Japanese scholarship to the study of pre-modern Chinese history. Educated at Toronto, Kyoto, and Oxford, he is currently Chair of the Department of East Asian Studies at the University of Toronto.